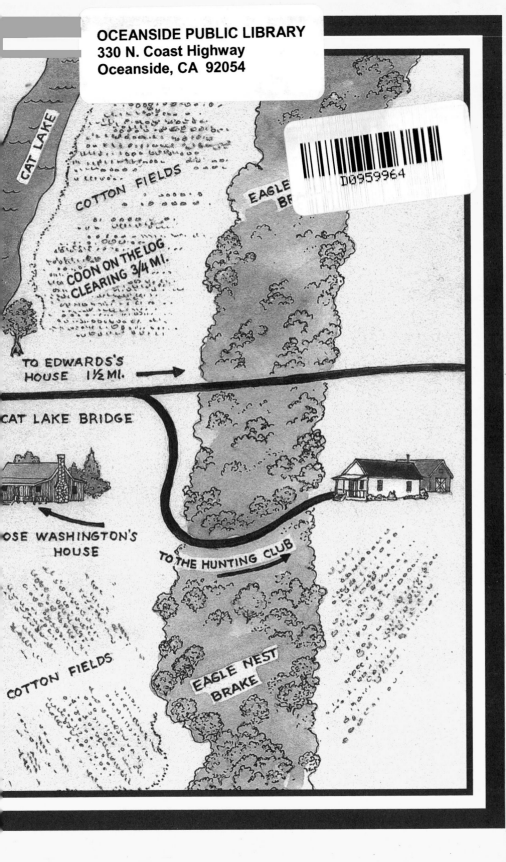

CAT LAKE

COTTON FIELDS

EAGLE
BR

COON ON THE LOG
CLEARING 3/4 MI.

TO EDWARDS'S
HOUSE 1½ MI.

CAT LAKE BRIDGE

OSE WASHINGTON'S
HOUSE

TO THE HUNTING CLUB

COTTON FIELDS

EAGLE NEST
BRAKE

ABIDING DARKNESS

ABIDING DARKNESS

A Novel

JOHN AUBREY ANDERSON

WARNER
Faith ®

NEW YORK BOSTON NASHVILLE

This book is a work of fiction. Names, characters, places, and incidents are the product of the author's imagination or are used fictitiously. Any resemblance to actual events, locales, or persons, living or dead, is coincidental.

Warner Faith
Hachette Book Group USA

1271 Avenue of the Americas, New York, NY 10020
Visit our Web site at www.warnerfaith.com.

The Warner Faith name and the "W" logo are trademarks of Time Inc. Used under license.

Printed in the United States of America
Originally published as *Black or White*
Warner Faith Edition: August 2006
10 9 8 7 6 5 4 3 2 1

Library of Congress Cataloging-in-Publication Data
Anderson, John Aubrey, 1940-
    [Black or white]
    Abiding darkness / John Aubrey Anderson.— 1st ed.
        p. cm. — (The black or white chronicles; bk. 1)
    Previously published as: Black or white.
    ISBN-13: 978-0-446-57949-0
    ISBN-10: 0-446-57949-1
    1. Children—Fiction. 2. Best friends—Fiction. 3. Race relations—Fiction. 4.
Mississippi—Fiction. 5. Spiritual warfare—Fiction. I. Title.
    PS3601.N544B55 2006
    813'.6—dc22   2005034007

For Nan

The Characters

A. J. Mason. An almost austere, grandfatherly type—and a dead shot with anything that fires a bullet.

The Bainbridge family. Halbert Bainbridge is wealthy and influential because of his willingness to immerse himself in corruption; Estelle Bainbridge is the personification of evil; Hal, Ollie, and French—the Bainbridges' sons—are adept students.

Among the people of the South, some elements are classified as "white trash" because they are poor, others because they're morally despicable. Pool Pommer fits in both categories—the former by birth, the latter by choice.

When Missy Parker attends Ole Miss, she attracts the attention of Hull Dillworth, David Patterson, and Pat Patterson.

Dillworth is the scion of a wealthy Delta family. He has what it takes to play football—or play the field—at Ole Miss, but chooses to invest himself in an on-campus Christian group.

David Patterson, a postgrad student from Texas, drifts into the Delta on the eve of a rift between Missy and Hull.

Pat Patterson, David's older brother—and the smarter of the two—is in the final stages of securing his Ph.D. in philosophy. Pat is a stellar example of the gulf that can exist between intellect and wisdom.

The Black Folks

Mose "Junior" Washington. The son of Mose and Pip Washington, and Missy Parker's best friend. He's fiercely loyal, energetic, reasonably compliant for an eleven-year-old boy, and sold out to Jesus Christ. Junior, Missy, and Bobby make up the three-member confederation referred to by local folks as "those Parker children."

Mose Washington. The great-grandson of a slave, he is the staid operations manager of the Parker Cotton Gin.

Pip Washington. Mose's wife, and combination cook and maid for the Young Parkers.

Evalina Daniels. Old Mrs. Parker's cook has been on the Parker Plantation since 1886. She's the mother of Pip Washington and Leon Daniels, both of whom live and work on the plantation.

Roosevelt Edwards. Mose Washington's right-hand man at the Parker Cotton Gin. If Rose chose to go grizzly hunting, the Sierra Club would insist that the bear be the one with the gun.

Emmalee Edwards. Roosevelt's thirteen-year-old daughter is everything a man would want his daughter to be—except thirteen.

Sam Jones. A former college student from Pilot Hill, Texas. He's quiet, respectful, and doing time at Parchman Prison Farm because he's black.

Blue Biggers. An easygoing loafer who'd sell his soul for two quarts of beer and a day uninterrupted by toil.

The Others

The rebellion took place in the great, bright reaches beyond time and space; one third of the angelic realm followed Lucifer, the highest angel—"the perfection of wisdom and beauty"—in his rebellion against God. Now, because the first man allowed Lucifer to persuade him to taste a sample of his rebellion, you and I are appointed to struggle, not against flesh and blood, but against the rulers, against the powers, against the world forces of darkness that God banished from heaven. This conflict—into which every human is born, and in which we all take sides—will continue until that foretold day whereon God will be pleased to melt the elements of the universe with intense heat.

ABIDING DARKNESS

CHAPTER ONE

Summers were mostly reliable.

They always followed spring. They always got hot. And they always promised twelve weeks of pleasure to the three children at Cat Lake.

The summer of '45 lied.

The whole thing started right there by the Cat Lake bridge.

They were playing their own version of three-man baseball when Bobby knocked the ball onto the road near the end of the bridge. Junior was taller and faster, but Missy was ahead in the race to get it. Bobby and Junior were older, but Missy was tough enough to almost keep up, and the boys usually held back some so they didn't outdo her too much.

Missy was still a few yards from the ball when it rolled to a stop near the only car in sight. A boy taller than Junior stepped from behind the far end of the car and picked up the ball; he was followed by two more boys—one younger than Missy and another almost as tall as a man.

Missy slid to a stop in the gravel and yelled, "Hurry! Throw it!" Junior jogged up behind the girl and waited.

A heavyset man in a rumpled suit was standing in the road

by the driver's door; he allowed himself a long look at the girl and whispered something to the boy with the ball.

The boy nodded at what the man said and backed toward the car's rear bumper. The tallest boy moved up to stand by the man.

The fat man eyed Junior, then looked up and down the deserted road before beckoning to Missy. "Why don't you come closer, and he'll let you have it?"

Missy ignored the man, walking past him as she advanced on the boy with the ball. "Give it."

When she passed the taller boy, he fell to his hands and knees behind her and the one with the ball shoved her over his back. When Missy hit the ground, all three boys laughed. The man grinned.

In the near distance, a foursome of well-armed witnesses—tall, bright, and invisible—stood at a portal between time and eternity and watched Bobby Parker leave home plate and sprint for the bridge.

One of the group said, *It begins.*

Junior Washington's guardian answered for the remainder of the small assembly, *And so it does.*

The three guardians conferred quietly about the events taking place before them; the archangel watched the unfolding drama in silence. The quartet—guarded by the wisdom of the ages against restlessness—waited patiently for a precise instant in time that had been ordained before the earth was formed.

The middle kid was plenty bigger than Missy, but she came up off the ground ready to take him on. When she waded in, the tall kid grabbed at her. Junior got a hand on the strap of Missy's overalls and yanked her out of the boys' reach. He held her back with one hand and popped the tallest kid in the nose, hard enough to knock him down.

When the boy landed in the gravel, the man started swearing. He reached into the car, jerked a mean-looking billy club from under the front seat, and turned on Junior. "Okay, Sambo, let's see h—"

Bobby was short steps from the trouble, running wide open, when the archangel broke his silence. *The long-awaited time is come.* He pointed his bright sword at a point between Bobby and the man with the club and said, *In the Name of Him who sits on the throne, and for the Lamb—go there and turn the tide of evil.*

Bobby—barely slowing when he got to the confrontation—tripped over thin air and rammed the business end of the bat hard into the man's back. The man lurched forward, stumbled over the boy Junior had knocked to the ground, and sprawled on top of him.

Knocking the man down wasn't what he'd planned, but Bobby knew better than to back off from a pack of bullies; he was talking before the man rolled over. "You keep your hands to yourself, mister."

The red-faced man struggled to get up, cussing and pointing the club at Bobby. "Son, when a boy hits me, he steps over the line to manhood. That means you'll get the same beatin' I'll be givin' this nigger."

On the Parker place, Negro folks were called *black* or *colored.* For the children, transgression of that rule meant someone was going to get his mouth washed out with soap. Missy and Junior froze when the man said the forbidden word; Bobby didn't.

When Bobby squared his stance and drew back the bat, the man rethought his position. "You better put that down, boy."

Bobby was only twelve, but he knew serious trouble when he saw it—and he was the one holding the bat. "I reckon not." He and Junior and Missy had made a law about standing up for each other, and these strangers had chosen to be their enemies. If the man made a threatening move, Bobby was going to swing for his head and deal with the consequences later. "You're on Parker land, mister, an' you best be gettin' off."

The baseball bat had the man stymied. Exertion and frustration soaked his collar with sweat. "This isn't your land. It's a public road."

Bobby said, "That might be, but the land on both sides of the road belongs to the Parkers—an' that's us." He looked the man up and down. "You ain't from around here, are you?"

The man's wide mouth and thick lips were not unlike those of a bullfrog; small, widely-spaced teeth and flesh-draped eyelids contributed to his reptilian appearance. "What if I'm not?"

Bobby cracked a hard smile. "'Cause if you was from around here, folks would've told you not to mess with the Parker kids—that's us, 'specially the black 'un an' the girl." He pointed the bat at Junior and Missy. "That's them two."

From within the car a woman's voice said, "Let it go, Halbert. Don't be getting heated up over some white trash."

When the woman called them *white trash*, Missy puffed up and started for the car. Junior grabbed the strap of her overalls again. "Stay quiet, Missy."

The girl jerked loose and glared at Junior, but she stayed where she was.

The tallest boy got into the car, holding a hand to his bloody nose. The other two weren't ready to leave.

The man looked at the car and back at Bobby; he didn't want to leave either, but he wasn't going to argue with the woman. "Git in the car, boys." His tongue came out and made a circuit over his fat lips; he let his gaze rest too long on the girl, and he spoke to her last. "You'll get yours, Little Miss Blue Eyes. Just you remember Hal Bainbridge said so."

The woman in the car leaned across the seat. Facial features that had been cast to portray beauty were twisted into an angry mask. "Halbert!" she snapped, "I told you to shut up and get in the car."

The two smallest boys were the last ones to climb in. The one who had pushed Missy said, "I'll be back."

Missy made a face.

When the Bainbridge family withdrew, a creature that had been traveling with them stayed behind.

The being that remained on the Cat Lake bridge had been working his vile mischief in the Bainbridges' lives for years. His brief observation of Missy Parker, however, ignited a hatred that far exceeded anything he had ever felt toward Estelle Bainbridge. He petitioned his leader, the high-ranking villain who was assigned to the Bainbridges, to let him stay at Cat Lake and work his evil on the girl and those around her. The one to whom he answered hated to grant any request that might strengthen the position of a subordinate, but he hated humans more. So it was that the malevolent being stayed behind while his former superior and dozens of their kind moved away with the Bainbridges.

The spirit-being assayed his intended victim and was encouraged by what he saw. The girl was self-willed, self-centered, and self-confident—all traits that made her more susceptible to his influence. Early pieces of his plan were arranging themselves before the Bainbridges' car was out of sight. He would recruit his own team of underlings from the demonic realm. When he and his chosen confederates were in place, he would formulate a plan to destroy the girl's life—maybe in bits and pieces over the coming years, maybe catastrophically in a single day. There might even be a way to use the Bainbridges to help bring her to ruin. And, if the opportunity presented itself, he would do the same to the two meddlesome boys.

When the car was moving down the road, Bobby turned on Missy. "You can't be startin' fights with boys bigger'n you."

"I didn't start it. He did."

Bobby watched the car. "Well, don't be messin' with folks like that. That man had somethin' wrong with him, like he was mean or evil or somethin'."

"I ain't scared of the boogeyman."

"I don't mean like that. I mean grown men who stare at little girls like that—stay away from 'em." He watched the car disappear behind a curtain of dust. "An' if that bunch comes around here again, you head for me or Junior, you hear me?"

The girl directed her wrath at her brother. "You're not my

boss, Mr. Bobby Parker, an' I'll have you know I ain't a little girl."

Bobby was still learning that he needed to tell Missy to do exactly the opposite of what he wanted done, but he knew who carried the most influence over her. "Tell 'er, Junior."

Junior picked up the ball and offered it to the girl. "Do like he says, Missy. A growed man that'd speak bad to a lit—to somebody not big as him has got somethin' wrong inside 'im. That man had the devil in 'im."

She turned her back on the ball because she wouldn't be bribed. "Well, if a' evil man shows up again, an' I can't whip 'im by myself, y'all can help."

The boys took that as a concession and followed her back to their baseball field.

⸙

Amanda Allen Parker was the first girl born into the Parker family since the Surrender. Maybe they had spoiled her or maybe she knew she was special. Whatever the cause, "Missy" Parker was a young lady who didn't just give orders—she laid down the law for those who drew near.

When they didn't call her Missy, everybody on the Parker place and most people in town just referred to her as *the girl*. The petite picture of brown-haired Southern charm endured the company of women when she had to, but she preferred the attention of the males of her domain.

The Old Parkers and the Young Parkers lived out south of town in two nice houses set back from the west side of Cat Lake. They got good shade from a stand of oaks planted by their ancestors and the cool of a lake breeze when the wind was right.

Bobby Lee Parker ran the Parker Gin; young Bobby looked as if he had been spit out of his daddy's mouth. Young Mrs. Parker played bridge, went to the garden club and Missionary Society, and tended her yard. Old Mr. Parker farmed ten sections of cotton land, played dominoes, drank coffee, and visited with his friends. Old Mrs. Parker, the genetic source of the girl's spitfire personality, stayed close to home and baked things.

The Washington family—Mose, his wife Pip, Mose Junior, and little Pearl—lived across the lake from the Parkers. Their home was set back in a stand of pecan trees planted by the same hands that put down the Parkers' oaks. Mose had been born in the cabin and inherited the house and forty acres of good sandy land from Pap, his great-granddaddy. Back behind the cabin, a full section of Old Mr. Parker's cotton land separated Mose's place from the trees of Eagle Nest Brake. Pip, her brother Leon, and her momma Evalina "did for" the Parkers during the week. Mose was Mr. Bobby Lee's overseer at the gin.

When she became old enough to walk, the girl went where Old Mr. Parker went. While he drove, she stood beside him, one arm on his shoulders, the other holding on to the seat back. When he played dominoes at the pool hall, she sat on his lap. It was the men at the pool hall who named her Missy—she and those same men called her granddaddy R. D. Trips to that establishment diminished in frequency after Pip had to switch her for "cussin' in my kitchen."

Once she started to Mrs. Smith's kindergarten, Missy's day-to-day activities became even more curtailed. She countered by playing hooky when she'd had her fill of finger painting and stories about animals made of gingham and calico and velveteen.

After the second time she was called away from her Thursday morning bridge game to hunt for the girl, Young Mrs. Parker taught Pip how to drive. For the next two years, Pip was called into town about twice a week to retrieve the girl from the pool hall. When she was captured, Missy's complaints were drawled in a little-girl bass voice.

On her first day of first grade, the girl and the staff at the elementary school encountered the first in a series of unique obstacles. The magnitude of the initial confrontation was probably connected with the fact that Missy was on a first-name basis with most of the men in Moores Point, including both bankers and both white preachers.

Missy finally came out of her chair when the first-grade teacher persisted in calling her Amanda.

Hoot Johnson, the school's janitor, attracted by the mounting sounds of battle, abandoned his dust mop and intervened to contribute his unsolicited—and uninhibited—opinion. The girl's reaction to what Mr. Johnson had to say didn't help the situation.

The teacher made a strategic blunder when she decided she would enlist the aid of the principal. The principal made the mistake of showing up, and the tension multiplied geometrically.

Someone eventually called the pool hall and let Old Mr. Parker know about the conflict.

When he got to the school, the farmer didn't have to guess where the girl was; the war in Europe could not have been heard over the commotion coming from the first-grade classroom.

The adults in the room—a smattering of teachers, the principal, and one vocal janitor—were all yelling at the girl or each other. The other first-day first-graders—joined by two brand-new teachers who had made the mistake of coming to see what on earth the noise was all about—were all cringing in the farthest corner of the room. The girl, who seldom found it necessary to yell at anyone, especially an adult, was keeping her voice down. She was, however, employing the teacher's chair in order to be at eye level with the other combatants.

There was Missy, standing in the chair, her tiny fists at her waist, leaning into the principal's face, her Dutch boy–cut brown hair popping back and forth as her miniature bass voice cataloged the things she didn't like about his institution. She took passing note of her granddaddy's presence but continued with her business. She reasoned that if R. D. needed to talk to some of these folks, he was gentleman enough to wait his turn; if he needed to see her, he'd wait until she was finished. And wait he did. Leaning on the door frame and giving himself a manicure with his favorite Case pocketknife, the cotton farmer stood by and waited for a break in the storm.

When a majority of the folks finally stopped to catch their breath, Old Mr. Parker put away his knife. He got everyone settled down, borrowed the teacher's chair from the girl, and presided over the formation of a multifaceted truce.

In the future, the school's staff would call the girl Missy; she was old enough to decide what her name was. In return, Missy would address the Truitt Elementary School's principal as Mr. Franklin, not Jimbo, for basically the same reason. Missy would address Mr. Johnson, the school's janitor, as Hoot because he and the girl were good friends and both preferred it that way. And, one of the teachers crouching in the corner would be released from her contract before the girl moved up to her grade level.

The last point of the truce was a little vague and never resolved to the girl's satisfaction. It had something to do with whether she could stand on the teacher's chair, balanced against how many adults were "raisin' sand for no good reason" when the girl needed to make herself heard.

In the pool hall that afternoon, Jimbo Franklin said, "You know somethin'? That girl ain't always pliable, but she's almost always fair. I musta been about a bubble offa plumb to take that teacher's side." The sages in the pool hall, including Hoot and R. D., nodded. They agreed with every word.

During the next year, the second grade tolerated her well enough; the reciprocal wasn't always true.

She was three feet tall in the summer of '45, on the slender side of a pound an inch, with what Scooter Hall called "about eight ounces of eyelashes" strategically situated around midnight-blue eyes.

When the sun was out, the three older children at the lake—two Parkers and one Washington—were inseparable. Junior usually deferred to white folks of all ages, and both boys required themselves to yield to most adults. The girl's deference, however, was never offered capriciously; people of all colors and ages were evaluated on a case-by-case basis, and any recipient of her respect had earned it.

For those times when they stepped away from the rest of the world, the children—like a tiny nation—followed an often-argued tangle of laws they had fashioned for themselves.

For three months every summer, and at any other time the children were together, their respective parents—who never knew what might be coming next—waited for the "other shoe to drop." Or as Old Mr. Parker put it, "for the next shoe to crash through the floor and take most of the house with it."

That spring, the three had used up practically a whole Saturday morning arguing about what to name the boat.

The year before, they had procured the building materials for the vessel by tearing the siding off a dilapidated cotton house. Pip's brother Leon, who took care of things around the Parkers' houses, was perfectly content to cater to the girl's every whim. Missy traded him two of Old Mr. Parker's cigars for his help with the boat. Leon sawed the boards, helped the children nail them together into something that would almost float, and showed them how to put tar in the cracks "so it don't leak too bad." The finished product looked like a pauper's coffin: roughly seven feet long and two feet wide, with two-foot sides. They swamped it so often the first month that Pip told them, "Y'all could use it for one o' those summarines." Missy made a new law that only one person could stand up in it at a time, and they kept slopping on tar until they got so they could stay most of the day on the lake without sinking, unless somebody broke the rule. Pip complained, "When they git outta that confounded piece o' junk, they're so black I can't tell which one's Mose Junior." It wasn't the kind of craft a person would want to venture out in while wearing Sunday clothes.

The argument about the christening surfaced because Bobby wanted to name the boat after his hero. Mose Junior said he thought it might be good to name it something out of the Bible, but he cared more about getting started with the painting. When it came right down to it, Missy didn't really care what they named the dadgummed boat; she was just tired of Bobby getting his way just because he was twelve and she was seven. Bobby countered her objections by claiming they were a democracy, then bought Mose Junior's vote with the promise that Junior could do most of the painting.

They "happened across" a can of white house paint on the top shelf of the tool shed and made a paint brush by tying a wad of pine needles together. Unraveling the boat's actual name, called for the reader to do a little traveling. The lettering was white and bold; the spelling was close. Junior's GENRALROB worked its way down the starboard side; around the corner, the bow showed Bobby's neatly done ERT. The arrangement of the general's middle initial and last name on the port side was Missy's responsibility—they came out EEEL. The craft was one of their greatest accomplishments and they were rarely near the water without it.

Young Mrs. Parker took some snapshots of the paint-splattered trio standing by their pride and joy and gave one to Pip. The two mothers kept the cherished photographs on their dressers until the day they died and occasionally laughed together at speculations of what kind of grandchildren they would see from the mischievous threesome.

They had no way of knowing that the three little figures in the pictures were never going to have children.

CHAPTER TWO

The lady who was in the car during the children's encounter with Halbert Bainbridge was his wife, Estelle. Until the demons took full control of her mind, will, and emotions, the woman's entire life had been scarred by a long and twisted series of poor choices followed by pain.

Her father, Billy Smith, was the son of an Arkansas share-cropper, her mother, his childhood sweetheart. Hand in hand, the young couple blended hard work with a willingness to live modestly and a propensity for sniffing out undervalued land, all of which moved them toward prosperity. The young farmer surprised his wife with their first home when they discovered that they were going to have a baby.

Their daughter was, as the Bible says of Rachel and Esther, beautiful of form and face. They named her Estelle, after the most godly woman they knew—her paternal grandmother.

Billy Smith lost his wife when Estelle was twelve, and he committed the grievous error of trying to bring his daughter contentment by granting her generous access to his bank account. Partly because her father indulged her, but mostly because she had a bent toward wickedness, her grandmother's name became the only thing about the child that was remotely related to godliness. The beauty with which God had chosen to adorn her went unappreciated, and she brandished her father's prosperity and position in the community like a sharp stick.

Prosperity became moderate wealth, and by the time Estelle graduated from high school, her father's abundance allowed her to choose whatever college suited her fancy.

A smaller college might have offered the beautiful freshman a chance to become a woman of grace, but it was not to be. She was attracted to a prestigious—and costly—university in the northeast for a number of reasons: She couldn't remember a time when she wasn't ashamed of her heritage, she was tired of the meddling people at the small-town church, and she had visions of marrying a man who would ensure her a place of prominence in New England society.

Her dreams of marriage to the scion of a wealthy family were quashed shortly after her arrival on campus. Her college classmates turned out to be the pompous products of "old money," and those who weren't jealous of her beauty were intolerant of her origins, her accent, and her artificial overtures of friendship. The world had turned on her again. It was too late to register at another school, and she wouldn't go home in defeat, so she withdrew into herself.

The beauty's self-inflicted isolation attracted the attention of Stanley Tatum.

Tatum was tall, dark, and handsome—and accustomed to ostracism; he was the only Jewish person in the entire freshman class. The two social lepers became allies, and in so doing, attracted another outcast. Halbert Bainbridge, the third side in their triangle, was a scholarship student who waited tables in the dining hall; he was short and sly—and starving to be a man of consequence.

Poor choices will always precede grievous consequences, and the sharecropper's daughter became pregnant before semester break. She told her lover, only to find out that love had nothing to do with what had happened to her. Tatum disappeared into the canyons of Manhattan on the last day of classes, but not before telling Bainbridge of Estelle's plight. The man who hungered for wealth and power saw the opening and stepped through.

Bainbridge reasoned with Estelle that the embarassing prospect of showing up pregnant and unwed would be worse than having him for a fiancé. The two plotted and planned for several hours, finding out in the process that they were a matched pair; he was the cunning one, she the more contentious. They decided that Bainbridge would break the news of her pregnancy to her father.

Estelle had no illusions about Bainbridge's proposal and no qualms about accepting it. She believed that with her father placated—and probably elated at the prospect of having a grandchild—she and Bainbridge would have access to the kind of funds it took to become influential. They thought politics would serve them well.

She and her new fiancé showed up in Arkansas on a bleak afternoon four days before Christmas; Billy Smith met them at the train. They stood on the station platform while an angry wind beat against them and Bainbridge explained to his prospective father-in-law that they were going to have a baby.

During her extended absence, the man's daughter had written him five letters—four demanding more money and one to inform him that she was getting married. Bainbridge's smooth words did nothing to cushion Smith's jolting realization that he had been too lenient with his only child. Steam escaped from the locomotive as Smith listened, and his decision came faster than the forbidding wind could dispel the fragile vapor.

He waved aside talk of a wedding and put them in his car. He drove straight to the courthouse and advised them that they could be married by old Judge Hughes or they could pay for their own wedding.

They were married and back in the car fifteen minutes later.

From the courthouse, they went to the Smith plantation's commissary. Mr. Smith ordered a week's worth of food, a month's worth of staples, and some kitchenware, and helped the clerk load the provisions into the trunk. The last stop was a shotgun house on the back side of the plantation.

Smith invited them to get out of the car, and his daughter said, "I don't feel well."

"Suit yourself." Her father kept moving. "C'mon, Hal."

Smith pointed at the land around them. "This is four times more'n what me an' her momma started with, son—a hundred an' sixty acres of the best bottom land I own. You git the house free; I git a quarter of what you make on the cotton. Y'all can sign for what you need at the commissary, an' we'll settle up when the crop's in."

Bainbridge was relieved that Estelle had stayed in the car. "This is more than generous, Mr. Smith." He stared at the cold dirt. "We'll try real hard."

"That'd be a good idea, boy, 'cause my lawyer'll be back in town soon's deer season's over, an' I'm changin' my will." He rested a warm hand on Bainbridge's shoulder. "The good Lord knows I did that girl real bad when I spoiled her, but I can't go back an' change that. What I can do is give y'all a chance to git your lives goin' in the right direction. I'll give y'all five years to git settled on a section of your own land, then me an' you'll talk partnership. In the meantime, if I die, everything I own goes to my church."

Bainbridge pulled his coat closer in an effort to shut out the wind. "Thank you, sir. We can make it."

"I'll be prayin' for you." He started to take the groceries out of the car. "You best git your wife out of the car an' show her around. I got things that need doin'."

"Yes, sir."

The newlyweds stood on the porch of their honeymoon cottage and watched him get into the warm car. Before he drove off, he rolled down the window and said, "I'll expect y'all up at the big house for dinner on Christmas."

Bainbridge put his arm around his bride and tried to look brave. "Thank you, sir. We'll be there."

There was no Christmas dinner that year.

On Christmas Eve, a fire of unknown origin destroyed the Smith house. Billy Smith, his invalid mother, and his mother's nurse perished in the blaze.

Deer season ended a week later.

The spirit that had been brought to Cat Lake by the Bainbridges was a demon—a fallen angel. That his name was unpronounceable on this side of the wall between time and eternity was of little consequence . . . that he was a faithful follower of the author of evil was worthy of note.

He had been an angel, created by God and given the privilege of standing for all eternity in the glory of his Creator's presence. Then, in the great, bright reaches of eternity past, he and untold millions of his kind—a third of the heavenly host—had followed Lucifer in a rebellion against their Maker and were cast out of heaven forever. Now, based solely on his capacity to hate, Missy Parker's enemy ranked as a midlevel lieutenant in the hierarchy of demonic forces. He had not had a home for untold thousands of years, but roamed the earth, stepping from page to page through history in search of those whose unguarded lives could be decimated by his malevolence.

In the late spring of 1945, as summer prepared to launch itself at the cotton country of the Mississippi Delta, the demon lingered near Cat Lake because he had a new, focused passion: He wanted to be the instrument of this favored girl's death. He chose to make his headquarters below the surface of the quiet lake because the deep darkness suited his nature.

He had singled out Missy because she represented all that he loathed. She was happy, beautiful, and loved; he was none of those things, nor would he ever be. Killing her would not make him happy, but her death would bring lifelong pain to those around her, and his solitary function—his duty, the reason he existed—was to broadcast pain. The demon let the girl live untroubled for a week while he watched her . . . and planned.

At the end of those seven days, he devised a plan that would shatter the lives of all who knew her and would force Missy's friends to watch her being killed. When he couldn't find the animal that his scheme called for in the waters of Cat Lake, he expanded the scope of his search. He went eight miles east and moved for two days and nights through the thick grass, water lilies, and moss-hung cypress trees at the edges of Mossy Lake—seeking, listening. The quick-tick heartbeats of small mammals, birds, and cold-blooded reptiles came to him, every one too puny to suit his purpose. He wanted to kill the girl in a way that would strike fear in the hearts of all who ever heard about her death. He wanted a fierce and aggressive animal for his purposes. He wanted something the appearance of which would cause grown men to shudder. Something sinister. Something devastating.

He wanted an alligator.

His intention was to invade the creature's mind, take its possessed body to Cat Lake, and use it to do his will. He was just imagining how he would use the giant's teeth to shred the girl's flesh when he heard the heartbeat. What came to him was the deep *thug-gish, thug-gish* of something big. His practiced senses told him that it was as large as a human; he pictured a one-hundred-pound animal. And it was, only more so.

It slipped effortlessly through the shallow water around the cypress trees. Not a whisper of sound accompanied its passage. At first, he was too shocked to believe what was before him. It was beyond all he could have hoped for. He moved closer, undetected, then became motionless and watched as it glided away from him. He knew immediately that it would be the key component in a stunning triumph.

His mind ricocheted from thought to thought as he followed, watched, and plotted how he would use it. Alligators might generate fear; this beast was terror with skin on it. From behind, he inched closer still.

Its head whipped around in his direction; its heart rate escalated. It knew he was near. It couldn't possibly see or hear him, but it *knew*.

He was amazed for the first time in long ages. He had wanted an alligator, but instead he got this special creature.

A six-foot-long cottonmouth water moccasin.

The demon's invasion of the snake's body was immediate—and the animal's resistance was instantaneous and forceful. Every being and animal he had ever possessed had resisted strongly; the snake was no different. He overlaid its will with his own and seized control of its mind before it could do damage to itself. He was in complete control of its body faster than it could flick its tongue.

When evening came, he left Mossy Lake with his prisoner. It took him two nights, traveling only in darkness, to get back to Cat Lake. Patience was not one of his virtues; it was a means to an end.

The captive snake was a waspish representative of an aggressive species, but it had met its match—its new master was the personification of unrestrained wickedness. At Cat Lake water moccasins were plentiful, so at his direction the demon's minions spread out and harvested for themselves the largest of the poisonous creatures; their singular goal was the destruction of the girl. Near midnight, on the twelfth day after the altercation on the bridge, the demons gathered in their captured snake bodies at the south end of the dark waters and planned the girl's death. Any individual reptile in the collection possessed enough venom to kill three people the size of the girl; as a group they would take her life and leave horror in its place.

You have been selected because of your cunning, the leader told his underlings. *Our time will come soon. Until it does, we must remain alert and poised to attack. The one we will kill is the favored of many. When we kill her, we will break the spirits of her friends and family, and we will spread myriad doubts about the Enemy among the churchgoing fools in this miserable place.*

His words were beyond human understanding and exuded a stark hatred of anything living. That which emanated from the creature could never be described in human terms because nothing in the languages of mankind could capture the depth and strength of the dark one's desire to destroy.

Unveiled contempt blended itself into snarled responses. This hatred for all things, even themselves, was the defining characteristic of the demon's race, and he was the leader of this group only because his capacity to allocate evil was stronger than any of those who answered to him. Beyond his strength, however, the demon and his followers were allied by a powerful, eternal bond: their harmonized and overpowering hatred of the Enemy. There had never been, nor would there ever be, a time when they hated anything as much as He whose will they ceaselessly plotted to obstruct.

The demons looked forward to that promised day when they would be cast into the lake of fire; their rejection of God had assured it. While the clock ticked toward that day, they would sow evil in such a way that people would question the power of God; in so doing, the demons would influence as many of the humans as possible to accompany them into eternal death. The might of their supreme leader, the prince of the power of the air, would overshadow any thoughts of God when the demons pulled back the veil and showed horror to the humans at Cat Lake.

The child's daily routines were predictable, and her enemy's plans were well considered. The killing would not take place in the water. Historical accounts of people who had fallen into swarms of snakes were rare, but they were not unheard of. What they would do to this girl must never be mistaken for coincidence. The child was to be their main target, but they would have the resources to attack any of the humans foolish enough to come to her aid. Their strategy called for them to start by slashing the child's flesh with their fangs, wounding her as deeply as the cruel syringes would allow. When her would-be rescuers drew near, the demons would inject her with enough of their poison to ensure her death, then save their remaining venom for those who would attempt to save her. In the second stage of the battle, the demon-possessed serpents would see how many of the interfering humans they could assassinate. The dark angels would continue to use the captive water moccasins to attack the humans until the flesh of the snakes' bodies was rendered useless. No one would ever mistake this orchestrated attack for an accidental snakebite.

The council of war ended. In the dark waters of the lake, the V-shaped wakes caught pieces of starlight as the assassins glided away . . . to hide and wait in the coffee-colored waters.

The lake became still. Quiet. The moonless night was only a pale shadow against the approaching darkness.

CHAPTER THREE

Signs had been posted in all the towns within fifty miles for a month before the contest. Sunday, June 3, was the announced day for the Mississippi Delta Hunting Club's annual Coon on the Log competition. People all over that part of the state knew about the coming event on Cat Lake.

When the appointed Sunday finally came, gallons of Brunswick stew simmered in black cooking pots over open fires; Bedford Maxwell and some of the other club members had been up at the north end of the lake cooking since the previous afternoon. Their concoction contained very little beef but was heavy on venison, squirrel, game birds, and black pepper. Bottles of beer were iced down for the men who would want it, with Cokes for the rest. Those who wanted to drink something harder would bring their own; Mississippi was a "dry" state.

The event attracted men, boys, and coonhounds from most of the Delta and from as far away as the hills. About ten o'clock, the early arrivals came out to "help Bedford with the stew," which meant they would be half drunk when the first hound hit the water.

That morning, the pastor spent the whole sermon droning on about being ready. He said "be ready" in every other sentence.

Our job, he said, was to be ready to step up and get the job done when the moment came. A. J. Mason smiled. Brother Frank Smith talked as if he would have them all pack a lunch every time they left the house in case somebody was unexpectedly called away to Africa or someplace.

Mason was fifty-six years old. He'd been a Christian since the first year of the current century. A quiet man, but warm enough, he was serious when it was called for but carried a willingness to smile or chuckle. He had been born in Moores Point, and he figured he would die there. Well secluded from all beaten paths, the small town had two banks, three grocery stores, two drugstores, a Methodist church, a Baptist church, and a gin.

Mason thought he relied on God, but he'd never seen a miracle. The man read his Bible and prayed, but he'd never heard God speak. In fact, the activities of God seemed sparse and unspectacular in the Delta. Be that as it may, because he didn't take his praying lightly, when the preacher invited the congregation to pray silently about being ready, Mason bowed his head. He told God that he wanted to be ready, that he wanted to hear well if God called on him, and that he didn't want to ever do anything to embarrass his Lord.

He closed his silent prayer, saying, *Lord, if anything ever happens here I'll be real surprised, but that doesn't keep me from wantin' to be ready. I'd be obliged if You'd see fit to keep me sharper than most. Amen.*

After the service, Mason said his good-byes and got into his car to drive home. He put his toe on the starter and the engine caught. Intermixed with the sounds of the engine starting, he heard someone nearby say, "Be ready."

A. J. Mason wasn't a nervous man. He didn't jump, but he did sit back and look around the car. Nothing. The front seat was as empty as he already knew it was, and the nearest person outside was Reese Pemberton. Reese had woken up from his nap in the pew and was heading home to take up where he'd left off. Mason looked in the backseat. More nothing. He craned his neck to check the floor in the back. An empty pair of his rubber boots. His ears were playing tricks on him.

Sunday dinner at the Masons' house usually included Mason, his wife, their six children and their spouses, and what appeared to be about fifteen or seventy grandchildren. Normally there'd be seven men present, but two sons and a son-in-law were gone to the war. It was Mason's custom to leave the house after his Sunday nap and spend the afternoon riding the county roads looking at the crops and shooting up two boxes of .22 cartridges.

To wake himself from his daily nap, Mason always used a trick his daddy taught him. He wrapped his fingers around his pocketknife and let his hand dangle over the side of the bed. When he dropped off to sleep, his fingers would relax and the knife would hit the rug by his bed and wake him up.

The sounds of the house were just drifting away when someone standing near the head of the bed said, "Be ready."

He bent his elbow and looked in his hand. One Case pocketknife. He had been awake.

It had been the same voice. Not Brother Smith's voice, somebody else's. *Strange*, he thought.

Just before two o'clock, he got down his rifle, made sure there was a round in the chamber and the magazine was full, and left to go shooting. He put the rifle on the car's front seat and backed out of the driveway.

"Daddy!"

He stopped in the road and let his youngest son walk over to the car.

"Would you take this thing out an' shoot it?" He held out a rifle, a pump-action .22 Winchester. "I'm thinkin' 'bout buyin' it from Frost, an' he says it's a good gun. Would you mind lookin' it over?"

"Glad to." Mason finessed the gun through the car window so that it wouldn't get scraped or be pointed at the boy. After giving it an expert once-over, he said, "Looks clean enough. I'll shoot it this afternoon."

"I 'preciate it."

The boy walked back to the house. Mason made a place on the front seat for the pump. He put the car in gear and remembered the voice's message. *Be ready.*

The family didn't think much about it when Mason came back into the house to get his shotgun and a box of shells. In his hands, a good .22 would take care of almost any imaginable circumstance. His choice to confront the unimaginable was another pump—a Winchester twelve-gauge loaded with double-aught buckshot.

He put the shotgun on the backseat to keep it out of the way.

An hour after the last church let out, most of the Coon on the Log contestants and spectators were moving into place. Vehicles of all sorts lined the county road. Men and boys and dogs trudged down the dusty turn row by the Parkers' cotton field on their way to the clearing by the lake. Owners staked out their coon dogs and registered them for the contest. As people continued to arrive, things got louder. The men visited with old friends, told lies about their dogs, and drank beer and bootleg whiskey. Boys of all ages chased each other around the trees and into the nearby fields; they stomped down about an acre of knee-high cotton, tormented both dogs and men, and generally made nuisances of themselves. The dogs, somewhat better behaved than most of the boys, bayed, sniffed each other, and, when the boys weren't near, slept in the shade of the cypress trees.

Mason's shooting sessions usually took place out north of town on the Quiver River bridge. He'd toss up pebbles the size of marbles and bust them with the .22. Out of a hundred shots he would always miss less than half a dozen, sometimes none. The clean little pump didn't disappoint him. Winchester could be relied on to make a fine gun, and he was partial to them. He shot up most of the cartridges and loaded the rifles to go down south of town. He'd visit for a short while with the other members of the hunting club and make it home in time to hear the evening news.

Flowers and rose bushes, under Pip's careful hand, grew near Pap's grave. She was on her hands and knees among the flowers, wearing a pair of Mose's old khaki pants under a long skirt, her hands and arms covered with dirt. Sunday was the day Pip liked most; she wouldn't allow herself to do what she called "real work," but she would happily exhaust herself while she puttered around in her yard.

On the cabin porch, Pearl was teaching her doll how to have afternoon tea. The first-grader was still in her Sunday dress, a concession from Pip because the county's youngest lady rarely got a speck of dirt on anything.

As soon as he got home from church, Mose Junior swapped his wool pants and Sunday shoes for overalls and bare feet; he was watching in the direction of the bridge. The sounds from the clearing on the other end of the lake drifted on the water to the cabin in the pecan trees.

"Momma, how come them mens don't jes' shoot the coon?"

Pip was too busy to talk about white men's foolishness; something about June weather made the weeds grow as if they were being fertilized. Without looking up, she said, "*Those* men."

"Yessum. Those mens."

"Men."

"Yessum. Men."

"Go ask your daddy, son. He's the one knows 'bout huntin'."

"Yessum." The boy shook his head and walked away. *Have mercy. How come I had to do all that work fuh nuthin'?*

"It's 'cause you need to talk right," Pip said.

The boy kept walking; he was used to her reading his mind. He made it to where Mose was working with something under the hood of the old truck. "How come they don't jes' shoot the coon, Daddy?"

"How's that?" Mose didn't look up either.

"I say, how come them mens don't jes' shoot that coon, the

coon on the log? How come they sends the dogs out in the water after 'im?"

Mose kept at whatever he was doing for a moment longer.

Over by Pap's grave, Junior's momma muttered, *"Those* men."

Mose came out from under the hood and smiled in the direction of the dirt-covered English teacher; baggy clothes and yard dirt couldn't hide the fact that she was one of the prettiest women in Allen County. *"Those* men ain't wantin' meat, son. It's like a race." He waved at the black water. "They puts a coon on a log out in the lake 'bout thirty or forty feet an' turns a dog loose from a startin' line on the bank. They jes' seein' how fast the dog can git out there an' git the coon off'n the log an' fetch him back up on dry ground. The dog what's the fastest takes the prize." Mose stuck his head back under the hood.

"How long does it take?"

Boys an' questions, he thought. He chuckled, straightening from what he was doing. "Sometimes kinda slow like, sometimes faster. I reckon it pretty much depends on the dog . . . an' the coon."

"Looks like to me they gonna get they dogs all skint up by that coon for nothin'."

Mose nodded. "I reckon that's so. A coon is a sho' 'nuff mouthful for a swimmin' dog."

The boy considered his next question, knowing the answer. "Can we go watch it?"

"Bes' not, son. The white mens be drinkin' some. Bes' stay here 'bout."

White men who were drinking didn't worry Junior; he was the fastest fifth-grader at Stark Elementary. In fact, he could outrun everybody in the whole school except that long-legged Gentry girl. On top of that, he had been a Christian since Easter. The Bible made it real clear that God was with him every minute. His momma showed him where the same book said every child had his own personal guardian angel that didn't do anything but watch over just that one child. His momma said his angel had his hands full. He wasn't sure how he could still be afraid of snakes when he knew he had Jesus in his heart and the angel guarding him, and he prayed about it every night. His momma told him that the good Lord would get him over being afraid of snakes when He saw fit; the angel would be there either way—God said so.

The gathering at the north end of the lake kept his attention. "I reckon we can still play on the bridge?"

Mose looked up toward the long, low bridge. The heat was heavy, and the kids could swim at the bridge. He said, "I reckon. But you keep a eye out. Stay on this side. An' you boys watch out for that girl." He was shaking his head. "She don't know to be afraid of nuthin'."

The boy would do what his daddy said; he and the boy and that girl would play south of the bridge while the white men stayed north. Unless . . .

"Daddy? Is them mens—those mens gonna be shootin' up there?" The boy was scared of snakes, and nothing else . . . almost.

Mose knew of no reason for the boy to be afraid of a white man with a gun, but the concern had surfaced twice this week. "No, no, boy. They won't be havin' no guns. Mistah R. D., he don't allow it no more 'cept for them men in the boat. You three do yo' playin' an' jes' stay clear of them doin's on the other side of the road."

Junior thought he might ought to tell his daddy about the dream, but he didn't. "Yessuh."

The dream was probably the only real secret Junior had. He and Bobby and the girl pretty much told each other everything, but Junior kept the dream about the man and the gun to himself because he didn't understand it. It seemed like every morning for a week he had come awake with the same memory of the dream.

In the dream he's in terrible pain; his body feels as if it's on fire. A white man is falling out of the sky holding a big gun. In his dream he's on the ground and he can't breathe right. The man is yelling something he can't hear. The pain is increasing. Then a voice he's never heard speaks straight to him, real calm-like. "Tell him to shoot. Tell him to hurry and shoot." He feels more pain. The man shoots and shoots. Then he wakes up.

He looked across the lake to see if the two Parker children were out in the yard yet. The yard was empty. He turned to see his daddy watching him.

"You okay, boy?"

He knew he would have to tell his daddy about the dream eventually; it was heavy on his mind. This would be as good a time as any. As he looked up at Mose something moved in the corner of his eye. He turned to see Bobby and Missy running across the Parkers' yard, heading for the boat. They waved. He could tell Daddy about the dream tonight. He turned away toward the bridge. "Yessuh, Daddy, I be jes' fine."

"C'mere, boy."

Uh-oh, he knows. He turned and plodded back. Bobby and Missy would beat him to the float.

Mose bent over and rested his hand on his son's shoulder. "I got somethin' I wants you to start doin', boy. I wants you to keep yo' eye on that girl. Bobby watches pretty good, but four eyes is better than two. You be sure an' watch out that girl don't get hurt."

His daddy didn't give him many orders, and he didn't want to balk, but Missy didn't take much to being watched after. He offered a small explanation. "Daddy, she don't listen to me. She don't listen to nobody."

From a boy who had hardly talked back since Easter, it was a strong response. "Well, son, she ain't careful enough, an' that's a fact, but we needs to be troubled some 'bout them that ain't Christians. They needs more protection than us. It gives 'em time to hear the truth."

"So they can hear 'bout Jesus an' git to go to heaven?" He couldn't bring himself to say the other word. He had told the two white children about Jesus a hundred times, but they weren't interested. He'd prayed for them every night since Easter, and he worried that he'd get to heaven and they wouldn't be there.

"Somethin' like that."

"What if she don't listen?" Junior asked.

"She don't need to listen, boy. You can watch after her like the angels watches after you . . . quietlike. You can do that, can't you . . . like a man?"

"Yessuh. I can watch her quietlike . . . like a man." *I guess that's all I can do*, he thought. *That girl is bad 'bout bein' fracshush.*

"I knowed I could count on you." His daddy straightened and said, "Go on, then."

Mose Junior took off for the bridge. He just might beat them there. He was fast.

Bobby and Missy paddled up to the float just as Mose Junior clambered down the ladder.

An immediate altercation took place over what the afternoon would be used for. Missy and Mose Junior wanted to see who could jump the farthest from the bridge. Bobby, who didn't like to admit that he was afraid of heights, wanted to try catching turtles or crawdads. The two younger kids stood on the float, and Missy demanded a vote. Bobby, declaring that the democratic process didn't apply on the high seas, pushed away and left them to do whatever they wanted. The two daredevils raced for the ladder, both yelling, "I'm first!"

Bobby pulled a book about how to fly airplanes out of his back pocket and settled into the sticky bottom of the *GENRALROB ERT EEEL*.

Artesian springs fed Cat Lake. Its waters were a weak tea amber color in the shallows; out from the banks, its surface became a mirror-finish black. From the deeps below the children, a voice darker than the waters said, *Move the boat away from the other two.*

Thirty minutes later, Mose Junior was in the water after making "the longest jump ever done." He looked to see if Bobby had observed the record breaker, but the boat had moved out from the floating platform. Neither boy noticed that the tiny craft was barely drifting, making headway into a mild current of fragrance coming from Old Mrs. Parker's honeysuckle.

Junior swam toward the large float tethered to the bridge pilings. Reaching from the lake's surface up to the bridge railing, a ladder was nailed to the nearest piling. It provided access to and from the floating platform for those who might want to climb down to fish or climb up to jump.

The float was the previous year's summertime project. The kids, with the help of Leon, had built the float with materials gleaned from around the shop and lumber that had come from the sides of a fairly good cotton wagon. Leon's wages consisted of the entire contents of one box of Old Mr. Parker's cigars. Missy had extended an open invitation to R. D. for the float's use, since he had provided the lumber, labor, and cigars. He shook his head and thanked her for the gracious offer.

Because Old Mr. Parker had seen too many demonstrations of the girl's powers, Leon got off with a mild lecture. "Leon, you can't be lettin' that girl tell you what to do. She an' them boys will have you helpin' 'em tear down all the cotton houses an' then they'll start on this'n." He indicated his own home.

Leon respected his boss, but like most of the men around Moores Point, black and white, what he felt for Missy Parker bordered on worship. He laughed at his boss's words, saying, "Yassuh, Mistah R. D., I reckon you right, but I swear that girl don't know she jes' a baby. I reckon she gonna be a trial for some po' man."

"I reckon." Parker had come to the same conclusion when the girl was two years old. "But if you're fixin' to let 'em start tearin' down houses, you let 'em start on yours."

The girl topped the ladder in time to watch Mason's car drive onto the bridge. She waited for him to get closer so that she could jump while she had an audience.

Mason heard and saw a sharp, dust-drenched *phoosh*. The front tire on his side gave up some pressure. He grappled a little with the steering wheel to counter the slight swerve and slowed to a stop less than five feet from where the waiting girl stood. As the car stopped, there was another muffled explosion from the tire; dust from the bridge floor drifted back along his side of the car. He'd never blown out a tire so slowly. The abrupt maneuvering had caused the rifles to slide against the far door; he put them back in place and opened his door to survey the damage. *Hmm,* he thought, *that tire's less than a week old.* A closer inspection showed a precise cut in the sidewall. *Now, how 'bout that. Looks like somebody slit that thing with a straight razor.* He looked behind the car on the bridge . . . not so much as a large rock. He rubbed his jaw while he pondered his situation. *Hmm.*

Missy Parker had long since concluded that there were some men who would never come up to scratch, but A. J. Mason was next to R. D. for being worth her favor. Patience wasn't her long suit, however, and she had shared enough attention with a messed-up old piece of rubber. She teetered on the bridge railing, and demanded, "Hey, A. J.! Watch *me!*"

When he stepped from the car, Mason wasn't conscious of bringing the rifle with him.

From his place in the coolness beneath the float, the dark spirit said, *Now.*

CHAPTER FOUR

Something touched Mason's shoulder, and a voice that was becoming familiar said, "Pay attention."

He looked around. There was no one on the bridge with him but Missy Parker—a skinny, brown-haired little thing getting ready to jump from the bridge rail.

Every day for the rest of his life, he would recall that she had been grinning. She was turning away from him; the movement lifted the short-cut hair in seeming slow motion, moving it up and away from her like strips of ribbon on a fast carousel. A halo of water droplets escaped the brown tendrils and caught the afternoon sun like dozens of transparent pearls. The pearls arced away from the girl and fell in a perfect circle. Water ran down brown legs from the rolled up overalls, her knobby little knees bent, her body leaned out slightly, tanned arms lifted, and her knees began to straighten. And he'd remember how fast the grin changed to something else.

She still had her feet on the railing when she looked down and saw the snake.

A useless scramble of windmilling arms only delayed the inescapable plunge. Almost invisible against the black water, the snake coasted to a stop directly beneath her and waited.

She and the snake looked into each other's eyes.

The snake was waiting for her.

The girl's futile attempt to regain the railing cost her any chance of controlling her fall toward the waiting killer, and gravity inevitably overcame her efforts. She had time for a single panic-charged flash of face at Mason and a scream as she toppled from the rail. "Bob-beeeeee! Help meeeeee!"

Bobby looked up from his book in time to watch Missy cartwheel off the railing. He was startled to discover that the boat was at least a hundred yards south of the bridge. The last thing his daddy had said to him before the screen door slammed was, "Watch out for your sister."

She was still falling when the next scream came in one long, drawn-out syllable. "Ssssnnnnaaaaaaaake!"

Bobby grabbed the short paddle and dug it into the water.

Most of the men in the vicinity were accustomed to hearing children at play. Everyone who heard that first scream knew the girl was in trouble. The men at the hunting club's gathering turned to see Missy plunge into the lake. Bobby Lee started running for the bridge.

Just offshore from the hunting club's activity, Ruddell Noble and Horton Milstead were manning the coon-tenders' boat. The two men heard the long squeal and looked up just in time to see the girl's splayed body careen into the water below the bridge. Her second scream reached them as she hit the water.

Ruddell watched the girl's wild entry and yelled, "That's Missy! Unloose that line! We'll take a look!"

Milstead was already jerking the rope free.

Ruddell yelled again. "An' throw off that empty cage!"

The coon-tenders' job was to move back and forth between the lake bank and the log in a ten-foot boat to bring out coons, rescue dogs, and such. Ruddell Noble's responsibilities also included the care and maintenance of a small outboard motor, a brand-new one. Brand-new because the last motor had been a casualty of the previous year's festivities.

Ruddell was the more vocal of the two. He was seventy years old, crotchety, and pretended he couldn't hear a church bell ring if he were standing in it. He was also the club's self-appointed, official boat-driver-in-charge, and he didn't suffer his assistant coon-tenders lightly. His orders were screamed in a hurricane of words, followed by scathing criticism, regardless of whether or not they were carried out well. He didn't know anything about Horton Milstead, except that he was at State College on the GI Bill. He figured the youngster was a lazy good-for-nothing because he was using up the government's money on schooling.

Horton, within the last two hours, had made a cool assessment of the boat driver: Ruddell was crazy. He decided that if God sent another flood, he would choose to drown before he'd get back into a boat with Ruddell Noble.

In '44 a coon managed to escape from one of the cages. It scampered between the tenders' legs, climbed up on the motor, and did a belly flop into the lake. During the course of the getaway, Ruddell made an attempt to shoot the fugitive, but his reaction time was trailing the coon by about half a pint. In rapid succession Ruddell managed to blow a hole in the boat's hull, shoot the gas can, and blast a cavity the size of a Garrett snuff bottle in the Johnson Seahorse motor. The unscathed coon paddled off to the far shore. Ruddell and his assistant coon-tender avoided personal catastrophe by jumping into the lake just before the gas can blew up.

Scooter Hall correctly observed that it was a minor miracle that Ruddell hadn't burned down the lake.

Junior was at the float when Missy screamed the dreaded word. His climb from the water to the deck, normally a struggle, was made in one fluid move.

Do not kill her. Do not bite her. Do not harm her. Drive her to me. The dark voice under the float made the instructions clear. *I will kill her while they watch. When she is dead, we will deal with the other two and whoever comes near us.*

Missy had screamed all the way to the water. When she tried to re-fill her lungs, the water choked her. She had landed on the snake, but it had missed biting her. Missy was still underwater and didn't know where right-side-up was. Panic shut down her reasoning process. She struggled for breath and tried to yell for help while fighting the water. The darkness below the surface that she was so accustomed to had become her enemy. The snake had to be nearby, and she was looking for it when she saw the sunlight through the water. The next thing she saw was the black S-curve of the snake's silhouette between her and the light. She had to go past where it was or drown where she was. She tried to angle away from it, stroking upward. She knew it was going to bite her.

Mason had watched the girl's fall and strode to the railing.

"Be ready," said the voice in his mind.

God, please don't let me be going crazy, he prayed.

He brought the rifle to his shoulder and snapped off the safety, tracking the barrel in a circle just outside where he expected the girl to reappear.

He was leaning out over the railing when her face materialized out of the amber water. He had been searching but hadn't seen a snake. He was hoping it was a false alarm when Missy gurgled a choke and a scream at the same time. She was facing away from the float. Two feet out from the tip of her nose he watched the snake's head barely break the surface. It was followed by an immense body.

Have mercy. It was a monster longer than the girl. Subconsciously Mason prayed, *Lord, help us.*

The snake stirred its body enough to move an inch closer to the girl's face, then stopped. The girl was already backpaddling furiously.

CHAPTER FIVE

What Mason "saw" when he fired a gun was different.

He never had been able to teach anyone how to shoot, mainly because his method was so completely unorthodox. He didn't swing his gun to "track" moving targets, and he didn't bother with a gun's sights. When shooting birds on the wing, he just pointed at the spot where the bird was going to be when the birdshot got there and pulled the trigger. If his target wasn't moving, he just looked at where he wanted the bullet to go and squeezed off the shot. It didn't make much sense to other shooters, but you couldn't argue with success. A. J. Mason could shoot quail on the rise with a *.22* rifle.

Mason didn't bother to breathe, relax, aim, or make any other preparations. He looked at the dead center of the narrow spot on the snake, right where the triangular head joined the fat body, and touched the trigger.

The men tending the coons looked back toward the bridge in time to see A. J. Mason shoot into the water near the girl. It was worse than they first thought. Ruddell Noble was R. D. Parker's brother-in-law, and the girl in the water was his favorite great-niece. Ruddell yelled at Horton to hang on, jerked the starter rope once, and moved the throttle lever all the way to the right;

the engine was still coming up to speed when he rammed the tiller hard over. Horton managed to grab a handhold just as the boat tilted forty-five degrees to the side, swapped ends, and accelerated back through its own exhaust smoke with the engine running wide open. Ruddell pointed at the shotgun, yelling, "May as well get that thing loaded!"

Horton was already digging in his pocket for the shells.

Now was not the time to sink the boat—Horton decided to leave the chamber empty.

The bullet tore the snake's head off, but that didn't calm the girl. The snake's body, instead of sinking out of sight, began rolling and twisting, thrashing and sprinkling a froth of red bubbles onto the girl. Missy tried to back away and push water at the contorting thing at the same time.

Mason stole a glance at the float. Mose Junior was huddled as far as he could get from the action. Mason drew in his breath to call to the boy to go to her, but no one else could help her . . . except him.

The girl didn't know that. "Bobbbeeeeee!"

Missy didn't see the next snake, but Mason did.

Ruddell leaned forward and tossed the empty cage overboard. Missy couldn't weigh much over thirty pounds. *Lord, she ain't big enough to handle a snakebite. If you'll just take care of her, I'll start back goin' to church. I promise.* He stopped praying long enough to hear another shot, then raised the ante. *An', Lord, I'll quit drinkin'. I mean it.*

The giant-bee whine of the engine couldn't drown out the girl's pleas for help. Ruddell reached behind him to hold the throttle against the stop. They were too far away—way too far.

He and Horton watched A. J. shoot into the water again, then again, and one more time.

A. J. don't ever miss. What did he have to shoot so many times? A gator? Sweet Jesus, don't let it be a gator.

Ruddell's eyes strained to take in the details at the bridge.

Mose Washington's boy had rolled up in a ball. He was holding his hands over his ears and squeezing his eyes shut. The old man continued to pray. *I promise. I mean it, Lord. I promise.*

Horton threw an uncertain look at the screaming motor. "Will that motor put up with bein' run so hard? It won't quit, will it?"

Ruddell shook his head. *Dadgummit! A college boy could always be depended on to ask a stupid question!* He didn't want to argue at the top of his lungs but was disgusted that the young fool would pick a time like this to wonder about the engine's worthiness. *I tuned this thing myself, college boy,* he thought. *I'd bet my own life on it.*

The giant bee left. The motor that master mechanic and official boat-driver-in-charge Mr. Ruddell Noble of Moores Point, Mississippi, had tuned himself didn't cough. It didn't sputter. It didn't stumble. It quit plumb cold.

Ruddell had the starter rope in his hand before Horton's mouth could fall open. He wound the rope around the engine's flywheel and yanked on it.

Nothing.

Mason had killed too many snakes.

The demons were keeping what was left of their hosts on the surface. They writhed near the girl and contaminated the surface with mucous-thick redness. She was getting tired. "June—" A drawn breath. "—yurrrrr!"

Bobby Lee and a herd of men raised dust in their race toward the bridge.

Ruddell rewound and pulled the rope.

Horton looked toward the scene of the battle. The little colored boy was standing and looking wide-eyed in their direction. He waved his arms for them to hurry. Horton turned back to watch Ruddell making continued, fruitless attempts to start the motor.

Junior watched Ruddell's boat and thought, *Why did them white mens stop? Are they scared of the snakes like me? Is the man on the bridge the one I dreamed about?*

Moses Lincoln Washington Jr. could hear his daddy's words. *I wants you to keep yo' eye on that girl.*

And his own. *Yassuh. I can watch her quietlike.*

Horton looked back to the bridge in time to see the colored boy sprint across the float and lift himself in a long jump that would land him in the midst of whatever was causing all the shooting.

When Horton turned back to his partner, Ruddell looked him straight in the eye and said, "Pray."

He'd figured that Ruddell was a prime candidate for the insane asylum at Whitfield; now the old man's brain had unraveled because of a torn-up outboard motor. The only thing he could think of to say was, "Huh?"

"You heard me. Pray!"

"Whaddayou want me to say, Ruddell?" His eyes strayed to the shotgun on the seat between them. *I guess I could pray you ain't fixin' to go beeserk an' kill me.*

Ruddell cocked his head, then nodded as if he had just heard the answer to Horton's question. Horton watched in fascination as Ruddell Noble turned and dropped to his knees, smack dab in front of the quiet motor. Noble said, "Lord, I can't do it, but You can. If You're gonna have us help her, You gotta be the One to start the motor."

Horton didn't know what was in the water with the two kids, but it couldn't be as scary as being in a boat with a man praying to an outboard motor. He looked back at the action. Several bunches of boys were streaming across the bridge toward the shooter. He wished he were with them, or even back in France.

Mason watched Mose Junior land in the water next to the girl. He didn't think it would help anything, but it seemed good for the girl not to be alone. He heard the boat motor quit, and thought, *That ain't good.* Having someone to snatch the kids out of the water might bring the nightmare to a wakening. Maybe.

The first crowd of boys arrived at the scene. When they saw all the blood and twisting snakes, they yelled questions at each other, they yelled at the girl and the colored boy, two started throwing up for no reason, and a disordered squad of preschoolers turned and took off to fetch their fathers.

Taking his eyes off the water for a fraction of a second, Mason found a familiar face—Todd Stiles's boy. He yelled over the bedlam, "Stiles! You know how to handle a gun?"

The boy peered over the railing and yelled back, "You want me to go in there an' git 'em outta the water, Mistah Mason?"

"Nonono," Mason answered all in one word. *We're not having a war with the water.* He beckoned him closer with a head jerk and asked him again, "Do you know about guns?"

"Yessuh." The boy's voice wasn't shaking too badly.

One of the taller boys stepped over the rail at the ladder.

Mason caught the move from the corner of his eye and looked up to yell, "Hey!" The boy stopped.

Mason had the urge to be closer to the water himself, but he could do more good from where he was. And he didn't need any more people cluttering up the area around the two kids. His eyes back on the water, Mason told Stiles, "Tell him we don't need more people in the water, son. I don't want to shoot into a crowd."

The Stiles boy looked at the kid by the ladder and shook his head. The vice commander told the other kid, "Don't let nobody down there."

Mason had to shout at Stiles over the screaming of the boys. "Can you reach in my front seat an' get that other .22 an' bring it over here by me? It's loaded. Can you do that?"

Before the boy could reply, Mason's rifle went off for the sixth time. *Where are they comin' from?*

"Yessuh." The boy didn't jump when the rifle fired. He

glanced over the rail to see the result. He was scared, but he could still function.

"Go on then, son. I don't know what's goin' on here, but that's about the sixth snake I've shot. They're after those youngsters, an' me an' you gotta hold 'em off."

The boy turned away.

"Stiles!"

"Yessuh?"

"Look on the seat an' bring those cartridges."

In seconds the boy was back with the rifle. "What you want me to do now?"

Mason had been thinking. His face was grim, resolute. Ready. "Go back to the car an' get me that shotgun."

The boy came back. "It's here, Mistah Mason, an' the shells. What do we do now?"

"Do you know about prayin', boy?"

Stiles didn't answer as quickly as before. He wasn't going to have to pray in front of all these boys, was he? Finally he said, "Yessuh, I reckon I pray some."

"Okay. I want you to stand right here next to me an' hold that .22 ready an' watch for snakes. I don't know what's goin' on here, an' I'm not sure how many we're gonna have to kill, son, but if I empty this gun I'm gonna have you reload it while I shoot that one there. We gotta be ready. Understand?"

"Yessuh."

"An' I want you to pray that I don't miss. We'll use the shotgun if we have to."

"I can do it."

"An' tell one of those boys to drive that car off the bridge."

Mason never took his eyes off the two children who were centered in the conflict below him. *Lord, is this the* ready *I prayed about?*

The demon couldn't do anything about the old man on the bridge, but he had enough lieutenants to outlast him. He spoke to his henchmen. *Distract the black one. Do not kill him . . . not yet.*

Mose Junior was trying to drag Missy toward the float while she fought the bodies of the snakes. The girl couldn't keep fighting for long, but the possibility of children drowning wasn't in the forefront of Mason's thoughts; he was worried about running out of ammunition. If he ran out of bullets, people would have to be sacrificed to go down into the battle and bring the two children out. He'd go first and maybe get them both before the venom rendered him useless. For now, he was wondering how many snakes there were in the lake and what was going on below the black surface of the water. Even as the thought went through his mind, Mose Junior made a noise for the first time.

A pealing, sustained wail resonated down the lake.

The watching crowd collectively sucked in its breath when the boy's arm came out of the water. Camouflaged against the child's black skin, and initially mistaken by Mason for some kind of hideous swelling, were the tight coils of yet another huge moccasin. When the boys on the bridge saw what was on Junior's arm they leaned forward in unison, then got their breath back and became his chorus. No questions, no advice—just terror in audible form. Even as it cleared the water, the snake buried its fangs in the boy's skinny black shoulder. It was the first time anyone on the bridge had seen a snake strike a human. The pitch of the screaming that couldn't increase somehow did. The Simpson boy fainted.

For as long as he could remember, Junior had secretly believed that one day he would get bitten by a snake, but he wasn't prepared for this. He'd read it in a book at school. *Almost all snakebites in humans occur below the knee.*

The bite was everything the boy had feared it would be. The sharpness of the pain radiated all the way to his waist. Just the shock of having it happen made him almost rigid. The pressure of the snake's mouth had wickedness in it. When he turned his head, the snake stared back at him. Mose Junior looked into the orange-golden eyes and knew he was looking at the devil.

The boy's vision started to blur. He could feel himself losing consciousness. *I can't faint, Jesus. Please don't let me leave this baby out here amongst all these things by herself. Help me. Lord, where's my angel at?*

The coolness of the lake took away the heat in his body. The cold body on his arm was tightening its grip. He thrashed around until he could get his free hand on the snake. He grabbed it below its head and tried to jerk it loose.

Mason killed a snake that was moving in on the girl, then turned his rifle on the boy. He hesitated long enough for his last shot to echo down the lake and, without changing expression, shot twice into the blackness by the boy's hand. The boy, still screaming, peeled off the crippled serpent and threw it from him. The partially destroyed animal started a disjointed struggle to get itself back to the boy. It could still kill.

Mason cut its head off with the next bullet, then dropped the firing pin on an empty chamber.

He held the rifle out to Stiles. The boy took the empty gun and offered the pump. "That'n has one in the chamber, Mistah Mason, an' I'll load this here automatic."

"Take your time, son. You drop those bullets in the dirt an' it'll get in the guns."

"Yessuh."

Mason didn't want to hurt the boy's feelings, but a careful man needed to know. He cracked the action far enough to see the bright brass of the chambered cartridge. He closed the action, thumbed back the pump's hammer, and snugged the curve of the butt plate to his shoulder.

Ready.

CHAPTER SIX

At the cabin Pearl Washington's eyes came open. She sat up in her momma's bed, listening. She looked around the room for a moment, rubbed her eyes, then crawled off the bed. She took a more careful look around the room, then carried her doll over to the little window on the north side of the house.

Outside the window the dog stood with his ears cocked toward the bridge.

The child stood at the window and studied the activity at the bridge for awhile, then went over and touched her momma's arm. "Momma?"

Pip didn't move. If she stayed still, the child might go off and play by herself.

The child patted Pip's arm insistently. "Momma."

Well, a five-minute nap is better than none. She opened one eye and looked into a serious mirror six inches away. "What is it, baby?"

"They's a lots of goin's on at the bridge, Momma."

Pip digested this while her brain was coming awake. "What kind of goin's on, baby?"

"The white mens is all runnin' 'bout an' wavin' they arms. They's heaps o' mens on th' bridge."

Pip opened her other eye.

Her first thought was that Mr. R. D. hadn't let her and Mose help pay for the cotton trailer the children had torn up. He had laughed and said it was the most entertaining thing they had done so far. Mose spent a lot of money on a box of cigars for the man, and he and Pip had their own separate, no-nonsense visits with Mose Junior and Leon. Mose Junior and Leon fared pretty well with Mose; neither of them wanted another encounter with Pip. She had taken a pecan branch and just about worn the pockets off Mose Junior's britches. She tapped Leon's chest with the same stick and promised her brother the identical prescription if he ever let those children talk him into anymore foolishness. "I swear, Leon, that girl can get into more mischief than a pet coon, an' I don't need you coaxin' her along. You hear me?"

It was the most words she'd used on him in a month. Thereafter, he managed on two-for-a-nickel cigars and always seemed to be out of pocket when the kids needed help with their construction ventures. Trifling with Pip was a sure ticket on the train to pain.

Pip closed her eyes for a moment. *Lord, please don't let it be somethin' those three children have done.*

The five-year-old was always shy. Today she was troubled. "Momma?"

"Yes, baby?"

"I thought I heard my Bubba yellin'.'"

Pip rolled out of the bed and walked to the cabin door. Mose had the old truck running and was up to his shoulders under the hood. She walked out into the shade of the porch and looked north. She didn't see any smoke. She couldn't hear anything over the sound of the truck.

Well, the bridge isn't on fire, an' I truly thank You for that, Lord. The children didn't play with matches, and the boys had given up smoking since Old Mr. Parker caught them in back of the chicken house with a pack of his Lucky Strikes. Mr. Parker saw no reason to play favorites between the boys. He tore the Luckies open, counted out each frightened boy an equal share, and said, "Eat 'em." The aftermath was worse than the time they got into Leon's watermelon wine, and the boys still didn't like being around tobacco too much.

From what she could tell, there were a good many people

on the bridge, and another big bunch seemed to be in a foot race or something at that hunting club doings.

People who claimed to know about snakebites said they burned something awful. The arm that suffered the bite didn't work quite right yet, but it didn't burn much either. Mose Junior managed to hook some crippled fingers onto the girl's overalls and headed for the raft. Missy was kicking her feet, but whether it was to help him or to fight snakes he didn't know. Her breathless screams were lost in the noise from the crowd.

Mose Junior got the girl to the float and looked out to see that Bobby was still pretty far away. Lake water gleamed on a black shadow that obscured part of the letters on the boat's bow, and he thought, *Bobby's fixin' to have his own troubles. I reckon I gotta git this girl outta the water by myself.*

He held one of her overall straps until Missy got her hands on the float, then pushed and encouraged her while she used him for a ladder. When she stepped on his shoulder, it didn't seem to hurt as much as it had a few seconds before.

When Missy finally made it out of the water, she quit screaming and collapsed on her back.

Bobby saw the snake mount the front of the boat just after Mose Junior did. He brought the short paddle back and swung it in an arc that met the serpent smack on the side of its head. The black thing was driven sideways with a solid *thunk*.

The activity in the boat caught Mason's attention just in time for him to see the snake immediately remount the boat. The angle was perfect; the distance wasn't—the boat had to be fifty yards away. *Help me.*

A. J. Mason was almost sixty years old. He'd been shooting rifles and shotguns since he was old enough to understand what the trigger was for . . . training for this day . . . becoming a man who was ready. Bobby was cocking the paddle for another swing when the incoming bullet centered itself on the snake's spine and drove pieces of it through the white *R* in *ERT*. Bobby yelled and went over backward as if the bullet had hit him; with the quickness of a spring toy he bounded to his knees.

What was left of the snake's head was crazed—and less than three feet from him. Its eyes glared at him from the front seat of the little boat, its mouth opened and closed rapidly, bouncing itself around on the seat and making a sticky, clapping sound. The boy took the paddle, hands trembling, and swept the evil thing into the water. *What's happening?* he wondered.

Go to the boat. Come in from the other side and wait for my command.
Two more snakes left the middle deeps of the lake.

Mason made a quick survey of the water beneath him and looked back at the struggling boat. Bobby was fighting for more speed out of the awkward little craft, pressing on toward the float.

Mason said to his helper, "Keep an eye on that boat. If he yells, or you see somethin', you tell me."

"Yessuh. This here automatic's loaded again, Mistah Mason. You want it?"

"One in the chamber?"

"Yessuh."

"Show me."

Stiles understood. He pushed the plunger far enough to crack the action open. Bright metal peeked out of the rifle's chamber.

"Good work," Mason said. "Let's swap." He lowered the hammer on the pump, they made a quick exchange, and he told the boy, "Top that one off."

"Yessuh."

From the corner of his eye he could see the boy slide the pump's magazine open and start inserting more bullets. He nodded to himself. *Good! This war ain't over, Lord, an' I 'preciate You sendin' me this boy.*

Pip didn't want Mose to bang his head on the hood, so she stood back, picked up a small rock, and tossed it against his leg. When he looked around, she smiled and walked closer. She didn't like to raise her voice, even to be heard above the noise of the truck.

Mose turned around, grinning as he watched her walk toward him. In spite of his efforts to convince her, she didn't know she was beautiful. "Short nap."

She was used to the grin and tried to ignore it. She got close and pointed her finger. "They're doin' somethin' up on the bridge."

Mose turned to look and pulled a rag out of his back pocket. When he was at the gin, he wore khakis because he was the head man. Today he had on faded overalls. He wiped his hands while he considered the large crowd stirring around on the bridge. Some folks thought he moved slowly; Old Mr. Parker knew he was deliberate. When he got some of the grime off his hands, he reached into the truck and turned the key.

The sounds of the engine died soon enough for them to hear a rifle shot followed by two more. They had time to look at each other just before the next shot sounded. People shooting off the bridge was a common enough thing for a Sunday afternoon. Mose heard his son's voice ask him again, *Daddy? Is those mens gonna be shootin' up there?*

Mose smiled. "Well, I don't see no smoke. That's somethin', ain't it?"

Pip's laugh was as pretty as she was. "Ain't it the God's-honest-truth."

The screen door slammed behind them, and Pearl came out on the porch clutching her doll. "Daddy, I heard my Bubba yellin' up yonder at the bridge."

Mose looked to see what the dog was doing. The dog was leaning forward slightly, sniffing, studying the bridge. As if sensing a question from Mose, he looked at the man and made a whuffing sound.

Below the float, a huge black body stirred impatiently. *Attack the one in the boat. Attack him! Draw the attention of the one on the bridge. The time has come to kill the girl.*

Mose Junior finally made it onto the wooden platform and collapsed beside Missy.

Mose held his hand out to Pearl. "I reckon me an' you an' yo' baby bes' walk up there an' see what yo' Bubba's yellin' 'bout."

Pearl grinned and put her hand in his.

"Well, there's Mose Junior, right yonder on that ol' float," Mose said as he looked up.

Falling in behind them, Pip looked over her shoulder at the gravesite. *The weeds will be there later.*

The dog trotted out to be in front.

Two snakes came to the surface on the far side of the boat. They closed rapidly on their objective, cutting broad wakes in the flat water.

"Mistah A. J., there's some more at the boat!"

Mason looked up to see Stiles pointing at a pair of V-shaped wakes on the far side of the boat.

He cast a make-sure glance at the children on the float, then focused his attention on the boat. It was still a long way out, and Bobby was almost directly between him and the snakes. The sun's glare was in a bad spot, and the black forms in the water were all but invisible.

Lord, that's a bad shot. Help me.

Overhead, a single small cloud chose that moment to move between the sun and the lake. When its shadow cast itself on the water, the triangular shapes of the moccasins' heads stood out as if carved in relief. Mason made a downward gesture with his hand, but Bobby didn't understand.

Mason had time to try again. He motioned for Bobby to get down.

Now that he and Missy were out of the water and closer to the crowd, Mose Junior felt safer. The screams were still coming from just over his head, but the intensity had lessened slightly; the people had calmed some. His shoulder barely bothered him, but the encounter with the moccasin had drained his energy. He didn't feel like moving, but he crawled to the girl's side and said, "C'mon, I don't want to be down here no more. We needs to get up the ladder in case they comes up on the float."

"Okay. You first."

I wants you to keep yo' eye on that girl.

Yessuh. I can watch her quietlike . . . like a man.

"Cain't," Junior said, sucking in the good air. "You got to go first."

It was Missy's nature to insist on having her way. Junior watched as her brows drew together and her mouth took on the familiar firm lines.

Have mercy, Junior thought, *I tried to tell Daddy she was frac-shush.*

From above their heads, the sharp crack of the rifle told them the war wasn't over.

Junior looked out at the boat and watched Bobby fall into the bottom of it under a shower of water. The rifle fired again and more water drenched the boy. Junior looked back at Missy.

In that same moment he felt the float lurch and pitch under them and assumed somebody had climbed down the ladder to help them. He was thankful, but he was too distracted to turn and see who it was.

The screams of the people on the bridge changed to sounds of hysteria.

His attention was drawn from the girl back to the boat. *Why would they make so much noise?* he wondered. *Mistah A. J. missed him by a mile.*

Mose and Pip saw the impact of the bullets near the boat. *Have mercy!* thought Mose. *Why would Mistah Mason be shootin' a gun so close to that child?*

He could see Mose Junior and Missy safely on the float along with a lopsided stack of old tires or inner tubes. He turned to Pip and said, "Maybe we bes' hurry."

As far as the girl was concerned, the worst was over. When the float tilted she also assumed that someone had come for her—for them; the swells of hysteria from the bridge made no sense. She turned her head and shaded her eyes, squinting into the sun at the faces of the folks lining the rail. Boys she knew, some from her school, were leaning over the rail, wild-eyed and screaming incoherently. They were pointing at something below the bridge. She followed the gestures to see what was so exciting.

Her eyes took a couple of seconds to adjust to the relative darkness below the bridge.

First her brain allowed her to assume that someone had dropped makeshift life preservers in the form of a couple of small inner tubes. At the same time another part of the same brain nagged at her. *Inner tubes aren't heavy enough to make the float sag.* She didn't care.

As her eyes grew more accustomed to the dark under the bridge, she could see that the inner tubes were moving.

Near the foot of the ladder, the float sagged under the weight of the monster moccasin as it undulated back and forth around itself while the demon maneuvered it into position for its first attack. There was no real need to hurry. The one on the bridge was shooting at the snakes near the boat with a puny rifle, a weapon that could never stop the serpent near the ladder. His time had come. His prey couldn't escape.

The sound from the crowd became a shrill, sustained scream.

The measure of the crowd's fear passed across the water to Mose and Pip. Turning loose of Pearl's hand, Mose started to jog. The dog was out front, whining for him to hurry. Pip and Pearl followed.

When Mose Junior saw what Missy was looking at, reality tried to make its way into the consciousness of both children at the same time; both firmly resisted it.

The thing on the raft was bigger than both of them. Snakes weren't that big, not even in nightmares. Its ugly body was slithering back and forth over itself.

The girl scrambled to her knees. Reason fragmented and fled on the sound of her scream.

Mose Junior sprang to his feet. *Lord Jesus, send me my angel. Lord, send us a lotta angels.* The skinny little black boy grabbed the girl's overalls and dragged her to the far corner of the float.

Missy jumped up and reached around to hold him, but he pushed her off and yelled something.

The watching crowd didn't understand why he would push her off. Questioning anger barely tainted their screams.

Almost all snakebites in humans occur below the knee.

She grabbed at him again, eyes filled with the kind of terror only a child can experience or exhibit.

Junior held her off and yelled, "Ally up!"

She shook her head and tried to pull close. He rebuffed her again but held his arms out to her. They were near the edge of the float now. The snake was fully coiled.

The color of anger emerged from the panic on the bridge. *Why wouldn't that colored boy help her?*

Junior continued to yell. "You gotta git *up*! He'll git you. Ally up, Missy! C'mon, now! Git *up!*"

She partially choked off her next scream, emitting a shrill wheening sound and nodding at the same time.

The snake's head rose out of the mound of coils and drew back. The movement of the black body embodied all things unholy.

Months of training to be world-famous acrobats took over. She put out her two hands; he crossed his hands and met hers. In a move that belonged to ballet, Missy planted her foot above

Junior's knee, and with his last measure of adrenaline he carried her in a perfect vault onto his narrow shoulders.

He regained his balance and squared himself at the monster just before it hurled itself at his chest.

When he turned away from killing the snakes at the boat, Mason saw the same thing the children had seen. His first impression of the dusky black thing was akin to theirs: *Where'd the inner tubes come from?* His confusion was short-lived.

The girl twisted through the air in some kind of trick and landed like a circus performer on the boy's shoulders. The boy sagged away from the snake, then straightened just as its head came out of the coils. The monster's head, as broad as an ax blade, drew back to strike.

The men who were almost to the bridge got the news from a wave of boys who were running to escape the terror. "It's snakes! They're everywhere! Missy an' that colored boy are in the water with 'em!"

Bobby Lee could see part of what was happening. When he saw the black stack of coils he thought the same thing his daughter thought: *It's a couple of old tires.*

Mason watched the monster's white mouth open and draw back. It lashed out of the coils, arcing out across the short space while the shooter's mind made its unorthodox calculations. There was no way to sever a head that large in one shot, so he'd just have to do as much damage as he could. Mason looked at the point where the copper-bright eye was going to be when the bullet got there and squeezed the trigger.

Mose and Pip were close enough to see the girl do her trick jump onto their son's shoulders. They had watched the pair practice the move a thousand times, but they had never seen the children get it right.

They watched as Mason rewarded the children's performance by shooting at them.

Against the dark backdrop of the bridge pilings, a heavy shadow landed on the float hard enough to cause one side to sink beneath the water.

Mose realized what it was and began to run. Pip, not far behind, screamed at him to hurry.

Bobby Lee was sprinting and sweating. Tears streamed down his cheeks, and his overtaxed lungs felt as though he were sucking in flames. He saw the giant snake's head come out of its coils. *This can't be real.*

Bobby Lee Parker didn't go to church because he didn't have the time; he didn't need it, and as far as he could tell, the men who went weren't any better off for going. In that moment, though, he knew where his only help would come from. *Lord, just tell me what You want me to do an' I'll do it. Please . . . anything . . . just don't let that thing hurt my girl.*

The hollow-point bullet hit the snake in the center of its eye and knocked its head off-line just enough. Its gaping mouth brushed under Mose Junior's upraised arm, and the nightmare landed in a spray of blood on the wooden deck.

Keeping the girl on his shoulders, his knees bent under the weight, the boy wobbled across the deck to the ladder. While he stood with his back to the enemy, the deck rose and fell, transmitting the message of something heavy behind him . . . something moving. He held the girl's legs, trembling, waiting for the attack he knew was coming.

When Missy got her hands on the ladder, her weight left him. When she was safely on her way up, Junior grabbed a rung and followed. Some boys grabbed the girl's arms, and he looked up in time to see her disappear over the railing. More hands came down, reaching for him, yelling for him to hurry.

Mason held his fire when the boy tottered past the snake. The enemy, sheltering its ravaged head behind its body, gathered its coils for another assault.

Mason waited. He couldn't see the snake's head anymore, and there was no good reason to shoot a .22 into a body that big.

Mason knew there was only one explanation for what was happening on Cat Lake. Demons. Real, live, just-like-in-the-Bible demons. Satan's angel-demons. He remembered Bible stories about demonic activity. The only way to stop the demons was to totally destroy the body they were using or cast out the demons. While he waited for the head to reappear, Mason prayed that the demons would be defeated. *Lord, I can't stop this, but You can.*

When the snake's head came out of the coils, the bullet's exit wound was visible. At the back edge of the monster's mouth, bright blood ran freely from a hole the size of a quarter. Mason had a perfect view of the other eye. It would be over in less than a second if the demon needed the snake's eyes. He looked at the center of the good eye and moved his finger.

Above the screaming of the crowd, he heard the emphatic snap of the firing pin falling on a chamber as empty as death itself.

Mose and Pip were close enough to the bridge to see the monster clearly. Mose was running. Pip was praying.

The bloodied mouth opened and presented its fangs as it flashed across the short space.

A. J. Mason told his eyes to close.

They didn't.

Mose Junior already had his other foot on the ladder. He was looking up into the terrified eyes of the people who were reaching down for him. Two boys grabbed his wrists and pulled hard. A driving weight slammed into him from behind, breaking their grip and hurling his body into the ladder like a thrown doll. The snake's huge fangs, like scaled-down meat hooks, embedded themselves in his back and locked there; a pot of boiling grease poured inside his chest. The faces of those who would help seemed to fade. He clutched at the ladder, but his arms had to surrender to more weight than they could support. He was pulled back, twisting and screaming, descending into the only hell he would ever know.

Mason's face paled as the snake dragged the thrashing boy away from the base of the ladder. "Well, I reckon that's about enough." He handed the rifle to Stiles and grabbed the shotgun. He turned for the ladder, working the slide to make sure the chamber contained a shell. "Don't waste any .22's on the big one," he ordered.

Missy was curled up in a fetal position on the rough planking by the ladder, her hands pressed hard to her face. Some of the boys were trying to comfort her. The first men were running onto the far end of the bridge.

Down on the deck, the snake had released the boy and was coiled almost under him, using him for a shield.

Bedlam reigned on the bridge. Mason had to yell to be heard. "Move 'er back, boys." He turned to Stiles. "Toss me that box of shells."

Stuffing handfuls of shells in his front pockets, he swung his leg over the rail. He was getting a grip on the ladder when the first group of men got to the scene.

Bobby Lee Parker was out of breath. Sweat stained his shirt and streamed down his face. Pushing a boy aside, he knelt by his daughter. "Is she all right?" Looking from the girl to Mason, he yelled, "Where's Bobby? What the devil's goin' on?"

Devil is right, Mason thought, but he ignored the questions. "She don't need you right now, Bobby Lee, but I do." He had to yell, too. "Git that .22 an' watch out for me!"

The Stiles boy, now a veteran of the war at Cat Lake, thrust a rifle at Bobby Lee. "This'n's loaded an' ready."

Bobby Lee Parker was past being scared. He'd been listening to the shooting for more than a minute while he ran for the bridge. His daughter was curled up with her face hidden against her knees and wouldn't look up. Bloody water ran from her clothes onto the bridge. "Listen, A. J., I don't—"

Mason held up a hand to interrupt him. He pointed at the rifle, looked into Bobby Lee's eyes, and clipped his words. "We ain't got the time, Bobby. Shut up an' git over here." Starting down the ladder to where the snake was waiting, he growled, "Shoot anything that ain't human!"

The snake watched him coming.

The Stiles boy stepped to the rail and snugged Mason's little automatic next to his cheek. He swept it back and forth to get its feel, then waited. *Lord, I cain't shoot like him, but You can.* Mason was between young Stiles and the big snake, but the boy killed two of the black beasts that showed up at the edge of the floating battleground. He heard Young Mr. Parker's rifle fire once.

When the rifles were empty, all they'd have left was the shotgun.

Mason watched the snake release the boy and retract itself, coiling, a seeming grin showing on its blood-covered snout. It was watching him. The snake's tongue stayed in its mouth; the demon wasn't interested in Mason's scent. The man had to go down the ladder one-handed, maneuvering to keep the shotgun bearing on the monster. If he fired immediately, he wouldn't be able to pump out the spent shell. That meant waiting until he was on the deck to shoot again. The shotgun wasn't as precise as the rifle. He needed to be closer.

The snake's actions would dictate Mason's next move. If it came for him, he'd shoot.

The boy struggled like a drunk and made it to his hands and knees. He was partially blocking Mason's clear view of the snake.

The snake struck the boy again, and Mason dropped the last few feet to the deck. Somewhere in the background, he heard the outboard motor come to life.

Horton had been watching the bridge while Ruddell prayed. He watched Mason start down the ladder and spoke to God for the second time in his life. *God, that man is goin' into a tough place by himself, an' he sure could use our help. If You're really there, I reckon You're the One that got me out of that fiasco in those woods . . . an' You can get us to where we can help Mr. Mason. I never did thank You for gettin' me out of those trees alive, an' if You're really there, an' if You really got me out of that mess, I appreciate it. I reckon You're all we got.* He turned around to look at the still silent motor . . . just in time to see it start.

Ruddell was on his knees in front of the motor, hands clasped, head bowed, eyes closed. The Johnson motor was as quiet as the surrounding lake water one moment and running at a healthy, midrange power setting the next. Ruddell bumped his head on the motor when the prop bit into the water; the collision knocked his hat to the boat's deck.

Noble ignored the hat, grabbed the tiller, and opened the throttle to the stop.

Mystified was not a strong enough word to describe Horton's initial reaction. After the motor started of its own volition, the thought passed through his mind that he might be safer in the lake. He was totally immersed in something he didn't understand.

Ruddell joined him in being a little wide-eyed about what had happened. "I reckon God done it. I prayed; He answered. You ever seen anything like it?"

Horton looked from Ruddell to the motor, then back to Ruddell. He waited a full ten seconds before he said, "Oh yeah. I've seen somethin' like this a couple of times." *An' God got me out of it when He was good an' ready.* Staying in the boat would be fine. He bent and picked up the shotgun.

Ruddell nodded without hearing him. The boat driver's lips weren't moving when the scream of the engine moved far enough into the background for Horton to distinctly hear a voice say, "Be ready."

The words echoed through him while he jacked a shell into the shotgun. He fed another shell into the magazine, looked the gun over, and turned to face the bridge.

Mason's feet hit the wood as the snake wrapped its body around the boy; its fangs were now buried in the child's chest. The boy got the bloody head in his hands and pushed it away, but the snake's body had completely encircled him.

The boy's face was a contorted collage of pain, effort, and resolve. He looked straight into Mason's eyes and said something the man couldn't hear over the bedlam on the bridge. The boy spoke again. All other sounds seemed to recede as the white man heard the little black boy say, "God said you got to shoot him, right now." A. J. Mason thought the boy tried to smile.

He put the gun's muzzle by the child's hands and pulled the trigger. The beast's head came off in an explosion that covered man and boy with a layer of red gore. The coils continued to tighten, and Mason could hear the green-branch snap of cracking ribs. He put the muzzle back against the still deadly giant and pulled the trigger, then again, severing the thing's body in two more places.

Huge pieces of the snake fell free. Mose Junior threw the head out and away from him. The head was tumbling through the air streaming blood when Mason shot it the first time. He chambered another shell and fired, transforming the largest remaining piece into unrecognizable shreds. Bits and pieces of snake were sprinkling the lake's surface just as Bobby ran the *GENRALROB ERT EEEL* into the deck.

The war was over.

The deck, Mason, and Mose Junior were painted with blood and bits of sticky flesh.

The crowd on the bridge was catching its breath. The hot air carried the musky odor of snake to them. Mason ignored his surroundings and dug in his pocket for more shells.

The shooters on the bridge relaxed.

Bobby stepped onto the float while the approaching outboard bawled for attention.

The incoming motorboat closed on the bridge at full speed. Horton was on one knee in the bow holding the shotgun.

The approaching motorboat was on the far side of the bridge pilings when the last snake slid undetected onto the float behind Bobby Parker.

The little boy who wasn't scared of anything but snakes saw the killer as it coiled itself to strike. He lunged past Bobby as the snake struck and managed to thrust his hand between the incoming fangs and his friend's leg. The needles stabbed the pink palm dead center. Junior tried to close his hand on the snake's head and struggled to get a grip on its body. The snake managed to twist free and bite Mose Junior once on the arm and once in the face before he could control it. He ended up sprawled on his stomach with one hand wrapped around the snake's head and the other gripping its writhing body.

Ruddell cut the throttle late, and the incoming rescue team rammed the float hard enough to hurl Milstead headfirst into the aftermath on the deck.

Horton Milstead, twenty-year-old freshman at Mississippi State College, former member of the 101st Airborne Division, and decorated veteran of the D-Day invasion, was three days away from not celebrating the first anniversary of his getting shot four times. He tucked the gun in close, led with his off shoulder, and rolled once when he hit the wooden deck. He came up in a crouch and made a 360-degree sweep with the shotgun. When he had assured himself there were no other threats, his gaze came to rest on the thing in Mose Junior's hands.

Mose Junior had made it to his knees. He was holding something he couldn't release, waiting for Horton to act. Horton gritted his teeth when he saw the holes in the boy's chest and arms. He looked into the boy's eyes—the eyes of a man with a mission. The two, who had never seen or heard of each other, were brothers.

Horton got close to the boy holding the thrashing, four-foot-long killing machine and said calmly, "Buddy, you just hold him out away from you so I can cut 'im in two, then you throw the head in the lake. Does that suit you?"

The black boy nodded and held the snake in front of him. Horton put the muzzle against it and blew it to smithereens. The boy threw the severed head into the water.

Mose Junior no longer had the strength to hold himself up. The remains of the snake fell from his hand as Horton caught his arm and let him sag to the deck. Junior rolled onto his back and smiled up at Bobby.

Bobby could only stare, wide-eyed, at what was left of the thing that would have killed him.

Horton watched around the edges of the deck while he fed a shell into the shotgun.

CHAPTER SEVEN

Mason reloaded his shotgun and handed it up the ladder. Next, he sent Bobby up the ladder and told Horton he'd be smarter to get back in the boat. Horton just shook his head. No one was going to make him get back in that boat, not while he was still holding a shotgun.

Up on the bridge, Bobby Lee got the full story several times over. Missy was safe in her grandfather's arms. Bobby Lee hugged his son long and fiercely at the top of the ladder, then climbed down and knelt by Mose Junior. "Junior, your momma an' daddy will be here in just a minute."

"Yassuh." Mose Junior looked at his surroundings. The float looked like a well-used slaughter table. "Bes' get me up on the bridge; Momma got no business down here." He struggled to sit up but couldn't make it. He swiped a hand across the red mess that covered his chest and wiped it on the deck, which was almost as bloody. "Boss, if you would, y'all needs to wash me off so Momma don't have to see all this here blood. She gonna be plenty upset enough."

Mason, not trusting his voice, nodded his agreement. The boy couldn't possibly live.

The realization of what could have happened to the Parker children was sinking in for both men. Bobby Lee struggled to harness his emotions but failed; he wept steadily while he dipped his hat in the water and passed it to Mason. Silently, Mason rinsed the boy's chest, arms, and face. He finally managed to say, "That's better now, son. You ready to go up on the bridge?"

The boy smiled. No white man had ever called him "son." "The bridge ain't nuthin' but a stop, boss. Ain't nuthin' but a short stop."

Mason was sliding his arms under the boy when Bobby Lee stopped him. "Mistah A. J., if it's all right with you, I'd like to carry him to the top."

Mason understood and nodded. "I'll go first. You hand him to me."

Bobby Lee knelt by the boy. "Son, I'm gonna have to move you around some to get you up there. It'll hurt, but it'll just be for a minute."

Mose Junior smiled. Now Mr. Bobby Lee had called him "son." He knew they were doing it because he was going to die. *That young white man with the shotgun called me Buddy 'cause he knowed I was doing what had to be done*, Junior thought, *just like a full-growed man*. The boy smiled. He'd done what his daddy had told him to do.

The boy was small enough that Bobby Lee could manage to carry him and climb the ladder.

Horton took one more look around, then followed them.

They got Junior to the top of the ladder just as his momma ran up. She held both of her fists against her mouth while Mason reached across the rail and took the child from Bobby Lee. Mason turned and helped Pip lower her son to the bridge deck.

Blood seeped freely from the puncture wounds in his chest. The boy reached out and put his hand to her face, saying, "I know'd you'd come."

She tried not to sob. Her face twisted and she smiled. *"Knew."*

The boy nodded solemnly, then smiled. Their joke. "Yessum. I knew."

His daddy was at the boy's side, holding Pearl. Mason had just told Mose that the boy saved Missy and Bobby. Mose put his girl down and knelt next to his son's head. He knew as soon as he saw the boy's eyes that it was almost over.

Mose Junior said what all young boys would say in the lull following guns shooting and people yelling. "I didn't do nothin' wrong, Daddy."

Mose smiled at his son and shook his head. He didn't have much time to tell the boy what he felt. "Son, you ain't ever been nothin' but a good boy. An', God help me, I'll be a proud man all my life 'cause you my son."

What he said pleased the boy. "Thank you, Daddy." Almost formal.

Pip pulled him close and said gently, "Quiet now, boy. Don't be tryin' to talk."

The boy looked at his mother and shook his head. "I'm dyin', Momma. Cain't nobody do nuthin' 'bout that."

His momma's first tear came. "You're not gonna die, son. You rest yourself, now."

He looked up at her. "Don't be tryin' to hold me here, Momma. The good Lord jes' lettin' me visit with you for a spell 'fore I gets to go to Him." He wasn't a boy anymore. "He knows I got to tell you somethin'."

Pip placed her hand on his head and brushed gently across the beads of lake water that sparkled in his wiry hair. "You stop that talk—"

Regardless of age, gender, or color, some folks who are holding hands with death see things from a different plane. Junior's lips parted in a knowing smile. Without his consciously hearing it, his instincts had already told him his remaining time on earth was measured in priceless seconds. The eleven-year-old boy, who had never called her anything but Momma, said, "Hush, woman."

She clamped her hand over her mouth in a futile effort to stifle the moan that escaped from her heart. She leaned over him, as if she could keep her body between her son and eternity. The wells of her eyes poured tears as she tried to pull him closer. "Baby, you got to—"

His eyes had closed. He forced them open and signaled his arm to move to her, but all he felt was coolness where his body was supposed to be. He said, "I tol' you to hush, now. I cain't be takin' yo' words with me, Momma, but you can keep mine here."

His forehead continued to frown while he smiled up at her. It was an expression a man would adopt if he were explaining something complex to an adored child. "You the best momma a boy ever had."

She resisted what she already knew. "Baby, you need to be quiet or—"

The boy shook his head like a patient old man. "Have mercy, woman. I ain't got no time to be quiet here. Ain't gonna be no quiet where I'm goin'."

A shudder gripped him and ran the length of his body. The woman moaned deep in her chest.

"Momma?" His eyes came open, but he looked right through her.

"I'm right here, baby."

The tremors came and went with the rise and fall of his chest. "Momma, you got to tell them white chillun 'bout Jesus. They didn't never understand."

The woman's mouth worked, but no words came out.

"Momma?"

Pip put her lips to his ear and forced out words. "I'm here, baby. I'm right here." His shudders had moved into her body and became a constant tremor. She pulled him closer to her while she wiggled her knees under his back, trying to get more of his body into her lap. The swelling was moving across his face now.

His tone changed—not to fear but to wonder. "I can't see here no more . . . anymore." Another smile. "But I'll see you in heaven, won't I?"

Tears coursed down her cheeks and splashed on his chest. "Baby, please—"

He made a shushing sound to silence her. "Listen to me, now. You an' Daddy, Momma . . . y'all got to tell Bobby an' Missy . . . you got it to do . . . don't trust it to nobody else. You got to finish for me." He took a deep breath. Tears that were scattered on the dusky darkness of his chest trembled in the sunlight. "Talk to me, Momma."

"I'll do like you say, honey. I'll tell 'em."

"Make sure they know." He seemed to breathe even more deeply. Only one thing mattered now. "They don't know, Momma. You got to see to it."

"I'll make sure."

"Momma?" The cloud had gone. His eyes were fixed on some point out past the sun.

"I'm here, baby. I'm right here."

"Are you holdin' my hand, Momma?"

Pip grabbed his swollen hand and grasped it in hers. He was dying before her eyes, and all she could do was cling to his hand and watch. The soft curve of his ear was against her lips. She managed a whisper. "I'm holdin' it, baby. I'm right here holdin' it."

He seemed to relax at her words. His eyelids drifted down. "I love you, Momma. I'm—"

The broadening distortion brought on by the swelling gave way to the familiar soft smile she had seen so often, loved so much—the same smile she sometimes saw in her mirror. Then came a slow transition to a frown. He had only seconds left. A struggle to breathe. A small victory in the struggle. Again the smile, slightly stronger this time. His last words were whispered in a soft, breaking sigh. "You tell ... my daddy ... I watched out for her ... like a man." A single bright tear sparkled in the sun as it found its way from her chin to the center of his small, dark chest and rested there.

It didn't move.

The boy's thoughts became welcome pictures ... firm remembrances ... ever special ... the warm woman ... the strong man ... the lake with the dark water. ... Then his thoughts turned away ... called ... drawn ... to another place with newer memories ... where there is no darkness.

The boy's smile broadened for a moment, then slowly faded. The woman watched his face, staring with hopeless anticipation at his closed eyes, praying, begging God to lower the barrier for one last, priceless moment. *Lord, please . . . please just let me hear his voice one more time. Let him just speak to me . . . one miracle . . . just one word, Lord . . .* knowing her son would never move again.

She drew him even closer in her lap. With a trembling hand she gently brushed the water droplets from his arms and chest. She wiped her eyes so she could see him better, then her hand came back to his quiet cheek and rested there, her tender fingers touching the swelling that continued to move across that sweet face she loved. She moved her hand and reached around him, squeezing her son as close as her strength would allow. She bowed over him, rocking back and forth, humming to him. The man who knelt beside her put his arm around her shoulder, drawing her and their son to him. The woman used the strength of the man's arms to gather her son ever closer, snuggling herself and her son against the man's chest.

Some men near the woman—the few black men and even some of the white ones—reached up and took off their hats.

For long minutes the crowd stayed still, silent, almost reverent. After awhile, though, most of the white men wanted to talk about what they witnessed and started to pull away. They made their way back to the place where the steam rose off the Brunswick stew. They stood in the shade; the bottles came out, and they began to tell each other the story they would retell for the rest of their lives.

Bobby Lee Parker was backed against the bridge railing, shoulders sagging, eyes closed. He held one of his son's hands in both of his; lake water trickled from his hat and blended with his tears. Bobby stood with his knees trembling, clinging to the railing. He kept his back to the crowd, watching his own tears fall to the surface of the lake. The little girl was high in her grandfather's arms; pink water seeped from the sagging cuffs of her overalls and streaked Old Mr. Parker's khakis. The girl kept her eyes on the two black people who knelt over their son in the middle of the bridge; her attention wavered only to exam-ine the area around her granddaddy's feet for snakes. She had yet to speak.

After awhile Mose straightened slightly and said to Pip, "We bes' take him home now." He reached out his arms to slide them under his son's body.

The woman raised her head and looked up at him. If they took him home, they would have to put him in that hard ground by Pap's grave. "Not just yet. I'll just hold him a bit longer first." She looked into the man's eyes and showed him the origin of the boy's soft smile. "We can go soon enough, can't we?"

The man nodded and shed his first tear. "Yes, baby. We can go soon enough."

Old Mr. Parker and Mason heard the exchange. Parker looked down at one end of the bridge and said, "A. J., you go tell those people down yonder. I'll walk—"

"Uh-uh." Without taking her eyes off the kneeling couple, the girl shook her head and interrupted. "A. J.'s got the gun. He stays where I am, an' I'm stayin' right here."

The two men looked at the girl, then at each other. They knew her too well to be completely dumbfounded—or to argue.

Mason called the Stiles boy over and said, "Go get another boy, an' go tell the folks in those cars waitin' to cross the bridge I said to wait just a short while longer. This ain't the time to be havin' somebody gettin' impatient an' startin' a fuss."

The two black people huddled over the still body of the boy—a portrait of loss painted on an old wooden bridge.

Missy said, "Lemme down."

Her granddaddy put her down.

She hooked a finger in Mason's belt loop and said, "C'mon." She took small steps until they were next to Mose's shoulder.

Mose looked up, first at Mason, then at the girl. She knelt next to him and rested her hand on his knee. He patted her hand without speaking. She stayed quiet for so long that Mose forgot about her. The girl sat on her bare feet, waiting silently until Pip noticed her, then asked the person who should make the decision, "Can I touch him?"

Pip looked down at her son. She started to shake her head. Her face came apart again when she tried to explain to the child; new tears came when she said it for the first time. "He's gone, baby. He's already dead."

The firmest lower lip in the Delta trembled. "I know. I just didn't get to tell him—" Her first tears came when her voice broke. The little girl knelt there in the dust by Mose and cried silently, unable to stop, not caring that she couldn't.

Pip reached for the child's hand. "Here now, baby. You come 'round here on this side an' jes' help me hold him for a minute. He's not here anymore, but I'll bet he's watchin' from heaven right now."

Missy let Pip lead her around Junior's body. The little girl curled up against Pip and wept, clinging to the woman's blouse with both fists and sobbing like a young widow. The men couldn't watch; they lowered their heads and hunched their shoulders in an effort to escape the heart-scalding sounds. Pip snuggled the child under her arm and cried with her.

It was long minutes before Missy could get her breath. When she did, she reached out a small hand, pink-tinged with dried blood, and rested it on the boy's Bible-black chest. Speaking between ragged breaths, she swore to her friend, "I don't know how . . . an' I ain't sure when . . . but I'll pay you back, Junior. An' that's a promise."

CHAPTER EIGHT

They buried the boy right next to his great-great-grandfather.

All the Parkers and lots of other white folks came to the funeral. Two men from the colored church brought the rockers off the porch for Pip and her momma to sit in. Pearl sat on Pip's lap; Mose stood beside them. The boy's parents chose the pallbearers—Old Mr. Parker, Mr. Bobby Lee, Bobby, Leon, Mr. A. J., and one other person lowered the boy into the ground. No one had ever seen a woman or a girl for a pallbearer, but the girl was Mose Junior's best friend, and it was fitting.

The following Saturday, Pap's grave was more than twenty years old. The boy's was five days new.

After the funeral, Pip seemed to just disappear inside herself; she didn't cook, she didn't talk, she didn't even go to work at the Parkers'. Mostly she sat on the porch and rocked, occasionally disturbing whatever cat was in her lap to wander out to stand over the grave and maybe pull up an imagined stray piece of grass.

Pearl had given up trying to include her momma in her conversations with her doll. The child got impatient enough to approach her daddy with her concerns. "How come my momma won't talk to me?"

Mose's gentle voice had acquired an even softer quality.

"Give her time, baby. Momma's got a lot on her mind right now. Jes' give her a little time."

Mose had stayed home from the gin for two days after the funeral, then started going back a couple of times a day because there was nothing for him to do at the cabin. The women from the church came out most days and clucked over Pip and Pearl. They noised about so much that the dog either went hunting or went with Mose to the gin.

A. J. Mason stopped by the Washingtons' every afternoon to check on them. On the first few days, he just said a few words to Mose and drove off. On Friday he watched Pip while he talked to Mose; on Saturday he walked up to the porch to speak to her.

Mose stood around for a few minutes while Mason said things at Pip. When Pip stayed silent, Mose excused himself and wandered down to the lake with the dog.

Pearl was inside taking her nap while the shade from the trees kept the heat down. A sparse breeze came up from the lake, cooled Mason and Pip some, then went in the front door to cool the little girl as well as it could.

"How come God would take a boy like that?" Pip had asked the question every other minute for six days, sometimes in her mind, sometimes into the silence that surrounded her.

Mason answered, "I don't know much about God, Pip, but I know about folks. That was no boy."

She hadn't been hearing everything people said to her. "Hmm?" She forgot to say, "sir."

"I say, that was no boy. That was as much a man as God ever made. Most I've ever seen." Flashes of what he'd seen came, and he squeezed his eyes shut in an effort to drive them away. "Most I ever want to see."

She moved back and forth in the rocker, and he stood by the front steps. Normally hospitable, Pip didn't think of inviting Mason to sit. He didn't notice. She talked into the gaps when he paused, not noticing whether she was responding to what he said, just speaking what came into her mind. "He wasn't even twelve years old yet . . . just a baby . . . so small. . . ." Her voice trailed off.

"I watched what he did." Mason blew out a long breath

through pursed lips. He pushed the heel of his hand hard against one eye, then said, "I saw it. There's not a man living anywhere in the world that'll ever do a braver thing. Ever. Never has been, never will be. I'd—" His voice caught. More memories of the boy's deliberate sacrifice tightened his chest. He didn't look at her because he knew he'd cry again.

The emotion in his voice worked its way into Pip's world. She stopped the slow back-and-forth motion and pointed herself at his face, waiting for him to speak again.

He rubbed the heel of the other hand across an eye; his voice had become husky. "I don't know a man in the world . . . or a woman . . . who would want anything more than to have their son become what your son was." He used both hands this time, pressing them hard against his eyes for a moment before he spoke. "He faced the meanest, most dangerous thing he knew about, the thing he was most afraid of, an' he did it to save the life of somebody else."

Pip gave lengthy consideration to the words, then said, "I thank you for sayin' that. It's right kind of you."

The rocker began its journey again. Mason stared at the porch by her feet.

Mason said the next words without thinking. "That's what Jesus did."

The rocker halted. "What?"

Mason stood in his own quiet for a moment, considering. He had her attention now. He made his decision. "There's more, Pip."

The rocker hadn't moved. She waited. "Yessuh?"

He was having a hard time. He looked up at her like he was admitting something he had done wrong, then said, "I knew somethin' was gonna happen."

Traces of fog drifted away from the edges of her thoughts. The rocking chair and the bit of breeze stayed still. "Sir?"

The voice he heard last Sunday was real, and he told her about it—all of it.

When he finished his story, they were both silent. Then she asked, "You told anybody else yet?"

"Not yet . . . except my wife." If he told folks that he had heard the voice, they'd haul him off on the next train to Mississippi's insane asylum down at Whitfield.

The rocker took up its journey again. Mose stood down by the lake with the dog. Out behind the house a dove's cooing came from the brake. Pip thought more about Mason's story, then came almost completely out of the fog to warn him. "I don't think you oughta tell anybody about that."

"I'm afraid you're right, but it's a shame." He looked down and noticed that he was holding his hat. "I know in my mind that it was an angel or something. It had to be important."

"I 'spect it was, myself. But it's bes' not to be expectin' even a preacher to understand. People say they believe in God an' angels an' such, but they get skittish when folks talk about 'em like they're right here with us."

He nodded. Whitfield.

The breeze came back and stirred through the dust on the porch. She remembered what Mose told her and looked out at the old truck. "What was it cut that hole in yo' tire?"

Mason was staring at the ground, remembering the voice. His head jerked up. "What's that?"

"Mose said he saw that cut in yo' tire at Mistah Scooter's fillin' station. He said that cut was fine as a razor an' long as his hand."

"That's right." Whatever made the cut slit the sidewall wide open.

"Mistah Scooter said the tire was new."

Mason nodded. *Brand-spanking new.*

"Mose brought the tire home with him." She lifted a single finger from the arm of the rocker to point with. "That's it on the truck yonder." She gave her attention to the finger while it moved back to where it had been. The fog shrouded her thoughts for a moment, then receded. "He went out to the bridge an' looked at where the tire blew all the dust off'n that bridge. Accordin' to them marks on the bridge, you must of driven twenty feet on a tire that couldn't hold any air . . . but did. It blew a little patch of dust off in one place clean down to bare wood, then went twenty feet an' blew plumb out."

Mason divided his attention between Pip's face and the tire. "What's he think happened?"

She let the rocker coast to a stop and said, "He said it looks like to him somebody cut that tire, then held it closed. He said they let the rest of the air out when the car got where they wanted it to stop. Every bit of the dust was blowed off right there by the ladder."

His chest rose and fell. "An angel?"

"He thinks so."

A light wind moved the tops of the pecan trees.

It was Mason's turn for consideration. He passed a hand over his mouth and looked down at the man by the lake. He moved away from the porch to the yard. "I'm gonna go visit with Mose for a bit." He put his hat back on and listened to the rocker start to creak as he turned away.

Pip was already asking, *If the angels were right there, Lord . . . if they had their swords right there in their hands, how come they didn't step in? Why would You let an innocent little boy like that die when a single angel could've stopped it?*

The dog met Mason halfway and escorted him to Mose. Mose waited for Mason to speak.

"She said you think there was an angel there."

Mose frowned and cut his eyes toward the house. "I done told her to keep that to herself, Mistah A. J. Too many folks thinks I cogitates too much on what God thinks."

"I don't." Mason stepped up beside the man, and they considered the blackness of the lake's surface. "Somebody's gotta think about God, Mose. He told us *all* to."

Mose wasn't sure. The doubts of past decades were creeping back in. "Things happen different from what we expect, angels or not." He bent over and picked up a twig, fooled with it for a minute, then tossed it back on the ground. The dog didn't completely understand the action, but he examined the twig, just in case.

"How do you mean?"

Mose looked over his shoulder at the graves. "Pap birthed me hisself an' named me hisself . . . Moses Lincoln Washington . . . right there in that house. Said I was named for fine men who was set on freein' their people. The day before I buried Pap, I promised him I'd raise my children to tell folks 'bout the only thing that counts—Jesus; the only One what can save anybody. Me an' him sat right there on that porch on his last day, an' he told me to git to know God an' to make Him known, an' to tell my children. . . ." His voice trailed off.

On the last day of Pap's life, Mose sat with him on the little porch and enjoyed the evening breeze. The cypress trees on the west side of the lake filtered the last of the sunset. Pap alternately sipped his coffee and clutched the cup to himself like the remnants of a warm fire.

The old china cup, a refugee from a long-ago trash pile, was as timeworn as the fingers that grasped it. The old man studied the little bit of liquid in the bottom of the cup, swirled it to pick up any stray grain of sugar that might be left, and poured the last of the bitter sweetness into his mouth.

Mose sat on the steps and watched the old man inspect the bottom of the cup.

Pap, after satisfying himself that the last dram was gone, said, "Boy"—He never called Mose anything else—"there ain't never gonna be no drink better than coffee."

Mose smiled his gentle smile and spoke the words the old man expected to hear. "'Cept in heaven, I reckon."

The frail old man nodded, and spoke as he bent to put the cup by the rocking chair. "'Cept in heaven is right, boy. Gonna drink from the fountain that don't never run dry. A sho'nuff pure river of living water." His twisted old hand, made ugly and beautiful at the same time by a hard life, made a waving motion of water flowing. "Clear as crystal, proceedin' straight out of the throne." The old man smiled. "Now that's a drink to shame the best cup of coffee on the place."

The young boy smiled and nodded. He had no doubts that what the old man said was true, and he liked hearing him say it. It was the angels that worried him.

He asked Pap what the rest of heaven was like.

"Don't know, boy. But I 'magine if we knew, we wouldn't cling to this earth the way we do." Pap could talk as good as any white man and better than most. "I reckon if we really knew, we'd swim to the bottom of that lake an' hold on to a root 'til we was drowned."

The boy allowed this to soak in, then asked, "Did you ever see a angel?"

"*An* angel," Pap corrected. "No. Never did."

"How do we know they're there?"

"The Bible says we each have us a guardian angel. Each one of us. I always go with the Bible."

"Did my momma have a guardian angel?"

"Yes, she did."

The question nagged at Mose fairly often. "Then how come she died?"

"It ain't the job of the angels to decide whether or not we die, boy. That's the Lord's job."

The boy pressed the subject. "But you believe the angels are there?"

"Most certainly do." Pap moved his hand around. "There's at least two guardian angels right here by us—one for me, one for you." The old man let the boy study his surroundings, then asked him, "Do you believe they're there, boy?"

The boy pondered some more, then answered, "I reckon I ain't sure sometimes, Pap. I ain't never seen one."

The old man took the stance he always took. "Well, the Book says they're all around us. I reckon I'll stay with the Book."

More pondering by the boy. Pap had been staying with the Book for more than eighty years; it never let him down. Mose made his decision: "I reckon I'll go with the Book myself. I can't see 'em, but they're there."

"Goin' with the Book is the thing to do, son," Pap said, resting a hand on the boy's shoulder. "But you can't be doin' it just 'cause I do."

It was a serious time. "I don't reckon I'm stayin' with the Book 'cause of you, Pap. I figure I'm gonna stay with it 'cause I believe it's true."

"It won't let you down, boy. The Book an' Him that wrote it won't never let you down."

The boy looked out over the lake. "My own angel."

Pap nodded. "When the battle goes fierce, there's more."

"When the battle goes fierce?"

"Mm-hmm. Them angels what followed Satan out of heaven can't be nothin' but wicked. The angels what stayed with the Lord won't never be nothin' but good. The great battle between good an' evil's gonna be goin' on 'til Jesus comes back to rule His kingdom, an' God says me an' you an' the other Christians gets to fight on His side." The old man pulled himself forward slightly to add emphasis to his next words. "So what me an' you needs to do is make sure that when we gets to heaven, we wearin' scars we got from fightin' the good fight. You understandin' me?"

The boy thought he understood. "Yassuh."

Pap leaned back and napped for a minute, then woke and smiled at his last sunset.

When the sun was gone, Pap said the same thing he had said every few days for as long as Mose could remember: "Boy, you need to do two things for your whole life. You got to know God better every day, an' you got to make Him known. If those two things cost you food an' shelter, then go hungry an' sleep in the wet, but you spend every day of your life knowin' Him an' makin' Him known . . . an' you bring yo' babies up to do the same. You hear me?"

"I hear you, Pap. An' I'll do it."

Pap smiled right at him and said, "I reckon you will, boy. I reckon you will." Then he closed his eyes, settled himself back in his rocker, and died.

The only flowers at Pap's funeral were the few scraggly roses that a hot September left on their only bush.

Pap was born a slave on the Parker place more than eighty years before and died without seeing the inside of a church with stained-glass windows. He didn't want a church funeral.

The casket was a clean bedsheet. The stitching by the thirteen-year-old boy was careful but not expert.

Mose stepped into the grave. He picked up the small corpse, knelt, and placed Pap gently in the ground.

The boy climbed out of the hole and knelt beside it. "Lord, Pap said he didn't want no whole bunch of people sayin' things an' caterwaulin' 'round him. He said You an' him was all his funeral needed."

The Lord, Mose, and the angel were by the grave while Mose spoke. The dog was the only other attendant. He was Mose's dog, but he had stayed close to Pap for the last week or so.

Mose went to the porch after he buried Pap and stayed there all day. At sundown he was still remembering and reminiscing, thinking of the two things his Pap had stressed: Know God and make Him known.

The next week he went to work in town at the Moores Point Gin.

Mason picked up the same little piece of wood Mose had dropped and rolled it back and forth between his fingers while he waited for Mose to speak. The dog's attention was fixed on the brake; he was listening to the dove.

Mose had spent the years since Pap's death studying the Bible and telling all sorts of folks, including his children, about God. "Ever since Easter, Junior ain't cared nuthin' 'bout nuthin' except for tellin' folks 'bout Jesus," he said to Mason. The question from his younger years came back. It nagged at him. "It don't make no sense that God would allow a boy like that to die if the angels was right there with him. That boy done said he was gonna tell the wide, wicked world there wasn't nuthin' but Jesus standin' between them an' hell—'cept he wouldn't say *hell*. Leon come to me an' claimed the boy was 'bout to drive him straight into Whitfield."

The only worthwhile response Mason could think of was that he and Leon might could keep each other company. *What do you tell a man who has just lost his only son?* The colored preacher at the funeral said something about God wanting Mose Junior up there in heaven with Him, but the preacher said it was because Junior was such a fine boy. Mason didn't like that explanation; neither did Mose.

Mason looked at the ground and prayed. *Lord, I don't know what to tell him. I never lost a child. An' besides, I'm a white man; why would he listen to me?*

"Mistah A. J.?"

Mason looked up.

"Was you prayin'?"

"Kind of."

"What'd you pray?"

Mason told him, and it made sense to Mose. "What do you think, Mistah A. J.?"

Mason arranged his thoughts, then spoke. "I think your pap was one of the finest men I ever met, an' I'd stick with every word he said. I think you're cut from his cloth, so I think you'll do it. I think your boy was the bravest Christian man I'll ever know, an' I can't believe that God would let a man that was committed to Him die for nothin'. That makes me believe that what's gonna come out of this could be mighty important. God don't consult with me, but I've got no reason to think anything else. He just don't make mistakes."

The *GENRALROB ERT EEEL* rested lopsided against a brush pile on the far side of the lake. Some of the letters on its side were below the water. Mose seemed to study it before he spoke. "I reckon maybe you might be right."

A. J. Mason was long gone when the dog snuffled. Mose looked up from doing nothing to see Young Mrs. Parker's car turn down the road to his house. He was waiting with his hat in his hand when the car came to rest in the shade of the pecan trees.

Pearl came to the front porch to see who the company was. She held her doll in one arm and walked down the steps to be closer to the white folks.

Young Mrs. Parker stepped out of the car wearing a yellow

dress that showed up against her tanned skin. She smiled and spoke to Mose before she reached into the backseat. Missy came out of the passenger's side and rounded the front of the car. She edged along the front fender, her hands in her pockets. Mose spoke to the girl. She nodded but kept her eyes on her toes.

Mrs. Parker said, "I brought y'all a ham."

Mose could smell it before she turned around. When he saw the size of the thing, he mentally started listing the folks he would be taking the extra meat to. "That's right fine, Miz Susan. We much obliged."

The white lady started toward the porch. Her step was almost reluctant, her smile tentative, questioning. "Uh . . . afternoon, Pip." The words were no stronger than her smile.

Pip moved enough to turn toward the voice. On most other days she'd have risen in the presence of her boss lady. "Miz Susan?"

The visiting woman came to a stop at Pip's feet and looked down at the meat as if wondering where it had come from. "I brought y'all a ham. I suppose it's kind of big. . . ." She set the platter on the edge of the porch; her smile faded to pale confusion, as did her words. "I didn't know how to . . . I mean, I already burned one trying to do it myself . . ." Her words started to come in pieces that didn't fit together right. "Pip, I'm . . . sorry . . . I can't cook like you . . . an' your boy died . . . an' then . . . I burned the other . . ."

The quiet woman in the rocker watched the white lady. Susan Parker's departure from the conscious world triggered Pip's reentry. "Mose!"

Mose dropped his hat and caught the woman from behind just as her knees folded.

"Here, now." Pip was beside him in a moment, helping him move the woman to the porch steps. "Turn her like this. That's it. That's it. Now sit her right on this top step here." They guided and carried the woman to a place on the step. "Right here. That's good. There now."

Pip was back. "Take that meat in the house an' bring me some fresh water an' a clean cloth."

The gin's boss man was sweating. He could handle men, meat, water, and washcloths; he didn't do too well with fainting white women.

By the time he got back, Pip was sitting on the step with the woman's head in her lap. Miz Susan was weeping quietly. Pip nodded at him to put down the water and towel.

Missy came close enough to make sure her momma was still alive. Pip was too busy to notice the girl, but Mose nodded and smiled encouragement at her.

Pearl saw her daddy smile at the girl. She watched her momma comforting the white woman like she would a child, then looked at Missy. Missy was watching her own mother. The two girls looked at each other; Missy followed Pearl's eyes when she looked back up at her daddy. The little black girl was wearing a neat cotton dress made from flour sacks; the white girl was wearing overalls rolled up to her knees. Pearl eased sideways to be next to her daddy and slipped her hand into his. This was too much for her young mind—her brother dying in front of her eyes, the funeral, and now this white woman taking her place in her momma's lap. She was unsettled.

Pip told Mose, "Take Pearl down to the lake an' look for crawdads or somethin'."

Pearl pulled on her daddy's hand without taking her eyes off the white woman with her momma. Mose picked up his hat and slapped it against his leg. The dog made a last inspection of the stranger on the porch steps, then moved out in front of Pearl and her daddy.

Missy stood at the foot of the steps and watched her momma's face for a full minute. She finally turned and followed Mose and Pearl.

Mose and Pearl stopped at the water's edge. Missy was hanging back a little. The dog went back to get her and bumped her to be petted; he remembered good things about her smell. She rested her hand on his back and let him lead her to the lake bank.

She ran her hand over the dog's coat while she looked back at the porch. Finally, she turned to Pearl and asked, "Can I be with y'all?"

Pearl didn't share her doll or her momma. Sharing her daddy was a fact of life, but she didn't particularly like it. She was put off by Missy because the girl acted like a boy and never dressed in real dresses. She decided to relent only because the girl's momma might be dying and every real dress she had ever worn had come from the girl's closet. She nodded.

Mose said, "Sho' you can, baby." He took one black hand and one white one and turned to walk along the lake shore. "I tell you what we'll do. Let's us walk down here to this bridge an' see can we see us a turtle."

When he said "bridge" the two little hands retracted in unison. Mose stopped and turned around. Both girls were looking at him, feet planted and shaking their heads.

Missy spoke first. "I ain't goin' on the bridge no more."

Pearl backed her up. Firmly. "I ain't neither."

Mose dropped to his knees between the girls, and the dog turned back to see what was causing the delay. "How come y'all won't go to the bridge, ladies?"

Both girls stared at the long, wooden structure. The creosote-treated pilings were almost camouflaged against the black water. On the other side of the bridge, cypress trees along the lake's banks showed up against high white clouds. The blue of the sky painted the scene with peace.

Pearl didn't see the peace. "That's where Bubba died. I don't want to be there."

Missy backed her up. Firmer. "Me neither."

Mose sat back on his heels and rubbed his hands together. "Well, ladies, I'll tell you. I think maybe you're makin' a big mistake, here. That bridge is the place where the bravest thing in this here country ever happened." He pointed at Missy. "You were right in the middle of it. A boy what was scared of snakes took 'em on so's his friends could live." He nodded at the girls in turn and said, "He was yo' Bubba an' yo' best friend an' my son. I reckon I just like goin' up there so I can remember what a fine thing he done . . . what a fine boy he was. That bridge is like one of them memorials to a brave man. Folks will walk on that bridge long after I'm gone an' remember what Moses Lincoln Washington, Junior, done there."

He let the girls look at each other and think it over. The dove over in the brake cast its vote, and the girls decided to nod at the same time.

The man stood up, the girls took his hands, and they walked up to the bridge.

Mose sat on the dusty floor of the bridge by the ladder; Pearl sat across his lap so she wouldn't get dirt on her dress; Missy ignored the dust and sat cross-legged, facing Mose. Mose told the girls that what Mose Junior did was like what Someone else had done a long time ago.

At the little cabin in the pecan trees, Susan Parker sat on the dusty steps in her yellow dress and rested her head on Pip's shoulder. The white lady cried while Pip held and comforted her as if she were one of her own.

The girl was carrying a scrap of paper in her hand when she stepped out on the porch where her parents sat. The sun was down, and the katydids were tuning up for their evening concert. The bang of the screen door slamming shocked the katydids into a short-lived silence. Bobby Lee watched Missy march across the porch and asked, "Hey there, punkin, where you goin'?"

"R. D.'s." She had business to take care of.

"You stayin' the night?" Bobby was camping out with the Scouts. With Missy at her grandparents', he and Susan would have a rare evening by themselves.

"No, sir." She kept walking. "Goin' to borry a Bible."

A Bible? His bourbon tumbler slipped and hit the glass tabletop pretty hard; nothing broke. Bobby Lee Parker could not be surprised at anything the girl did . . . almost. He looked at the spill and a mild cuss word escaped his lips.

The small crash and equally small curse brought the girl's momma back from some distant place. She looked down at her hands, only half listening to the father-daughter exchange.

"Punkin, we got a Bible right here."

She slowed. "No, we don't. I already looked."

Bobby Lee looked at his wife for help, but she was busy studying one of her fingernails, smiling about something.

"It's in the cabinet under the bookcase, behind the checkers an' stuff."

"Yessir. Thanks." The girl changed direction.

"You're wel—"

The screen door banged again. The katydids paused again.

"What's she want a Bible for? The world ain't comin' to an end, is it?"

His wife only wanted to do one thing at a time, and the fingernail study took precedence over speculation of coming cataclysmic events.

Diminished traffic through the screen door allowed the katydids to sing in earnest. The ebb and swell of the night sound was more peaceful than any music mankind would ever make. The girl interrupted the concert to give a house-to-porch progress report.

"Daddy! It ain't in here!"

He looked at the fingernail student. "You wanna help her."

"No, thanks. I think I'll wait here and listen to the katydids."

He picked up his glass. "Comin'!" *Kids can't ever find anything.*

They found the Bible right where he'd said it was, except it was in the hall closet. He dug it out and asked, "What do you want it for?"

"Mose told me how to be a Christian." The girl waved the piece of paper. "He told me to look over these here Scriptures an' think about what they say. I figure I'll give it some thought."

What? "Honey, we're already Christians."

"Not accordin' to Mose, we ain't."

He hoped her being hardheaded would come in handy someday; right now it was a trial. "Punkin, you were christened when you were a baby; you just can't remember it. You've been a Christian all your life."

"That's what I told Mose, but he says it don't work that way. He says I have to choose for myself, an' I have to understand what I'm choosin'. To tell the truth, it don't even make sense to me that you could choose to make me a Christian." The girl liked making her own choices.

When she put it that way, it made even Bobby Lee stop and think.

Missy carried the book to the dining-room table, dusting it off as she went. Bobby Lee trailed along behind, almost smiling. She took the time to arrange the Bible, a pencil, and the sheet of paper, then opened the Bible and began to flip through the pages.

Bobby Lee took a sip of whiskey. "Can I watch?"

"Yessir. Do you know how to find the different parts?"

"Parts?"

"Yessir. Like this . . ." She stabbed the first penciled line on the paper. "Roman."

"Sure. Learned most of 'em when I was in Sunday school. It's the name of a book: Romans." He was practically a Bible scholar.

She nudged the Bible over so that it was in front of him. "Show me where—" She studied her paper again. "—where Roman is."

Susan Parker moved to the doorway of the room and listened.

"Lemme see. Acts . . . Here it is. Romans. Why?" The girl's daddy was starting to lean toward being mystified. His daughter thought she wasn't a Christian. His wife walked in the house an hour earlier with dirt all over her favorite sundress and didn't want to talk about it. What next?

In answer to his unspoken question, the girl said, "Mose told me it says in Roman chapter three, in —" She struggled with the strange language. "—verse twenty-three, it says we're all sinners."

Bobby Lee looked at his daughter as if she were a stranger who had wandered in out of the cotton fields. "Why would Mose think we're all sinners? Where would he get an idea like that?" *Confound your hide, Mose. I'll be up all night tryin' to get this notion out of her head.*

"Mose didn't say what he *thought*." She had a good memory. "He said it's what the *Bible* says. Says it's plain as black or white."

Susan Parker put the hand with the fingernails over her mouth. She was making a sound like she was coughing or couldn't get her breath or something. The sound made Bobby Lee frown.

The girl's finger worked its way slowly down a page. She found the verse and read it from the book. "Number twenty-three . . . 'For all have sinned, an' come short of the glory of God.' Sounds pretty clear to me."

"*All?*" Her daddy put his glass down. "Lemme see that."

She pushed the Bible back to him and crossed her arms on the table. The obvious had not escaped her. "I reckon God an' Mose think alike."

Her momma moved closer to the table, then asked, "What else did Mose say?"

The girl frowned at her paper. "A pretty good bit. In Roman, number six—" She moved her finger across the page. "—verse twenty-three, it says, 'The wages of sin is death; but the gift of God is . . .'" She struggled through the next word. "'E-tur-*null* life, through Jesus Christ our Lord.'"

The man's eyes followed the words in the book as she read from the paper.

"That means sinners either take the gift, or they don't git . . . uh . . . that life. What's e-tur-*null* mean?"

"*Eternal*," her momma pronounced. "It means forever and ever."

Her daddy pulled over the piece of paper to study it. "Did Mose write this on the paper?"

"No, sir. I did. He just told it to me."

"Did he use a Bible?"

"Why should he?" She shrugged. "He knows what it says."

The Bible scholar looked up at his wife. White teeth showed against tanned skin. It was the first time in almost a week that the man had seen his wife smile.

"What else did Mose say?" Susan asked again.

The girl's finger worked its way down through four more verses. Mose had given her a whole mess of things to think about.

The next morning, the girl walked over to R. D.'s house and through the back door. R. D. was sitting in his chair with his Sunday paper and his coffee. He didn't bother to look up when the screen door banged.

She was getting almost too big for her customary perch on the arm of his chair. "R. D., I wanna go to church this mornin'."

It was a law that if she needed to talk, he could keep the paper open in front of him, as long as he paid attention to what she said.

"Well, why don't you go get your momma to take you?"

" 'Cause she said if we went, we'd go to Billy's church, an' I ain't goin' there."

"Any particular reason?"

She thought Billy talked like a sissy, and she thought his son and daughter were mean, but she decided to employ diplomacy in her answer. "I reckon I wanna go where A. J. goes."

Parker folded the paper and looked at her over his reading glasses. "How come you want to go to church so bad all of a sudden?" The girl had stayed pretty much to herself all week, refusing at least three invitations to ride into town with him.

"Mose Junior was gonna tell the wide, wicked world 'bout how they could be Christians. He ain't here no more 'cause of me. I'm thinkin' I might ought to take his place."

"You want to tell people how to become Christians?"

"Nawsuh, I don't reckon I want to, but since Mose Junior can't, I figured I'd take his place." She usually didn't have to repeat herself to R. D.

"Why?"

It seemed pretty simple to her. "Seems fair, don't you think?"

He took a sip of coffee while he thought for a minute. The girl came up with some strange notions, but she was usually fair. He pulled out his watch, made some calculations, then said, "All right. Go get dressed."

She looked down at her fresh overalls. "Whatta I wear?"

R. D. went back to his paper and morning coffee. "Ask your momma."

She studied his khakis. "Whatta you gonna wear?"

It was a law that she wouldn't interrupt him and his paper just to pass the time. Without taking his eyes off the newsprint, he said, "Scat."

The church service wasn't near what she expected, and it dadgum sure wasn't anything worth putting on a dress for. Mose Junior told her what his church was like, but what she witnessed in the white church came up lacking.

The only moderately exciting thing was getting to watch Mrs. Haywood Puckett. The cantankerous old lady marched by, glaring at the girl and R. D. for being in the wrong church, and besides, it wasn't even Christmas. Her misdirected attention allowed the self-appointed member of the church police to bump into a doorjamb enough to knock her hat sideways. When it happened, A. J. grinned at Missy and winked. Missy grinned and winked back. Mrs. Puckett got huffy.

The four-person choir droned through the songs practically by themselves, then some lady got up and read a list of about a hundred people she wanted the two dozen folks in the congregation to pray for. By the time the preacher stood up, Missy had read all the names written on the stained-glass windows and was counting the metal ceiling tiles. Her Bible and piece of paper lay forgotten on the pew.

When Brother Frank Smith started up, he sounded as if he had been reading the girl's sheet of paper. In fact, it sounded as if he had been listening to everything Mose told her; he even talked about how Junior died to save somebody else. Missy picked up the Bible and opened it to where the pages were folded over.

Frank talked about her first two verses, then went straight to the very next one on her list.

"Romans five, eight says, 'But God commendeth his love toward us, in that, while we were yet sinners, Christ died for us.' Folks, that means God deliberately chose to let His Son die so that you and I wouldn't have to pay an eternal price for our sins. It's as simple as that. It says exactly what it means."

He talked along about that part, then said, "Turn to Ephesians two, eight and nine."

The girl went to the page in Ephesians that was folded over. R. D. read over her shoulder.

"'For by grace are ye saved through faith; and that not of yourselves: it is the gift of God: Not of works, lest any man should boast.'"

The words were clear to Missy, but Frank explained them anyway. No one would go to heaven just because he was good; nobody was good enough. It was just like Mose said. "The finest man in the town, even a preacher, can't go to heaven 'cause he's good. It's God's heaven an' His Son, so He decides; an' ain't nobody ever gonna be as good as His Son. Don't nobody get in 'cept them what believes in Jesus an' what He done on that cross."

The girl looked around to see how the rest of the people were taking the message. Lots of folks were counting the ceiling tiles; Reese Pemberton was asleep with his mouth open.

They visited with Frank Smith and some of the other folks after the service and headed for home. She thought maybe she ought to go to church with Mose next time.

The girl ate fast, told her grandmomma to save her some dessert, and left her place by R. D. before the rest of the Parkers had finished their Sunday dinner. She ran across the bridge and got to Mose's house while they were still eating. Pearl got quieter and snuggled close to her momma when Missy sat in the only empty chair at the table.

After they talked a little about the weather and the crops, Mose asked, "What'd you learn in church this mornin'?"

That was easy. "Nuthin', I guess." The girl liked being in the cabin because of the smoke smell.

"How come?"

"All he talked about was what you told us up on the bridge. Even used five of the same lines from the Bible."

"Verses?"

"Yeah, verses." *Verses that weren't very interestin'.*

"You decided anything yet?"

"Nope. Can't see right now how it makes any difference." *An' I've already wasted half of Sunday tryin' to figure it out.* "How will I know when I'm a Christian?"

"I reckon it comes to different folks different ways."

Pip nodded.

The girl said, "Well, I reckon I'll know if it hits me." She wasn't sure she would.

Mose smiled. "It ain't gonna run you down in the road an' bang you on the head, child. You'll be lookin' for it when it comes. It's 'tween you an' God. He'll tell you."

"Has God ever spoke to you?"

Pip got up to clean off the table; Pearl followed her.

"No, but I know I'm His 'cause of how I sees things now. Different from before."

"Did Junior change?" The girl already knew the answer. Junior argued with her every day about how she needed Jesus to save her. She always asked him what she needed saving from, and he told her the only way to get to heaven was to accept Jesus for who He said He was. He wouldn't say anything about hell. He wouldn't say the word.

"Oh yeah, Junior changed. You seen it yo'self."

She *had* seen it. For the last couple of months, she was occasionally able to talk him into doing mischief, but he didn't really enjoy it as much as in the past.

Summer moved along into July. The girl's visits to church, usually with R. D., became so commonplace that she wore her overalls; nobody seemed to notice. In late August, the picking season was on, and Mose and her daddy disappeared into the gin. They wouldn't come out 'til sometime in October.

She started school again in the fall and made use of a word she had picked up in church. Third grade was an *affliction*.

CHAPTER NINE

The sun wasn't up yet, but the day was. Old Mrs. Parker's rooster said so.

Missy sat on the gin's loading dock with a few hundred bales of cotton, swinging her feet and watching the bridge. Just before daylight, she saw Mose's silhouette against the promise of dawn and jumped down to run meet him.

He was halfway across the bridge when she reached him. "Mornin'."

"Mornin', Missy. You git outta bed to do the milkin' this mornin'?"

She passed on the humor. "I got somethin' I wanna tell you."

He had to stop or run over her. "Is that right?"

"Yep." She was all business. "I understand the whole thing now. I figured it out last night."

Mose knew the answer, but he asked the question anyway. "Figured out what, baby?"

"I figured out 'bout bein' a Christian. I'm gonna be one."

"An' how you gonna do that?"

"I been readin' them verses over an' over, an' it came to me. That verse in Romans ten: 'For whoever calls on the name of the Lord shall be saved.' That explains it."

"Well, there's a bit more to it, ain't there?"

"Oh yeah, all those other verses just explain it. But they don't make you a Christian—they just tell you where you stand with God. But if I believe in my heart 'bout what Jesus did for me, an' if I tell Him so, that does it."

The girl had come closer to explaining it than most preachers. "I reckon you got it figured out then."

They moved to the bridge railing, and the girl looked out at the lake. "I ain't prayed yet," she said, "to call on His name." She looked up at Mose and a pair of tears caught the purple-pink of the dawn. "I reckon I just wanted to be with you when I asked Him. An' I wanted to do it right here where Mose Junior died . . . on this here memorial bridge. Is that all right?"

He looked into the dark blue eyes, matching her tear for tear. "Baby, I'm right proud you done it this way . . . an' honored. An' I'm ready whenever you are."

The child took his hand and pulled him down to kneel with her by the old ladder. She said, "God, I 'poligize for waitin' so long to do this. It just took a while for me to get it all straight in my mind—an' in my heart. Me an' You both know I'm a sinner. I know You sent Jesus down here from heaven to die 'cause of my sins. An' I've figured out I need you in my heart—however that works—to save me. An' that's what I want . . . what I'm askin' for . . . prayin' for . . . is for You to save me. I don't think I can be good all the time, but I think I can keep on tryin' every day. Lord, You're all I need, an' I'm obliged to You for savin' me. Amen."

She stayed where she was for a minute, then looked sideways at Mose. "I reckon that'll do it."

The black man rested a hand on the little girl's shoulder. "I reckon it couldn't of been done no better. I'm proud for you."

"You reckon I'm a Christian now?"

"I reckon that ain't somethin' for another feller to try to call. Do you think you are?"

"I most certainly do, an' I figure God does too." She had something else on her mind. "Mose?"

"What is it, child?"

"Would you pray for me?"

"Already do, baby. Every day."

"Will you pray for me right now? That I'll be a good Christian?"

"Of course I will, baby. Let's bow our heads."

The man lowered his head to the wooden railing. His chest rose and fell once or twice before he spoke. "Lord, we just kneelin' here on this old bridge to ask Yo' blessin's on this here young girl. I pray, Lord, that You'll see fit to bring her close to Yo'self, that You'll make her heart to hunger to be a fine woman. Protect her good if You would. An' I pray, Lord, that she won't want nuthin' as much as she wants to know You—an' make You known. Keep us in Yo' care, Lord. Amen."

She studied his face. He had dust from the railing on his forehead. She moved an eight-year-old mother's fingers across his brow to brush it off. "Thank you, Mose."

He answered with a smile.

They rose from their knees and he resumed his walk to work. She slipped her hand in his and took him as far as the steps to the loading dock. When they got there the girl didn't turn loose. He looked down at her.

"Mose?"

"What is it, child?"

"I 'preciate what you done . . . showin' me them verses an' coaxin' me along an' all." She took a breath. "An' I love you."

"Have mercy, baby." He shook his head at the wonder of it all. "I reckon I love you like you was my own."

The girl grinned. "I almost am. I 'spect I'm gonna do what Junior set out to do. I'm gonna know God—an' make Him known. That makes me near 'bout yours, don't it?"

She whirled around and trotted off before the man could reply. He watched her cross the road and run down the driveway toward her house . . . and thought . . . and prayed.

From the darkness beneath the surface of the lake, a voice said, *She is no longer within our grasp, but she and those around her are not immune to our power. We will watch from here and wait, and our time will come.*

CHAPTER TEN

The cotton in the Delta was mostly picked, and work at the gin slowed to five or six days a week. Pip spent a nickel on seed, and the graves by the cabin were covered with rich rye grass.

On a cool Sunday afternoon, four days before Thanksgiving, R. D. and Missy arrived in the Washingtons' front yard. They pulled up just in time for the fall wind to pry an early pecan off the nearest tree. The nut hit the hood of the truck and landed on the ground. The planter stepped out of the truck, observing for the thousandth time that his great-granddaddy—the man who had decided to put the big house on the west side of the lake—had given the nicer spot to the cabin.

Mose came down the steps and greeted Old Mr. Parker at the door of the pickup. "Howdy, Mistah R. D. How y'all doin'?"

"Doin' fine, thank you." R. D. Parker extended his hand.

Mose, surprised and slightly flustered by the gesture, didn't know what to do except to shake it. No white man had ever offered to shake hands with him—even at the funeral. It just wasn't done.

Pearl, who was closely trailing her daddy, let her jaw go slack and dropped her doll when Missy stepped from behind the truck. The girl was wearing a dress.

R. D. cleared his throat. "Missy and I just came over to see if we could visit with you an' Pip for a minute."

Smoke rose out of the chimney and was spirited away by the wind almost before it left its mark. The fragrance that lingered was comforting, and Parker said so. "Wood smoke is about the best smell I know."

Mose nodded and agreed. "Yessuh—an' it's comin' winter. I reckon the fireplace is gonna be a right fine place to be in a week or two." He was distracted because he didn't see the dog. "Uh—y'all want to come in the house?"

The girl looked at Mose, then at R. D. The two men looked at each other, then at the ground. There was an instant of silence before Missy smiled; sometimes men moved too slowly. She held her shoulder-length hair back from her face with one hand and mounted the steps, saying, "That'd be real nice, Mose. If we go inside I can see Pip an' stand by the fire."

Mose finally spied the dog under the steps, just watching. It seemed strange that the animal would watch the white folks so closely without offering to come out. What was going on?

Pip was cleaning off the little wooden table when the four entered the cabin's front room. She stopped and started arranging chairs for the visitors.

"Afternoon, Pip." Missy's greeting was more subdued than usual.

Pip nodded at the girl and spoke to Mr. R. D. She shot a questioning glance in Mose's direction. He was busy thinking about something.

A measure of tension had come to the cabin in the pecan trees. The two men took positions inside the front door with their hats in their hands; neither could decide which foot to stand on. Pearl was trying to hold onto her doll and her momma's skirt and suck her thumb all at the same time. In sixty seconds, a peaceful Sunday afternoon had become anything but. Pip worked around Pearl to finish her housekeeping, the girl stood by the fire, and the two men looked about as comfortable as a pair of cats at a dog fight.

R. D. spoke first. He made a motion to take in Missy. "Well, it seems like we've been actin' almost mysterious. Every one of us have been knowin' each other a long time, but we just haven't ever been together like this . . . kind of makin' a social call . . . an' I guess that's kind of a shame." He seemed to be listening to himself and realizing that what he had said was too true. He picked back up. "Anyway, we came to see you to tell you what our family has decided."

While R. D. spoke, the girl stood with her back to the room and watched the fire.

Pip and Mose watched R. D.

The thinking process of most white folks was a mystery to most black folks and vice versa. Mose and Pip didn't have even a vague notion of what Mr. R. D. was talking about, so they both stayed silent.

"I can't think of a way to get to this slowly, so I'll just start." He shifted his feet again. "Mose, you an' Pip . . . an' you, Pearl . . . lost somethin' no one can ever replace—a son an' a brother. We're not here to try to make up for Junior bein' gone. Nobody could do that, an' it'd be unseemly to try. What we're here to do is to show you we 'preciate what he did for us when he gave his life for Bobby an' Missy. We've got somethin' we've got to do . . . somethin' our family has to do . . . somethin' we want you to have."

Missy had a big envelope under her arm; R. D. wasn't holding anything but his hat. Mose's mind raced. *Mister R. D. is goin' to offer us money.* Mose looked at Pip. Her head was already moving back and forth, already saying no. He caught her eye to make sure. She frowned at him, her lips compressed, her mind made up. *Good,* he thought.

R. D. continued. "Pickin' season's over an' all our cotton's 'bout in." He paused, then sighed. "I guess you could say we did good this year." He didn't sound happy about their good fortune.

What was happening was a kind thing, but it wasn't something Mose was comfortable with. He looked at Pip; she was looking at the floor. She'd already told him what she thought. Money was short, but he and Pip were mighty particular about how they came by it.

Parker paused a moment to gather his thoughts, then said, "If rich men could, they'd trade their money to be a man like your boy, but they can't. What we want to do is honor him by givin' to you out of what the good Lord has given us. We've got more land than we need; we've got the gin, an' we can buy more land if we want to. An' because of what your Junior did, we've still got both our children. So, our family's been talkin' it over for awhile now—" He waved a hand at Missy. "—and Missy's got a letter from each one of us to y'all, tellin' how much we 'preciate what Junior did an' how much we want to do what I'm fixin' to tell you. That land between your house an' the brake is good cotton land. We came today to give you an' Pip that land for as long as you live, from friends to friends."

Six hundred acres. Mose's mind actually went blank for a short while. Landowners among the Negroes in Mississippi were extremely rare. Mose and Pip were already almost rich by black folks' standards because they owned forty acres and the cabin outright. His job at the gin paid him better than what any farmhand in the Delta made, and he worked all year long. His eyes were on R. D., but he couldn't figure out what to say. He didn't need to ask what Pip thought; he knew. Finally, he said, "Mistah R. D., we most grateful that you'd want to do this for us, but the good Lord knows we can't—"

The girl anticipated his reaction. When Mose spoke the first word, she turned from the fireplace. He was going to shake his head, but his chin hadn't made a full round trip before she stepped across the tiny room and put her hand in his. He stopped talking involuntarily to see what she wanted.

The girl tugged gently on his rough hand. "Come sit over here."

Mose let the child lead him to his chair by the fire. She put the envelope on the table, and when he sat, she put her other hand on his arm. She spoke calmly, in that deep voice of hers. "I told 'em we couldn't all come 'cause it might've made you nervous. They sent me 'cause I told 'em you could hear my words better than most."

Mose watched her face and nodded. She was right.

The girl took a long breath, seeming to search for words. She was praying.

Mose waited.

Missy turned to Pip. "Pip, I know you don't want to do this

no more than he does, but it's important to us . . . to *me*. It's a special thing. They told me it was 'bout a lot of money, an' that y'all didn't have much. But it ain't 'bout money; it's 'bout 'preciation. My daddy says he owes God for me an' his son; my momma owes you an' God for her salvation. Bobby said you can have everything he owns 'cause of what Junior done." Missy's voice stayed even, low. She didn't cry, but her eyes were beginning to shimmer. She continued to speak the words she prayed about. "An' it's like all I am . . . all I'll ever be . . . started bein' born that day Junior died for me. The Bible talks 'bout the tithe . . . an' this here is ours. I figure this is how we get to show God that we 'preciate all He's ever done for us, all the things He's given us. We figure God used y'all to give to us, an' givin' this tithe to you is as good as givin' it back to Him. Puttin' it in your hands is puttin' it in His."

Pip had not taken her eyes off the girl. The child's speech was more than she could endure. She took her apron with both hands and wiped her eyes with it. When she nodded her understanding, the decision was given over to Mose.

R. D. was proud of the girl. His feet became still.

Mose hadn't changed his mind. He took the girl's hand in both of his. "Honey, it's a fine thing—"

He was going the wrong way so the girl interrupted. "It ain't a thing if it don't happen."

"Baby, I can't —we can't—"

She wouldn't let him finish. "Mose, it ain't right for me to keep interruptin', but this here is almost between me an' you an' God now. An' I need you to do this for *me*. It's real important." She paused while she took a breath and inched closer to him. "I've got God, I've got R. D., an' I've got my daddy. An' all three of 'em know you're as good a friend as I'm ever gonna have." Her expression stayed cloudless and her lip firm, but the first tear came. "Mose, I reckon most white girls don't get to have colored daddies, but I'm close. You ain't got Junior no more, but you've got me." Another breath. The slightest shudder. Another tear. Nothing but earnestness in her face. "You mind my words. This ain't somethin' you can figure right now, but someday you'll know you done the right thing by lettin' me an' my family do this for you an' yours. If it was the other way 'round, you'd want us to let you do it for us." Her voice stopped; her tears kept coming, slowly, making their way down quiet cheeks.

The only sound in the room was the crackle from the fire.

Pip dabbed at her eyes with one corner of her apron and watched Mose. The black man moved his eyes at intervals. He looked at the floor, the fire, out the window, at R. D. Parker. Every time his gaze shifted, it stopped for a moment on the girl's face. The girl never took her eyes off his. The firm lower lip eventually gave way to a smile as soft as her tears. She knew what was fair, and she was watching him come to know.

And finally, he did. "Baby, I reckon I just can't say no."

When the two embraced, R. D. Parker smiled and wondered at Missy's ability to sway people. *Thank goodness she usually wants what's right.*

Mose worked that six hundred acres 'til the spring of '52, the year they had the killing out at Cat Lake.

CHAPTER ELEVEN

In June of 1952, Bobby Parker was a pilot in the Air Force, fly-ing fighter jets in the air war over Korea; Pearl Washington was a tall eighth-grader; Missy and Pip had been studying and pray-ing together for nearly seven years.

The girl and her black mentoress had gotten their start the day after Christmas in '45. From the beginning, Pip had made it clear to Missy that she was willing to pray with her and she'd teach her how to study her Bible, but the girl would make her own choices about how often they got together. They prayed and drank coffee at the Parkers' breakfast table on weekday mornings before school. On Saturdays, the girl brought what-ever her grandmother just baked, and they prayed at Pip's house. Sunday was a busy day for Pip, but they started over early on Mondays. When the girl was sick, Pip came to her bed-side and they prayed there; the girl reciprocated on those rare occasions when Pip couldn't get out. Until just recently, the only time they missed a day was when the girl was out of town. Lately, though, the girl had decided she needed sleep more than she needed prayer, and the Saturday prayer times were the first to go. Seven years is a long time to remember a promise.

In thirty years, Blue Biggers never struck a blow at a man, woman, or dog. He didn't do those things for two reasons: he didn't have an angry bone in his body, and the action might call for too much energy. Blue was set up well and pretty good-looking on the outside; inside he was comfortable with being weak and worthless. When he was job hunting, the farmers that didn't know him hired him as soon as they saw him because he was tall, sturdy, and mild mannered. Women took to him because he was fine-looking and smooth talking. The women and farmers who chose to invest their time in him were always disappointed. Blue instinctively started well and got his boss's—or woman's—hopes up, but eventually he fizzled. His bosses and his women would wait months for him to hit his stride again, but Blue never met their expectations. He was never able to stay on any one farm for more than a year because his laziness caused his bosses too much aggravation—no less for his women. For the past ten years, he had been meandering his harmless way north from Yazoo City at a pretty consistent five miles a year. Now in his mid-thirties, with twenty years of sporadic labor behind him, his total accumulated wealth took the form of two gold teeth and a worn-out old car that was perpetually low on oil. His attachments to women, like his opportunities for employment, came according to mileage—about one every five miles.

Early on a blue-sky, spring-feeling Friday morning, Blue's latest investment in the female world notified him that she was fed up with his uselessness. Almedia Franklin, who was a foot shorter and half the weight of the affable sluggard, paid him the final installment on his investment with the hard end of a mean broom. He went flying out of Inverness at six o'clock, carrying an impressive knot on the back of his head, a quart bottle of warm beer, and a handful of gone.

The same Friday caught Missy still in bed an hour after Pip got to the house. Pip stood in the door of the girl's room and surveyed two hundred square feet of chaos. The corner of the girl's Bible was visible under a three-day-old stack of dirty clothes.

"Well, Missy, are you gonna pray this mornin' or sleep?"

The girl, who had been resisting the sun's steady march into the day, pushed herself up on one elbow. "What time is it?"

"Goin' on seven. Wake up, baby. The coffee's gettin' cold."

Long dark hair cushioned her collapse into the pillow. "Come back in five minutes."

Pip didn't have time to slow down. "I can't be traipsin' back an' forth between here an' my kitchen, woman. I've got house-work to do. Now get out of that bed if you're goin' to."

Missy swung slender legs over the side of the bed and pushed back her hair. With Pip watching her, she looked into the mirror next to her bed while she pulled her daddy's T-shirt tight against herself and grimaced. Nothing had changed since the night before. She let go of the shirt. "I'm almost fifteen," she pouted. "Every girl in my class looks like a girl 'cept me, an' God made me flat as that mirror."

Pip was busy harvesting the crop of dirty clothes. "Baby, you'll start growin' soon enough."

The girl couldn't hear her. She picked a tiny brassiere off the floor and frowned at it. "Two flat triangles for a girl with two flat bosoms. The only reason I wear it is so I won't be the only grown woman in Miss'ippi without one." She let the under-garment dangle and glowered at the image in the mirror. "I bet Marilyn Monroe was born with bosoms."

Pip stopped behind the girl, rested her hands on the droop-ing shoulders, and said, "Baby, it's not ever goin' to be about what's on your chest; it's about what's in your heart."

Missy stared at the bra and ignored her. "God shortchanged me."

Pip snatched the bra out of Missy's hands. "Have mercy, child. Didn't I just tell you I don't have time for this foolish-ness?" She shook the undergarment in Missy's face, then tossed it into the pile of dirty clothes. "Get out of that bed, get your Bible, an' get out there in my kitchen."

"How old were you when you got to have bosoms?"

Pip picked up the pile of laundry and was already out the

door; she didn't slow down to answer. Missy and everybody else in the whole house could hear her praying as she went down the hall. "Lord Jesus, give me the strength to deal with this foolish white child."

Missy hurled herself across the bed and looked around for something to kick, but Pip had picked up all the soft stuff. She swished across the room and yelled into the hall, "Well, I ain't prayin' no more. I've been beggin' Him for just two little bitty bosoms ever since Polly Ragsdale got those grapefruits of hers, an' I ain't got so much as a mustard seed to show for it."

Pip's voice came back from the kitchen. "*Haven't* got."

Thirty seconds later, Missy stomped into the kitchen. She threw the well-used Bible on the table, slumped into her chair, and glared at Pip as if the whole thing were her fault. "He made every confounded mountain in the whole world. You'd think he could spare me a figure."

Pip refused to be drawn into an argument. She leaned down and kissed the top of the tangled hair. "God an' time, baby, the whole thing is about God an' His good time."

"Humphf."

"Let's read some First Samuel. Go to chapter sixteen, verse seven."

"Is this gonna help me get some bosoms?"

Pip turned to the chicken she was cutting up and told Missy, "Read to me, an' we'll talk."

Missy thumbed her way to First Samuel. "'But the Lord said unto Samuel, Look not on his countenance, or on the height of his stature; because I have refused him: for the Lord seeth not as man seeth; for man looketh on the outward appearance, but the Lord looketh on the heart.'" The girl rolled her eyes. "Well, that's just peachy. You're tryin' to tell me that God doesn't care whether I look like a boy."

"Baby, I didn't write those words. God did."

"It's all the same." She slammed the book closed. "Nobody cares that I'm gonna grow up lookin' like an underfed pancake."

It was Pip's turn to roll her eyes. "Child, when you get your head fixed in one direction, you can shame a steam locomo-tive."

"Polly Ragsdale ain't as old as I am, an' she looks like she's got a pair of basketballs in her blouse. I don't—"

Pip had things she needed to get done; she interrupted without turning from the sink. "Missy baby, it ain't somethin' me an' you can fix."

"Well, why not? He could give me just two little bitty bumps without wreckin' the world, I guess." The fourteen-year-old bottle of vintage teenage stupidity was getting ready to cross the line, and she knew it. "I'm gonna end up bein' one of those flat-chested old women that's skinny enough to tread water in a garden hose, 'cept for a butt as wide as a Greyhound bus."

Pip kept after the chicken, waiting for a second before she spoke. "You know I won't stand for that kind of talk, Missy. Now say you're sorry an' read me somethin' that'll help us both."

Missy couldn't decide whether to blame God or Pip for her flat chest; she focused on the person she could see. "I ain't sorry, an' I ain't gonna say so."

The arm attached to the knife hand quit moving, and the hand that had been holding the chicken came to rest on the kitchen counter. Pip's back straightened and her head came up, but she didn't speak.

The girl seemed bent on proving that even the best teenagers can't always be counted on to show good sense. When Pip took her time responding, the girl issued the next challenge. "Well?"

Pip took time to rinse off the knife before she turned around. "You know I don't allow that kind of talk in this house, an' I won't take your sass. Now"—she pointed the knife at the girl—"you can take it back an' apologize, or you can go cut me a switch."

Missy compounded the effect of a string of imbecilic deci-sions by digging her hole deeper. "This ain't your house."

The only time Pip ever raised her voice was when she sang in the choir. She put the knife on the counter and conviction in her tone. "It may be your daddy's house, young lady, but while I'm in it"—she tapped the counter with an unyielding finger—"the language will suit *me*."

The girl stepped out of the hole and planted her feet firmly in midair. "I ain't apologizin', an' you ain't gonna switch me."

Pip, her lips pursed in thought, looked at the girl without rising to the challenge.

The girl was right; she was too old to be switched, but she wasn't too young to behave decently. The woman reached a decision and nodded to herself. She said, "Baby, God's work sho' needs stubborn folks, but the good Lord knows there's such a thing as bein' too stiff-necked."

The girl saw Pip take off her apron a million times, but she never saw the act take on the flavor of finality that she tasted in the kitchen that morning. Her best friend folded the apron neatly, put the garment in its drawer by the back door, and left.

The dirty clothes were piled in the laundry room, the partially butchered chicken was on the counter by the sink, the Bible was unopened on the table, and the girl was standing at the kitchen window watching Pip walk across the bridge toward her house in the pecan trees.

Three hours later, the girl walked back into the kitchen and looked at the cut-up chicken. She gathered up the pieces, marched out to the garbage can by the driveway, and threw them in.

Weekends in the Mississippi Delta always called for a temporary reclassification of a certain segment of the population; this sometime subgroup, comprising both blacks and whites, was classified by both sides of the color line as "nothin' but trash." On Saturdays, white folks and coloreds went about their business and did their shopping; on Sundays they mostly went to church and visited family. The trashy elements of both races spent all Saturday drinking, carousing, and moving back and forth between whatever juke joints were handy; they spent Sunday getting over their hangovers, cuts, and bruises.

For Blue Biggers, any day that wasn't Sunday was Saturday.

Blue spent all Friday morning doing what he did best, and a few minutes before noon he shut down the engine in his car and coasted across the Cat Lake bridge toward the Parker Gin. He wasn't coasting to save gas; his old Ford didn't have much in the way of brakes.

Immediately after turning the key, Blue knew that shutting the engine down on the bridge was a mistake; it meant he'd have to be slowing down over the waters of Cat Lake. Every man in the Delta knew about the lake and what had happened there, and Blue was definitely not the kind of man who liked being alone in a bad place.

Those who have been cast out of eternity to sow evil have no incentive to mark time. A voice that the demons beneath the surface of the lake had not heard for seven years pronounced a sentence. *It is time. The one we have waited for is here.*

The hound of hell selected four of his most vicious cohorts. *You will possess him. Subvert his will and wait for my instructions. It could be that he will be the instrument of destruction among our enemies.*

Moving as swiftly as a shadow striking the ground, and with no more fanfare, the four specters took the reins of Blue Bigger's mind, will, and emotions.

Even as his fear of the lake began to make inroads into Blue's mind, the bridge appeared to take on movement; the black waters appeared to surge and swell, obscuring the horizon. The illusion, probably brought on by the rap Almedia gave him with the broom, made him dizzy.

When the car cleared the bridge, he stomped repeatedly on the clutch, ground the gears, left the road in a cloud of dust, and managed to get the worn-out clunker stopped before running into the gin's loading dock. The gin's resident flock of pigeons, disturbed by the mechanical protests from the car, left the roof

of the gin for the safety of the sky. In those last few yards between the bridge and the gin, Blue sweated through his shirt.

Mose was busy on the upper catwalk inside the gin when the
car shuddered to a halt by Mr. Bobby Lee's office. One of the
two men on the catwalk tapped Mose on the shoulder and
pointed at the car. "That there's Blue Biggers. They don't come
no sorrier."

Mose nodded. He watched the driver jerk, bang, and cuss
the car's door open. When the man finally got clear of the car,
he put an unsteady foot on the door and kicked it shut. Mose
finished explaining to the men on the catwalk what he wanted
done before he made his way down the ladder.

Blue looked across the hood of the car and watched a slender white girl, as fine-looking as any grown woman he'd ever
seen, throw something in a garbage can and glance his way. She
was wearing a sleeveless white blouse and blue shorts. He lifted
his cap and nodded politely, but the girl didn't seem to notice.
Those who controlled his will had him watch the girl's ponytail
follow her back to the house. His thoughts told him, *That cute
little thing knowed I was watchin' her, an' she liked it.*

The pigeons were settling back onto the gin's roof when
Blue stuck his head in the open door of the gin office. What he
saw was common to gin offices throughout the world. Pieces of
broken gin parts and cotton lint held down the papers that were
stacked on every horizontal surface. The shelves of two floor-
to-ceiling bookcases sagged under the weight of grime-stained
ledgers. Time and use had worn the floor white, except for an
area that graduated to dark brown around the spittoon. Twenty
years of oily dust and cotton lint covered everything but the
white man who was tilted back in his chair with his feet
propped up on the desk. The only thing in the office that was
out of place was the open Bible on the fellow's lap. Bobby Lee
marked his place with his finger and gave his attention to the
new arrival.

Blue had paid the white dentist in Inverness twelve dollars

each for the gold caps on his two front teeth. When Bobby Lee looked up, the visitor displayed his only worthwhile assets.

"Mornin' to ya, boss. My name's Blue Biggers. I was wonderin' did y'all have any work?" Blue moved to prop himself against the door frame, missed, and collided with the nearest bookcase.

Bobby Lee didn't bother to get up. It wasn't even dinnertime yet, and the man was drunk. "Mornin', Blue. Just walk out there on the dock. I'll ring the bell an' Mose'll show up in a minute. I run the office; Mose runs the gin." Without bothering to sit up, he used his toe to press a button by the desk.

Out in the gin, an electric buzzer told Mose to come get rid of this drunken fool so Bobby Lee could get on with his Bible-reading.

Blue grinned wider and said, "Thanks, boss." He noted the Bible and was going to try to paint himself in a good light, but the first word of the phrase wouldn't come out. "Guh . . . Guh . . ." He struggled with the words and finally managed to force out, ". . . uh . . . bless you."

Bobby Lee nodded without looking up.

Blue was sauntering across the loading platform when he saw Mose. Mose wore neatly pressed khaki pants and a matching shirt, just like a white man. The out-of-work cotton chopper, who had never done a full day's work in his life, decided in that moment that he needed a job like Mose's. *A black man runnin' a whole gin*, he thought. *Oh yeah. I done found me a home.*

Blue pulled out the twenty-four-dollar smile. "Howdy. I reckon you'd be Mose."

"Mornin'." Mose had been running the mechanical side of the gin operation for several years; he hired and fired his own men, and he had dealt with enough troublemakers to spot this one when he stumbled out of his car. The man on the catwalk called it right. Mose stopped by one of the vertical support timbers and let Blue come to him; while he waited, he hooked one finger in his watch pocket and rested his free hand on the post. Hanging by a strap near the gin foreman's fingertips was four feet of what had been a hoe handle. Mose used the wooden club for everything from killing rats to poking into the gin stands. It was a versatile tool.

Blue accentuated his swagger some and kept walking, talking, and showing his teeth. "Well, I been figurin' to get me a job in a gin, an' I'm told this here is the place to go." His eyes went up and down Mose, appraising the smaller, older man.

Mose could smell the cheap whiskey. "No." He shook his head without returning the smile. "We ain't hirin' yet. Things'll be slow 'til July, an' we already got our men lined up."

Blue Biggers decided in that moment that he didn't like asking another black man for a job, he didn't like being turned down, and he didn't like people who were immune to his charm. He reached into his pocket, produced a crumpled pack, and shook out a ready-roll cigarette while he thought about what to tell this highfalutin' Uncle Tom.

"Don't be lightin' that up here," ordered Mose. "You know better than to smoke at a gin."

Biggers's building resentment for Mose took on breadth. If he wasn't going to get a job he might as well show these folks who they were messing with, and he'd start by whipping up on this old man. He stuck the cigarette in the corner of his mouth and spoke around it while he pretended he was looking for matches. The fingertips of the man who had been amiable and harmless until he crossed the Cat Lake bridge touched his pocketknife. "I reckon you gonna stop me?"

Mose shook his head in mild wonder; the man was worthless—*and* stupid. "I reckon I ain't." He used the watch-pocket hand to whistle and the other to lift the hoe handle off its nail.

The whistle caught Biggers by surprise. The man it conjured up turned his insides to cold soup.

While Blue stared, Mose pointed the hoe handle at the third member of the group. "This here's Roosevelt Edwards; he'll be the one what'll do any stoppin'." Blue was spending his time being impressed by the size of the new man while Mose hung the rat-killer that he wasn't going to need back on its hook.

Mose turned to Roosevelt and said, "Roosevelt, this here's Blue. He's leavin'. Right now."

Roosevelt nodded twice; once at Mose and once at Blue. Mose turned back to his work.

Blue rarely displayed good judgment, but that Friday was an exception. Edwards's arrival on the scene took the odds against him up to about four or five to one. He got the car door open on the first try and drove away from the gin without ever lighting his cigarette.

Friday morning became a mild-mannered afternoon and found the girl visiting her friends in the pool hall.

Things were slow at the service station, and Scooter Hall was in the third hour of his lunch break. "I swear, Missy, you get any taller an' you won't have to sit on them pillows to drive."

She was slouched against her granddaddy's shoulder, kibitzing the game. She pretended to frown so Scooter would enjoy the exchange, but her heart wasn't in it. "I haven't had to sit on a pillow since I turned thirteen, Scooter, an' you know it." She gave an inch of honest ground. "I just have to stretch a little to reach the pedals, is all."

"Well, I reckon by next year you'll be six feet tall."

Without pretense, the muscles that supported her face and shoulders melted a fraction of an inch. *Flat-chested and short.* "Maybe not. I'll be fifteen this fall, an' I reckon my growin' days are 'bout over. I sure wish I could've made it to five-two, but it don't look like it's gonna happen."

"Seems like you slacked off on cussin' some," someone else observed. "You must be gettin' too big for Pip to use a switch on you; that's good for somethin', ain't it?"

She was having a hard time staying interested in the conversation, and she didn't like remembering what she'd done to Pip that morning. "Well, first of all, Pip hasn't said anything about me bein' too big to switch. As far as cussin' is concerned, I guess I haven't completely broken the habit yet, but I got it bent pretty good." She sighed, remembering how she had just treated someone who cared about her. "Pip doesn't hold with me bein' down here too much."

Smart men don't take on inflexible objects, so Scooter ignored the reference to Pip. Within minutes he would regret his next question. "Don't you reckon God could make you tall if He wanted?"

Missy took another deep breath when God was invited into the conversation. She knew what He thought, and she knew Who her daddy would say the house belonged to. She said, "No doubt about it. God can make me any size He wants, an' He says so real clear." She sighed for the hundredth time. "But if it was me choosin', I'd sure be happy to get at least as tall as Debbie Reynolds, an' she's just a squirt." She hadn't thought about being short for almost five minutes, and the subject wasn't her favorite. She said, almost to herself, "You'd think He could take a couple of inches off of some tall galoot that's comin' down the pike and give 'em to me." The muscles in her face and shoulders melted a little more while she thought, *I'm short an' flat-chested an' stupid, an' Pip hates me, an' God's probably gettin' ready to kick my wagon-wide back end clear into next Tuesday.* Her heart slumped along with her shoulders. *An' I deserve every smidgen of it.*

There weren't any psychiatrists in her audience, but all the men knew she was dealing with things that were dragging her down. They wanted to feel sorry for her, but they were constrained by three realities: She was prettier than any woman any of them had ever seen, her voice had a quality that would shame Lauren Bacall, and teenagers almost always had tomorrow.

When she moped out the door, Fred Crockett turned to R. D. and spoke for the girl's friends. "She don't get it, does she?"

R. D. shook his head and spoke without taking his eyes off the game. "Never has. If women could rob beauty from one another, the female half of the world would've been waitin' in the street for her to step through the door."

Each man within hearing nodded and secretly wished he were forty or fifty years younger.

R. D. let his eyes go to the figure standing on the sidewalk with her hands stuffed in the pockets of her shorts. Spring sunshine highlighted the dark hair and tried to warm her shoulders. R. D. stood up and said, "Scooter, play out this hand for me."

When the old man reached the girl, he added his big arm to the sun's efforts. The girl stood on the main street of Moores Point and buried her face against the front of her granddaddy's khaki shirt and wept.

The men in the pool hall watched the girl cry; several cussed because they were helpless in the face of the cruel swirl-wind of adolescence. The one who cussed the longest was Scooter Hall.

Saturday morning the girl walked past her mirror on the way out of her room, paused long enough to get mad, and went into the kitchen to look at the clock. Almost ten-thirty in the morning, and no prayer time. The house was quiet enough to be empty. She opened the refrigerator and surveyed the contents; nothing met with her approval. She wrinkled her nose and shut the door. She lifted the lid of the coffeepot and saw that it was half full. She turned on the burner under the pot and looked back at the clock. It hadn't moved. She walked to the window and looked across the lake at Pip's house. Pip had walked out twenty-seven hours ago, and today would mark the third Satur-day in a row that the girl had ignored her quiet time. She thought maybe she could catch up with her praying tomorrow afternoon or maybe Monday morning before breakfast. Or, if Pip didn't come back, maybe she would just quit having a quiet time. Maybe it wasn't her fault if Pip wanted to be stubborn.

When the coffee was hot, she poured a cupful and stared out the window at the lake. *What the heck difference does ten min-utes worth of prayer make?* she thought. *I've spent hours asking for bosoms, an' I'm flat as that water out there.*

Her mother interrupted her thoughts. "Missy?"

"Ma'am?"

"Come drive me to the grocery store. I've got a couple of things I need to get for tomorrow."

"Yes'm."

The peaceful surface of the lake belied the evil being plotted in its depths. Satanic phantoms sat in council around their commander, encouraged by their conquest of Blue Biggers.

The underling who had been shadowing the girl reported, *She has isolated herself from the black one and forcibly resists the call of the Enemy.*

The archfiend could see the opportunity taking shape. *How does she use her life?*

She ignores the offered wisdom of the Writings and whiles her time away with the foolish things of the flesh.

The demon, who had been thwarted in his first attempt to kill the girl, intoxicated himself with the remembered execution of Junior Washington. *This time we will breach the barrier. We will use this black sluggard, first to deal with her friends across the lake and afterward to render her useless to the cause of our Enemy.*

§

Saturday morning found Blue Biggers in Moores Point, mad at Mose and drunk. Shortly after eleven he was standing in front of the Yellow Dog with a following of other black trash when Pip walked out of Failing's Grocery Store. He nudged one of the men and asked, "Who's that?"

The man nodded his agreement with Blue's taste in women. "That there's Mose Washington's woman. Name o' Pip."

"You talkin' 'bout that Mose what works at the Parker Gin?"

"That's the one. Only he don't just work there; Mistah Bobby Lee practically lets him run that gin by hisself. An' he got six hundred acres of good cotton land on the other side o' that lake."

Everything the man said made Blue more agitated. Mose, in Blue's convoluted mind, had all the things Blue deserved— a big job, a good-looking woman, and more cotton land than any black man in the state.

"An' that there is his woman?" The woman looked in their direction, and Blue was confident that she let her gaze rest on him a moment longer than was necessary. His twisted mind said, *Any woman who would look at a man that long must like what she sees.* Blue couldn't believe his good fortune; he might just settle with Mose and then take this woman away from him.

"Blue?"

"What?"

"They ain't like most folks. That was their boy what got killed savin' them white chillun. They different."

The man's eyes narrowed. "Yeah. So what." The words were a statement, not a question.

The loafer standing next to Blue wasn't drunk yet. "Blue?"

"What?" The traveler from Yazoo City didn't take his eyes away from Pip.

"Pip don't fool aroun', Blue."

"We'll see." Blue was showing the trademark gold. "Sometimes it just takes the right man."

Missy Parker chose that moment to park her car at the curb between Blue and Pip. When she stepped out, Blue said, "Well, I swear, that's that white gal from out by the gin. Y'all got more good-lookin' women in this here town than a man can abide."

When Blue's companion realized that he was talking about Missy Parker, he felt a deep chill. "That there's the Parker girl, Blue. Any white man in this town sees you lookin' at her an' you'll be dead 'fore noon."

Blue stared boldly at the young girl. "I ain't scared o' no white man."

The man with Blue enjoyed spending as much time as he could with people as foolish and lazy as he was, but he didn't seek the company of crazy folks. He stuttered a lame excuse and got away from Blue—fast and far.

By midafternoon, Blue gave up on Moores Point. Somebody said they needed hoe hands on Klondike Plantation, so he headed south of town to offer his services. When he drove back across the Cat Lake bridge, the darkness of the water seemed deeper somehow.

From the intense darkness that centered itself below the

bridge, the spirit's voice said, *They have brought him. We will use him to break the barrier.*

Blue had gleaned plenty of information about the Washingtons while in town, and it wasn't hard to spot the little house south of the bridge. The car left the road and headed for the cabin without his even thinking about it.

Mose left Pip napping and went out the back door of the cabin to do some Saturday afternoon fixing up around the place. Pip wasn't hard to please, but they had the money to make a few changes, and Mose had dragged his feet as long as he could. He heard the car coming and stepped around the corner of the house to watch Blue's beat-up old junker shudder to a gear-grinding halt in a cloud of gray oil smoke. The dog by Mose's knee was growling before Blue started to struggle with the car door.

The Moores Point grapevine was efficient, and Blue's comments about Pip around town had made their way back to the Washingtons before noon—Blue was trouble. Pip, though, had always ignored the Blues of the world; at dinner she'd told Mose to do the same. "You just let him go, baby, an' he'll move on down the road."

Mose watched the dust and oil smoke drift past the car and shook his head. *She sho' ain't wrong much, but she done missed it a mile this time.*

Mose had spent twenty years at the gin telling men what to do, and what he saw in Blue didn't measure up to normal. A man with wild-looking eyes would only come to the cabin if he wanted to make some real trouble.

Mose shook his head again while rapping his knuckles on the porch. He spoke loud enough to be heard inside the cabin. "Baby, bes' bring my gun to the door."

Blue was still being held prisoner by the car.

Mose stepped close and said, "Don't bother gettin' out, Blue. You ain't stayin'."

Blue ignored the uninvitation. He reclined into the passenger's seat and used both feet to kick the wreck's door open. He stepped out and moved his lips to display the gold. "Afternoon, *Mistah* Washington. Figured I'd stop by an' see how y'all was."

For a short moment Blue looked disoriented. He wiped the back of his hand across his face, squinting as if the sunlight hurt his eyes. "Where's Pip at?"

"Blue, you're drunk. You bes' be gettin' in that car an' gettin' on down the road."

"Ain't too drunk to know the bes' lookin' woman 'round when I sees her. I come to let Pip choose." He tried to laugh, and a dry, hacking sound came out.

Blue was twenty-five years younger than Mose and plenty bigger. If he'd been a smaller man, things might've taken a different turn.

Mose watched a prominent blood vessel in the other man's forehead swelling and receding in time with his heart. The man he was facing wasn't the kind who responded to reason—a good man could either take Blue's kind on or let them walk over him. Mose stepped closer to the man and said, "You come to the wrong place, Blue. You bes' leave Pip alone."

"Where's yo' stick at, Mose? An' yo' big bodyguard?" Blue stepped around Mose and approached the porch. "Hey, Pip!" he yelled. "Come on out here an' see what a man looks like!"

Mose warned him one more time. "Awright, Blue. You better leave Pip alone."

Blue turned around and snarled, "Ol' man, yo' day is over. This here young buck is steppin' in." The metal of the knife's blade winked in the warm sun, and things went past the last turning point.

Mose took a step away from the knife and put his hands out. Blue crowded into the space between them. The hair went up on the dog's back, and he moved in from the side. Mose tried to reason with the man. "Don't do this, Blue."

Blue might as well have been deaf. "I reckon I'll see that pretty little Parker girl after I take care of her ol' Uncle Mose." He swiped a hand over his eyes again. "Right now I'm fixin' to see yo' insides."

Blue had his back to the screen door when it opened and closed. From behind him, Pip said, "I reckon you better pull up there, Blue."

Blue's face was running with sweat. He growled his words.

"Not jes' yet, Pip. First I'm gonna cut this here ol' man, an' then I'm gonna talk to you. If'n you don't talk right, you'll be gettin' the same as him, an' I'll be on the road to see that little Parker girl."

The dog crouched, showing his teeth and growling.

An unconcerned cat sat on the edge of the porch and cleaned its paws; redbirds sang while a mockingbird family went through its repertoire. The even tone of Pip's voice fit its surroundings. "Not on this day or any other."

Blue looked over his shoulder into the barrel of a shotgun. Pip had the gun's stock snugged up to her cheek; the muzzle was centered on Blue's back. The woman didn't blink.

Mose drew a breath and let it out. He almost smiled. "I told you not to mess with her, boy."

Blue no longer had access to what it took to be scared. Pip was even prettier up close. "You ain't gonna shoot me, Pip. You too good lookin', an' I'm too much of a man. Me an' you gonna look good together."

While the two men watched, Pip came down the steps and across the yard to within six feet of them. "Blue, that'n standin' in front of you is what a man looks like, an' I ain't inclined to have anything to do with a cur dog. Now you back off away from him, or the good Lord Jesus knows I'm gonna give you what you came out here askin' for."

Blue made a wheezing noise when she said the sacred name. His voice croaked. "I don't reckon you'll shoot, Pip."

Pip had talked enough, but she gave him one more warning. "I've already said I would, Blue, an' I've already decided I will. You can end your sorry life somewhere else later, or you can end it right here . . . right now."

Blue was tired of talking. He pivoted away from the gun and whipped the knife in a short arc at Mose's chest. Mose grabbed his hand and the two went into the dust by the car. Mose came out on the bottom with both of his hands holding the wrist of the one with the knife. Blue swung his free hand hard at Mose's face. The fist didn't find its mark because the dog got Blue's wrist and sank his teeth in all the way to the bone. Blue screamed and shook loose. He got both hands around the knife's hilt and leaned on it. The knife was on its way to Mose's chest when the shotgun went off.

When Blue regained his senses, he was flat on his back in the dirt. His ears were still ringing, but he could hear a single mockingbird pick up its song. He looked toward Pip and saw smoke still curling out of the gun's barrel. He thought, *Son! Them folks in town was right. That woman don't mess around none at all. I musta been crazy*. He was about half relieved and half angry. He had been run out of Inverness by one woman and scared nearly to death by this one, all in less than two days. The half of him that felt relief was taking over. He put his head back to rest a minute. The sun glittered on the gold teeth when he considered how lucky he was. The good Lord had sure saved him this time. It was springtime cool in the shade under the pecan trees. He hadn't paused to listen to a mockingbird since he was a boy, but this one caught his attention; it sounded good, and he was glad he was alive to hear it. The shade grew darker, and he opened his eyes to see if maybe some clouds had moved in.

He knew his eyes were open, but all he saw was what he had been looking at his entire life—darkness. When he tried to speak, his mouth didn't move. Appreciation and relief left him—truth came at the speed of thought. He used surging emotional energy to soak himself with terror. The darkness around him took on substance. From out of the emptiness around him, Blue Biggers heard the first of an eternity of screams and recognized his own voice.

Mose got to his knees, then to his feet. He looked from Blue to Pip. Pip wasn't moving. The dog, his hair still up, sniffed at Blue. Blue stayed in the dirt.

The dust settled, the rest of the birds took up their songs, the cat had disappeared. The afternoon peace came back to the things around the cabin but not to the people.

The white man's justice could be expected to be whimsical at best, and the Washingtons couldn't take a chance on the possibility of Pip being sent to prison; Pearl needed her momma at home. When the sheriff came, he asked his questions, and they told the story just the way they'd rehearsed it.

An hour after the shooting, Pearl stood on the porch of the cabin with her momma; Old Mr. Parker and his daughter-in-law stood behind them. The young girl watched the white men take her daddy away to jail in the black car. One of the Washingtons' old quilts covered the form out under the trees, but it wasn't big enough to cover the stain on the dirt. They didn't have a quilt that big.

The trial in Indianola started at ten in the morning. By noon, the testifying was over. The jurors had already made up their minds, but they held back so they could get a free lunch at the county's expense and came back with a verdict before two o'clock.

Most white folks in the Mississippi Delta expected most colored people to shoot or cut one another on a regular basis. And they didn't care much one way or another which black folks went to Parchman, as long as it wasn't one of their good hands; colored folks going to jail was a way of life. Besides, it was coming summer, and the Parchman Farm was going to need cotton pickers.

The Parkers did what they could, but it wasn't enough. Not a single juror mentioned it, but when it came right down to it, it might've been the gift of the six hundred acres that got Mose sent to Parchman. Of the twelve white men on the jury, only one farmed more than four hundred acres of land; none of them were friends of the Parkers.

Pip sat in the balcony and held hands with Missy and Pearl. Susan Parker would have chosen to sit with Pip at the trial, but a white woman sitting in the colored section would just stir folks up. None of the white folks cared where Missy sat because she was too young to matter. When they pronounced Mose guilty, Pip cried on Missy's shoulder.

After the verdict was announced, some of the members of the jury apologized to Old Mr. Parker. They were quiet and respectful, and they told him they were sorry, but as one put it, "Yo' Mose shot that boy dead, Mr. R. D. There wasn't nothin' we could do."

The Negroes had to stand and watch while the white men sent one of their best to prison because the world had been done a favor. Every Negro who had ever known Blue knew he needed killing. They knew it was inevitable that someone would accommodate him. And they knew who had done the shooting.

R. D. got them to let Missy talk to Mose before they took him away. Mose stood by the sheriff's car while Missy told him, "It was my fault again, Mose. I said I'd take Junior's place, but I didn't. I got stubborn an' gave up on prayin', an' all I could think about was me."

"Now you listen to me, baby. The good Lord don't figure there's but one yesterday we can handle, an' that's tomorrow's. He forgave you two thousand years ago for all yo' sins, includin' not prayin'—an' there ain't nothin' you could ever do that I wouldn't forgive you for."

"But you're goin' to Parchman 'cause I was stubborn."

"God decided a long time ago what I'm gonna be doin' tomorrow—He done chose every step I takes." There were no tears in his eyes when he said, "You do like He says, baby . . . you put what's done behind you."

"I'm scared to make promises anymore."

"You just got to be choosy about who you makes yo' promises to, child. Promisin' a young boy that jes' died is one thing. Promisin' God takes a little more seriousness."

The deputy put his hand on Mose's arm.

Mose nodded and rested a shackled hand on the girl's shoulder. "I'm gonna be gone a spell, an' you the only one what's strong enough to watch out after Pip."

"Yes, sir. I'll try to take care of her." She couldn't bring herself to promise, but she'd do what he asked.

Mose got into the backseat of the car. Before they shut the door, Old Mr. Parker said, "I'll get you out, Mose."

Dante captured the spirit of Parchman Prison Farm long before white men ever saw that twenty thousand acres of sandy cotton land. From six hundred years in the past, across an ocean's breadth, he said, "Abandon hope, all ye who enter here."

CHAPTER TWELVE

Lost men don't need clocks.

In a world where a man spends every night locked in a dark chamber with a hundred desperate men, where he goes to work every day before daylight and quits after dark, where he drinks water or relieves himself only when he has permission, time is measured in seasons, not seconds. The convicts started getting the land ready at the end of every winter, planted cotton in the spring, chopped cotton in the early summer, and picked cotton till late fall. In the early winter, they killed hogs and cattle for meat. In the late winter, they started over. Parchman Prison Farm was neat and ordered—twenty thousand acres of cropland manicured by the hands and lives of twelve hundred hope-starved men. When they weren't plowing, planting, and picking, the prisoners were chained together and sent out to bring neatness and order to the shoulders of Mississippi's highways.

Every facet of prison life was segregated by skin color. Scores of work gangs—some black, some white—worked the cotton fields. Each gang had a driver, a prisoner who worked the prisoners. The drivers ran the prison and answered to the sergeants, a small company of mounted white men who were the overseers.

Each gang accommodated one other special prisoner—a shooter. The shooters were the counterpoint to one man's argu-

ment that Parchman inmates were slaves in striped clothing:
History tells us slaves were occasionally treated as though their
lives had value.

Mose was in his fourth summer when a mule-drawn wagon
came to the fields carrying Sam Jones. The tall young man,
more lost than most, slid off the wagon and stared around him.
He saw twenty men picking cotton under the eyes of a lean
white man on a horse. A solitary black man leaned against a
half-filled cotton wagon, his hands draped negligently over the
rifle he carried across his shoulders. One or two prisoners gave
Sam a quick look and went on with their picking. The man with
the rifle looked Sam over, weighed him, and went back to his
study of the pickers.

When Sam's attention came back to the white man, the man
beckoned and spoke to him. "Over here, boy." The overseer sat
straight and easy on the horse; he wore polished riding boots
and carried a clean .38 at his belt.

Boss Williams watched Sam's face while he walked over.
When the new prisoner got to the horse, he took off his hat and
looked up at the white man. The prisoners who were stealing
glances at the encounter grimaced; Boss Williams was shaking
his head. He said, "You never been in prison, boy?"

"No, sir . . . uh . . . boss."

Boss Williams looked at the boy while the pickers watched
and sweated. One prayed.

"What're you in for?" Williams sat on a good-looking roan
stud; every piece of leather on or near him had been hand-
polished by a convict.

"I was hitchhiking. Uh . . . boss."

"They sent you up here 'cause you were hitchhikin'?"

"Yes, boss. I was going back to college from my cousin's
funeral."

Some things in the world just weren't right. "Your cousin's
funeral?"

"Yes, boss. My uncle's son . . . died when he was seven

years old. The officer told me I was in the wrong place at the right time."

Boss Williams looked as if his dinner wasn't agreeing with him. "You ever pick cotton, boy?"

Sam looked around him. The fields were white—and endless. "No, sir, boss."

More prayers, especially by one old man.

In the midst of the organized madness that was Parchman State Penitentiary, the man who sat on the roan was one of the few people who almost reflected balance.

When the war started, Billy Williams lied about his age and joined the Marines. He was a perfect fit—he was born neat, he was good with a gun, and he paid attention to what was happening around him. He turned seventeen behind a machine gun on Guadalcanal and spent several lifetimes fighting his way to Okinawa. While on Okinawa, he chain-smoked cigarettes and watched the fleet being readied for the invasion of Japan.

On a hot Saturday morning, Sergeant Williams and several other Marines were picked for an easy detail; they were sent to guard a lone ship anchored well away from the rest of the fleet. Gossip about the isolated vessel's contents had allowed the GIs in the port to speculate on rumors that took in the possibility of gold, secret weapons, and whiskey for the generals. The enlisted men who were chosen for that morning's duty solved the ship's mystery minutes after boarding. The freighter was loaded from bow to stern with nothing but crosses—tens of thousands of white wooden crosses, ready for the men who would need them after the invasion of the Japanese homeland. Bill Williams and his sober young buddies hung their legs off the ship's stern and worked out the math in their heads. Eight square miles of Iwo Jima had cost them roughly a thousand men per mile; Okinawa had cost them another twelve thousand. One ship couldn't hold enough crosses to take Japan.

Coming up on ten years later, the still-alive former Marine had two heroes in the political ranks: He liked Harry Truman and the sitting governor of Mississippi. He liked Truman because the president had saved his life. He liked his cousin, the governor, because the governor had gotten him a good job.

Boss Williams never yelled; he spoke. "Preacher."

The convict who had been praying said, *Thank You, Lord!*
He shook his cotton sack loose and jogged the few steps to the
horse. Because the white man had called him, the old man
didn't have to ask permission to take off his hat. "Yessuh, boss."

Sam turned to look at the man next to him. Preacher was on
the lean side, with sharp features and white hair trying to show
in the fuzz on his head. The old man was fixing a noncommittal gaze on the gleaming toe of the white man's boot.

"Okay, Preacher. Take Slim here under your wing for
awhile. Git him lined out best you can."

"Yessuh, boss. C'mere, boy." The old man took Sam by the
arm and jerked him away from the man on the horse. The
younger man moved his arm to pull away, but the hand that
held him clamped down hard and added something to the tug.
"C'mon, Slim. Step on over here."

When they got away from the white man, Sam was frowning; he didn't like being pulled around. "Take it easy, uncle.
And my name's Sam."

The man kept moving and pulling. "Hush, boy. You need to
be listenin', 'cause what I'm fixin' to tell you will keep you
from gittin' a beatin'. An' I don't mean like in school, you
hear?" They were several rows from the man on the horse when
the old man finally turned loose of Sam. "First of all, boy, don't
never look no white man in the face."

"What?"

The old man spoke in a hushed voice. "You heard it right.
If they speaks to you, you look at the ground, an' you keep
lookin' down 'til they tells you different."

Sam's mouth actually dropped open. The old man continued, "I snatched you away from Boss Bill 'cause he didn't want
to use that strap on you, what with you bein' new an' all. He's a
fine enough man, an' you been blessed by the good Lord 'cause
you on this here gang."

"He'd have hit me for looking at him?" Sam still didn't believe it. He turned to look back at the man on the horse.

Preacher couldn't have snatched the new man back any
more abruptly if he had turned to look at Medusa. "Boy, are you

hearin' me? Didn't I just tell you not to look at no white man's face? When yo' face is pointed at that horse you be lookin' at the ground."

The old man Sam saw looking at the polished toe of the white man's boot no longer existed—the man he had become was looking hard into Sam's eyes, waiting for a response.

"Yes, sir." Sam flexed his arm and massaged his bicep.

"That's better, that's good." The man nodded his head. "Would he hit you? I spent almost two years trying to get on that man's gang, boy. If you'd looked at any other white man on the farm, they'd have taught you a lesson you wouldn't never forget. Now, we bes' hurry along, an' I'll talk a little as we go. You ever pick cotton?"

"No, sir. Not a drop."

"Boy, I'm gonna tell you some of the rules. You gonna hear 'em, or you gonna get that strap laid on you. Simple as that. You understand?"

"Yes, sir. Am I supposed to call you Preacher?"

"My name's Mose Washington, but that don't count for much. What we call one another is small enough compared to what we become while we're at this place. You understand me?" Mose watched the boy's face.

In a long-ago life, during his second year at Tuskeegee, Sam hitchhiked home to Texas for Christmas. On Christmas morning he was sitting in the place of honor at the breakfast table— at his momma's right hand—when his momma said something to him that he didn't quite understand.

At six feet, three inches and nineteen years of age, he considered himself to be a grown man. When he didn't understand his momma, he made the mistake of saying, "Huh?"

Had he blasphemed God, the silence could not have stepped in any sooner or more emphatically. Forks stopped in midair. Everyone but his momma stared at him.

The lady at the head of the table, who weighed roughly half as much as her nearly grown son, was touching her favorite ceramic coffee mug to her lips. She didn't change expression, she didn't warn, and she didn't hold back. The mug—with coffee and follow-through—hit him in the center of his forehead and knocked him, along with his chair, confidence, and misconceptions, backward onto the floor.

When the not-too-grown-up-after-all man's vision cleared, his momma's finger was tapping the table by his plate. "Get back up here and finish your breakfast."

He gathered himself and the chair and rearranged both at the table; the confidence and misconceptions hadn't survived the tumble. Hot tears of embarrassment and pain stung his eyes; hotter coffee was dripping from his ears. His younger brothers, all seven of them, were trying, without any measurable desire for success, to keep from laughing.

"Now, then." His momma smiled at him as she touched a dishtowel to the tears and ears. "Don't be forgettin' to say 'sir' and 'ma'am' to them that are older than you. You understand me?"

Sam remembered what he told his momma and told Mose pretty much the same thing. "Yes, sir. I won't forget." He meant it both times.

Mose told him how it was going to be. He'd have to pick a hundred pounds that afternoon, two hundred the next day, and up from there. He wasn't to look a white man in the eye unless he was told to. He needed to take his hat off anytime he was near a white guard or talking to one. If he kept his mouth shut, he'd learn most everything else. The gang might sing some, but nobody talked much while working.

"See that man yonder—the one by the wagon?" He pointed at the prisoner carrying the rifle.

"Yes, sir."

"That's a shooter."

Sam looked at the man, taking in the striped pants and heavy rifle; the man turned his head to look back. "He's a trusty?"

"Partly. Mostly he's a shooter—name o' Po' Boy. If somebody tries to run off an' a shooter kills 'em, the shooter goes home that day with a pardon, no questions asked. If the runner don't die, the shooter stays here. Not many men run. If a shooter sees you even thinkin' 'bout runnin', he'll shoot you down an' walk right out that gate."

Sam looked at the shooter again and tried to figure out what the man reminded him of. "He doesn't move around much."

The new boy caught on pretty quick. Mose said, "Neither do snakes."

That was the shooter. A snake waiting in the Delta sun. Waiting for someone to step into his domain.

The friendship began that very minute. Mose helped Sam make his picking quota that afternoon, but by noon the next day, Sam's fingers were bloody and tender from their constant encounters with the briarlike tips of the cotton bolls. Mose picked his own quota and part of Sam's till the boy's fingers got toughened up. At the end of the first week, Sam could almost hold his own in the cotton field.

Two weeks after Sam got to Parchman, he and Mose were standing near a window and looking out at the night sky, trying to pick up any breeze that might come by.

Mose asked him, "Are you a Christian, boy?"

"I think I am. My momma's been taking us to church all our lives."

"You say you think you are? Don't you reckon you ought to know for sure?"

"I think that'd be a good idea."

"Do you believe in God?"

"Yes, sir."

"Do you believe Jesus was His Son?"

"Yes, sir, I believe that."

"Do you believe He died on the cross for yo' sins?"

"I do." Sam was confident.

"Can you recollect a time when you prayed for Him to forgive you of yo' sins, an' you told Him you want Him to be yo' Savior?"

Sam knew what he was like on the inside, and he spent enough time in church to know he couldn't measure up to God's standard; God expected Christians to live differently from other people. The reality of what his life was like made him feel empty.

His eyes stayed on the floor. "Well, Mose, I've been plannin' on doin' that, but I need to wait 'til I clean up my life some.

Before they put me in here I drank too much an' I cuss as bad as most, an' I've done a couple of other things I don't want to tell anybody about."

Mose understood. "I got news for you, boy. There ain't gonna come a time when anybody in the world is gonna get clean enough to come to Jesus. That's how come He had to come here an' die. You come to Him, you accept what He done, then He takes care of the cleanin' up."

Sam's head came up. He looked at Mose for a minute without seeing him, then looked back at the dark sky while Mose waited for him to speak.

Sam grew up in a home where his momma took him to church almost every Sunday, a church where the preacher made sure he told his congregation how to be saved.

He leaned close to the window, took the iron bars in his hands, touched his forehead against their cool surfaces, and, after hearing the most important words in the world almost once a week for twenty years, said, "I wonder why nobody ever told me that."

He tapped a bar with his fingertips and looked out at the night. "Can I pray right now?"

"Sho' can."

Sam lowered himself to his knees, Mose knelt with him, and Sam expressed his belief in what God had done for him and relinquished control of his life.

A few days later, Mose got the boy a tattered Bible, and they started through it together.

Mose taught Sam how to pray, study his Bible, and grow as a Christian; Sam was a good pupil.

Three weeks after Sam became a believer, the gang watched Boss Bill send him on an errand by himself, an unheard-of thing for a convict who had been on the farm less than a few years. Two days after that, a tall fellow they called Tree wanted to know if Mose could show him how to become a Christian.

Half of that year's cotton was still in the field when Mose got one of his regular letters from Missy. The girl wrote him strong words of encouragement every week; the letter he held in his hands was bad news. The only man in Mississippi who stood a chance of getting Mose out of Parchman early was dead and gone. Mr. R. D. Parker died peacefully in his sleep. Mose had eight years left on his sentence.

The weight of each cotton sack was determined by a balance-bar scale suspended from the back of a wagon, and the pickers each had a specified quota to fill. Every morning from late summer to late fall, the men would take the long canvas cotton sacks and work their way through the cotton fields. Each man would fill his sack, take it to the man at the scale, and have it weighed. After the weighing, the picker would dump his cotton in the wagon, return to the field, and continue to pick. The process was repeated over and over, sack after sack, until that year's cotton was gone.

The drivers worked their respective gang's scale, and if a driver could be coerced, the cotton-picking suffered. The bosses at Parchman had long ago figured out that if the man who was doing the weighing was the toughest man on the gang, then he didn't need to lie for any of the other convicts.

The pickers would start out together at dawn and move at different paces along the tall white rows. The first man would be back at the wagon with a full sack an hour or two after the start; thereafter, the men would come in at irregular intervals to have their sacks weighed and tallied. Some men were required to pick three hundred pounds a day, some five hundred, the older and more feeble as little as a hundred and fifty.

The men who weighed and tracked the daily picking could take small bribes in the form of nickels or cigarettes to lie about a sack's weight. Most didn't; the foolish ones did. The sergeants could watch for "shortin'," but their job was made easier if they knew their driver was immune to intimidation.

Will Green Henry was the driver who weighed the cotton

for Boss Bill Williams. He wasn't Williams's scale man because he was the meanest, but because he was the biggest and hardest. Will Green was as smart as any other man at Parchman, and he reasoned it this way: any man who was willing to have him lie was willing to have him get into trouble with Boss Williams. Being a scale man was the best job Will Green ever had at the prison, and lying for some no-account piece of black trash wasn't a good enough reason for losing it.

Once every year or so, some slick convict would show Will Green a knife or razor and say something like, "I'm gonna slack off some, Mister Scale Man, an' you gonna like it, or you gonna discuss it with my friend here," and he'd let the knife disappear into his clothing.

When threatened, Will Green always said pretty much the same thing. He'd point at the scars on his forearms and face and shrug. "Better'n you've tried it, boy, but you welcome to come on." He'd show the troublemaker the palm of his giant right hand and point to a scar shaped like an angry bolt of lightning. "I got this here when I taken a straight razor from a tough-talking boy what was plenty stouter'n you. I taken that fellah's han'—razor an' all—an' crushed it. Then I taken the pieces what was left of that cuttin' edge an' stuffed 'em in his mouth an' made him chomp down on 'em." He'd make a laughing sound deep in his chest as he turned to walk off, and he'd say, "You bes' listen to friendly ol' niggah, boy. Pickin' cotton is sho' 'nuff easier than tryin' to swallow one o' them straight razors."

Every now and then a troublemaker would follow through on the threat. Will Green might or might not get cut, but the other man always lost. For most people, losing a fight on the Parchman Farm carried with it the ingredients that made for a life-changing experience; losing a knife fight to Will Green Henry was always worse. Picking a few extra pounds of cotton was a whole lot easier than trying to get Will Green Henry to risk losing his job at the scales.

On a mild morning in late August, every man on the gang watched the old man struggle off the wagon. He was bent and weak—and in trouble. He knew how to stand and talk to Boss Williams, and that's what he did. When they finished talking, the boss shook his head as he watched the old man pick up a sack and shuffle out to the field.

Sam worked his way along so he could catch up to the old man just before lunch and traded a nearly full sack of cotton for the old man's nearly empty one. The old man objected, but Sam did the swap. Later that evening, when the sun was touching the horizon and the sky in the west was promising rain, the gang worked their way in from the field. On the way to the wagon, Sam swapped sacks with the old man for the second time. The old man was too tired to protest.

The old man got his cotton weighed in first. "Twenty over here, boss."

"It'll do." Boss Williams never said anything else when the weight was right. There never had been but two answers to Will Green's reports from the scale: "It'll do" or "Bring me that Black Annie."

Every boss on the farm had ready access to a Black Annie— a three-foot-long leather strap. The origin of the strap's name was secreted a century away in a dark past; its pronouncement melted the hearts of hard men. Annie's three-inch width could minimize the chances of cutting the back of the man taking the beating; its tapered thickness magnified the message of the man wielding it.

Sam's turn was next. He handed the cotton sack to Will Green.

Will Green hung Sam's sack over the hook and moved the weight out to where it needed to be. When the end of the bar tilted the wrong way, the driver tried again. It wasn't going to work. Sam was going to come up short, and there never had been but one answer for not meeting your quota. Just the week before, the gang had watched another man come up short. That man's trip to the infirmary netted two dozen stitches in places where the strap had made its worst cuts. Sam and Will Green broke new tides of sweat; the men standing near them stopped breathing. Mose bowed his head and closed his eyes.

Boss Williams was standing by his horse at the edge of the rows near the cotton wagon. He was facing the setting sun, one arm propped on his saddle, watching the promise of rain; an uninterested actor in a fearful drama.

The group of men glanced at the boss's back, then at Will Green, then at Sam.

Will Green looked at Sam and shook his head.

Sam looked sick and shrugged.

Will Green had to say it. "Thirteen short here, boss."

Boss Williams continued to look into the distance, answering without seeming to hear himself. "He'll do."

It was a new answer, and it flustered Will Green. He passed by the offered pardon and committed his own crime. "Boss, I said it was—"

The white man seemed preoccupied with his study of the thunderstorms lined up along the Arkansas side of the river. When he spoke, he didn't even bother to turn around. He just said a man's name. "Will Green."

Those two words said it all. Will Green Henry had just committed a sin greater than Sam's: He'd corrected a white man—a boss at Parchman—and questioned his judgment, all with just a small handful of words. Possible penalties scrolled through Will Green's head like dark oil paintings. He watched the white man's back while he tried to think of a way to make an excuse. He was agonizing over a way to avoid the inevitable beating when it occurred to him that the white man had just spoken to him in a manner that required an answer. The driver needed to show that he understood the man, and he became more frightened because he hadn't replied. The silence got louder; time slowed to the speed of sweat; the paintings of imagined retribution sped through Will Green's brain and shut down his ability to communicate. Will Green was rooted to the ground, staring at the white man's back while the rest of the prisoners looked on and waited. Several men sidled away from the wagon.

Mose got Sam's attention. He frowned at Sam and jerked

his head at Will Green. The boss was shifting his feet to turn when Sam Jones drew back his fist, took one quick step, and hit Will Green on the shoulder hard enough to knock the big man into the wagon. The smack of flesh on flesh was followed by an eruption from Will Green. "Yessuh, boss! Yessuh! He'll do! Yes*suh!*"

Williams's feet stopped moving. Behind the storms in Arkansas, the sky was a beautiful, deep red. He remembered Okinawan sunsets that had been almost as beautiful. "Next man, Will Green."

Will Green jangled the scale's bar and frowned at the next man in line. "Next man! Next man!" The next man was standing a foot away, his eyes as wide as a frightened child's, holding his sack an inch from the scale man. "You can't be hangin' back like a fool, boy. Step on up here."

Will Green grabbed the man's sack with palsied hands, got it on the scale on the second try, and knocked the scale weight into the dirt; a stir of warm breeze chilled him. Two or three of the other prisoners wiped their sleeves across wet foreheads.

Mose made eye contact with Sam, and neither man smiled. It had been close, but no one had suffered. The time for suffering was short days away.

CHAPTER THIRTEEN

Nothing about the cloudless afternoon was special.

The sun was unmoving and unrelenting. The convicts were picking endless rows of cotton. When a man's cotton sack got full, he emptied it into the wagon and picked up where he'd left off. Boss Bill Williams walked his horse here and there in the field. The only break in the routine came when Pepper Jack Bradley arrived.

Bradley, something of a celebrity in the Delta, was on his third extended visit to the prison farm; this time he was in for a double homicide. It seems two men in a tonk between Yazoo City and Belzoni got it in their minds to give him a short course in amateur knife fighting. What the men at the honky-tonk didn't know was that Bradley already possessed an advanced degree in the art.

The old wagon creaked when Bradley slid off the tailgate; his arrival giving evidence that the white man who assigned him to Williams's crew was not acquainted with a crucial piece of information. In fact, only two men at Parchman knew that Boss Williams's shooter—Po' Boy Thompson—was Pepper Jack Bradley's first cousin.

Pepper Jack took one look at the rifle in Po' Boy's hands and decided that he was going to be the first man in recent history to spend less than a day on the farm. That night, in the darkness of their sleeping quarters, he whispered to his cousin what needed to be done. The next morning, four or five hours after sunup, they saw an opportunity to make their move.

A short string of prisoners was lined up by the wagon to have their sacks weighed. Pepper Jack was coming out of the field, moving slowly, timing his arrival.

In women, the trait is called *intuition;* in men, it's a sixth sense—"seeing" something that isn't there.

The men in Parchman had no reason to be happy, but that morning found too many frowns for no apparent reason; the men were either anxious, or concentrating, or both. Mose was at the edge of the field, picking a few extra handfuls while he waited for a cluster of men to get their sacks weighed. Bill Williams would not classify himself as a perceptive man, but three years of fighting in the Pacific had sharpened his senses— the second time the stud snorted and stamped a nervous foot, Williams went with his instincts. He backed the stud and turned him to move farther away from the crowd at the wagon. As soon as the boss's back was to the shooter, Pepper Jack nodded to his cousin. Mose saw the signal and watched Po' Boy edge away from the wagon, moving so that he could have a clear shot at the white man. Bradley was swinging his sack off his shoulder; the shooter was bringing up the rifle.

Mose swept off his hat without asking permission.

Boss Williams caught the movement; his head came up, and his hand started for his waist. Mose looked into Boss Williams's eyes for the briefest instant, then looked behind the white man at the shooter.

The *snick* of the hammer coming back on the rifle got the attention of every man near the wagon. Men scrambled in all directions—most of them diving for the protection of the wagon or the cotton field. Williams was turning, his hand already on his belt gun, when Po' Boy fired. Williams's partially turned body presented less target for the shooter, and the bullet that should have hit his back dead center went up and across his chest. The impact knocked Williams sideways in the saddle.

Po' Boy hadn't been in the Pacific. The shooter made a whining sound while he overworked the lever on the rifle;

Williams was exhaling and looking at a button on Po' Boy's shirt when the pistol cleared his polished holster. Both men fired. The rifle bullet went across the back of Boss Williams's left arm; Po' Boy took the .38 slug in the middle of his chest and stayed on his feet. Boss Williams triggered the .38 again, sending a helpmate into a spot two inches from the first. When Po' Boy hit the dirt, Bradley sank to his knees by the turn row.

The horse stood for the jerking of the rider and the noise from the guns well enough, but the smell of blood made him jumpy. Boss Williams leaned over, slid from the saddle, and staggered when he hit the ground; he had blood on most of his upper body, and his eyes were starting to glaze. The prisoners froze where they were while the boss walked to Po' Boy's body. The ex-Marine put a bullet into the dead man's brain, straightened, and took a ragged breath. Sam took two steps and held out a hand to the white man. Williams took Sam's hand, put the gun securely in it, and tilted forward into his arms. Sam dropped the gun and caught the man.

Mose moved past Sam and lifted the rifle out of Po' Boy's hands. He worked the lever, stepped away from Sam and Williams, and turned on the prisoners.

The .38 was on the ground at Sam's feet. Bradley had recovered and was crawling toward it.

"Uh-uh." Mose backed another step, leveled the rifle at Bradley, and shook his head.

Bradley took a quick measure of the old man and decided to make his try later.

When Bradley turned away, Mose looked at the wound in Williams's chest and said, "We needs to git him to the doctor."

The rest of the prisoners came out of hiding and stood by the cotton field in a loose group. They divided their attention between Williams, Po' Boy, and Mose; Bradley was watching the rifle.

Sam helped the white man sag to the ground. "How're we gonna do that?"

"I'm gonna git on that hoss, an' you gonna hand him up to me."

"Then what?"

"I'm gonna take him to the 'firmary, an' you gonna be the shooter 'til somebody gits back here to help."

Sam looked around him at the faces of the men listening to Mose; they were all interested in him now. "What if somebody tries to run?"

Mose was grim. "I reckon choices ain't always black or white, son. You either kill 'em, or run with 'em, or somebody's gonna kill you. Can you do it?"

Blood was running from the white man and mixing with the tan dirt. "Yes, sir."

Mose pointed at the handgun by Sam's feet. "Hand me that pistol."

Sam did as he was told. Mose tucked the pistol in his belt, then climbed on the horse. He motioned Sam over. "Okay, hand him up here across the saddle."

They fixed the white man across the saddle, and Mose handed the rifle to Sam. The older man's eyes could be hard if they needed to be. He let his gaze move over the crew, then back to Sam. "You the shooter now—it's you or them. I'll try to git somebody back out here quicklike."

"Yes, sir."

Mose took the horse off at a lope, and Sam moved to the wagon.

The men in the group were eyeing the man with the rifle, trying to decide whether to try the new shooter. Will Green Henry broke the silence. "Settin' down here, boss."

Sam nodded his thanks, and said, "Sit down, Will Green. All of you that want to can take a break." He pointed the rifle at the dead man. "Pop Willie, you an' Bro cover him up." The two covered Po' Boy with a cotton sack, then joined the rest of the group squatting at the edge of the field.

For the next few minutes, Bradley watched Sam out of the corner of his eye. The killer was one of the biggest men in the prison—two inches taller and fifty pounds heavier than the recently appointed trusty. He leaned over and whispered to Proc Nelson, "I'm fixin' to leave here. You watch an' see."

Before Mose was a hundred yards away, Sam had figured out that Bradley was going to make trouble; he heard the whispering and ignored it. He could wait for Bradley to start the fight because the big man wasn't the kind to sneak up on a person. When the action started, Bradley would want an audience.

As soon as Mose was out of sight, Bradley said, "Gittin' a drink here, boss."

Sam moved across the narrow turn row, several feet from the prisoners and the wagon where the barrel hung. Bradley was watching Sam's eyes and pointing at the water barrel. The big man was excited about what was about to happen. The adrenaline had gone to work in his system, and he was smiling when he stood up.

Armed men at Parchman maintained a "halo"—a circle of no-man's-land—around themselves, and the convicts knew better than to violate the space. If a prisoner got too close, some sergeants or trusties would warn; most would shoot.

Sam shifted to his right to make room for the man. Without making eye contact, he said, "Get a drink."

The troublemaker put a dipper of water in his mouth and spit it in the dirt halfway between himself and Sam. The quiet talk around the circle of prisoners stopped. All eyes were on the two men.

"They say you been to college, boy."

Sam had made some decisions of his own while Bradley was biding his time. The newly appointed shooter looked the prisoner in the eye. "The rules haven't changed since your last visit, Bradley. Don't speak to me unless you're spoken to."

Bradley was slightly jarred by the even quality of Sam's voice; he expected the younger man to stammer or become flustered. He could have considered waiting, but he had already made his brag that he'd be the first convict in Mississippi to spend a single night at Parchman—he was committed. He stepped toward the shooter, and Sam backed up.

"Well, what's the matter, *boss boy?* Ain't you ever been this close to a real man before?" He thought maybe the college boy wasn't so tough after all.

Sam took another step back. "Leave it be, Bradley. I don't want to break a sweat, and this gun isn't for show."

Sam knew the confrontation was coming, but he didn't

want to kill a man if he could help it, not even a man who was willing to kill him. He gauged the distance between himself and the spectators sitting on the ground. He didn't think any of the other men would take part in the fight, but just in case someone else might draw courage from the killer's foolish move, he backed up a couple of more steps to draw Bradley away from the crowd.

Bradley followed, grinning. "I figure that gun is—"

Now is as good a time as any.

Sam Jones got his quickness from his momma and his moves from fighting seven tough brothers. He lifted his left foot as if to move farther away, and instead stepped toward the bigger man. He feinted at the man's worn belt buckle with the barrel of the rifle.

Bradley dropped a paw to brush the barrel away, and as soon as he moved his hand, Sam stepped closer and whipped the edge of the rifle stock into his face. The sound of flesh and cartilage giving way blended with the impact of the rifle stock on the bridge of Bradley's nose. Blood spewed into the air, and the big man swayed backward. Before Bradley could recover, Sam sidestepped to get a good angle, dropped his right foot back, and using the weapon like a long stick, he whipped the man across the side of his head with the gun's barrel. The pupils of Bradley's eyes rolled out of sight. He tottered backward for a second, then sagged forward; his knees gave way, and dust escaped from around him in a soft cloud as he crumpled into the dirt. The fight was over in less than five seconds.

The men on the ground, who had, predictably, not moved to intervene, looked at Bradley, up at Sam, and back at Bradley. Bradley wasn't moving. Sam was wiping blood from the rifle barrel with his bandanna; Bradley was leaking the red fluid into the same dirt that had soaked up the white man's.

One of the men recovered his powers of speech and whispered, "Mer-cee!" As a group, the spectators seemed to feel as if they were too close to the young man with the rifle, and scooted away slightly toward the cotton field.

A minute later Sam was holding the barrel of the rifle so that it caught the sun and inspected it closely. He could imagine his momma's voice telling him that there was no reason to wait for some white man to come out and bring order to an area where one of her sons had been made responsible. Without taking his eyes from the gun barrel, the youngest man on the gang addressed himself to the men squatting by the cotton field. "Break time's over."

Fifteen pairs of eyes were still welded to the man bleeding on the turn row dirt. When the young shooter spoke, it took them a second to realize that his quiet words were addressed to them and another second to process what he'd said. By the time three seconds passed, they figured out that he told them to do something and that they weren't doing it. Fifteen grown men went from lounging to standing on their feet fast enough to raise another small cloud of the light-brown dust.

It was thirty minutes later that the day's largest cloud of dust showed in the distance. A herd of trucks—carrying all manner of white men, shooters, guns, and dogs—was rushing out to salvage what they could of Boss Williams's crew. When they arrived, the men and dogs found an ordered scene—a former shooter stored under a cotton sack, Mr. Pepper Jack Bradley tied across a wagon wheel, and a tall young black man holding a .30-.30 while his crew picked the Parchman cotton.

A few hours later, just before suppertime, children stopped their laughter, talk, and games to watch the shiny black car with white doors roll down the gravel street in Jones Addition—the colored section of Moores Point, Mississippi. When it stopped in front of a neat little white house, every screen door on the street opened at the same time. An attractive woman wearing a plain dress and a blush of flour on one cheek stepped through the door of the neat white house. She stopped on her porch and wiped her hands on her apron while she studied the car. The whip antenna on the car was the only thing on the street that moved. The back door of the car opened and a tall young man, a complete stranger, stepped out of the car and smiled straight at the woman on the porch. The woman rewarded him with a noncommittal nod.

The young man by the car took in the nod and smiled wider. In a short blink of time Sam remembered the answer to one of a thousand questions he had asked Mose.

"Naw, I ain't worried 'bout her foolin' 'round. Pip ain't the kind." He shook his head in disgust. "The only fool what couldn't figure that out got me sent to this here prison."

"What about you?"

"You mean foolin' 'round with some other woman?"

Sam nodded.

Mose chuckled. "I reckon not. Me an' her been married more'n twenty years now, an' we got us a understandin': I don't look sideways at no other woman, an' Pip don't work me over with a yard rake."

Both men laughed.

When the next man came out of the car and smiled at her, the woman—who never raised her voice except to sing in the choir—screamed loud enough to send the children on the street scurrying for their mommas.

Pip and Mose weren't the kind of people who would cling to anyone, but they went to sleep that night—and the few they had left together—in each other's arms.

CHAPTER FOURTEEN

Mose and Pip and Sam were up the next morning before daylight, sitting in the kitchen's semidarkness, drinking coffee, talking, and stopping every few minutes to bow their heads and thank God for the men's freedom.

Sam would have felt out of place in a strange house with anyone but his hosts. Mose was the best friend he was ever going to have, and his years of listening to the man's stories about Moores Point and Cat Lake made him feel as though he had known Pip all his life.

When the sun came up, Pip ran them out of the kitchen while she fixed breakfast. The two sat on the porch and drank coffee like free men and waved at folks Mose hadn't seen in years. Over breakfast, Pip told them about things at the church and around town, and they all laughed like drunk people at stories that were barely humorous. Elation over the prisoners' release governed everything they said and felt.

By the time they finished breakfast, Sam was ready to go to Texas and have the same kind of homecoming with his own family.

Pip hugged him and asked, "Are you comin' this way again?"

Sam smiled. "I'll go see Momma first, then I'll probably be

comin' back through here next month on my way to finish college."

"In Alabama?"

"Yes, ma'am."

"Well, if you need a place to stop, this is it."

Sam said, "Thanks, I'd like that. I imagine it'll be a long time before any of y'all will be coming to Texas."

Pip said, "That's true, son."

Mose said, "We needs to call Pearl."

Pip looked at her watch. "She'll be at work by now. We better wait an' call her tonight."

Mose walked his friend downtown to the drugstore where the bus stopped. They talked about the weather and watched the sun bring another scorching day to cotton country.

The bus came, and they stood by it and shook hands. Sam said, "Mose, you saved my life at Parchman, and you stuck with me 'til I became a Christian. That means you saved my life twice."

Mose almost smiled. "You'd of figured Parchman out soon enough, son. I just made yo' learnin' process a little less painful. As for you becomin' a Christian, you an' I both know only God can do that. He just fixed it so me an' you gets to tell folks 'bout Him. He does the rest."

"And you told me." Sam smiled past the tears in his eyes. "I owe every day of the rest of my life to you. If you ever need anything, you call me, hear? *Any*thing."

"I need to know you gonna live yo' life gettin' to know Him better an' makin' Him known. If I know that, we'll both be happy."

Sam held up his Bible. "I'll be readin' it all the way home today, an' every day thereafter."

Mose put Sam on the westbound Greyhound. That evening would find the young man with his brothers at his momma's kitchen table in Pilot Hill, Texas. The whole family would go to church together on Sunday, and Sam would walk down the aisle and tell the preacher he wanted to be baptized.

Mose took his time on the way back to the house. He walked down Main Street in the shade of the store awnings, stopping whenever he liked to watch occasional tractors pass, all taking another load of cotton to the gin. The news of his release was out, and folks hitching rides into town on the cotton wagons would smile and wave; Mose would lift his hat because he wanted to and speak to the folks he knew. Dozens upon dozens of little black faces peeked over wagon sideboards and grinned and laughed; he grinned and laughed back. Saturday morning in Moores Point was getting off to a slow start, but no one seemed to notice or care—and no one yelled at him to hurry. The still, hot air around him felt like a fresh mountain breeze, and every time he put his hat back on, Mose would take a deep breath of freedom.

When he got back to the house, Missy was waiting for him.

He hadn't seen her in all these years because Pip and the Parkers were afraid to let her visit him at the prison. Having a white girl visit a black man at Parchman would have brought retribution that he might not've survived.

He smiled, shook his head, and took off his hat. "Honey, you done turned into a grown woman."

The years hadn't changed her grin. "Well, I guess my blouse won't ever stick out as far as Marilyn Monroe's, but I'm taller than Debbie Reynolds."

Pip shook her head in mock exasperation and swatted at her with a dish towel. "I ought to tan your hide." Mose and the girl laughed.

She couldn't let go when she hugged him; she held on tight and cried against his chest. He patted her on the back a little, then turned her over to Pip.

Pip smiled at the girl's tears. "It's okay now. He's home for good." Mose touched her shoulder once more and walked out to the backyard with his coffee.

Minutes later, still crying, she held Pip's hands and asked, "When are you goin' to tell him?"

"This mornin', I guess. I need to do it before somebody else blabs it out."

Pip knew for a month that she had cancer. The doctor told

her she could live six months—maybe more, probably less. She dreaded the trip to Parchman to tell Mose. God fixed it so she would get to tell him while he was a free man.

She looked around her at the neat little house. "I've been thinkin' we'd go back out to the cabin. We had a good life out there—a fine life. I guess I want to tell him out by the lake. Maybe we could just live out there 'til I die."

Missy started to cry again. "Pip, I don't want you to die. Who'll be my friend?"

Pip patted the girl's hand. "Here now, baby, it's just not somethin' we get to choose."

Missy's tears slowed and her lower lip started to firm up. "It's not fair."

Pip shook her head. "Don't be talkin' like that, honey. *Fair's* not a good word." The woman lost her only son when he was eleven years old, her husband had just come home from spending five years in prison for a crime he didn't commit, and now she was dying of cancer. She said, "We can praise the Lord that He's gracious, Missy. He tells us in the Bible that He's a just God. You've memorized the words that say so; don't forget them. He delights in lovin' kindness, justice, and righteousness. He says so. You an' I earned the punishment He chose to put on His Son. If God was fair, He'd have killed every one of us a long time ago."

Missy walked to the back door to watch Mose drink his coffee. "I'm not goin' back to school this fall."

"Why on earth not?"

"I'm stayin' here with you."

Pip went to the door, stood behind Missy, and put her arms around the girl. "I reckon not, baby." Pip was the one who had less than six months to live, and in the past month she'd spent part of every day comforting Missy. She pulled the girl close and her voice softened. "You know I can't love you any more than I already do, but that man out there is gonna need me to himself for this last little bit of time. We can't ask him to share, now, can we?"

"I guess not."

"I'm fixin' to run you off, but I want to tell you somethin' first. I want you to be careful who you spend your time with. Don't be goin' around with a man that won't lead you closer to God, you hear me? It's important that you marry a man who loves God more than he loves you."

Missy was staring at Mose. "I need to find me a man like that one right out there."

"That's right. An' you need to do one thing even more, baby."

"What?"

"You've got a strong heart, Missy, but it needs God's direction. You need to remember that two people have already died so you could live. Now, puttin' Mose Junior in the same sentence with Jesus is risky, but you need to remember that the Son of God an' a fine little boy both died so you could live this special life. You need to figure out how you're gonna use this great gift they gave you." She kissed the girl on the forehead. "Now, you scat."

"What're you gonna do?"

She squeezed the girl one more time. "I'm gonna get my Mose to take me out to that little cabin by the lake."

Missy went back to Ole Miss in September and came home every weekend to check on Pip and be comforted. October came and brought clear, cool days, and the cotton wagons made fewer trips to town. Pip and Mose would spend an occasional night out at the cabin, but the house in town became more comfortable for her. The first frost came in November, and by Thanksgiving it was evident that Pip was losing her strength. When December came, the trips out to Cat Lake stopped.

On Missy's first night home for Christmas break, Mose called and said that Pip needed to talk to her.

Cars were crowded along the street when Missy got to the house.

Mose met her at the door. When Missy stepped inside, a living room full of somber black people stood, not because she was white but because she was Missy Parker—and she was special. The ones she spoke to nodded or bowed slightly.

"Where's Pearl?"

"She's hurryin' from Jackson." He took Missy's hand. "I don't think she's gonna make it here in time."

Mose led Missy into the bedroom and sat her in the chair by Pip's bed. Pip was propped up in a sitting position with several pillows. The only light in the room came from a tiny lamp on the dresser. Even the dim light couldn't hide the fact that Pip's life was no longer ebbing away—it was fleeing.

Mose shut the door and moved to the other side of the bed. "She's here, baby."

Pip opened her eyes and reached for Missy's hand. "Come closer, child. Time's gettin' short."

Missy wanted to encourage Pip; instead she said, "It's too soon, Pip. It's happenin' too soon."

Pip still had the most beautiful smile in the Delta. "Not for me, baby. I remember holdin' my Junior out there on that bridge, askin' God to let me hear his voice just one more time . . . just once. It all seems like yesterday afternoon now." She touched Missy's face. "I'll tell you like Junior told me. I want you to mind what I say."

Missy nodded.

"You're as good a woman as I've ever known, Missy, but you've got to go beyond where you are. You won't be goin' by yourself. You understand me?"

"I understand. God's here."

Pip took a breath. "An' you need to get closer to Him."

"I will, Pip."

"The devil's here on this earth, child. Those snakes had demons in them . . . you know they did . . . an' they weren't after Junior. They were after you. There's no reason to believe Satan's angels are gonna leave you alone."

The three people in the dark room all knew that Missy was the one the snakes meant to kill.

"What do I do?"

"You soak yourself in the knowledge of God, Missy. You surround yourself with Him. You be like Mose's Pap said—you become a woman who knows God an' makes Him known, an' you bring those who come around you to do the same. But when you do these things, you need to be ready because the devil's goin' to fight you."

Pip closed her eyes and stayed still for a moment.

"Pip?" Missy's voice quivered.

"I'm still here, child." She opened her eyes. "God didn't give me you for my daughter, Missy Parker, but He let me have you for awhile to be by my side. I want to die knowin' you're goin' to make sure my boy didn't die for nothin'."

"Yes, ma'am."

"I want to hear you say it."

"I'll study to know Him an' speak to make Him known." She bowed her head over Pip's hand. "I promise."

Pip smiled and squeezed the girl's hand gently. "That's all I wanted to hear. You go on back to your house now, baby, I'll be seein' you in heaven."

Missy didn't try to hold back her tears. "Pip, let me stay. Please, Pip."

Pip cupped Missy's cheek in her hand and patted it one last time. "You'll see me soon enough in glory, baby. Now you go on out of here an' leave me with my Mose."

A week before Christmas, they buried her out at Cat Lake, next to her son.

CHAPTER FIFTEEN

Polly Ragsdale was talking when she came through the door. "I guess you know that nobody in this dorm is ever going to speak to you again, don't you?"

It was Monday afternoon. Girls in bathing suits roamed the halls of the dorm, all going to and from the roof to "lay out," building foundations for their summer tans. The midterm exam Missy was studying for was coming up Tuesday, and her skin hadn't changed color since Christmas.

The scholar stood up and stretched. "Let me guess. You've exceeded your one-couple-a-week breakup rate, an' everybody's gonna punish me because I'm your roommate." All Polly had to do to get a date invitation from most boys was make eye contact. Consequently, the majority of the girls at Ole Miss envied her or hated her, or both.

"I'm talking about *your* newest conquest."

"My *what?*" Missy knew exactly who Polly was talking about.

"Every girl on this campus is drooling to have Hull Dillworth glance in their direction, and you're the one he just invited to sit in the holy huddle with him."

"It's a plannin' meetin', not a marriage proposal. An' with at least one notable exception—" She pointed at Polly. "—the young ladies at Ole Miss are too sophisticated to drool."

"I wouldn't eat for a week if he asked me the time of day."

"You wouldn't miss dessert for a date with Elvis Presley." Missy got busy brushing her teeth so her roommate couldn't see that her hands were shaking.

Ole Miss was called "Mississippi's country-club college"; knowing God and making Him known was not the focus of most of the students there. So far, three years of college had netted Missy fewer than twenty dates because most college boys didn't flock to girls who queried them on their spiritual beliefs.

Missy—in a rededicated effort to grow spiritually—had gone looking for allies after Pip's death in December and joined a nondenominational Christian group. The group met once a week to sing, hear a short devotion, and discuss how to reach out to fellow students. The group's founder—and good-looking cause of Missy's promised ostracism—was Hull Dillworth. Two hours earlier, he had called on the hall phone and asked Missy to sit in on their Tuesday night planning session.

Polly was saying, "Margaret Clements went to high school with him; she says he's gonna be a preacher."

The toothbrush stayed in Missy's mouth. "Mmm."

"And she said some Ole Miss alums told him they'd buy him a car if he'd go out for football, but his momma told 'em to go jump in the lake."

"Mmm."

"Miz Dillworth says living for Jesus is more important than playing in the Rebel backfield."

"Mmm." Missy agreed with Mrs. Dillworth. Everything else Polly said was old news. The girls on campus wore out the rumors surrounding Hull Dillworth. He was said to have girlfriends in Memphis, Jackson, New Orleans, and at the University of Alabama; he had never dated anyone at Ole Miss.

Polly ticked off another known fact. "Besides, Mrs. Dillworth was a Memphis Hull, and the Hulls have got more money than Fort Knox."

Missy got control of her hands and washed off her toothbrush. "You can be my maid of honor."

Polly frowned. "It's bad luck to plan your wedding before he asks you."

"Is it bad luck for you to plan it?"

Polly picked up Missy's hairbrush and ran it through perfectly groomed blonde hair. "Elvis Presley would shave his sideburns and bleach his hair if he thought it would make him as good-looking as Hull Dillworth."

Missy agreed with her but said, "There's more to bein' a man than looks."

"Maybe, but being ugly won't make him a better man." Polly contemplated her image in the full-length mirror. "You think he'd ask me to a meeting if I started reading the Bible every day and memorizing verses?"

"Is it safe to assume that this would mean you would be wearin' Bible verses instead of tight sweaters?" Missy laughed and sat back down at her desk. "I'm probably still alive 'cause I didn't say anything to Pip about usin' God to attract boys."

"It might work."

Missy returned to her books. "Don't bet your sweater on it, cutie. You can read your Bible more, Polly, but all it's gonna tell you is to worry less about makin' yourself known an' more about knowin' God."

"How many times have you told me that?"

"Not enough for you to hear it, yet."

"There's more important things out there than memorizing the whole Bible."

"There's nothing more important than knowin' God an' makin' Him known."

"Mmm." Polly thought Missy had a one-track mind. She turned sideways and appraised her romance-interrupting profile. "Except for you, I'm the best-looking girl at Ole Miss."

It was a tagline for an old argument, so Missy changed the subject. "What time are we leavin' for the coast?" She was one of three girls riding with Polly.

"Noon Wednesday. The DKE party starts things off that night." Polly was facing the mirror again without seeing it. "Missy?"

"What?"

Polly's eyes stayed on the mirror while she tapped the hairbrush against her cheek. "We've been at Ole Miss three years, and Hull Dillworth has never even glanced at me."

"So?"

Polly turned to face her friend. "*Nobody* doesn't look at a girl that looks like me, at least not any man that's breathing. It's not natural. You must really be something."

Missy said, "Maybe it's Hull that's really somethin'."

"Maybe so." Polly turned back to her reflection. "I think I'll wait 'til after I'm married to start memorizing Scripture."

When the planning committee got together, Hull suggested that those who wanted to make the trip could meet in Biloxi during the coming spring break. They would play some, get some sun, and go out in pairs to tell the students on the beaches about Jesus and what He had done for them. The plan was approved unanimously.

At the end of the meeting, Missy suggested that the group start memorizing Scripture and doing a Bible study together. It was decided to table her suggestion until the April meeting.

The phone rang at the off-campus apartment of French Bainbridge. "Hello."

The caller said, "What're you doing over spring break?"

"I'm open."

"I'll be in Biloxi. Why don't you come down?"

"You got anything special planned?"

"I'll tell you when you get there. I'll be at that lighthouse at noon Friday."

"I'll be there, an' it better be good."

The weather was perfect for spring break. The skies were clear, the sun was hot, and the beer was cold. Several thousand college kids sweated, meandered in and out of souvenir shops and bars, yelled at each other and innocent civilians from cruising cars, and strolled the beach along U.S. Highway 90. A high percentage of these devotees of the sun were veterans of past celebrations in Fort Lauderdale, and they knew that the only difference between the east coast of Florida and the gulf coast of Mississippi was eight hundred miles' worth of gas and time. Plus, the police in Biloxi were more lenient than their counterparts in Florida. It didn't take a fraternity's math major to decide that they could spend more of their gas money on beer if they stayed in their own backyard, and they'd get better treatment to boot.

Every fraternity and every sorority from every white university in the state had a social affair scheduled for the long weekend of spring break, and the parties would all take place on the coast. In the distant past the events had been called galas or balls; present-day fraternities called the occasions house parties. The uninitiated observer would call them orchestrated opportunities for college kids to get drunk, augmented by live music. The magnitude of any given house party, and its ultimate standing in spring-break lore, depended mostly on the dedication and diligence of that particular group's social chairman and the size of his available budget. The event would last, depending again on money and enthusiasm, from several hours to several days. Every year, a small handful of parties would distinguish themselves to the point that most of the area's revelers would ignore the smaller parties and move from one major bash to the next, making their small contributions to the immortalization of the more notable festivities.

Missy woke early Saturday and went out by the motel pool to have her quiet time. She read in Ephesians about wives submitting themselves to their husbands and the strong direction for husbands to love their wives. She looked out at the blue Gulf and repeated the words to herself. "Let every one of you in particular so love his wife even as himself."

She'd spent more time with Hull in the past three days than

she had with any boy in the last three years. They ate meals together and went to two parties and a movie, and yesterday they had gotten separated from their group and walked the beach together until sundown. He laughed at the same things she did, liked the same things she did, and didn't feel compelled to cram words into interludes of silence. In three days he had not even tried to hold her hand.

Father, she prayed, *I think he could be a good husband. You know how weak I am, an' You know I need a strong husband. I know Hull's looks aren't as important as his heart, but he could have both, couldn't he?* She remembered Pip's warning. *Lord, I ask that you protect me. Guard me against my stubbornness an' impatience. You're the only One who can protect me from my own strong-willed stupidity.*

When she finished her quiet time, she got a newspaper and a cup of coffee and went back to the pool to soak up some morning sun while she thought about Hull. Being thrown together on the coast was one thing; she needed to prepare herself for things to be different when they got back to Ole Miss.

"Get up, Ashman."

Ashman's body was splayed faceup on the floor. He had fallen out of the bed during the night and been unable to mount a successful counterattack on the spinning mattress. He didn't open his eyes. "What time is it?"

"Noon." Frank Schafer was in the bathroom combing his hair and grousing. "Where's Hull? He took my car last night."

"Man, I don't know. Why would he want a junker like yours when he's got that T-Bird?" Ashman was a whiner.

"You'll have to ask Golden Boy. Where'd he go?"

Ashman said, "He left someplace last night with some girl . . . I think."

Schafer turned away from the mirror. "That's a lot of help."

"Look, man," Ashman cranked the whining up a notch. "I told you. Him an' me were somewhere . . . an' there were a bunch of people . . . an' there was this girl in one of those French bikinis . . . maybe Hull an' her left." He pushed himself into a sitting position against the wall. "You reckon he's passed out someplace?"

"C'mon, Ashman. Put your head on straight. Hull won't even drink grape juice."

"How're we supposed to get back to school?" He was inspecting open beer cans for contents and peeling strips of sunburned skin from his legs.

"When he took my car, he left me the keys to the Bird. If he's not back here by five, I'm long gone." Schafer walked out into the heat.

Schafer was looking at a couple of beer cans at the bottom of the pool and considering an early morning swim when Ashman staggered out of the motel room. He was adorned in dirty socks, a filthy T-shirt, and a too-big swimming suit with frayed boxers poking out around the edges. The sunburned zombie reeled stiff-legged across the grass, stumbled, and grabbed at the pool ladder—he missed by a long foot, and smacked into the water face first. When he surfaced, he stood in the waist-deep water, swished a mouthful through his teeth, gargled, and spit the water back in the pool. Schafer decided against the swim and turned toward the parking lot.

"Where you goin'?" The bather was removing his shirt.

Schafer didn't turn around. "Breakfast."

Someone had left the Saturday morning paper on a chair by the pool, but neither boy noticed it. A small story on the second page told of a young black girl who had been raped and beaten by two white men the night before. The white men had been driving a nondescript sedan.

Dillworth and his group of disciples scheduled their final get-together for noon on Saturday. When the meeting was over, he approached Missy. "Hi. Want a ride home?"

Missy's heart picked up speed. She smiled. "Are you goin' my way?"

He smiled back. "Most definitely. I can drop you right at your door. I'll spend the night in Greenwood, go to church with Momma, then go back to Oxford tomorrow afternoon."

They laughed and talked for most of the five hours it took them to get home to the Delta. For the first time, she felt she was fully recovered from Pip's death, and she told him so. She told him about Mose and Pip being as close to her as parents.

When they got to the Parkers' house, Hull walked her to the door. "*Psycho*'s playing in Greenwood tonight. Come eat supper at our house, and we can go to the show. I'll have you home by ten thirty."

"That sounds like fun. Come in an' wait while I tell Momma an' freshen up." The girls in the dorm were going to set fire to her room.

Supper at the Dillworth house was not the favorite part of Missy's spring break. The home was beautiful, but Mrs. Dillworth was formal and aloof. Mr. Dillworth wasn't quiet because he was stuck up; he was trying to be invisible.

Missy thought the chicken salad was bland, but she complimented Mrs. Dillworth on it anyway. The lady waited until their black maid left the dining room and whispered that the secret was to use white meat only; according to her, no one in her house was allowed to eat dark meat.

After supper, Hull and Missy excused themselves and got out of the house. He laughed when they got in the car. "Sorry about Mom and Dad. They mean well, but I think they're scared of college kids."

She said, "Your parents are great. An' everybody should be scared of college kids." They both laughed.

Thunderstorms to the west made the sunset especially beautiful, and he called her attention to it. She couldn't remember ever hearing a boy comment on the colors in the sky and decided it was the kind of thing she could put up with for about fifty years.

During the movie, they both jumped at the scary parts; she didn't scream but twice. When the guy got stabbed on the stairs, she grabbed Hull's hand and hung on until the credits ran. Hull didn't seem inclined to pull away.

They stopped on the edge of town at Alfonzo's and sat in the car to eat hamburgers and rehash the movie. She said, "I won't sleep for a week. An' I'm never closin' my shower curtain again."

He said, "I'd like to see that."

When she looked startled, he said, "Wait . . . wait . . . I mean . . . Good gosh, I don't know what I mean. That came out wrong."

She thought his red face was cute and got tickled. "Behave yourself."

"Yes, ma'am. Right. Sorry."

His face got redder, and she smiled.

They pulled away from Alfonzo's, and he said, "Tell me some more about Mose and Pip." So she did.

They were almost to her house when the first raindrops fell. While she was helping him put the top up on the convertible, he said, "Shoot. I was gonna get you to show me where Pip was buried."

His interest in something that was meaningful to her was the latest pinnacle of pleasure in a perfect weekend. "It's not far from our house. An' it's not rainin' hard enough to hurt us." She thought, *Lord, I don't want to second-guess You, but I think he's doin' pretty good.*

The demon that made the deeps of the lake his habitat watched the car cross the bridge.

His deputy said, *Is this the time?*

The leader had waited patiently for that night's ingredients to blend themselves together. He said, *It is.*

Is the one you've chosen not a follower of the Enemy?

He speaks the words, but he does not believe.

Do his words not breed harm to our efforts?

Contempt colored the leader's assessment. *He speaks peace with his neighbors, while evil resides in his heart. The Enemy's Word warns Its readers of him because his kind can be more dangerous to the Enemy's cause than you and I.*

But will the humans who hear him not be swayed to the Enemy?

The Enemy's Word says this one is like clouds without water, wild waves of the sea, casting up his own shame like foam. Those who ignore the Enemy's warnings against his kind will surround themselves with empty platitudes and on that final day will be condemned to the outer darkness with us and our kind.

Can they not escape?

Contempt became anger. *They can always escape in this life, fool. Did not the Enemy's Son die to save them from the coming eternal death? That is why our strong master obliges us to cloud their minds, so that they may hear only their own reasoning and not the Truth. It is our given task to see that they suffer while we wait for eternity to again close its doors on time. The time is swiftly coming when we will be thrown into the pit; until that day, we must work to turn as many as we can from the Truth.*

Missy and Hull turned down the road to the cabin and stopped near the pecan trees. A flash of lightning revealed a stack of lumber and a collection of carpentry tools on the front porch; someone had been working on the cabin. Hull pulled a jacket from behind the seat to cover their heads.

"Have you got a flashlight?"

"Don't need one. I'll leave the headlights on."

He came around the car to get her, and she led the way to the graves. Neither of them noticed the dark shape watching from beneath the cabin's porch.

They slipped and skidded through the mud, staying fairly dry under the makeshift umbrella. Raindrops, ignited by the lights from the car, cut streaks against the dark behind the tombstones. She pointed at each stone in turn. "That's Pap, that's Junior, an' that's Pip."

He stared in silence, then said, "You said she was like your momma."

"Mm-hmm." The darkness around them gave something to the moment, and she reached out to touch his hand.

He moved the hand to point at Junior's headstone. "And he's your brother?" The shower of bright meteors grew thicker.

She smiled. "Almost. He saved my life." The memory was one of her favorite things.

Behind them, the shape had moved from beneath the porch and was standing at its full height near the steps.

"But they're all ni—" Lightning struck a tree on the north end of the lake; the despicable word disappeared into a concussion of thunder.

His deliberate choice of the most repulsive word in her world ignited her anger. "They were *black*, Hull. I made that clear comin' over here."

"And they're your family." The escalating savagery of the storm seemed to add a gravel-coated quality to his voice.

In ten short seconds, he had ruined her entire weekend and earned her disgust. "That's right, buddy boy. They're my family."

"If they're your family, what does that make you?" His words were saturated with contempt; his hoarse growl no longer relied on the fierce storm. Lightning flashed, chiseling the handsome face into a gargoylesque caricature of what it had been.

Hull Dillworth's goodness had been nothing more than a paper-thin veneer wrapped around false promises, and Missy could hear Pip lecturing her for being too impetuous. There were a hundred questions she would ask before she ever got into a car with another boy—if she ever did. She stepped out from under the jacket and started back toward the car lights. "You can take me home."

The wind carried the dark shape to the nearest corner of the porch when the girl pulled away from the boy.

Dillworth spoke to her back. "They couldn't help what they were, but you're kin to them by choice. That makes you worse than them."

"I said, take me home." She thought, *Lord, I must need a keeper. I'm out here on a horror-movie night with a Norman Bates who's got Wally Cox for a daddy, a KKK grand dragon for a momma, an', judgin' from the way Norman here uses his brain, they're probably first cousins.*

"Not in that car."

"That suits me fine." She veered away from it. "I'll walk."

"You might." Dillworth had decided that Missy was going to get what the little black girl on the coast had gotten. "After I teach you what white boys like."

He caught up to her at the front of the car and grabbed her arm; he was bigger and stronger, but he hadn't spent enough time within five miles of the Parker place. The fact that he'd never heard the wise admonition to "watch out for that girl" was going to cost him.

She made a natural transition of modes from flight to fight when he grabbed her arm—when he jerked her around to face him, the abrupt turning momentum only accelerated the speed of her fist.

She hit him hard under the eye, and they both went into the mud.

The wind whipped and snapped at the thing from the porch, changing its shape, driving it toward the desperate struggle in the muddy yard.

Hull wrestled to gain control of her arms, got on top of her, and slapped her hard enough to stun her. When she stopped struggling, he pulled off his belt, looped it around her neck, and jerked it tight.

The rain was falling hard on her face, and she was strangling.

"Now—" He was breathing hard. "—you so much as twitch and I'll show you how I break a stubborn birddog." He grabbed her blouse at the collar and ripped it open down the front.

The car lights went off one moment, and the shape from beneath the porch was standing in the darkness at Dillworth's side the next. A voice as deep as a well came from the darkness around the looming black thing. "You're in trouble."

Something cold and wet wrapped itself around Dillworth's neck and lifted him off the girl; he started gasping for breath and grabbing at the restraint.

The darkness said, "Be still."

Missy rolled to her hands and knees. The rain tried to wash the mud from her back while she pulled the belt from her neck and choked air into her lungs. She caught glimpses of a thing the color of the night, swirling and changing shape, holding Dillworth on his tiptoes. Whatever had him looked huge.

The darkness holding Dillworth said, "Boy, you can't see it in the dark, but that cold edge you feel against your neck is the bad end of a hatchet. You make a move against me, an' I'll split your skull." It almost picked Dillworth up with the noose. "Understand?"

Dillworth gasped and tried to nod.

The hood of a poncho fell away and the shiny black shape became a man. He turned to Missy. "Are you okay, ma'am?"

She took the knuckles of her hand out of her mouth. "I hurt my hand when I hit him. An' I'm gonna have to tell five thousand people at college why I've got a black eye."

Dillworth was making choking sounds.

The man jerked the belt. "Shut up." He turned back to Missy. "Sorry I didn't get to him sooner."

"Me, too. I had to go all the way to Greenville to get this dadgummed blouse." She kept an eye on Dillworth, holding the edges of the blouse together with one hand while she sucked on the knuckles of the other. "Who're you?"

"Name's Patterson." Lightning streaked across the sky; thunder followed. Rain bounced off the blade when he pointed the hatchet. "I was just passing through, and my car quit. I was sleeping under the porch, there, waiting for morning to bring enough light for me to see how to get her going again." He tapped Dillworth's chest with the blade. "Friend of yours?"

Missy had her own question. "What do we do now?"

"We take care of you first." She didn't look like the kind of person who needed much care. The women in West Texas had a reputation for being pretty tough, but they could take lessons from this one.

"I need to go home." She pointed at the lights across the lake. "I live over there."

He gestured at the convertible. "We can take his car." Huge raindrops beat the car's hood.

"No." Her hair was plastered to her head, her clothes were muddy and soaked through, but she'd had her last ride in the Thunderbird.

"Well, we can use his battery. Go turn on the headlights."

When she came back, Patterson asked, "What about him?"

She shook her head slowly back and forth while she chewed the corner of her mouth. "He's an idiot. When we get to my house, you can try to help me talk my daddy out of killin' him." She gestured at the belt around Dillworth's neck. "You might need your choke collar for Daddy."

Dillworth made a moaning sound, and Patterson jerked on the belt to shut him up. "You're serious, aren't you?"

"You're doggone right, I'm serious. If Daddy doesn't kill him, some man in town probably will." She examined her middle knuckle, put it back in her mouth, and talked around it. "If they don't kill him, the sheriff'll put him in jail. Either way, his datin' days in this state are over."

Patterson pulled Dillworth close and peered at his face. "You sure? He looks like a handsome devil—" He grinned. "—except for the swollen eye."

"Then you date him." Standing in the rain was no longer romantic. "Are you gonna walk me home or not?"

"Just a minute." He pursed his lips while he thought, then pointed up past the pecan trees. "You go on up toward the road some 'til I get him turned loose."

"Why can't you turn him loose with me here?"

"Because I don't know if he wants to behave. Just go wait over there for a minute." The next lightning strike was brighter. "And stay away from those trees."

"Well, don't take all night."

More thunder rumbled. Missy turned her back and walked past the cabin.

Patterson turned his attention to Dillworth. "Okay, sonny boy, I'm going to give you some slack on this belt, and you're going to behave, or I'm going to tap you with this hatchet. Understand?"

Hull nodded.

Patterson slipped the belt over Hull's head and stepped back. Hull went to his knees, gasping for breath.

Patterson said, "When you get up, you get in that car and get lost. Clear?"

Hull nodded and watched the hand holding the hatchet relax.

Patterson was bigger than the man kneeling in the mud, but not as quick. Hull came off the ground fast, his fist took Patterson hard on the chin. The bigger man went backward, arms flailing, and hit his head when he crashed into the edge of the porch.

Hull used both hands to snatch the hatchet free.

Patterson's head cleared. He watched the man's face split into a grin that became wild laughter and, finally, shrill screaming. Hull posed in the glow from the car's lights, the hatchet raised like an executioner's axe.

When Missy turned, sustained lightning worked its way across the base of the clouds and illuminated the scene. Patterson was on his back at the porch; Dillworth stood over him with the hatchet, screaming. She was sprinting back to the two men when the sweep of the hatchet blade traced an arc through the wicked blue light. She added her voice to the screaming.

Just as the hatchet fell, Patterson jerked to one side.

Dillworth missed his mark by an inch and buried the blade in the wood of the porch. His screaming got louder and became prolonged screeching, and Patterson threw himself into the rain-dimmed light behind his attacker.

Missy slid in the mud by the steps and fell almost at Hull's feet. She pulled herself up, and her hands found a piece of scrap lumber by the porch.

Hull was screeching louder, struggling to free the hatchet.

Missy went down again and scuttled backward through the mud, distancing herself from the man she had been laughing with an hour earlier. Patterson grabbed her from behind and picked her up. He reached for the makeshift club. "I'll take that."

She pulled away and pointed at a stack of scraps. "Uh-uh, you get your own. If he comes for me again, I'm gonna save my daddy a trip to Greenwood."

He followed her eyes to the scrap pile, then looked at Dillworth. The crazed man was jerking from side to side, cursing

ABIDING DARKNESS

and screaming, trying to get the blade out of the wood. When he got it free, he would use it on them.

Patterson picked up a length of pine the size of a baseball bat and stepped close to the thing that had been Hull Dillworth.

"Let it go, boy!" he yelled.

Dillworth braced himself with one hand on a porch post; the other grasped the hatchet and tugged in time with his grunts. He could no longer hear Patterson.

"Let the hatchet go, I said!"

Missy was yelling. "Quit talkin'! Quit talkin'! *Hit him an' stop him!*"

Dillworth was immersed in madness—if he got the blade loose, they were dead. Patterson knew the girl was right; he just hated to hit a man who wasn't fighting him. He didn't have a choice.

Patterson took a batter's stance, aimed at the most exposed part of the man's body, and swung the pine club at the hand braced on the porch post. The heavy piece of pine was shattered on impact, and so was Dillworth's hand. A sound that only a wounded monster could make pierced the wetness of the night, and Dillworth abandoned the hatchet to grab at Patterson. Patterson jammed the splintered end of his club into Dillworth's stomach and felt it tear flesh.

The thing stopped screaming. It reached past the shortened weapon, lashing out hard and accurately with its good hand. Patterson fell into the mud on his back.

Missy was in close. She drew back to swing, but lost her footing and her club. Dillworth got her by the throat and threw her onto the porch and held her there.

Patterson was back on his feet. He smashed the thing in the back with his elbow and grabbed a fistful of hair. The thing turned away from Missy.

Missy reached across her body to grasp the handle of the hatchet. *Lord, help me,* she prayed.

The handle moved in her hand, and the blade came loose. She scooted off the edge of the porch, got both feet planted, and cocked her arm. "Hey, Norman!"

The monster turned, and the flat side of the ax head—powered by anger, adrenaline, and one of the best backhands in the Delta—hit him dead center in the mouth. Hull Dillworth was down, and out.

They dragged him to the car and threw him across it. Coursing rainwater washed a spreading stain from the car's hood almost as fast as it flowed from the wound made by the hatchet.

"C'mon. Let's get you home."

She slipped in the mud, and Patterson caught her arm. She jerked away and snapped, "I can walk by myself."

CHAPTER SIXTEEN

Missy didn't want conversation or the poncho, and Patterson was content to trail along behind her. By the time they got to the bridge, the storm was letting up.

When they got to the back door of her house, the rain had almost quit. She said, "Let me go first. Daddy doesn't know you."

She was at the back steps when the door opened.

"It's just me, Daddy."

Bobby Lee Parker looked past her at Patterson and stepped into the doorway. "I thought I heard somebody scream a few minutes ago."

"You probably did."

Bobby Lee was wearing his robe and slippers and carrying a large revolver in his right hand. "Good grief, Missy, you're soaked." When she stepped into the porch light, he saw the torn blouse and turned his attention on Patterson. "Who're you?"

"This man's name is Patterson, Daddy. I had some trouble with Hull."

Bobby Lee's eyes narrowed. He was still looking at Patterson. The thumb of his right hand moved to the gun's hammer. "What kind of trouble?"

"I'm fixin' to tell you." She took a jacket from a peg by the door and turned her back to put it on. Bobby Lee let Patterson pass, and the two men followed her into the kitchen.

When Missy stepped into the brighter light, Bobby Lee saw the bruise starting to show on her cheek and the marks at her throat. He turned to Patterson and his thumb took a firmer grip on the gun's hammer. "You want to tell me what kind of trouble we're talkin' about here, mister?"

Patterson lifted his hands away from his sides and nodded at the gun. "First, I want her to tell you that I'm the knight in shining armor here."

The storm had waked Bobby Lee and his wife, and he was out of bed because they thought they heard a scream. Now, he's standing in his kitchen with a mud-covered stranger the size of a draft horse who's just brought his daughter home with her blouse torn and her eye swelling shut. His words took on edges, and the barrel of the gun tilted slightly. "I asked *you*."

Patterson told Missy, "Tell your father I'm a nice man before he shoots me."

Missy took the time to hand Patterson a dish towel and got her first good look at his face. He was barely older than she. "It's okay, Daddy. He stopped Hull before things got too rough."

"What things?"

Patterson looked at the gun that was still pointed in his general direction. "Tell him again."

"Daddy, this man saved my life tonight. Do not shoot him unless he keeps tellin' me what to do, okay?" She dropped into a chair at the kitchen table and glowered at Patterson. "There." She started blotting at her hair with another dish towel.

If she was thankful, she was concealing it well. Based on her conduct since he stopped the assault, Patterson could believe she might get more excited about losing a checkers game and more appreciative if he'd changed a flat tire on her car.

Bobby Lee relaxed his thumb and looked from the girl to Patterson. "Her mother an' I were prayin' for her when the storm came up, an' it bothered me when we heard that scream. Is somebody gonna tell me what happened out there?"

"Like she said, that fellow she called Hull got a little out of hand, and I stepped in."

"Things that are 'a little out of hand' don't cause bruises or tear blouses. How'd she get marked up?"

"You might want to ask me, Daddy. I'm sittin' right here."

His daughter was home and relatively safe. Bobby Lee took a deep breath. "Well?"

"We stopped at the cabin so I could show Hull Pip's grave, an' it was like he went crazy. He grabbed me hard, an' I went for his nose. We ended up in the mud an' wrestled around some 'til he slapped me silly an' put his belt around my neck." She pointed at Patterson. "He got Hull off o' me."

Bobby Lee cocked his head slightly and stepped closer to her. When he spoke, he seemed even calmer. "Hull Dillworth slapped you an' choked you with a belt?"

Missy forgot about being mad and fixed an earnest gaze on Patterson while she spoke to Bobby Lee. "He did. But I'm okay now, Daddy."

"Mm-hmm." Bobby Lee nodded. He looked out the window. "Is he still over at the cabin?"

Missy's towel stopped moving. Her eyes were pleading with Patterson.

Patterson said, "I doubt it. Are you planning on killing him?"

Bobby Lee's face went pale. He looked at the floor and rubbed his cheek while he thought. "I appreciate what you did for her, son. I'll take it from here."

"He's already paid a high price."

The father's lips were compressed into a thin, bloodless line. "Like I said, son, I'll handle it. My job is to make sure men know better than to touch her."

"She said you'd kill him." Patterson took off the poncho. "No man from my part of the country would blame you if you did."

Some quality in the young man's voice caught Bobby Lee's attention. "You sound like you'd do somethin' different?"

"I've already done it." He folded the poncho while he talked. "He hit her, and he spoke roughly to her. I used a piece of lumber on his hand, and she wrecked his mouth with a hatchet. That's enough for you to sleep on."

Bobby Lee took a long minute to consider what the man said. When he put the gun on the table, Missy started sponging at her hair again.

"Okay, we can sleep on it." Bobby Lee pulled out his cigarettes. "Where're you from?"

"West Texas."

"Where're you stayin' tonight?"

Patterson said, "I was sleeping under the porch of that house. My car's broken down on the other side of that bridge."

"You got any dry clothes?"

He had an easy smile. "In the car."

"I'll change an' take you to get 'em. You can stay with us."

Patterson checked the girl's reaction; she noticed and nodded at him. He said, "Thanks. I think there were some critters under that porch with me."

Bobby Lee changed clothes and came back. Patterson followed him to the door.

Missy said, "You forgot your gun." She was still slumped in the chair, dabbing at her hair and dripping on the floor.

"I don't think I'll need it now."

"Take it anyway." She pushed the gun across the table. "Hull was a snake."

A communication that Patterson didn't understand crossed between father and daughter.

Bobby Lee walked back to the table. "Okay, you go get a shotgun an' wait in your momma's room 'til we get back."

She got up and walked out of the kitchen.

Bobby Lee picked up the pistol and stuck it behind his belt. "Let's go git you some clothes, boy."

Missy had come back to the kitchen door. "Uh . . . Mr. Patterson."

Patterson turned around.

"Thanks."

Her voice sounded like she meant it. Patterson smiled. "Yes, ma'am. You're welcome."

Missy stood where she was for a moment. She didn't understand it, but when most men got close to her they acted as if they were blowing fuses in their brains; maybe this man was different. She came around the table, stood close, and looked up at him. "I don't know your first name."

The left side of her face was swollen and turning blue; water dripped from tendrils of mud-plastered hair; her clothes and shoes—except for the oversized work jacket—looked as if she had been in a pen full of unruly pigs. He couldn't imagine a shade of blue darker than her eyes. "Uh . . . David."

"I'm Missy Parker." The blue eyes studied his face when she offered her hand. "What do you think is the most important thing in the world, David Patterson?"

It was probably the most important thing anyone had ever asked him. He wanted to say something that would please her, but she kept looking into his eyes. "Getting myself back to Texas before I starve, I guess." He was regretting his choice of words while they were still on their way from his mind to his mouth.

"Oh." Her shoulders drooped; the hand he was holding went limp. "Well, I guess we can give you all the food you can carry."

Before he could react, she was walking away, speaking to the floor. "Thanks again for rescuin' me."

He watched her leave while he struggled to think of the words that would stop her. If they had been alone, he could have called her back to ask her how he should've answered her question. But they weren't, and he couldn't, and he'd never know. She disappeared through the door.

When the two men were settled in the truck, Patterson said, "Tell me why she had to get out the shotgun."

"It's a long story, an' you can get her to tell it to you tomorrow." Bobby Lee took the time to light a cigarette, then asked, "What'd you do to Dillworth?"

"The scream you heard was when I broke a two-by-four on his hand. She did worse damage to his mouth."

Bobby Lee blew smoke at the windshield and put the truck in gear. "I'll call the sheriff tomorrow an' let him handle Hull."

Patterson's car was a well-used Chevrolet. When Patterson opened the door to get his clothes, Bobby Lee said, "Let's see if she'll start now."

"She won't. The generator went out on me, and I used up the battery nursing her this far."

"I'll take a look under the hood."

"It won't help. She's dead as a hammer."

Bobby Lee popped the hood. In the light from his pickup he could see that one of the wires to the generator was hanging loose; he fastened it back to its post. What he had read in the Bible and the things that he had seen happen around Cat Lake made him assume God's intervention first and coincidence never. "Give 'er a try."

Patterson said, "The battery's graveyard dead," but he slid behind the wheel and pressed the starter because the man asked him to. The car started smoothly, and the interior light came on. Patterson said, "I'll be darn."

Bobby Lee nodded. He'd have something to tell his wife and daughter when he got home.

When they got back to the house, Bobby Lee said, "You want to go to church with us in the morning?"

Patterson had his trunk open and was looking at three or four boxes of books. "Well, I don't have to work on my car, but I need to get over to Arkansas to see about a job."

"What kind of a job?"

"Pipeline. I'll work 'til fall and head back home to start school."

"You want a job here?"

Patterson was distracted. "I think somebody's been in my trunk."

"They steal something?"

Patterson shook his head. "There wasn't much to steal. But

they . . . it looks like it's been cleaned out. I mean, somebody cleaned it."

Bobby Lee looked in the trunk. It was kitchen clean. "How 'bout the inside?"

"When I left it tonight, it was pretty messy. Now all the trash is gone and the floors are clean. That's why I looked in the trunk."

Bobby Lee said, "Imagine that."

Patterson let the trunk lid fall. "You said something about a job? Doing what?"

Bobby Lee pointed across the road. "Workin' over there at that gin."

"Is it your gin?"

"Yeah, but my manager does the hirin'."

"You think he'll hire me?"

Bobby Lee smiled for the first time that night. "You tell him what happened out here tonight, an' he'll probably give you my job."

Bobby Lee got Patterson settled in a spare bedroom and went to tell his wife and daughter what happened at the car.

Missy sat on their bed and brushed her hair until Bobby Lee finished his story. "So you think God broke his car down on purpose an' sent him to take care of me. Then He cleaned it out an' recharged the battery."

"Dead batteries don't recharge themselves." Bobby Lee was nodding, and Susan was backing him up. He smiled knowingly. "And, yeah, angels cleaned out the car just so you'd know that Patterson's being there was God's doin'. What do you think happened?"

"I think I need to start takin' more time decidin' what I think. G'night."

Patterson didn't sleep much and was in the kitchen before daybreak. The coffee was ready, but the kitchen was empty.

He poured a cup and walked to the back door. Light from the kitchen window barely made it to a figure sitting at a table on the back porch.

He stepped through the door. "Morning."

She didn't turn around. "Mmm." She sat with her feet curled under her in the chair, holding her cup near her lips and taking an occasional taste without putting it down.

When she didn't say anything else, he sat down and arranged his chair so he could see to the east.

When the predawn sky turned pale pink and it was light enough to see the cypress trees by the lake, he brought the coffeepot and refilled their cups. It seemed both strange and appropriate to sit in the near darkness with an attractive woman his own age without remarking on what the coming sun was doing to the sky.

When the sky was shading to blue, she got up and went into the kitchen.

Patterson wanted to talk to her, but he didn't want to be pushy. He had gotten an hour of sleep and spent the rest of the night thinking about her and her question. He stayed on the porch and let his mind go back over the same ground for the millionth time and tried to figure out how best to answer her.

When the sun finally made its way to the porch, he got up and walked into the kitchen. The night before, when her hair was plastered with mud, he thought the girl was the prettiest woman he had ever seen. The sight of her in plain jeans and one of her dad's starched shirts made it difficult for him to breathe, and he could feel his face getting hot.

Missy waved at him to sit, then filled his cup and sat down before she said anything. "You're up early." If she cared, she was good at hiding it.

"Habit, I guess. You're up early, yourself."

"Mmm. I guess I've been waitin' for Hull to bust down the door." Patterson thought she was hoarse because of the belt being around her neck, but her dad hadn't mentioned it. She said, "So, what does a knight in shinin' armor do for an encore?"

He laughed quietly. "Hard to say." He watched her eyes. "I

was headed for Arkansas, but your dad offered me a job at the gin."

"Mmm." She didn't care about that either.

Susan Parker came in after sunup, met Patterson, and thanked him for taking care of their daughter. She was as warm and pleasant as her daughter was cool and distant. Bobby Lee came in when the biscuits were done.

They were finishing breakfast when the phone rang.

Missy said, "Hello. . . . Yes, sir, he's right here." She looked at her father.

"I'll take it in the den."

When he came back into the room, his wife looked at him. "Who was it?"

"Joe Tom. He's lookin' for Hull Dillworth." He looked at Patterson. "Joe Tom Rogers is the sheriff over in Greenwood. The Biloxi police called him because they want to talk to Hull." He got out his cigarettes. "I told him what happened out here, an' he's gonna pick Hull up."

Susan Parker quit eating. Patterson was starting on his sixth biscuit.

Missy stirred her coffee and picked up the cup. "Why'd he call here?"

"Mrs. Dillworth said Hull hadn't been home yet. She told Joe Tom you might know where he was."

Missy couldn't remember anything she liked about Mrs. Dillworth. "If I'd had a gun last night, I could lead 'em straight to his sorry carcass."

Bobby Lee nodded. "I 'magine. Joe Tom'll be comin' by here after dinner to ask you a few questions."

Missy said, "Well, he better hustle his bustle. I'm goin' back to school as soon as dinner's over." She pushed back from the table. "I'm gonna get ready for church."

Her mother said, "Are you okay?"

Missy said, "Yes, ma'am, I'm fine. But I'll be better when they put the sorry dog in jail."

When she walked out of the room, Susan turned to Bobby Lee. "What do the Biloxi police want with Hull Dillworth?"

"It's not good."

She waited.

"They think him an' another man hurt a young girl in Biloxi this week."

"How badly?"

"She died yesterday."

Susan Parker tried to keep her hands from shaking. "Bobby Lee, what if he'd—"

He reached across the table to hold her hand. "He didn't, honey, 'cause God was lookin' out for her." He turned to their guest. "David, we're gonna pray for a minute or two. I want you to know you're welcome to join us."

Patterson was sliding his chair back. "No, sir, y'all go ahead. I'm gonna walk around for awhile." When he stood up he added, "Maybe I should have stayed out of it and let you kill him last night."

Bobby Lee said, "God decided those things, son, not me or you. You did fine."

Patterson walked out to the middle of the Cat Lake bridge and looked at the water. Missy's question had to have something to do with God. Her dad wasn't surprised that she had asked, so he must know the answer. He saw Bobby Lee step into the backyard and walked back to the house.

Bobby Lee met him at the road and walked him to the back porch. "Have you decided what your plans are, yet?"

"Well, I can't live here forever, but the offer of a job at the gin is a bird in the hand. If you're still receptive, I'll stick around for awhile."

"Good. See Mose Washington at the gin in the mornin'."

Patterson looked at the gin. "Is he easy to find?"

"Yep. Black man, green pickup, starched khakis." He smiled. "He's not as tall as you, but you won't notice it."

"I'll be there."

"Are you worried about Hull?"

"No, sir. Hull was a coward; he's long gone by now."

"Don't try to predict him too much. He could fool you."

"Missy doesn't seem too worried."

"Missy's different from most women. She handles what she can an' lets the rest handle itself. If he's got any brains left in his head, he'll go where he won't cross paths with her."

They went inside and sat at the kitchen table; Bobby Lee smoked and Patterson filled their cups. Patterson took a bite of the last biscuit and washed it down with a swallow of coffee. "Are you gonna tell me why she had to get a shotgun out last night?"

"I'll tell you what. Missy needs a ride back to school this afternoon. We'll eat dinner with my momma after church, then you can run Missy back to Oxford in our car, an' she can tell you the story on the way."

Patterson grinned and held up the last bite of biscuit. "Does your mother cook this well?"

"You'll have to judge that for yourself."

"And y'all are going to church this morning?"

"Mm-hmm. You interested?"

"I guess. It'll beat sitting here by myself."

Bobby Lee picked up his Bible and walked to the door. "I'm gonna spend some time out on the porch before we go. We'll leave about ten thirty."

When Patterson came out of his room at ten fifteen, the three Parkers were around a table on the back porch, holding hands and praying. He went back in his room to wait for ten thirty.

Patterson was noncommittal about the preaching, but enjoyed meeting the people there. Missy's black eye got fewer comments than he expected. Apparently, it wasn't her first. Word of the previous night's events had made it to town before them, and every man in the church came over to shake Patterson's hand.

Sunday dinner at Old Mrs. Parker's wasn't a loud affair, but it was lively. Evalina, Pip's mother, still cooked for whichever Parker household needed her, and she had been warned to fry extra chicken for Patterson. Old Mrs. Parker still did her own baking, and she made an extra half-dozen rolls for the big man. He pleased her when he ate his allotment of rolls and two pieces of pie.

They were drinking coffee when the phone rang. Evalina said it was for Missy.

Missy said, "Hello?"

Then, "Yes, ma'am."

Then, "No, ma'am."

Her face started getting red while she listened. Finally, she said, "Mrs. Dillworth, your precious little boy got away from here last night without gettin' skinned alive thanks to my daddy's generous spirit. If he ever comes within twenty feet of me again, he won't be so lucky."

Patterson watched the people around the table. The rest of the family was listening, but no one appeared inclined to help the girl express herself.

Missy listened again a brief moment, then held the receiver away from her ear and glared at it while she spoke at the mouthpiece. "You can blame anyone you want to, lady, but if that sweet momma's boy ever comes around me again, you can bet a platter of your segregated chicken salad I'm gonna pay him what he earned last night."

She slammed the phone back on its cradle and turned to her audience. "That woman is about two sacks short of a bale."

Old Mrs. Parker was blowing on a fresh cup of coffee. "You got a gun in your purse, baby?"

"Yessum, an' I'll keep it there 'til they lock him up."

Bobby Lee told everyone, "I'm havin' David drive her back to Oxford this afternoon."

The red in Missy's face became luminescent; if she'd been a year younger, she'd have stomped her foot. "I don't need a dadgummed bodyguard."

"No—" Her father was calm. "—but you need a ride. Your car's still at school."

"Oh." He was right. And again, she spoke too soon. "I'm gonna go pack."

"Are you plannin' on talkin' to Joe Tom?"

"Yessir, if he pushes back from his dinner table soon enough to get here before I leave."

He didn't.

The trip back to Oxford took two hours, and Missy spent the first hour telling Patterson the whole story of the war at Cat Lake. She told the story often enough to be able to judge the reactions of most people, and Patterson was a skeptic.

"You don't believe it, do you?"

He mulled over his answer. "I don't think I have to believe it for it to be true."

"Well, that's honest enough."

"Can I ask you something?"

"Sure." She leaned over to change the radio station.

"You keep using the word *demon*." He smiled. "Now, I don't want to get thrown out of the car, but do you really believe in demons?"

"Do you believe in God?"

"Of course."

"Well, He believes in demons."

"And so do I. I just wanted to know if you really did."

"Yes, I really do, an' I don't like bein' tested."

"Can I ask you about something else? Last night in the kitchen you asked me what I thought was the most important thing in the world, and you didn't like my answer. What did you expect me to say?"

Missy stared out the window for awhile before answering with a question. "What're you goin' to do tomorrow?"

"Probably start work at the gin, if your dad's manager will hire me."

"My Mose—Junior's daddy—is daddy's manager at the gin."

Patterson let the information sink in. "That's why your dad knew he'd hire me—'cause I helped you out last night."

"That's right. I'm almost Mose's daughter, an' you probably saved my life."

"Well, I don't know if I'd go so far as to say I saved your life."

"I would. Hull Dillworth couldn't have done what he was gonna do to me an' let me live."

"Why would you go out with a guy who would pull a stunt like that?"

He was learning that she didn't always rush to give an answer. "He had something wrong with him that I didn't see. Next time I'll look closer."

"How?"

She didn't want to tell him. "I'll take my time."

"You didn't answer my question."

"About what answer I was lookin' for last night?"

"Yep."

"There isn't a right or wrong answer. The answer just tells me what you think is important."

"Well, I said something about starving, but I was wrong."

"Oh?" She was pushing buttons on the car radio again.

Patterson said, "Yeah. I had a chance to make an important statement about what I believe—"

Buddy Holly entered the conversation and washed out the rest of what Patterson was saying. The girl closed her eyes and hiccuped along with "Not Fade Away."

CHAPTER SEVENTEEN

The parking lot in front of Missy's dormitory was three acres of suitcases, tennis rackets, and golf bags, all with sunburned coeds attached. Missy directed David Patterson to a parking spot, and he got out to help with her bag.

She tried to beat him to the trunk. "I'll get it."

Patterson already had the bag in his hand. "Look, Missy, I work for your dad now. And even if I didn't, I ought to be helping you with your bag."

Missy put her hand on the suitcase grip with his. "But you *don't* work for me. An' I *don't want* a chauffeur. An' I *don't want* any help."

"I need to tell you one thing, Missy."

She had to listen because he still held a grip on her suitcase. "What is it?"

"If the answer you've come up with to that important question is better than mine, why would you shut me out without telling me what it is?"

A car brushed by behind her and someone called her name. Missy didn't hear her friend because her attention was fixed on what David Patterson had said.

Last night she had asked him a question that could tell her whether or not he was a Christian, and when he gave every indication that he wasn't, she turned her back on him. Missy

Parker, the girl who said she wanted to know God and make Him known, possessed the open secret of eternal life, and she refused to share it. Instead, she used her beliefs as a criterion to determine whether to befriend the person to whom she owed her life. She thought, *If I won't be friends with people who aren't Christians, who will I talk to about how much God loves us?* This guy holding her suitcase and smiling at her had caught her red-handed, and she didn't like it.

She said, "Is that all?"

"Yes, ma'am." Patterson almost laughed out loud at her stubbornness, and she reddened under her new tan.

He got back into the car and grinned. "I'll see you the next time you come home."

Missy thought, *Not if I can help it.* She dropped the suitcase at her feet and watched him leave.

"*Who* was that hunk of *hombre?*" Polly stood at her elbow, watching the car drive off.

"That's the jerk my daddy just hired to work at the gin, an' be my chauffeur an' bodyguard."

"What'd you do with Hull?"

"Not enough. He's still alive."

Polly divided her attention between the departing car and Missy's black eye. "Huh?"

"I'll tell you later."

Polly watched the car until it was almost out of sight. "This bodyguard-gin-worker-chauffeur . . . have you got your stamp on him?"

"Never."

"Oh? What's wrong with him?"

"Everything. He's nice, smart, an' good-looking. An' he saved my life." She swiped at the tears on her cheeks. *An' I just got through treatin' him like a fungus.*

"Can I have him?"

"Dear heart, you can have every confounded one of 'em. I'm gonna be a nun." She picked up her bag, and Polly followed her to their room to hear about Hull.

On the Tuesday after spring break, the police found Hull Dillworth's car on the Mississippi River bridge at Greenville. Sheriff Joe Tom Rogers and the Biloxi police waited for news that his body had showed up downriver, but it never came.

Four weeks after his disappearance, one of the wealthiest families in the Delta held a memorial service for its only child. Fewer than six people attended.

At the cabin, on the night of the attack, the lightning had given Missy a good look at Hull's eyes. They matched those of the snakes that tried to kill her when she was a child. The little handgun stayed in her purse.

Bobby Lee wasn't happy with the way the telephone conversation was ending; he smiled anyway when he said the only words the listener wanted to hear. "Yes, ma'am. I'll take care of it right now."

He leaned forward to put the telephone receiver back on its cradle, rubbed the bridge of his nose under his reading glasses, then went to the door of the office. He searched the gin loading area but didn't see who he was looking for. His lips tightened, and he moved out into the midmorning sun to look down the narrow corridor between the gin stands.

"David!" The gin wasn't running, but Bobby Lee always yelled when he was talking to anyone near the large machines. Twenty feet away, Patterson stepped into view.

"Yessir?"

"What're you doin'?"

Patterson pointed into the recesses behind the machines. "Greasing these strap wheels."

"Okay, remember where you were on that." He was frowning as if something had left a bad taste in his mouth. "I got somethin' else I need you to do." He turned away and motioned for Patterson to follow.

Bobby Lee shuffled back to his desk, shoulders hunched under the weight of getting the gin ready for summer while catering to the women in his life. He was pushing things around in the desk drawer when Patterson got to the office.

"Momma just called. Leon's down in his back, an' she needs somebody to help Evalina at the house." Leon's back gave him trouble about this time every year. Bobby Lee finally found what he was looking for and held out a broken piece of yardstick to his helper. A single key was attached to it by a short cord. "Take that pickup out there to my house. Susan an' Momma an' Evalina'll have you settin' up tables an' haulin' stuff for the garden club's spring bash tomorrow. Just do whatever they tell you."

"I can do it. Are they having anything to eat?"

Bobby Lee didn't smile. "Yeah, an' you bes' stay out of Evalina's way while she's cookin' it."

Evalina puttered and muttered and ordered him around in the kitchen while he set up tables and polished silver. She fed him three ham sandwiches and a gallon of sweet tea at noon, then put him to work washing windows. Before he left that evening, Old Mrs. Parker said, "Do you have a dark suit, David?"

"Yes, ma'am."

"Good. You put it on and be back here at seven in the morning to help Evalina. You can carry the trays and heavy things out to the tables just before the ladies get here."

"Yes, ma'am. I'll be here."

He was walking to the truck when a car pulled into the driveway. Missy Parker opened the door and waved at him. He waved back and Missy motioned to him.

"Hi. How's school?"

"Almost over." She was smiling. "Lemme guess. Leon's back's botherin' him again."

Patterson laughed. "Leon's a smart man."

"Yeah, he gets that way every spring." Her hair caught the

late afternoon sun when she laughed with him. The smile stayed, and she said, "I have to ask you to forgive me."

"For what?"

"For a million things, I guess. My lack of appreciation, my stubbornness, just my actin' like an all-around spoiled brat. I'm really sorry."

He laughed again. "I'll forgive you if you'll ride over to Indianola and get a hamburger with me."

Her smile faded. "Is it okay if I take a rain check?"

His smile left with hers. "You bet. Anytime."

The silence lasted until he said, "Well, I guess I'd better be going. They've got me doing butler duty in the morning. G'night."

She let him take several steps, then said, "David?"

He wasn't smiling anymore. "Yes, ma'am?"

"It's not you, okay? It's me."

He tried to be nonchalant. "Sure. I understand." He didn't.

Bobby Lee was waiting for him when he took the truck back to the gin. "Well, you survived."

"Yes, sir. If I make it through tomorrow, I'll be home free."

"Thanks for helpin' out." Bobby Lee started to leave and turned back. "Say, have you been over at the huntin' club lately?"

"That's the old house and barn back behind Mose's cabin, right?"

"Yeah." Bobby Lee pointed to the east. "Back east of Eagle Nest Brake. You been back there?"

"I've been over there, but not in the last week or so. Is it okay to be back there?"

"Oh, sure, it's on our land. A couple of the boys thought they saw a white man back there yesterday an' the day before, but it could've been anybody."

"You want me to tell folks to stay away?"

"Naw. It's probably just kids, an' they can't hurt anything." He was grinning when he got in his truck. "Have fun tomorrow."

"Thanks a lot."

Bobby Lee drove over to check on the hunting club. It was deserted.

The luncheon the next day wasn't really fun, but David was thankful that it put him in close proximity to Missy.

The ladies from the Moores Point Garden Club started arriving at eleven thirty. For the next thirty minutes, Patterson carried trays and food. Missy greeted and visited. While the ladies were eating, he made the rounds, doing things a waiter would do. By midafternoon the luncheon was over, the ladies were gone, and the kitchen was clean. He checked outside, but Missy was nowhere to be seen. Evalina called him to come sit down and eat.

He was on his second sandwich when Missy breezed into the kitchen barefoot. She was wearing Bermuda shorts, her ponytail splayed across the back of one of her daddy's shirts, talking to whoever might be listening. "I'm on the way to Indianola to play tennis wi—" She stopped.

David Patterson was sitting at the kitchen table with Evalina, and the cook was resting her hand on his arm. When David saw her, he stood.

Missy appeared transfixed.

Evalina frowned at her. "Missy? What's the matter with you?"

The girl came out of her trance and laughed at herself. "Sorry, I guess I had too much coffee this mornin'."

"Humphf. Too much somethin'."

David said, "Shall I drive you to the club, miss?"

The joke went over her head. "No, thanks. I'm pickin' up Polly." Missy was looking in his direction without seeing him, frowning slightly, a study in concentration.

David picked up the rest of his sandwich and walked to the back door. "Well, I'm taking the rest of the day off."

Missy followed him. "Me too."

When they got to her car, he opened the door. She stopped and rested her hand on it.

"Are you going to play barefoot?"

"Hmm?" She was still frowning, squinting in the direction of the kitchen.

"Are you going to play tennis without your shoes?"

She looked at her feet. "Ohmigosh! I don't have any shoes on."

She looked through him again.

"Missy, are you okay?"

Her ponytail stood straight out when she whirled around and started back for the house. "No, I left my brain in my shoes again."

David watched her run into the house, then shrugged and walked toward the bridge.

When Missy got to the kitchen, Evalina was putting something in the refrigerator. "Evalina?"

"Mm-hmm?"

"You touched him."

Evalina stayed at what she was doing. "Did what?"

"Him. David. You touched him. You put your hand on his arm."

The cook turned her back to the refrigerator. "Baby, you sure you feels all right?"

Missy walked around the table and stood by the cook. "Evalina, I've known you all my life. You've never touched a man or boy, woman or girl, black or white, with anything but the business end of a wooden spoon. You were restin' your hand on his arm."

Evalina closed the refrigerator and stood with one hand on the door, frowning at the girl. "Baby, I don't know what's gotten into you."

"What made you do that?"

"Why did I put my hand on him?"

Missy nodded.

Evalina went back to her kitchen work. " 'Cause we love each other."

"You're in love?"

Evalina stopped to stare at Missy for a second, then put both hands on the counter and bowed her head. "Sweet Lord Jesus, jes' send the chariots for me right now 'cause I can't stand no more of this."

"You said you loved him."

Evalina rolled her eyes. "Don't talk foolishness, child—I'm past seventy years old. We ain't *in* love; we love each other—the Bible says for us to love one another."

"That's for Christians, Evalina. He's not a Christian."

The cook put her hands on her hips and dark clouds on her face. "Who says he ain't?"

"He said it himself. I asked him what the most important thing in the world was an' he said it was food."

Evalina shook her head. "My, my, my."

"What's the matter?"

"When did you ask him 'bout all this important stuff, child?"

Missy remembered the exact moment. "We were standin' in this kitchen after the thing with Hull."

Evalina thought about that. "Did he ever see you in the light before that?"

What difference could that make? "No."

"Was you close to him?"

"I guess so." *I was a foot away.* "Maybe."

The clouds cleared on Evalina's face. "Missy, baby, you ain't never cared about it, an' you ain't goin' to now, but you ain't like other womenfolk. You the prettiest white woman in the Delta, an' that probably means the whole world, an' you got somethin' 'bout you . . . somethin' that comes out sometimes when you look at folks. Men who ain't never seen you before have a hard time catchin' up with what they seein', an' it takes 'em awhile to make their brains work it all out. You take all that an' hook it to them blue eyes, an' it's a credit to that boy that he could look you in the face an' still make his mouth say any words at all."

"An' he's a Christian?"

"Only him an' God can know for sure, baby, but if he ain't, he don't know it."

Missy looked at the back door. "Where'd he go?"

"Just now? I 'spect he went to the house. That's what he said."

"What house?"

Evalina pointed at the kitchen window. "Mose is lettin' him stay over there at their old house on the lake."

Missy was at the door when Evalina called her back.

"What?"

"Child, when menfolks look you in the eyes, they don't do too good. The bes' thing you can do is keep yo' eyes to yo'self."

Her instincts had guided Missy to protect men from her powers since she was twelve years old; she knew Evalina was right.

She said, "Great. Maybe I can get a job as a witch doctor."

Her angel watched the girl hurry to the car and said, *Here am I, my leader.*

You are chosen to be the instrument of our Lord's strong protection.

Yes, leader. What would be the measure of my intervention?

See that her life is spared, so that she may stand and speak.

Would He have her know of His protection?

He would.

And what of the man, leader?

The leader smiled because he had been told of the man's destiny. *Send me his guardian.*

Missy was halfway across the bridge when she realized she had no plans for what she would say. *Lord, You must think I'm a complete idiot, an' I'm sure he does. I don't want to marry the man, but I would like for him to know I'll be his friend. Would You fix it so I don't make all this worse when I talk to him?*

The rockers were back on the porch, with a cat in each one. Missy parked under the pecan trees and pushed the car door open. David Patterson was leaning on an old push mower, watching her; one of the cats shifted to a more comfortable position.

The smell of cut grass drifted on the breeze, and Pip's few bushes were trimmed. When Missy put her foot on last fall's leaves, the sensation told her she left her shoes on the other side of the lake. "Hi."

"Hi." He left the mower. "Your tennis date stand you up?"

His smile was polite, but that was all. He was probably wondering if she was going to start calling on him twice a day to kick him in the knee. *Where do I start, Lord? I'm over here talkin' to him, an' I haven't thought of what to say. Why didn't You break my car so I wouldn't get here so fast?*

She took the only reasonable option that offered itself—she pointed at the little gravestones and lied, "I thought I'd come over an' check on our little cemetery."

"Mmm." He ignored the graves and concentrated on the downcast blue eyes. His smile started slowly and spread. "I'd wager that you don't lie very often."

She could look back now and recall that he never talked like a country boy. "Guilty." She grimaced. "I guess maybe I'm . . . sort of . . . not very good at it."

He enjoyed her discomfort. "If you were a spy, you'd be standing in front of some impatient guys with rifles, smoking your last cigarette." He pointed at the rockers. "Come have a seat in my confession booth, and let's talk about it."

She moved a cat and sat down. Tranquillity came to her at the remembered peace of her childhood. "I have some special memories of bein' out here on this porch."

"With Pip?"

She closed her eyes and let her head rest against the back of the chair. She could remember the smell of the lake and the smoke of yesteryear's fires. "Mmm. Pip an' Mose an' Junior an' Bobby." She hooked her feet on the rung of the chair and withdrew into a quieter place.

He watched her while she remembered.

When she opened her eyes, he was looking at her. She blushed and directed his attention away from her face. "I forgot my shoes again."

"Mmm." That face was something a man would write home about. He already had.

"How long have you been livin' here?"

"Mose let me move in when I went to work at the gin."

"Gosh, I can't help but envy you." The afternoon sun came in ripples from the surface of the lake; a mockingbird cocked his head at them from a lower tree limb. "I wonder if this is the most peaceful place on earth."

She had never impressed him as a person who was interested in peace. "Could be."

"The inside always smelled like wood smoke."

"It still does." He'd never seen this measure of serenity in her, and he wanted to help prolong it. "C'mon, I'll give you a tour."

"I'd like that." She put the cat back in the chair when she stood.

When they got inside, she laughed. "What a mess! Pip would have a fit if she saw this place."

The bed was made and the kitchen was ordered, but writing materials were piled everywhere. A portable typewriter on the dining table was trapped in the center of a stationary whirlpool of books and notebooks, loose pieces of paper, and pencils. Most of the books that hemmed in the typewriter were large and had the word *theology* in their titles. Her fingers traced over several of the books, and she hefted the nearest one.

"Eschatology." The reality of the present was eroding the tranquility left by her daydreams. "What in the dickens is eschatology?"

"The study of last or final things."

She could feel herself coming awake in the middle of a fast-moving nightmare. The frown spread to her words, and she gave him an order. "Tell me that you are *not* a preacher."

"Okay." He snuffled into his hand and fought the smile. "I start my final year of seminary this fall, so officially I'm not a preacher."

"Officially." She strode to the window, stayed two seconds, and stomped back. "That's just peachy. You're almost a preacher, an' I only need two more semesters of college to *officially* qualify me to be a village idiot." She picked up the three-pound version of *Things to Come: A Study in Biblical Eschatology* by J. Dwight Pentecost, Th.M., Th.D., and the room shook when she slammed it onto the table.

Patterson employed a fake senatorial tone. "Well, I'm confident that in your case most upper-echelon institutions would be glad to waive the postgrad requirements based on your past history of—"

"You stop that!" This whole thing was this smart aleck's fault. The fingernail full of accusation she put against his chest was small and cute but devoid of any known properties of peace—or nail polish, for that matter. Her recent quest for tranquillity was suspended. "You didn't tell me you were a preacher."

His smirk told her he was having too much fun. "And I would've conveyed this information to you during which of our extended conversations?"

She snatched the fingernail back and made another round trip to the window. When she got back to the table, he made a show of putting a protective hand over the typewriter.

She gave up and sat down at the table. "If God killed Christians for bein' stupid, I'd be in real danger."

He took the chair across from her and shook his head. "Oh, I emphatically disagree."

"Thanks for that much."

"Mmm. I think you'd be safely in heaven."

She left the cane-bottom launching pad and landed next to the table with both fists clenched at her sides. "He's right, God!" she yelled. "You're still lettin' me be impatient *an'* stupid!" As soon as the words were out of her mouth, she crossed her fists on her chest and replaced the anger with shock. "Is that blasphemy?"

He was bent over, laughing and holding onto the table with one hand while he motioned with the other for her to wait.

She plopped all 102 pounds back in the chair and watched his shoulders shake. "This is *not* funny."

He dried his eyes on his shirt sleeves. "And I'm not laughing."

She pulled the eschatology book close with both hands, and he moved back to distance himself.

She giggled. "I'm recovered . . . I think. Why would someone study about prophecy?"

"Well, if you're asking a serious question, I think an understanding of prophecy increases our sense of urgency. If you're still dodging the issue you came to discuss, the answer's the same. There're some real bright men out there who think we don't have much time left."

"For tellin' people about Jesus?"

"Or anything else. The necessary ingredients are in place for the end times."

"The end times?"

He tapped the eschatology book. "The Rapture, the Tribulation, the Antichrist, Christ's return."

Her brow wrinkled. "I don't know too much about those things."

"It's important stuff. You can take that book with you. If you read it, you'll know more than nine out of ten preachers know."

"Thanks." She propped her elbows on the volume and pointed at the partially completed page in the typewriter. "You're writin' a paper?"

"A letter to my brother. That's the first draft."

"You write a first draft of a personal letter?"

"Yeah. I have to get things off my chest first, then I'll rewrite it so that I don't sound too pushy."

"So, he's not a Christian?"

"Not yet. My sister's a believer." He touched the typewriter with a knuckle. "Pat's a doctoral student in philosophy— too smart for his own good. He and I keep a debate-type dialogue going via the mail, and this is my latest installment."

"What about your parents?"

"Mom and Dad were killed in a car wreck two years ago. They were good people."

"Were they Christians?"

"Mom was. I'm not sure about Dad."

"Mmm. Ex-wives?"

"Nope." He could show a wicked grin when he chose to. "Or girlfriends."

"I didn't ask." Her face could turn red in a single heartbeat.

He had let her stall long enough. "Okay, tell me why you're over here."

Missy pushed the eschatology text into the center of the table. Ex-wives and girlfriends were forgotten. "I didn't know you were a Christian."

"You mean all this is about me being a Christian?"

She took a deep breath. "I was a pill because I didn't want to date you because I wasn't interested in goin' out with a non-Christian. I came to apologize . . . or somethin'."

With one click, all the little puzzle pieces snapped into place. He was on his feet. "So, does this mean we can ride over to the Dairy Freeze tonight and get a hamburger?"

She said, "Don't you have any questions or anything? Aren't you interested in how I got myself in such a mess?"

He hooked a thumb in his belt and drawled, "Lady, I've got a feelin' that this here ain't yore first rodeo."

He had her pegged. "Well, don't you at least want to listen to what I believe?"

"Sure, but can't we swap life histories over a hamburger?"

"Okay, okay, okay." She stood. "First, I have to go get my shoes." She walked to the door while he went toward the kitchen. "Pick me up at my house."

"I'll be right behind you."

The late afternoon sun flickered at her off the silver-bronze surface of the lake, causing her to squint at the silhouette standing on the top step. The sweet smell of new-mown grass had given way to something rancid.

Hull Dillworth was back.

CHAPTER EIGHTEEN

Well, if it's not Miss Missy Parker." The words emerged from a foul tangle of hair and whiskers. Weeks of accumulated filth covered the remnants of the clothes he'd been wearing the night he attacked her.

Missy looked past him. Her purse and its contents were strewn on the ground by the car.

"Don't tell me you're thinking about this." He brought her handgun from behind his back and stepped closer. "Now, you wouldn't want to use this on a friend, would you?" He cackled, and rotten gaps showed where most of his front teeth had been. The smell of him made her gag.

"Don't like the way I smell? I like that, Missy-prissy. I wanted to be good and ripe for our last meeting. You may not live much longer, but I've cherished the thought of how much you're going to hate the closing minutes of your life."

She got her voice back. "You're crazy, Hull."

"No, he isn't." Patterson was standing in the door behind her. "He's possessed."

"Well, well, well. Just what I've been waiting for . . . a reunion of the Cat Lake Class of '58. You can try to be a hero, big man, or you can live and watch what I do to her." The malignant evil in Dillworth's voice clashed with the haunted expression in his eyes. "When I finish with her, I'll give you something to remember me by." He held up a disfigured hand, its fingers curled like cruel talons. "Something like one of these."

Patterson knew from where their only help would come. He said, "Demon, I order you in the strong name of the Lord Jesus Christ to come out of this man."

The mouth cackled again, and a different voice hissed, "The Enemy's Word says our kind only come out with prayer and fasting, preacher boy. We're too strong for your weak words."

Patterson put his hands on Missy's shoulders. "The Lord Jesus names Himself as our powerful protector, demon. I speak my words in the strength of His name and order you to come out of this man."

"Not while we need him." The thing that had been Dillworth pointed the gun at the center of Missy's chest. "We have plans for this one—alive or dead. The snakes did not kill her, but this time the world will come to know what we did to her because we will leave you alive to tell them."

Patterson moved to get closer to Missy, and the demon said, "Stand still, fool. You cannot protect her from us."

The girl took a half step forward. "You'll have to kill me before I—"

Patterson made a grab for her arm and missed. "Missy, don't provoke—"

The only warning she got was the fleeting impression of a grimy finger tightening on the gun's trigger. She was conscious of the sting of the powder from the blast even as the force of the bullet lifted her from the threshold and catapulted her body into Patterson. He caught her full weight in his arms—sagging and twisting with the impact—fought to keep his feet, and managed to guide her fall to the floor. The gun boomed again, and the second bullet went over his head and broke something in the kitchen.

Missy's world tilted and turned red, then dark. She felt herself doing slow-motion cartwheels into a deep void. . . .

Then she felt nothing.

Patterson released Missy and turned back to the threat.

The demon moved through the doorway as calmly as an under-taker and pointed the gun at the girl. Patterson came out of his crouch and took two long steps, hurling himself into the line of fire. Man and beast crashed into the wall by the door, taking a stack of books and papers with them. The demon threw the bigger man back, turned the pistol on him, and pulled the trig-ger. Patterson was moving toward the gun when it went off—he took the bullet high in his chest. He got one hand on the gun and seized Dillworth's neck with the other. He body-slammed the demon into the wall and tried to wrestle the gun from him. Instead of trying to escape, the demon attacked him.

Patterson was six inches taller and seventy pounds heavier than Dillworth, but he was no match for the forces that inhab-ited the smaller body. Shrill, screeching sounds came from its mouth while it jerked itself from side to side, kicking Patter-son's legs and body with both feet, poking at his eyes with its free hand, and trying to bite him in the face.

The big man slid the demon along the wall, got it to the door, and pinned the gun hand while he shoved the rest of its body outside. When the demon went through the opening, Pat-terson slammed the door and trapped the arm with the gun.

Patterson put his full weight against the door and the demon's screeching turned into the laughter of something de-praved. A door panel cracked under a blow, then splintered, and the thing's deformed arm forced its way through the hole. The crippled claw grabbed at Patterson while he fought the arm holding the pistol. He managed to wrestle the gun from the beast, pointed it along the trapped arm, and pulled the trigger. The demon emitted another screaming laugh and left flesh on the edges of the splintered panel when it jerked its claw back. In the following instant, pieces of wood exploded into the room and the beast rammed its head through the splintered hole. Pat-terson abandoned the skirmish with the pinned arm, put his weight on the thing's head to wedge it in the hole, and shot it in the temple.

Sinister utterances and overlapping screams—a cacophony of unholy sounds—erupted from the pinned beast's mouth;

they were accompanied by impossible gyrations that threatened to tear the door from its hinges.

Patterson remembered the stories of the war at the lake and knew what had to be done. He pulled down hard on a handful of the creature's hair, jammed the muzzle of the gun against the base of Dillworth's skull, and started back on the trigger; he had to sever the captured man's spine. The beast surged against the door. Its head came up and lifted Patterson off the floor, and it jerked back through the hole.

When the beast came against the door again, David knew he wasn't going to be able to kill it. Dirty fabric showed where the beast was pressed against the door. David gasped, "Only You can save us, Lord," and shot twice into the thing's body.

The cloth disappeared, and a thousand screams hurled themselves against the door. The screams were drowned out by a harsh boom that could only come from a shotgun. The shrieks redirected themselves toward something outside, and two more explosions from the shotgun brought a silence that made the world around the cabin seem suddenly empty.

Patterson's knees started to give, and he slid down the wall. Until now, he hadn't had time to care that he'd been shot. He looked at his chest, and mild shock set in when he saw the blood. He kept an eye on the door while he crawled to Missy.

"Missy?" He used her shoulder to roll her over.

She had blood coming from the side of her mouth and from one nostril. Her eyes were closed, but her chest rose and fell, and he couldn't see any blood on the front of her shirt. When he felt for her pulse, her eyes fluttered.

"Missy? Can you hear me?"

Her eyes came full open, widened, and she tried to pull away.

"Missy, it's me. You need to be still; you've been shot."

She remembered and her eyes followed her hand to her chest. She put tentative fingertips near her heart and winced when she put pressure there. "He hit me in the chest," she croaked.

Patterson leaned close to look; her shirt wasn't even wrinkled. Patterson said, "You aren't bleeding."

She looked at her clean fingertips and pressed them against the fabric again.

There was a noise behind him, and David turned in time to see the door start to move. He leaned across to protect her and leveled the gun at the opening door as Bobby Lee stepped inside. "Easy, boy. Easy now."

Patterson lowered the gun. "Hurry. She's been shot."

Mose came into the room carrying a shotgun. "By that white boy?"

Patterson pointed at the door opening. "Yeah. He shot her."

Bobby Lee started praying silently as he knelt by the wide-eyed girl. "Missy? Can you tell me where you're hit, baby?"

She rested her fingertips on the tender spot in the center of her chest and moaned when she tried to raise her head. "He . . . shot me."

Bobby Lee put a trembling hand on her forehead. The blood from her nose and mouth could mean she was bleeding internally. "Just lie back, baby. Where did he shoot you? Show me where."

"Right here." She stirred the fingers in a small circle over the spot. "It hurts."

Bobby Lee leaned closer, his eyes darting back and forth across the front of her shirt. "There's not even a hole in the shirt—there's no blood." He looked at Patterson. "What happened?"

Patterson was pale. "Not sure. The gun wasn't two feet away when he shot—it knocked her into me. She was shot."

"Well, she ain't now. Can you explain that?"

"Maybe . . . after I finish a semester in angelology, maybe later."

Bobby Lee lifted her hand to look at her chest. "Well, heaven will have to be where the answer comes from, 'cause the bullet didn't hit her."

"Good, 'cause we don't need but one casualty at a time, an' I got a hole in me big enough for both of us."

Bobby Lee noticed the spreading stain on the boy's chest for the first time. "You just hang on, son. We'll have y'all at the Greenwood hospital in twenty minutes."

Mose went to get the car.

It was after midnight when the doctor came out to the waiting room. He pulled his scrub hat off and dropped into a chair to massage his scalp. "Well, it turns out your boy's big and tough and lucky. Where's Susan?"

Bobby Lee said, "In Missy's room—probably on her knees. David's gonna be okay?"

"He'll be out of here in less than a week. The bullet glanced off a rib and went across his chest without ever getting close to anything vital. Didn't even crack the rib. He's gonna be sore as the dickens, but the bullet should've gone through his heart." He propped his feet on another chair and dug out a cigarette. "What's the latest on Missy?"

"She's tryin' to sleep." Bobby Lee started pacing. "I'd appreciate it if you'd look at her. She's not scratched, but Frank said the X-rays showed three cracked ribs, an' her chest is sore." He stopped to look out the window. "He . . . that thing shot her point blank an' knocked her off her feet, an' all she got was some bad ribs, a bloody nose, an' a busted lip."

"I'll look in on her before I go home." He concentrated on flicking his ashes into an empty coffee cup. "Frank told me Hull Dillworth's body is downstairs in the morgue."

Bobby Lee stayed at the window.

The doctor said, "Frank said he was a mess—smelled like he'd been dead a week."

Bobby Lee said, "He's probably been decayin' for years. I made a mistake when I didn't kill that snake last month."

Dr. C. J. "Sandy" Fancher had two daughters at home. "When he comes to, you tell your Texas boy this hospital trip is on the house." He took a last pull on his cigarette and snuffed it out. "Let's go take a look at Missy."

Bobby Lee waited in the hall while the doctor examined Missy. When he came out, Susan Parker came with him.

"Momma?" the girl was whispering.

Susan stepped back. "Yes, Missy?"

"Stand where I can see you."

Susan moved back into the room, and two men stepped close to her before the doctor spoke. "Well, her chest looks like she got kicked by a mule, but she didn't get shot."

Susan took Bobby Lee's hand. "What do you think happened to her, Sandy?"

"Only God knows. The evidence of blunt-force trauma is obvious." The doctor looked at the floor and rubbed the back of his neck. "I've been a surgeon for sixteen years, and there's no way a thinking man can do this job and not believe in God." He looked at the couple and shrugged. "If we have our facts straight, she was shot with a .38 from a distance of two feet. Day after tomorrow she'll have a bruise from her chin to her navel, and her ribs will be so sore she'll cry if she sneezes, but that's all. In six weeks, this'll be nothing but a bad memory."

Susan said, "What about David?"

"Barely worse, considering. They can go dancing as soon as they feel feisty enough."

The doctor went home to sleep; Bobby Lee and Susan went into Missy's room to thank God for the lives of their daughter and David Patterson.

Missy woke at noon on Sunday. When she saw what the hospital was offering for lunch, she said, "I'd rather hurt in my own bed an' eat Evalina's leftovers while I do it."

Her mother helped her drape a dress over her head, then left to check her out of the hospital and bring the car to the door. Missy stood by the bed to wait.

The orderly who brought the wheelchair for her was a gray-haired black gentleman.

"No, thanks," she said. "I'll walk."

His smile was as gentle as he was. "Sorry, miss. Hospital rules. I gotta take you all the way to the front door."

"I cracked some ribs. It'll hurt me to get in an' out of the chair."

The smile waned. "I'm powerful sorry, miss. I just does what they tells me."

"I don't." The dark brows came together. "Do you know who I am?"

The wrinkled old face became expressionless; confrontations with persistent white women were the worst part of his job. "Yes, ma'am." He pulled a piece of paper out of his shirt pocket. "You be Miss Amanda Allen Parker."

"No, sir." She made the mistake of shaking her head, and winced. "I'm Missy Parker, from Moores Point."

"You don't say." He squinted slightly and gave her a careful inspection. "From out at Cat Lake?"

She nodded, more slowly this time. "That's me. I'm Mose Washington's almost-daughter."

It has to be her, he thought. *Not hardly tall as a jelly glass, no-nonsense eyes that couldn't get no bluer, an' cantankerous as a dry wind.*

The old man stood straighter, and the smile was back. "They ain't a Christian black man in the Delta don't know 'bout you, honey. I'd be much obliged if you'd let me walk along with you to yo' car."

"First, I need to go see the man who came in with me."

"You be with Red Justin now, baby. You can go anywheres you please."

"Will you get in trouble?"

"Don't you worry none 'bout that, now. I reckon God calls the righteous to watch out for them what He holds close to Hisself—for His chosen." He almost bowed. "You'd be one of those, an' I'd be the one what watches out for you."

"His chosen?"

"Oh yes, baby, oh yes. The good Lord knows He done already saved you from the demons twicet—He done chose you for somethin' *special*."

Red walked her to Patterson's room. The hero was conscious, but just barely.

"David?"

When he saw her, he grinned for several seconds before he said, "She just gave me a shot."

She grinned back. "An' you're swacked."

"I feel great."

"I'll be here tomorrow to check on you an' bring you some real food."

"How long has it been since I ate?"

She looked at his empty lunch tray. "Fifteen minutes."

He mumbled, "Miz Parker's rolls," and closed his eyes.

Susan Parker didn't like it, and Evalina pouted, but nobody bothered to waste any breath trying to get Missy to stay home the next day. Mose drove the car, and she guarded a basket carrying a dozen rolls, one fried chicken, sliced ham, and a dozen stuffed eggs. The jars wedged in the back seat carried two gallons of sweet tea. On the seat by the tea was a three-layer chocolate cake. Mose drove carefully, but every joint in the pavement was like a hammer blow to her chest. When they got to the hospital, sweat was running in lines from her temples, and her blouse was damp.

She felt lightheaded when she stepped out of the car, but wouldn't admit it. Mose ignored her protests and stayed at her elbow until they reached David's room. They found him with Red Justin, discussing the theology of the end times.

Mose and Red went to get the food, and Missy took Red's place at the foot of the bed. "Well, I hope you're hungry, 'cause Granny an' Evalina sent everything but the deed to the kitchen."

"Did you think to bring my Bible?"

"It's in the car. Mose thought he had to escort me up here first."

"You look pale."

"I can't imagine why."

He looked sick but was in good spirits. He said, "And you're sweating."

"I take it that's a special compliment for your girls back in West Texas?"

"Sorry. You're perspiring."

"Girls in the South don't perspire—we glow."

"You're glowing through your shirt."

"I've been slavin' in the kitchen."

"Uh-huh. Tell that to someone who didn't get shot in the chest the same day you did."

She didn't bother to smile. "Hurts, doesn't it?"

"Only when I laugh." It was an old joke, and neither of them did. "Your mom ought to shoot you again for being out of bed."

"I haven't thanked you for savin' my life."

"Mmm. Have you figured out why the bullet didn't hit you?"

Her eyes went to a spot over his head. "Oh, it hit me all right. I felt it."

"Then why are you up walking around?"

"Like Daddy says, we probably won't know 'til we get to heaven, but I think an angel stepped in."

"You could be right."

"You sound like you're doubtin' again."

"Not a chance. I know God can do whatever He wants; I've just never seen an angel intervene. It's a new thing."

"Folks still call what happened back in '45 the 'War at Cat Lake,' so that makes me a veteran. I've never seen an angel either, but I've seen spiritual warfare up close, an' so have you."

"Red says that Cat Lake thing happened because you're a special person."

"Red's makin' a fuss over somethin' that happened fifteen years ago."

"Mm-hmm. To hear Red tell it, it happened again Saturday."

"It does look like it, doesn't it?" It didn't make sense. "Why would God do that? Why didn't He just give Hull a heart attack or somethin'?"

"Well, last time you took a new direction in life," David said. "But there's not much of a parallel here, except for it happening at the lake and you getting off pretty much unscathed. You didn't walk away with a new mission in life, and I'm not dead."

"Red was pretty good at givin' you the details."

He nodded. "And I've been prying information out of Mose for a month. What now?"

"Have you told your brother an' sister?"

"Called 'em this morning. My sister took it pretty well; Pat's coming in on the bus tomorrow. Says he's never known anyone who's been shot and wants my autograph."

"He sounds like you."

"Mmm. He's quicker academically—" He grinned. "—but not as tall, charming, or good-looking."

"I can't wait."

"Yeah." His mind was busy. "Say, how about we make a little pact?"

"About what?"

"Pat's more likely to listen to you or Mose than to me because guys don't listen to their younger brothers, especially if they think the kid brother's chasing a fairy tale. You or Mose, or both, tell him about Christ, and I'll do the same for someone you love."

She took her time considering. "I don't have anyone close to me that's not a believer."

"You can have a rain check . . . anyone you choose . . . even swap."

She was thinking about it when Mose and Red came into the room with the food. She said, "Mose, David has a deal for us."

"You don't say."

David outlined his proposition, and Mose said, "I can't be promisin' a man to do somethin' I don't have no control over. Sometimes a man don't want to hear 'bout Jesus, an' when that happens, we have to go on to the next man."

Mose had said it well, and Missy nodded her agreement.

David said, "You're right. I guess I get a little carried away where Pat's concerned."

Mose continued. "I won't make no agreement, but if he'll listen, I'll tell 'im."

David said, "Missy?"

"Sure. No contract, but I'll share with him for as long as he'll listen." She gave second thoughts to the commitment. "Is he real smart?"

"Too smart."

"Smart people are hard to talk to."

Red had been quiet. "He ain't smart as the Lord, Miss."

"Good point." David was uncovering the rolls. "Who wants to say the blessing?"

Red saw the chocolate cake. "Is one of these here paper plates mine?"

David smiled. "It is."

The old man said, "Bow y'all's heads, if you would, an' let's us go to the Lord in prayer."

Mose took Missy back to the hospital the next day with another load of food and was reenacting his role as her unwanted escort when they crossed the lobby. She was facing the mirrored wall by the elevators and blotting her face with a damp handkerchief when an image caught her eye; she couldn't believe who was walking up behind her.

She frowned at the reflection and continued patting her cheeks. "Do you mind tellin' me what in the dickens you think you're doin'?"

He was directly behind her shoulder now, and she could see his eyes but not the smile; he looked shorter in the mirror.

He said, "How are you?"

She stopped what she was doing and looked directly at the reflection. "Personally, I think we both ought to be in bed."

The effect of her eyes took his brain into the third stage of anesthesia. "Sweetie, if that's an invitation, you just find us an empty room in this place, and you and I will be fixed up."

She turned too fast, and the pain made her blanch. She looked up; the mouth was the same, but the smile was cocky. She forced a hiss between her teeth. "You aren't David."

He thought, *Oh great. Tell me I didn't just say that to a perfect stranger who, besides being perfect, is my brother's friend.*

Instead of apologizing immediately, he opted for trying to be glib. "No, ma'am. I'm Pat, the evil older brother." He offered his most gracious smile in hopes that it would cover up his stupid remark.

The abrupt onset of pain, coupled with his fresh attitude,

fired her anger; the perspiration became a deluge. "I can only assume you're tellin' the truth about bein' evil. Feel free to add *rude* an' *uncouth* to that list an' use me for a reference."

"I really apologize." He'd made a big mistake, and this girl was as tough as David said she was. "My mouth gets a little ahead of my brain occasionally. You must be Missy Parker." He moved to extend his hand toward her, a gentle gesture of conciliation.

The hand that caught his wrist was quick, hard, and black, as were the eyes of the man it belonged to. The man's quiet voice was more arresting than any hand. "Don't be touchin' her, white folks."

The girl turned her back, leaving him to deal with Mose.

Patterson turned out to be as smart as the girl was tough. Instead of trying to pull his hand out of Mose's grip, he relaxed and transformed himself into an impeccable gentleman. "I have to apologize again. I was out of line, and I'll keep my hands to myself."

Mose helped him step back from the girl and released his wrist.

When the three walked into David's room, Pat held his hand out and started toward his brother.

David said, "Don't touch me, you idiot, and don't make me laugh."

Pat froze and his mouth fell open. He looked at his brother and the light dawned. He turned to Missy and noticed the damp sheen on her face. She had a dark blue smudge showing where the blouse met her throat. He said, "I'm really not an idiot, honestly. I just forgot about how sore you must be. I apologize."

Missy didn't respond.

David struggled to sit up, and the effort turned him the color of the bed sheets. "You hurt her?"

"No, thank goodness." He pointed at Mose. "This gentleman rescued me from that blunder."

"If you haven't met, this gentleman is Mose Washington." David moved only one finger to point at Missy. "He's next to being her father, and he's my boss. Mose, this is my brother, Pat."

Mose nodded, and Pat stayed where he was. David said, "Missy, this is Pat. Pat, this is Missy Parker."

The stark white walls of the room were more important to Missy than the introductions.

Pat said, "We've met."

"Really?" David's chest was too sore to allow him to fully express his impatience. "Then that might explain how my friends managed to form some impression of you."

His brother was getting tired of being the villain. "Possibly."

David looked at Mose and Missy. Mose and Missy looked somewhere else.

After a few seconds of silence, Missy said, "C'mon, Mose. We'll find Red an' see if he likes pecan pie."

As soon as they were out of earshot, David said, "Okay, genius, how bad was it?"

"What makes you think it was that bad?"

"Because both of 'em like me, and both of 'em would spot you for my brother a mile off, and under normal circumstances they'd accept you and like you. But if you were on fire right now, neither one of 'em would walk across the street to spit on you. What'd you do?"

Pat told him what happened in the lobby. He colored it in his favor as much as he could, but the biased edition still sounded crude.

"You said you wanted to go to bed with her?" David's voice forgot it was in a hospital zone. "Good gosh, Pat!"

"I told you it was temporary insanity." He thought, *Only a blind man could survive a first-time encounter with her and maintain his ability to reason.* "What'd *you* do the first time she looked at you?"

"Oh." David remembered he'd gone temporarily braindead. "Well, I'll tell you something, bro, it's not just the eyes; it's the whole person. It's like she has some kind of spell over everybody she meets—in that little town *and* out at the lake. That old man just got out of prison for killing a man—if you had touched that girl he'd probably be on his way back up there tomorrow. The people in that town over there—Moores Point—

and the people out there at Cat Lake are different from anything you ever saw or heard about, and that girl is second only to God Himself in their estimation."

"So?"

"*So*, Dr. Brainboy, you need to act like all that tuition money you're spending is helping to make you smarter. *So*, if she doesn't like you, the whole countryside will hate your guts, and it'll spill over onto me. *So*, you need to go make things right with her and Mose."

"Forget it, Davey. That's all water under the bridge now."

"Hey, man, you're my brother, and I love you, but you're not listening. You make friends with her in the next few minutes, or, as they say in the movies, you get out of town before sundown and take your sorry reputation with you. And you need to get it done before anyone else finds out what you pulled downstairs."

"She acts like she might be stubborn."

David knew he'd won, and his smile was wicked. "That's just a pretense. Behind that façade lurks a heart as soft as aged oak."

"Humphf."

"One piece of advice."

It didn't take Pat Patterson long to get tired of advice. "You should learn how to do something besides give advice, preacher."

"My preacher days are over."

Pat was sidetracked for the moment. "Are you kidding me?"

"Folks don't want a preacher who's killed a man."

Pat said, "David, don't turn loose of being a preacher 'til you've had a chance to think it over."

David grinned. "Thanks for the spiritual guidance. We can talk about it after you set things right with Mose and Missy."

Pat didn't like being coerced. "Okay, okay. You got any more advice, little brother?"

"Win Mose first; he's more forgiving."

"I thought all Christians were supposed to be forgiving."

"Save your debating skills for the girl, big boy—you're gonna need 'em. Go see Mose."

The unwilling diplomat stuffed his hands in his pockets and walked over to glare up and down the hall. "Which way would they go?"

David was tired, and his chest was hurting. "Buy a map."

David was right; Mose was the forgiving type.

When they finished talking, Pat thanked him for understanding and said, "Well, I guess I'll go see if I can find Missy."

Mose knew what the boy could expect from his next audience. "If don't nothin' else work, ask her how much is seventy times seven."

"Seven times seventy?"

Mose smiled and shook his head. "You got to say it right. Seventy times seven."

"Seventy times seven."

"That's it."

"What is it, a code or something?"

Mose nodded wisely and smiled. "You just ask her."

Pat did the math in his head and came up with 490. He walked the corridors of the hospital thinking about the answer. *Four-nine-oh . . . forty-nine oh . . . four-ninety. It has to be some kind of secret Mississippi code.*

Pat eventually found her in the hospital kitchen, talking with a pair of black cooks and a black man she called Red. When she saw him, her face darkened.

"Excuse me, Missy . . . uh, Miss Parker."

She didn't care what he called her. "What?"

"Could I talk to you for a moment?"

"You *are* talkin'."

"Could we talk in private?"

The cooks forgot their preparations and drew closer to the conversation.

She said, "Go ahead an' say what you've got to say."

Aged oak is a lot softer than any part of this woman. "My brother tells me I've got to get things ironed out between the two of us or go back to Texas. Do you think you could forgive me for making that stupid remark?"

"I forgive you."

He could see it wasn't going to work. "I hate to sound picky, but you don't look like you forgive me."

"Forgiveness doesn't have a facial expression. I look like this 'cause I don't like you."

He pulled out David's car keys and toyed with them. He said the next words because he was obligated. "Look, what I said was really stupid, and I'm sorry. Do you think we could just start over—like we were meeting for the first time?"

"People never start over."

One of the cooks stage-whispered, "Watch out, now."

Missy spoke without looking over her shoulder, "You stay out of this, Sis."

Pat said, "I'm kind of at your mercy here."

"I'm not the merciful type."

Pat looked at her while he ran the edge of a key back and forth over his lower lip. "I'm beginning to see that."

She didn't respond.

He caught the girl's act and concluded two things: The people in Moores Point needed to be more careful about picking their goddesses, *and* if David wanted to visit with him, he could load his bullet-riddled carcass into an ambulance and haul it to Texas.

Well, it's not like I didn't try. He tossed the keys in the air and caught them. "Adios, Miss Christian."

He had his hand on the bar that opened the door when he remembered. He turned to her and said, "Tell me, how much is seventy times seven?"

Their reaction looked rehearsed. All four people in the kitchen stared at him first, then the three black people turned in unison to stare at Missy.

The cook who had whispered at her earlier said, "Oh yes, baby, he done asked the right question now."

Missy's face turned crimson from her collar to her hairline; she took her surprise out on the cook. "I told you to stay out of this."

It was the most fun the cook had had in a month. "I don't reckon, not while you lookin' at the boss of this here kitchen."

Both cooks were grinning at her; Red turned his back and covered his mouth.

It *was* a code.

Missy walked to Pat and said, "Push that door open an' let me out. We can't have any privacy in here."

When they reached the hall, they could hear Red and the cooks laughing. Pat looked at the girl, and her smile emptied his lungs. He resolved to keep his mouth shut for a full minute. If he tried to talk now, he might ask her to marry him.

Sixty seconds later he was breathing almost normally and said, "Okay, I give up. I ask you a math problem, and you decide to change your mind? What kind of language is that?"

She was nibbling on the corner of her mouth and thinking. "Mose told you to ask me that, didn't he?"

At first he thought he could take the credit. "I just—" He took a quick look at her eyes and in that moment resolved that he would never again try lying to her. "Yes, he did, but I don't know what it means."

"It means a lot of things. One, you got Mose on your side; that counts the most. Two, we can start over from scratch. An' three, if you're gonna be a doctoral candidate in philosophy, you're gonna have to start readin' your Bible."

"I don't have a Bible."

"An' four, if you're goin' to be a philosopher, you're gonna have to get a Bible."

Pat and Missy were smiling when they walked into the hospital room. David wasn't.

Sandy Fancher had cut David's bandages off and was pressing his stethoscope to the patient's chest. A nurse was poised on the other side of the bed.

Missy went to stand by the nurse. "What's wrong?"

David's color was too gray, and he didn't smile. "My chest . . . hurts."

CHAPTER NINETEEN

Missy looked at Sandy Fancher. "Is he okay?"

"He's going to be fine. I've got an oxygen tent on the way that will give him some relief 'til we find out what's going on."

David's gaze went from Missy to Pat. "How'd it go?"

Missy said, "Mose rescued me—again. We got things straight."

"You forgave him." He calmed. "That's good."

She smiled and patted his hand. "It's not like I had a choice."

Fancher was busy. "Okay, troops, y'all get out and let me get set up in here. You guys can visit later."

Pat came close enough to touch Fancher's arm. "I'm his brother. Is there anything I can do?"

"Everything's being done. He needs rest and quiet for now."

"And he's going to be okay?"

"He's going to be fine. It's safe to assume that the blow to his chest bruised him worse than we thought. Why don't y'all move into the hall and give us room to set up the oxygen tent and hook him up to some EKG leads."

Missy didn't move. "Do we have time to pray before we go?"

"Make it quick."

She took David's hand and bowed her head. Fancher was listening to his patient's chest. "Lord, please heal him. Please keep him well. Lord, I'm scared. Amen." She felt him squeeze her fingers and looked up.

"Thanks for your prayers." He looked more rested.

"Prayer always works." She felt relief. "You look better already."

His smile took too much effort. "I was wrong."

"An' you're willin' to admit it?" The pain in her chest reminded her not to laugh. "What were you wrong about?"

"I was wrong twice. I said you didn't have a new mission in life."

All thoughts of laughter fled when the memory of his words cascaded over her. *You didn't walk away with a new mission in life, and I'm not dead.* Something cold and empty spread itself through the place where her chest pain was. She put her other hand on his and shook her head; her voiced trembled. "No. No. David—"

"You said, 'For as long as he'll listen.'"

"No, David." Her first tears splashed on the bed sheet. "David . . . please . . . you can't!"

"You . . ." His eyes fluttered and closed. ". . . promised."

She could feel the strength leaving his fingers. "David?"

"Okay, y'all. Get out of here and let us work." Fancher straightened and took off the stethoscope. Two nurses were wheeling an oxygen tent into the room when he stopped them and pointed at the one in front. "Push that thing out of the way." Then to the one behind her, "Call down and get me an OR." The snap of his fingers was a whip-crack. "Now."

Missy stood by a window overlooking the parking lot. Pat paced.

She kept hearing David's words. *You didn't walk away with a new mission in life, and I'm not dead.*

Mose came. When he heard about David, he went looking for Red so they could pray. Missy prayed where she was. *God, it scares me for him to be like this. Would You take care of him? Please.*

Bobby Lee, Susan Parker, and Old Mrs. Parker had been in the waiting room an hour by the time Fancher finally got there.

There was never going to be a good way to tell someone what he had to say. "This isn't good news."

Pat stood near Missy. They waited. They knew.

"He's gone." Fancher looked exhausted. "We couldn't save him."

She could still hear his voice: *You didn't walk away with a new mission in life, and I'm not dead.*

Pat walked in a small circle and came back to where he started. "He was okay when I got here."

"No, he wasn't okay." Fancher lowered his body into a chair and dug out his cigarettes. "He was a strong man, but he never had a chance. Apparently the shock of the bullet caused—or aggravated—an aneurysm in his aorta. It ruptured. There was nothing anyone could've done."

You're wrong there, Doc, thought Missy. *Now I've got another mission in life, an' another one of my friends is dead.*

The small crowd was silent. Pat took Missy's place at the window.

Red said, "I think it'd be good if we was to pray."

Everyone in the room looked at Missy, and she nodded. "Would you lead us, Red?"

Fancher stood with them while they bowed their heads and held hands; Pat maintained his vigil over the parking lot. "Lord, You give us the privilege to stand before Yo' throne of grace an' thank You for this here young man an' for his life. I don't know what he done 'fore he come here, but I know what he done last Saturday, an' we're all blessed 'cause You sent him here to save this special girl's life. Lord, You let David come to You today bearin' the scars of the battle with evil, an' I ask that You'd see fit to allow us that same honor. Amen."

On Friday afternoon David had been dead three days. Missy walked into the kitchen and told Evalina, "I'm goin' over to the cabin an' feed the cats."

She had been spending every afternoon at the cabin because the solitude suited her mood, and there wasn't anywhere else she wanted to be. The chance for a special friendship with the easygoing young man was gone now, and their only real conversation had taken place at the cabin. She enjoyed sitting in the rocker now, remembering their brief time together.

Evalina wanted to hold Missy in her arms and comfort her, but the girl was still too tender to touch. Evalina settled for touching her arm. "Don't you be stayin' over there 'til dark, now."

Missy said, "I'll be home for supper." She got to the door and turned. "Evalina, I—"

Evalina was touching her apron to her eyes.

"Are you cryin' about David?"

"Maybe. I guess I don't rightly know."

Missy remembered the cuss word that had earned her a switching from Pip. It came to her mind frequently now, every time she thought about losing her newest friend. It surfaced with every breath when she cried. "I'm tired of cryin'."

"Oh, I know that, honey."

"He was a good boy, wasn't he?"

"Yes, baby, he was fine as he could be."

"Why do my friends always have to die? What's God tryin' to do?"

"Missy, that old man knowed what he was talkin' about."

"What old man?"

"That Red Justin over at Greenwood. Now, he ain't no prophet, baby, but he sees things other folks misses. If he said you was special, then you better be gettin' yo' life ready to be special."

"It doesn't make sense that God would pick one person to be more special than another, Evalina, 'specially me. We're all Christians—all equal."

"Being equal don't mean bein' the same, baby. We all have our special gift; He says so in the Book. That means we all part of the body. We all equal, but we ain't all the same. We each got a special, unique gift."

"I'm just me, Evalina, a twenty-year-old girl from Miss'ippi cotton country who'd rather go barefooted than go to Memphis."

"He don't choose famous city folks every time, child."

"I wonder what Pip would tell me if she was here?"

"Pip would tell you to be listenin', child. You listen an' let God tell you what to do."

"Well, if anybody comes lookin' for me, I'll be over at the cabin, cussin' to myself an' listenin'." She walked out the door with the cuss word making steady rounds in her mind.

She was sharing her lap with one of the cats when David's car rolled to a stop under the trees.

Pat unfolded himself from the old Chevrolet. "Hi. Mose said you'd be over here."

"Hi. Come an' sit."

A south breeze barely kept the surface of the lake alive. Birds came and went in the trees, visiting, building nests, caught up in the excitement of summer's approach.

They rocked for five minutes before he spoke. "I don't know if I've ever been in a place this peaceful. Do you come over just for the quiet?"

She wasn't sure. "I think I come because I can remember better when I sit here."

She watched the sun sparkle on the lake and wished for more peace. Places weren't peaceful, and peace wasn't dictated by events; peace found its origins in an understanding of God. The man who sat by her didn't know God. That meant he didn't know real peace, and she'd promised his brother she'd tell him about Jesus for as long as he would listen. *God, how am I supposed to explain spiritual things to a man who's gettin' a doctor's degree in philosophy? Red would say he's not as smart as You, but what about me? There's so much I don't know. I'm a hotheaded girl who can't do anything but say cuss words in my mind when things don't go the way I think they should. Lord, would You draw me closer to Yourself? Would You remind me why I'm still here an' Junior an' David are gone? Would You make me a woman after Your own heart? An', Lord, would You forgive me for cussin'?*

She looked at the gravestones at the edge of the yard. "We won't ever quit missin' him, will we?"

"I guess not. I still miss my mom and dad."

Her eyes stayed on the little graveyard. "Two of my best friends are buried right out there. I barely got to know David, an' now he's gone, an' I feel lonesome."

"He's gone, Missy. There's nothing we can do but go on with our lives." He wiped his eyes on the backs of his hands.

She moved her fingertips on the cat and watched the lake play with the sunlight. "Do you believe in God, Pat?"

The voice was soft enough, but the tone wasn't. "You mean the God who just let my kid brother die?"

She kept looking at the lake. "David knew God, an' he knew what was happenin', an' he was smilin' just before he died."

"I don't want to fight, Missy."

"Do we have any reason to? I didn't ask the question to make you mad."

"You strike me as the type who might generate a little more heat than light."

"That's not exactly true." She wanted to smile. "I'm afraid I tend to generate a *lot* more heat than light. Why don't we make a swap? You're a philosopher, so you can teach me how to win an argument. An' I can use what you teach me to help you understand how wrong you are about God."

"I'm not wrong, Missy. I've been over all this with David."

"But what about everything the Bible says? Do you just ignore that?"

"Missy, David understood that I don't believe what the Bible says about God. It's an ancient document written by a bunch of men who died two thousand years ago."

"But it's true."

"Nobody can prove that."

"Then can we just talk about what we believe? Just talk?"

"I'd like that, but we'd better hurry. I'm going back to Texas day after tomorrow."

"Oh."

He motioned at the cabin door. "I just came out to pack up

David's stuff, his books and all. When do you go back to school?"

"Sunday, I guess. I can be sore up there just as good as I can here."

"Will you tell me something?"

"If I can."

"What does 'seventy times seven' mean?"

"It means Mose is really smart." She smiled and teared up again. "He was usin' you to remind me that I was supposed to forgive you. It's a long story—in Matthew, I think—where Jesus tells us that we're supposed to forgive a person more times than we could ever keep track of."

"If you did that, people would take advantage of you."

"No, it's not like being a doormat. But we—that means Christians—aren't supposed to build barriers based on things that don't matter in the long run."

"That's being a doormat."

"Pat, I might have to be prompted sometimes—like Mose used you to remind me back at the hospital—but you an' I are havin' this conversation because I chose to forgive you. So, what have I said or done durin' the time you've known me that would lead you to believe that I'm ever goin' to be a willin' doormat?"

It was the first time he'd heard her say his name, and it sounded good. And she looked directly into his eyes the whole time she was talking. He decided that there was no such thing as a doormat made of assertive alligators with midnight-blue eyes.

When he regained part of the muscle control that had been sabotaged by her eye contact, he pointed at the cabin door and slid forward in his chair. "I guess I'll get started."

Mose had sent someone to fix the cabin door and clean up the mess, but Missy wasn't interested in being inside. She said, "I'll stay out here an' wait. I still don't like to move around."

"I won't take long. If nothing's changed, he'll have four boxes of textbooks and a bunch of half-filled notebooks."

She remembered the book. "Can I keep one of the books for awhile? He was goin' to loan me a book on prophecy that he said I needed to read. The title says somethin' about the future."

"Heck, you can have 'em all. I won't be reading them." He stopped with his hand on the door. "Missy, we can talk about God 'til trees quit making oxygen, but the answer's always going to be the same—man has evolved into a being who can find fulfillment *in* himself, *by* himself. Theology books can't change that, and the people who're paying attention—the ones who understand mankind—have already figured that out."

He waited, and when she didn't say anything, he said, "You're not talking."

She kept her eyes on the lake. "I have to stop an' pray 'cause you're smarter than me, an' I want God to help me say the right thing."

"Well, call me if you two come up with anything revolutionary." He went into the cabin.

The sounds that came from inside the old place melded with the creak of her rocker. The mockingbirds fussed at a jay; the jay fussed louder.

Missy pushed the rocker gently with her toes and prayed, *Lord, if I'm gonna be able to talk to him I need to know more, an' I need to know it sooner. Would You teach me how to talk to all those people who are too smart for their own good?* She continued to watch the lake without seeing it. *Would You help him stop an' consider You? Would You give me some words to make him see the truth? An' would You make him be a little nicer?* She closed her eyes. *An' would You forgive me for thinkin' cuss words?*

Missy and the cat were dozing when the sounds inside the cabin ceased; she woke up ten minutes later when Pat came onto the porch. She didn't bother to open her eyes. "Finished already?" When he didn't answer, she looked up.

He stood just outside the door, looking at nothing—a book in one hand, a piece of typing paper in the other.

"Pat?"

He moved to the other rocker and sat down. "He was writing me a letter."

She remembered the letter and chastised herself for not thinking to destroy it. "That's right. He told me that it was the first draft, but he needed to tone it down a little so you wouldn't get your feelin's hurt. Okay? He knew it was too . . . hard."

He gazed at the sheet for awhile, then out across the lake at the sky. "It's fine."

The book on his lap looked familiar. "You found the book?"

"Mmm. In there on the table." He put it by his chair.

Her watch told her he'd been packing for thirty minutes. "Did you finish?"

The sky kept his attention. "Finish?"

"Did you get everything packed?"

"Some, I guess."

He obviously didn't want to talk, and she preferred the silence. She helped him watch the clouds while the cat slept.

The breeze turned from the lake, and the new leaves hissed against each other, sounding like sand being sprinkled over a tin roof.

"This is Mose's house?"

"Mm-hmm."

"But he doesn't live here?"

"Not anymore. He lives in town."

"What would make a man want to leave here?"

"Different things, but I think he'll move back out here pretty soon."

"What things?"

How could she explain the events that moved Pip to town? Her voice got softer. "His wife died."

"Did you know her well?"

Her whisper was like the leaves brushing against themselves. "She was my best friend." Her first tears came, and she wiped her eyes with a handkerchief.

"I'm sorry."

"Me, too. I miss her." The handkerchief came into play again. "She always knew what to do."

He nodded as if he understood. "That was David."

"David saved my life."

"Mose told me. I can't think of anything that would have pleased him more than giving his life for someone like you."

"Did Mose tell you about his son?"

"Mose's son?"

"He didn't tell you." She pointed at the grave markers south of the trees. "That's Mose Junior's grave in the middle. He saved my life when I was seven years old."

"In the lake?"

"Yeah." She knew he wouldn't understand. "In the lake."

The recollection of what he found in the cabin distracted him, and his attention went back to something in the sky. The cat purred, and the birds became more civil; the breeze went here and there around them.

She had almost dozed off when he said, "He mentioned you in the letter."

What would he say about me? "Oh? He didn't really know me."

"Oh, really?" He smiled for the first time and winked at her. "Maybe he was just perceptive about both of us. Listen to this." He looked at the paper. "'Hi Bro. Well, I've met your match. I told you my boss's daughter was beautiful, but I didn't tell you how stubborn she is. I've had two short encounters with her, and I'm here to tell you that if you and this woman pooled your resources, you could drive Sigmund Freud nuts. More on that later.'" He took a breath. "'About your stance on self-reliance, someone has rightly said that the man who looks within himself to provide for his own sense of significance has gone blindfolded into a cloud-covered midnight to search an unlighted alley for a black cat that does not exist.'" The hand holding the paper fell to his side.

The girl flinched when she tried to lean forward. "Pat, I heard him talk about you. He wouldn't say anything to hurt you. He wrote those words because he wanted to make a point. We all do it. He thought he was goin' to have a chance to go back an' rewrite it . . . to soften his words. He loved you."

"I understand. I loved him, too."

She grinned at him. "An' he told me that he secretly thought you were a lot more stubborn than me."

He grinned back. "And he told me that he secretly thought you were a big liar."

"Don't make me laugh."

"Sorry."

It was confession time. She said, "He didn't bother to keep it a secret with me."

Pat was surprised. "David told you that you were a liar to your face?"

"An' he told me I wasn't any good at it."

"That's our boy."

The grins softened. They enjoyed thoughts of their "boy" and listened to the leaves whisper secrets.

Pat picked up the book. "*Things to Come.*"

"That's the one."

"Ironic, don't you think?"

"I don't understand."

He passed the book to her. "Something was coming."

The slick finish of the dust jacket was freckled with a thousand specks of burned gunpowder. In the center of the book was a scorched place surrounding a hole she could put her finger in. She didn't have to hold the volume to her chest to know that its dimensions would exactly match the rectangular outline centered in the bruise on her chest. Her fingers trembled as she opened the book. Wedged tightly into the pages was the mushroom-shaped bullet meant for her heart. Her vision blurred; the book slipped from her hands and hit the floor. Dust flew, and the cat jumped. The birds stopped singing.

Pat said, "I'm sorry. I should've warned you."

She shook her head and new tears came. "It's okay. I just didn't expect to see the bullet hole."

There was no reason why she should. She could distinctly remember leaving the book on the table before she walked to the door and encountered Hull.

Minutes passed, and the birds renewed their songs, the cat purred, and the breeze stayed close by.

Pat was looking at the book. "I guess that explains why you weren't shot."

"Mmm."

The scene came back to her in slow motion. She stepped toward Hull and saw his finger tighten on the trigger. David spoke her name. She put out her hands, and the blast from the gun went between them. David had been a full step behind her when Hull shot. She could remember leaving the book on the table, and David left the table before she did.

She thought, *An angel can go from one side of the galaxy to the other in an eyelash. That means my angel can make a round trip from that table to that door an' back before a bullet can travel down a gun barrel.*

Pat was watching her.

She said, "I'll bet that hole is dead centered."

"Why?"

She smiled to herself. "Oh, it just looked like it was in the middle." *An' because angels wouldn't do things haphazardly.*

He was examining the front of the book.

If I tried to tell him an angel protected me, he'd leave this place so fast the vacuum would pop my ears.

He looked up. "It looks close to me."

"Mmm." In her mind, she pictured Red Justin nodding wisely and saying, *I told you so.*

His fingers studied the pockmarks of burned powder on the book. She petted the cat.

When he started to put the book down, she said, "Can I hold it?"

He handed it to her. "You're welcome to keep it. In fact, you can have them all if you like."

She would like. "Can I pay you for them?"

"You were his friend, Missy. And beat-up theology books aren't in demand where I'm going."

"Thanks. That's special."

She touched the book to her cheek. The powder flecks reminded her of how R. D.'s whiskers had felt when he needed a shave. *Thank You, God. You've saved my life from more than one killer. If David was right, an' the Rapture's comin' soon, I want to make You known while I can. Would You focus my heart on the things of You? Would You make my remainin' time on earth worthwhile? An', God, would You give me the words to say to this man?*

Pat misinterpreted her move with the book. "Were you and David . . . uh, close?"

She said, "I only got to really talk to him once."

"Once?"

"Yeah. Just one time." She was musing. "It could've been more, but I messed up."

"I could've sworn you two were good friends."

"I think we were."

"How can that be?"

"You want the truth?"

He hardened, and the peaceful setting took on some of the attributes of a war zone. "Never mind. It's the Christian thing, isn't it?"

"It's a special thing, Pat." The words came out sounding more caustic than enlightening.

And he returned fire. "Well, I've got a question. If Christianity's so fantastic, why do you have to try to wedge it into a conversation?"

"Let me tell—" She jerked forward, clasped her chest, and fell back.

"Missy." Pat sat up. "Take it easy." He started to stand.

Pain drained the blood from her face. "Sit," she hissed. Anger and resolve sharpened her features and fired her eyes. The cat abandoned its unstable bed.

"Missy—"

She thrust one hand at him palm out; the other clutched the arm of the rocker while she tried to take small gulps of air. "You just . . . wait . . . one . . . confounded . . . minute."

He sat back in the chair and surrendered with his hands. "Look—"

Her eyes narrowed, and she began a renewed effort to pull herself upright in the chair. "Just because—"

When her eyes started to glaze over, he stood and caught her shoulders.

He eased her back into the chair and pushed it back toward reclining. "Take it easy there, toughie." .

CHAPTER TWENTY

She kept her eyes closed and gripped the arms of the chair, sucking air in short, careful breaths. When her color started to return, she said, "That was unfair. I didn't wedge anything into any conversation, an' you know it. You asked me a question, an' I answered it." She paused to draw a shaky breath. "People who spew sarcasm an' ridicule to make their point don't have a point."

Pat knew she was right. "Let's pretend you just took a tranquilizer, okay?"

She didn't bother to open her eyes. "Forget the tranquilizers."

"Uh-uh." He shook his head. "Let's pretend you took *six* tranquilizers, and they had some effect. Nod slowly if you comprehend."

Her eyes came open so she could glare at him. She nodded.

He spoke slowly and clearly, hoping to give her something besides anger to focus on. "Very good. Now, count to ten or something before you answer. Okay . . . do you not, as a Christian, have a plan to occasionally tell your fellow man about your faith? Nod if you do."

She thought, *I'm supposed to have a plan to know God better an' make Him known*, while she glowered at him and said, "I do."

He held out a pacifying hand. "Think about this. If some of the people you tell these things to refuse to become Christians, are you going to kill them?"

"Don't be stupid."

"Beat them?"

"This is ridiculous."

"Then how do you plan to accomplish what you say you want to do?"

She recited what she knew she needed to do. "I need to learn to be as effective as I can be at tellin' people about Jesus, so they can come to know God through His Son."

"Then, if your plan doesn't include annihilating your opposition, you have to learn how to sway people to your side without attacking them. A man can't learn anything if you're holding a blowtorch to his face."

She made herself rest her head on the chair back and watch the breeze ripple the lake. The clouds were arranging themselves haphazardly in the sky. She wondered if he still thought the place was peaceful; she didn't. This man was an unbeliever, and he had just given a secular interpretation of the Scriptures that said she was supposed to treat people gently so they might be drawn to Christ.

She said, "Havin' a bad temper is not fun."

"Then get rid of it."

"Sure. Do you get angry?"

"On occasion." He sounded smug. "When it suits my purpose."

"Like an actor?" She refused to be a fake.

"You say that you want to make yourself effective, to learn to know how to respond. Acting is what you need to do—what you should train yourself to do—while you're thinking about your next move."

That made sense. If an unbeliever could train himself to be effective, maybe he could teach her the same techniques. "Can you teach me to do that? To stay calm?"

His smile was so much like David's but so different. David's smile always looked genuine. "Well, people have managed to train most other species of wild animals."

She checked her first response, then said, "I can be a good student if I want to."

"Okay, I don't have anything else to do for the next day or

two. We can try having you take a short course and see how far you get."

"When do we start?"

"I can start you on your first lesson right now. You just caused yourself extreme pain because you were responding to sarcasm and words that you thought were unfair." He held up two fingers. "The second thing you need to learn about influencing someone is to avoid letting the other person provoke you emotionally. You have to become emotionless. Ignore the person and his tone—even his argument, if you can't use it against him—and disregard any ridicule or sarcasm. Know all you can about your subject and stick to one thing—the promotion of your position."

"I don't want to trick people."

"Don't worry. This is not about manipulation; it's about getting the other person to stop listening to *himself* long enough to allow himself to hear *you*."

"I can do that. You said that was the second thing. What's the first?"

"The first principle may give you some trouble." He held up a finger. "Do not launch a physical attack on your opponent, especially if you don't have the strength to stand up by yourself."

She didn't smile. Their eyes locked for a moment, and she looked away before it became a staring contest.

He noticed. "Wow. That was amazing."

"What?"

"You abandoned the fight on purpose?"

"I didn't surrender. I'm goin' to start pickin' my battles."

He said the same curse word that had been making its way in and out of her mind since David died, then added, "You're a quick study."

She said, "Thank you. I credit my mentor."

"That's good." He was going to be a great professor. "A little flattery. A distraction."

"Would you do me a favor?"

"What's the favor?"

"Would you not cuss while you're teachin' me?"

"I think you can be more effective if you learn to say 'curse' instead of 'cuss.'"

She didn't want to sound like a phony, but decided he might be right. "Okay. Curse."

"Profanity offends you?"

"Not particularly. But I'm tryin' to quit, an' I'm scared that if I hear it, I'll slip an' repeat it."

He sat back. She waited while he thought, his steepled fingers tilted out and back to touch compressed lips. Then he nodded and said, "Okay, here's the deal. I'll try not to curse, and you never ask anyone to do something like that again."

Her cheeks turned pink, but she kept her tone neutral. "May I ask why not?"

"You're amazing. Five minutes ago, if I had told you not to ask a person to quit cursing, you'd have cracked another seven ribs turning your chair over. You *are* a prodigy."

"Thank you." She dropped her chin and plucked at the sides of her jeans in a modified curtsy. "May I ask why I shouldn't ask people not to cuss . . . curse?"

"Very good. Mild humor, and you came back to your question." He leaned forward. "And the answer is, because you can't show them your throat, Missy—your weaknesses. If you ask some people not to curse, you've given them a weapon, and they'll use it to distract you. Simple."

"Mmm." He was right. "Okay."

Two beings stood in white light, watching the humans on the porch.

The shorter one said, *Tell me.*

The one at his side replied, *She knows now that her life was saved by an angelic messenger.*

Good. And is she seeking to make our Lord known?

She has a renewed passion and is diligently applying herself to the task, but she relies too much on herself and the ways of the world.

Stay close to her. She may yet learn Who holds the power.

What of the man? Will he come to know?

The answer to redemption's mystery resides in our Father's heart, not mine. Guard her well.

The taller angel's next words comprised one of his favorite phrases. *For His glory.*

At six thirty, Missy looked at her watch. "Supper's ready at my house. Come eat with us."

He hesitated. "I'm not sure that's a good idea."

"Where will you go?"

"David talked about a hamburger place in Indianola."

"The Dairy Freeze."

"That's it. I'll probably eat there."

"Where are you gonna spend the night?"

"I'll find a place."

"Come stay with us. It'll be part of our deal."

"What will your parents say?"

"The blessin' at every meal, so don't make any rude remarks at the table."

"Anything else?"

"Well, they probably won't shoot you for not bein' a Christian if that's what you're worried about, but there is this." She eased out of her chair. "God an' His Son are special to us, an' they come up in our conversations. Are you comfortable with that?"

He smiled the almost-David smile. "My mother was a Christian, so I'm used to the lingo."

"What about your daddy?" Missy was scared to hear the answer.

"Dad was a college prof at Tech. He didn't need God."

"What does bein' a professor have to do with needin' God?"

"Well, he was an intellectual. He seemed to think about the needs of mankind more than Mom did."

"An' your mom?"

"Mom didn't get to go to grad school. She taught school so Dad could go."

Missy said a short prayer, then asked, "Who was the smartest, your mom or your dad?"

Pat's initial answer came too quickly. "Oh, it was Dad by a—" His own recollections interrupted him. He frowned slightly, and the rocker stopped. He hunched forward and looked down at nothing while he remembered.

She waited until he said, "Nobody ever called Dad."

"What?"

"People called Mom all the time. She was always on the phone, answering questions about this issue or that problem. She had friends from all over that part of the country who wanted her opinion on everything from raising children to politics."

"An' your dad?"

"Dad was quieter." He was still remembering. "But he always bragged about Mom."

"Why didn't people call your dad?"

Because Dad never had any real answers, he thought. But he said, "I have no idea."

The two spent all day Saturday together, most of it on the porch at the cabin keeping the cats and birds company. He gave her pointers on how to sway people to her way of thinking, they cried together when they talked about David, and he packed some of David's books to take to his sister.

On Sunday morning, Pat had coffee while the family ate breakfast, then got in David's car and left for Texas.

At Sunday dinner, Missy said, "I'm thinkin' about going to summer school. Is that all right?"

Bobby Lee stopped eating and leaned on the table. "A new interest in academics?"

"Sorta. I may want to take some courses in philosophy. I can take a light load this summer an' graduate in December if I want to."

"Mmm." He and his wife glanced at each other. "Any particular reason?"

She saw the exchange between her parents. "Well, it's not

'cause I want to marry a Texas philosopher, if that's what you're thinkin'."

Bobby Lee picked up his coffee cup. "Then what is it? You seemed content to take your time up 'til now."

She was using the tines of her fork to trace patterns in her mashed potatoes. Her mother and grandmother waited for her answer.

The girl said, "David was just barely my friend, but I promised him I'd tell Pat about Jesus for as long as he'd listen. Pat's a lot smarter than I am, an' I want to be able to make him understand. It looks like to me that I don't have a choice."

"So you want to take more courses to help you know how to talk to him."

"Somethin' like that. I've been readin' that book on prophecy about Jesus comin' back. It explains the Rapture an' the prophecy about the comin' Tribulation."

"And?"

"An' it could happen any day. When it happens, Pat won't go to heaven with us unless he's a Christian."

"What'd your book say about when it's supposed to happen?"

"It didn't say when it would happen. In fact, it made it pretty clear that no one but God knows when it'll be. But it told how most of the ingredients—the events of history an' things in the world—are in place. About the only thing that was needed was for Israel to become a nation again, an' that happened back in '48."

Susan Parker mused, "I wonder why it hasn't happened?"

"Because God's patient," Missy said. "He says He's not willin' that any should perish."

"And everybody that's left after we're raptured goes to hell?"

"No, ma'am. After we're taken up, there's a seven-year time called the Tribulation. People will continue to have a chance to become Christians for seven years."

"Then what's the difference between now and the Tribulation?"

"Satan's beast will be here. We'll all be gone, an' most people are gonna think the world's a better place without us. This beast—this leader of a group of ten nations—will become the world's most prominent political figure, an' he'll arrange a peace between Israel an' some nations in the Mideast. For three an' a half years the world will have peace, an' the people who aren't Christians will give him all the credit."

"Then what?"

"Then he'll declare himself to be God, an' the people of the world will believe him. The last three an' a half years of the Tribulation will be a time of intense sufferin' an' horror, especially for Christians, an' later—toward the end of the Tribulation—God's gonna pour His wrath on the earth."

Her mother tried not to sound skeptical. "Doesn't it seem strange to you that we haven't heard about this before now?"

"It's probably because we haven't been around people who've bothered to study what the Bible says about prophecy. Most people aren't interested."

"And you understand it?"

"No, ma'am, but David told me if I'd read this book, I'd know more than most preachers. An' y'know, I believe he was right. The book makes sense of the whole thing."

Bobby Lee had been listening and thinking. "You said 'most.'"

"Sir?"

"When you were talkin' about the Rapture, you said 'most of the ingredients.' What's missin'?"

"Well, an army of two hundred million, for one thing."

"Two hundred million? The Bible says that?"

"One nation's army, a nation east of Israel, is going to launch an invasion with two hundred million men. It says so in the book of Revelation, chapter nine, I think."

He thought for a second. "Okay. How big is communist China's army?"

"Who knows?"

"Then things may not be as urgent as you thought. What else?"

Susan Parker answered, "A group of ten nations directed by

one leader. That doesn't sound like something that's gonna happen any time soon."

The girl had her mind fixed on the needed course of action. "We can't know that."

Bobby Lee said, "Maybe, but there're some things we *can* know."

"Like what?"

Bobby Lee smiled. "I haven't been workin' on my debatin', either. Let me think about it an' we'll talk next weekend."

Susan asked, "So what happens after summer school?"

"I can finish at Ole Miss this December an' go out to Texas for grad school."

"In philosophy?"

"Yes, ma'am. I want to train myself to think an' reason, an' I want to be good at it. Pat's almost too smart for his own good, an' I want to be able to make myself heard on his level. I want to tell him about Jesus 'til he hears me or runs me off."

Bobby Lee said, "Honey, I've never even heard of a girl like you before, much less had one for a daughter. An' I think you need to learn how to say clearly what we all know is the truth. People need to hear it. An' I want Pat in heaven with us, but havin' you take off for Texas is something I want to think on for awhile."

"I think it's important," Missy said.

"Yes, ma'am, I've heard what you think." Bobby Lee put his napkin on the table and smiled at his daughter when he stood up. "An' I said I'm gonna take a week to decide what *I* think."

Mose and Bobby Lee prayed all that week about the coming encounter with the girl. On the following Friday, they were sitting in the gin office when Missy's car pulled into the driveway across the road. When the car stopped, Mose stood up.

Bobby Lee said, "Where're you goin'?"

"Someplace else."

"Humphf. I hear all this talk about how you're her almost-daddy, an' then when things start heatin' up you ain't around."

Mose was holding his hat in one hand, rubbing his chin with the other, and staring at the stain around the spittoon. "I had me some fine mules in my time, but I can't recollect ever wantin' to stand where I knowed one of 'em was fixin' to kick. I reckon I'll find me a quiet place out here an' pray for y'all."

"Humphf." Bobby Lee stood up and went to the office window.

The girl was coming across the road to the gin, taking her time, the effect of the broken ribs barely showing. He wondered for the millionth time why God would choose to make such a special woman his daughter. Under the right circumstances, she was the personification of a quiet day in spring, but when motivated—as often as not for a righteous cause—she could become a summer storm. The only person in the family who came close to having her temperament was his mother, but Granny had long since cultivated a felt need to be diplomatic. The girl's tendency had always been to charge into a situation, declare war, and then attack the people who didn't ally themselves with her. He smiled and thought, *If we could harness thunderstorms, Christianity could use a million just like her.*

He went out to meet her, and she started talking before she got to the loading-dock steps. "What did you decide?"

"I've been fine, sweetheart. An' you?"

She didn't smile. "Are you gonna let me go to Texas or not?"

"Come in an' have a seat."

"Where's Mose?"

He turned and walked over to sit behind his desk. "Where he can't get hurt if you start pullin' down the gin."

"You aren't gonna let me go, are you?"

"An' that's not all." He pulled out the bottom drawer of the desk and used it for a footrest when he tilted his chair back.

"What else?"

He was leaning back, his fingers interlaced behind his head. "I have it on good authority that you're goin' to like my decision."

"Says who?"

He didn't smile. "God."

She started to glare at him and thought better of it. She

turned her back and walked over to stand in the doorway. After a long moment she said, "I'm gonna go see Momma."

"Okay."

"I'll be back."

"I'll be here."

Fifteen minutes later, he watched her leave the house and walk to the bridge. She stayed there awhile, then came back to the office.

She came behind the desk, sat in his lap, and put her head on his shoulder. "Hi, Daddy."

There were times when she didn't just change moods, she became a different person. "Hello, sweetheart."

"How've you been?"

"Good. You?"

"Not too good, I guess."

He could feel the dampness of her tears. "Can I help?"

"Two of my friends died savin' my life, an' I miss them."

He rocked her like a six-year-old child until she quit crying.

When she could talk, she said, "You were right. I like your decision."

"Good. Mose will be glad to hear that he's not gonna have to rebuild the gin."

She stood up. "I'll go tell him."

"What about summer school?"

"I'm not sure yet." She stopped at the office door. "Daddy, all my friends keep dyin'. First Junior, then Pip, now David. I barely knew him, an' he died savin' my life. How long is this gonna go on?"

"You're askin' me somethin' I can't answer, sweetheart."

"Would you be scared if you were me?"

"Scared of what?"

"Of havin' friends."

"Well, you've got me an' your momma an' Mose an' Granny an' Evalina an' Leon. And none of us are scared."

She sighed. "I'm scared Pat might die if we get to be friends."

"Well, that might not happen if he stays in Texas."

"That's another good reason to like your decision."

She found Mose in the back of the gin and waited while he finished showing some men how he wanted a piece of equipment situated.

"Well, what did yo' Daddy say?"

"He said you were a 'fraidy-cat."

He chuckled. "I just know when I ain't needed."

"I'm not goin' to Texas."

"Mm-hmm."

"You knew."

"Since last Monday when I come to work. Anybody what knows yo' daddy knows he ain't gonna let you go galavantin' off to where some man is. The man's job is to come to the woman."

"That's old-fashioned thinkin', Mose."

"What womenfolks wears is fashions, an' they can change, baby, but the way men thinks never will. Simple as that."

"How will I tell him about Jesus?"

"You can figure that out for yo'self."

"Mose, he'll be a college professor next year. How am I supposed to convince him?"

"Convince him?" Mose beckoned and moved to a bench in the shade. "Come over here an' sit down."

She followed and sat.

"Now." Mose tapped on the palm of one hand with the index finger of the other. "You've done got way out ahead of yo'self an' you goin' 'bout this all wrong. The secret about how we become Christians ain't somethin' a man can work out in his mind. The Book says in Romans ten, verse nine, 'That if thou shalt confess with thy mouth the Lord Jesus, an' shalt believe in thine heart that God hath raised him from the dead, thou shalt be saved.' He says in verse ten, 'For with the heart man believeth unto righteousness, an' with the mouth confession is made unto salvation.' The convincin' job belongs to God, not you. An' it all happens in the heart."

The Bible was clear on that point; Mose knew it, the girl had forgotten it. "You're right. I was gettin' ahead of myself."

He shook his head. "It's more than that. You the kind of person that wants to see things gettin' done, an' that's real good. But sometimes we tangle up what we think is our job with what

God says is His job. He lets me an' you be a part of what He does by lettin' us tell folks about Him. But if we step over the line into His territory, He'll slap us on the fingers. God calls us to live the life an' tell the folks, an' leave the rest to Him."

"You're right. An' I can't talk to Pat's heart."

"There you go. You just tell him what God says—God'll decide when he hears it."

The girl was smiling.

"What you thinkin'?"

"I'm thinkin' that this is the perfect time to ask Daddy if I can go to Europe with Polly this summer."

"Have mercy, child, you scary." Mose stood. "There ain't no way a college professor can keep up with yo' mind. I know *I* ain't interested in tryin'."

Old Mrs. Parker ate supper with her son's family almost every night. That evening, after the blessing was given and the food passed, she said, "Well, Missy, have you decided how you're going to spend your summer?"

"Polly's goin' to Europe, an' I was thinkin' I might like to go with her," Missy said.

If Bobby Lee heard her, he didn't show it.

The girl looked at her mother and grandmother. Her mother covered a small smile. Granny winked and touched a finger to her lips.

Two bites later, Bobby Lee said, "What about summer school?"

She had it all figured out. "We can use the tuition money we save to pay my way to England."

"What about Pat Patterson?"

"I'm gonna keep my promise to David, but I'm gonna do it by writin' him letters."

"Mmm." He put a forkful of food in his mouth, chewing for a moment before he said, "He called today."

CHAPTER TWENTY-ONE

It was the girl's turn to be silent. When she spoke, she said, "Pat talked to you?"

"Called this afternoon. Says he wants to work here this summer."

"What'd you tell him?"

"That I'd have Mose call him Monday."

"Are you gonna hire him?"

All three women waited for the answer.

"Should I?"

The girl sat with her elbows on the table, pinching pieces off her roll, turning them loose, and watching them fall onto her plate. "Not for me."

"Mmm. Why not?"

She looked up. "Because the only reason I'm goin' to spend time with a man who's not a Christian is so I can tell him how he can get to know God. It wouldn't be fair to date a man I won't marry. Not to him—not to me."

"Would you like to tell that to Patterson before he drives all the way over here from Texas?"

She grinned. "No-o-o-o, uh-uh. I'm not gonna start answerin' questions that he ain't askin'. He could be plannin' to bring his new bride, for all we know."

The girl's grandmother thought that was funny.

Bobby Lee did too. "Okay. I'll tell him."

Old Mrs. Parker asked, "Why does the boy say he wants to come here?"

"He says it's peaceful here, an' he wants to work on some writin' over at Mose's cabin."

Missy said, "You need to tell him he can't work in a gin durin' pickin' season an' get anything done on a dissertation."

"I figured I could have him follow Leon around an' help out over here, run errands an' stuff."

"Gotcha!" Missy poked her father in the side. "You've already decided to hire him."

Bobby Lee spoke around a bite of chicken. "Yep. But only if he understands that you aren't part of the package."

"Well, if he eats half as much as David," Granny said, "I'd better start bakin' tomorrow mornin'."

The subject of Europe died. The girl looked at Bobby Lee, then at her grandmother. Old Mrs. Parker touched her finger to her lips again and moved her head slightly from side to side. Missy waited.

After Bobby Lee asked to be excused, he pushed away from the table and put his hand on Missy's chair. "Let's me an' you ride over to Peavine's an' see if he's got any ice cream."

They sat in front of the Dairy Freeze and ate soft ice cream from paper cups. Five minutes after they arrived, Missy's side of the car got busy with a steady stream of high-school and college boys. It never failed; something about her sitting in front of the Freeze caused the local boys to be attacked by a passion for ice cream. They spoke to Young Mr. Parker and talked cotton for a bit, but mostly they just wanted an excuse to see Missy up close and hear that husky voice. So far, Bobby Lee watched four boys walk off while they were still looking back at her and bump into a metal support post that held up the curbside awning. It would be only a matter of time before one of them rendered himself unconscious or knocked down part of the building. For Bobby Lee, the parade of wide-eyed boys got old; for Missy, it was another day in the life of a reigning duchess.

During a rare lull, he said, "What if I say no?"

"About Europe? Heck, Daddy, I don't care. I don't even know if I really want to go."

"It makes my job easier to let you go. That way, I don't have to worry about you an' Pat gettin' to like each other too much."

"It won't help my argument for Europe, but I can cut your worries some. Pat has what it takes to be a good man, but without God he's nothin', an' I don't want a nothin' for a husband. In fact, I'm not sure I want a husband, period."

"Mighty brave talk."

"Yes, sir. An' I could stumble—" She scraped her spoon around the sides of her cup. "—but you an' Momma an' God an' Mose could catch me." She held his wrist and snared a spoonful of his ice cream.

Another carload of boys pulled up next to her. They got out, paid a prolonged visit, and walked inside. Two of them had been to the Dairy Freeze three times in the last half hour. Bobby Lee shook his head. Maybe he could send her to the Arctic 'til she was thirty-five. "There's one other thing."

"Sir?"

"You're gonna write to Pat?"

"If he'll read the letters."

"Then do this—remember that diplomacy hasn't always been your strong suit. The Bible says in Second Timothy for us to correct our opponents with gentleness because God may see fit for them to repent an' come to know the truth. Work on that. You're dealin' with a man who has a terminal disease; you don't have to be sweet, but it wouldn't hurt to be gentle." He handed her the rest of his ice cream. "A man who's standin' in midair can't be pinned down, so keep the play on your own court without gettin' stubborn. Stand in one solid spot, hold the Bible in one hand, an' offer him gentleness with the other."

"Okay, I'll do that. An' in return, the next time we come over here, you have to get chocolate on your ice cream instead of this strawberry mess."

On the last Saturday in May, when Pat Patterson showed up at Cat Lake, Missy was on her fourth day in Europe. There was a new Bible waiting on the table in the cabin. Inside the Bible was a note written in block letters on pale-blue notepaper.

> *Dear Pat,*
> *I swept out the cabin. The Bible is for you. If you decide to read it, I recommend that you start with the book of John.*
> *See you in late summer,*
>
> > *Missy*
>
> *P.S. I'll pray for you every day.*

He sniffed the page; it smelled like blue notepaper.

At supper that night, Bobby Lee asked Pat, "You got everything you need at the cabin?"

"Yes, sir. Thanks."

"You got enough money to make it to payday?"

Pat smiled. "I do. But thanks."

"Well, we'll be leavin' here about ten thirty tomorrow mornin' if you want to go to church with us."

Pat touched his napkin to his mouth. "Can I have a rain check?"

"Many as you want. We'll have Sunday dinner at Momma's house about twelve thirty, an' you're welcome to come."

"Thank you, I'll be there."

"Good. We can line out what your week's gonna be like."

Pat hesitated, then said, "The church thing—is it really okay if I don't go?"

Bobby Lee said, "Pat, the most important thing a man can do is come to know God—to accept Christ as his Savior—but nobody can cram it down your throat. It's somethin' you have to want for yourself. So is church."

Susan and Old Mrs. Parker nodded, and Pat relaxed.

Bobby Lee introduced Pat to Leon early on Monday. It was decided that Mose and Leon would share the white boy, with

Mose getting first choice. By the end of the first week, the three had worked out a schedule that suited the two bosses and the doctoral candidate.

Pat got off at five o'clock every day and went back to his cabin. He ate dinner with the family on Sundays, and Bobby Lee and the Parker ladies picked him up one or two evenings a week to ride to Indianola for ice cream or a movie. Otherwise, he stayed to himself.

Inside of two weeks, Pat, Mose, and Leon were regularly taking their noon break together, sitting in the shade to eat whatever Evalina fixed for them.

On a warm Wednesday they were finishing their lunch when Leon asked the white boy, "You goin' to prayer meetin' at yo' church tonight?"

Mose, who had just leaned back to take a short nap, sat up. He knew what the answer was going to be, but he wanted to hear it.

Pat said, "I don't go to prayer meetings."

Leon was doing a thorough job of cleaning the last shreds of meat off a chicken wing. "Yeah? How come is that?"

Pat said, "I don't believe in God."

The chicken wing was forgotten. "It ain't good to joke like that, boy." Leon wiped his hands on his shirt.

"It's just what I believe, Leon."

Leon looked over both shoulders, as if afraid that someone might think he was a part of this great transgression against his God. He leaned close to Pat and whispered, "That ain't right."

Pat was patient with the old man. "It is for me. I have a belief different from yours."

"No, no. I mean *you* ain't right. If you don't believe in God, boy, you can't believe in nothin'."

"Every man has beliefs, Leon."

"Who told you that?" Leon looked at Mose for help, but Mose had heard all he needed to hear; his eyes were closed. "Pat, the man that don't believe in God would be better off if he was this here chicken."

"Chickens can't do things to help their fellow man, Leon."

Leon leaned away from Pat and studied his face, frowning slightly. "Boy, you say you gonna be a college professor, but if you don't believe nothin', then you ain't got nothin' to teach nobody."

Leon was a good man, but he hadn't been to college, and Pat knew he rarely read anything but his Bible. "I believe I can teach them that men can bring themselves to better things—fuller lives, greater accomplishments—without relying on ancient beliefs and myths."

The white-haired yardboy said, "Is that what you gonna do?"

Mose opened one eye.

"I don't understand what you mean, Leon."

"Are you listenin' to the words that come out of yo' mouth, boy?" The old man was gentle. "You say you gonna tell college folks they can make theyselves better just 'cause they believe they can, an' then you gonna tell 'em not to believe in nothin'."

"You don't understand, Leon. I meant that all of us—all mankind—can bring our world to do better things. We can make this a better place to live. You and Mose and the Parker families are doing that."

"Watch out, now. Me an' Mose an' these other folks are tryin' to point folks to God, not to a empty life."

"But you've made me a better man because I've gotten to know you. Maybe someday I'll do something that will make you think you're a better person because you got to know me."

Leon started shaking his head before Pat finished talking. "You ain't payin' attention, son." He leaned over and rested a warm hand on Pat's shoulder. "Lemme tell you what I understand real clear. You done gone an' let them people in that college fill yo' head with foolishness an' yo' heart with emptiness. Men like me an' Mose have lived our lives watchin' folks doin' plenty of talkin' 'bout goodness, while they was thinkin' 'bout evil."

Mose went back to his nap.

242

On Saturday, Mose and the dog drove over from the gin and found Pat on the cabin porch with a Bible in his lap. A mish-mash of blue papers marked places in the back half of the book.

"Readin' anything special?"

"Missy left me a note and told me to read the book of John. And she's sending me verses to read almost every day."

"That's good. You learnin' anything?"

Pat ran his thumb over the edges of the pages. "Some of it doesn't make sense to me."

"Mm-hmm. Lemme see that Bible a minute." He opened it near the middle and said, "Jeremiah thirty-three, three says, 'Call to me an' I will answer you, an' will tell you great an' hidden things which you have not known.' That's God sayin' He'll help you if you ask Him to. Some folks calls it His phone number."

Pat spent some time with his own thoughts, then said, "Would you tell a lie, Mose?"

"I wouldn't like to, but I might."

"But you're a Christian."

"I am that. But I'm also just a man."

"But you wouldn't do anything wrong."

"I should've had you here to tell that judge that 'fore he sent me to prison for killin' that man."

"Killing?"

"There's a lot what's gone on 'round here you don't know nothin' 'bout."

"But I've been around you. You've got a good heart."

"Not accordin' to the One who can see inside it." He hefted the book. "If we was to look back a few chapters, it would say my heart is deceitful an' desperately wicked, an' nobody but God can understand it. You know, when it comes right down to it, I don't think I've ever had a genuine pure thought."

"May I see that?" Pat took the book and flipped through the blue note sheets until he found the one he wanted. "I got this from Missy yesterday. It tells me to go to Jeremiah thirty-three, three and read it—says it's God's phone number."

"Mm-hmm, an' you wants to know are me an' her in ca-hoots. That's how come you asked if I'd lie."

"Something like that."

"Well, I know I'd lie to protect my family, but ain't nobody in no danger here. We ain't workin' against you, boy. Fact is, I ain't heard from her 'cept through her daddy."

"So what do I do?"

"Well, I might think on what two people done told me to do."

"Where do I start?"

"Why don't you ask God to show you?"

"Mmm." He didn't like the answer.

"What does Missy say?"

Pat fanned the edges of the notes. "Just to pray, and some Scriptures to read."

"Then that's what I'd do. Ask Him to show you, an' read the book."

"So all I can do is just pray and read?"

"You don't know no better, but you just said the only ways we got to talk to God—to pray an' to read."

"Anything else?"

"Tell you what, if you want to know more about that book, you pray to God to show you what He wants you to know. Then you study over those readin's, an' I'll come see you next Saturday an' we can talk some more." He stood. "An' pray you don't die."

"Pray I don't die? Why?"

Mose was almost to his truck. "'Cause regardless of what you say you believe, you don't want to go to hell."

Pat shook his head and smiled. "It's hard to be scared of something I don't believe in."

Mose came back to the porch steps. "Lemme tell you somethin', Pat." He pointed a finger at his friend. "You needs to be more careful how you think about God. If He ain't real, you ain't lost nothin'. If He's who He says He is—an' He is—you'd be a fool to get caught treatin' Him slight."

That was Pat's third Saturday in Mississippi.

On the next Saturday, when the two men and the dog were settled on the front porch, Mose said, "You still readin'?"

"I've been through the book of John about five times now."

"That's mighty good. What've you learned about Jesus?"

"He was a good man and a good teacher, but I already knew that."

"Then you had to find out He was God."

"What? Why do you say that?"

" 'Cause He said He was."

"That doesn't mean He really was."

"You just said you knew He was a good man, but He claimed He was God. Either He was God or He was lyin'. There ain't no middle ground, is there?"

Pat hadn't caught the significance of Jesus' claim until Mose pointed it out.

Mose asked, "You been prayin'?"

"Seems like a pretty good bit."

"For what?"

"That if there's really something great and hidden in the Bible, that God'll show it to me." He changed the subject. "Are you going to move back out here when I leave?"

"I 'spect so. That house in town got too many people 'round it."

"But it's close to your church, isn't it?"

"I don't care 'bout bein' close to a church buildin'." He gestured at the lake. "I like bein' out here where it's quiet."

Pat looked at the little graveyard. "Your son died out here."

"Mm-hmm."

"People don't talk about what happened very often."

"Oh, they might if I ain't around. They think I git sad."

"You don't?"

Mose patted the arm of the rocker. The dog opened an eye to see if he was being summoned. "Maybe, but not like you think. I miss the boy pretty fierce, an' it would be good to see him as a man, but I wouldn't trade what he did for a million lifetimes."

"Nobody ever told me the whole story."

"Well, I reckon I'll let Missy or Mistah A. J. tell it to you. They seen it all up close."

"People say that the snakes were demon-possessed."

"An' that Dillworth boy was possessed when yo' brother an' Missy got shot."

"How can you know that?"

Mose made a decision before he answered. " 'Cause I'm the one that put 'im down."

"Everybody says Bobby Lee killed him."

"Mm-hmm."

Pat figured it out. "Bobby Lee had to tell people he killed him because Dillworth was white and you're black."

Mose nodded. "Dillworth was the second man to get killed right here in this yard. Pip killed a fellow named Blue Biggers here back in nineteen an' fifty-two. That's three killin's that them demons was involved in."

"Are you scared it'll happen again?"

"It might happen again, but I got no call to be scared. They can't touch me 'less God says so."

"Why?"

" 'Cause I'm His. I'm a Christian. Whatever comes to me has to get by Him."

"Maybe there aren't really any demons."

"Don't be talkin' foolish, boy. When Dillworth come off this porch at me, he was already dead. Yo' brother had shot him twice in the heart an' once in the side of the head."

Pat was hearing this for the first time. "What'd you do?"

"I done what needed doin'—what Mistah A. J. Mason done to them cottonmouths back in '45—I blowed his head off with that shotgun."

Quiet came to the porch. Mose rocked, Pat leafed through his Bible, a dove cooed from nearby. Pat said, "Is it okay for a person who doesn't believe in God to pray for something?"

"You said you was already prayin'."

"I mean for something besides Bible stuff."

Mose's chair stopped moving. "The girl."

"What makes you think that?"

Instead of answering, Mose said, "You might as well stick to prayin' about havin' Him show you Jesus, Pat, 'cause she ain't gonna look sideways at you if you ain't a Christian. Besides, you don't even know her."

Pat had heard a few stories about Pip. "How long had you known Pip before you knew she was special?"

Mose was fairly trapped. The memory of that first moment came to him often. "Less than a minute, I reckon."

He fished a packet of gum out of his pocket and took his time pulling a piece out, remembering. He offered the pack to Pat and received a headshake. He said, "I worked at the gin up in town 'til I was growed, then come out here to work for Mr. R. D. One day he told me to go over to the house to help out Miss Evalina. I'd just carried one of them great big glass punch bowls in from the kitchen counter an' put it on the dinin' room table. When I looked up, Pip was watchin' me, frownin' 'bout where I put it. I been thankful ever since I wasn't holdin' on to that bowl the first time I seen her 'cause I know I'd of dropped that thing an' busted it to smithereens."

"Then I'm going to include Missy in my prayers."

Mose put the gum in his mouth and stuck the paper in his pocket. "How come?"

"I'm not sure."

"Mm-hmm." The corners of Mose's mouth turned up. "Seems like you might lie quick as me, boy."

He and the dog stood. "Well, do what you want. They yo' prayers."

Pat studied all Saturday afternoon and took the evening away from his books to drive to Indianola. He pulled up to the Dairy Freeze out of habit and ordered a milk shake. Most of the boys in sight were sprinkled in close proximity to a white convertible full of beautiful young women; Polly Ragsdale was sitting behind the wheel. She saw Pat and waved.

When Pat returned the greeting, Polly left the all-American beauties in her car to entertain the boys and walked to his car. Every male over ten watched every step of her journey. Pat thought the city council in Indianola could possibly save a few lives if it drafted an ordinance that made it unlawful for Polly to walk within sight of a street where men were operating moving vehicles.

She spoke without smiling. "Hi."

"Hi there. I thought you were in some foreign country with Missy."

She opened the car door and made herself at home. "I got back a couple of days ago. Missy was goin' to Switzerland, and I was going crazy."

"So, what brings you home?"

"Bad food, lumpy beds, cold showers, and no iced tea. In fact, there wasn't any ice, period, except in the water pipes."

"Most people get past the hardships and enjoy the scenery."

She looked at the boys draped on her car—some talking to the girls, the rest trying to keep an eye on her. "I was ready for a change."

"Europe wasn't a change?"

"Not really. Same boys, same words, different dialect."

"And Missy stayed?"

"Yeah." She looked to make sure she wasn't missing anything back at her car. She wasn't. "She was goin' to Switzerland and some other places. Said she'd be home the middle of August. What've you been doin'?"

"Working for the Parkers and hitting the books. That'll be the story of my life for the next month or two."

"Are you almost finished?"

"I'm getting close."

Polly was bored. She got ten calls a day from boys who'd heard she was home. Pat was different, almost aloof, and he was the newest and best-looking man in the area. "Aren't you dating anybody?"

"Don't know anybody."

"You know me."

She had a Hollywood smile and skin that would shame a Coppertone ad.

"When's the last time you went on a date in a ten-year-old car?"

She laughed. "Never—'til today."

"Wanna go to the movies?"

Pat an' Polly, she thought. *It even sounds cute.* She pulled the door closed. "Let's just ride around."

"What about your car?"

She dismissed it and its precious cargo with a wave. "It knows the way home."

The incredibly cool coeds lifted nonchalant hands toward their friend and continued being beautiful for their audience.

Every male eye at the Dairy Freeze watched one of the most beautiful girls in the state ride off in an undeserving old Chevrolet. The radio in the convertible was playing "Poison Ivy," and a couple of the kids were singing along with the Coasters.

CHAPTER TWENTY-TWO

Sunday morning found Pat at his table, working and drinking coffee. When midmorning came, he pushed his books back and took his cup to the porch for a short break; he didn't bother to sit down because he didn't have the time. White clouds were building in the west, promising needed rain for the young cotton. He leaned on one of the porch posts, enjoying the mild breeze, and watched the Parkers' car leave for church. He looked at his wrist; if he got busy he could squeeze in another hour and a half of work before he had to get cleaned up for Sunday dinner.

Three minutes after he sat back down at the table, he noticed the air in the cabin was getting thick and the books boring. Two minutes later, he was walking between rows of knee-high cotton, going toward Eagle Nest Brake with his Bible in his hand.

Tall trees overhung the room-sized clearing he found. The surrounding woods filtered out the thoughts and sounds of the world and cooled the breeze that came looking for him. Birds felt free to come near to forage through the dead leaves, paying admission for their intrusion with color, motion, and music. He sat with his back to a huge oak and read from the book. After a few minutes, the birds forgot he was there, and so did he. The notes on the blue pages were committed to memory, but he referred to them over and over, reading and rereading the passages to which they sent him. After thirty fruitless minutes, he closed the book.

Well, I don't know if this is thinking or praying or talking to myself. I keep reading these words, and they still don't mean anything. Mose and Leon talk like they have a God who's their friend, but I don't feel anything. I keep reading, and everything I see keeps on being words. He was looking at the center of the clearing. *This book claims God can show His power to people. If You're there, how about giving me some kind of encouragement? Maybe just a peek at something only God could do?*

He was thinking the last of these thoughts when a redbird came out of the trees and landed scant inches from his feet. The bird hopped once, flitted its wings, and perched on the toe of his shoe. It fixed him with its bright eyes and cocked its head as if it had just asked a question and wanted a response.

Wow! Is this a peek?

He was going to reach out to the bird, but it flew when he twitched his fingers.

Well, maybe not. He frowned at another failed attempt to contact Mose's God.

He moved to get up and was arrested by a thought, or rather a hint of a memory. Was it important? Something Missy said? A phrase? Or was it something he said to Missy? He stood up, and the thought came closer. *Something about trees?* He turned in a full circle, looking at the trees. Then he remembered.

He remembered saying, *Missy, we can talk about God 'til trees quit making oxygen, but the answer's always going to be the same; man has evolved into a being who can find fulfillment in himself, by himself.*

Those were the words. *'Til trees quit making oxygen.* He repeated the phrase several times while he looked at the woods and got lost in thought. *Now there's a puzzle for you, boys and girls. Which came first, the chicken or the plants that make its oxygen?*

Minutes passed. He looked at his watch. Dinnertime was coming.

When he got to the edge of the brake, he saw that the clouds were spending their energies becoming more serious. Lightning flashed to the west; the thunder waited several seconds and likened itself to the sound of an advancing war; individual raindrops pelted him when he got into the open, and he started to jog. He was in the middle of the field when he remembered that he hadn't prayed about Missy. He kept jogging, grinning and praying his way through the cotton.

God, I don't really need a redbird, but how about some kind of acknowledgment that You know I'm down here praying while I run through this rain? It doesn't have to be anything special. You know, like maybe a trace of perfume on one of her notes, or maybe You could use one of those lightning bolts to tattoo her name on my chest.

Mose's week-old warning came as clearly as if the man were whispering in his ear. *You needs to be more careful how you think about God. If He ain't real, you ain't lost nothin'. If He's who He says He is—an' He is—you'd be a fool to get caught treatin' Him slight.*

The weight of his thoughts slowed him to a walk. He stopped. A line of heavy rain approached the lake while he stood in the middle of the cotton field, nodding and listening to Mose say the words again: *You'd be a fool to get caught treatin' Him slight.*

Pat slipped off his shirt, wrapped the Bible in it, and dropped to his knees in front of the advancing storm. *If You're out there, God, You know he's right, and so do I. I . . . uh . . . I apologize. I'm going to keep looking for You, and I'll take whatever help You want to give me, and I'll try to be respectful.* He wavered, then forced himself to add, *If it suits You, I sure would like to see Missy Parker again before I go back to Texas. Umm . . . amen.*

He looked at the wall of rain and measured the distance to the house; he was going to get wet. While he watched, a stream of sunlight forced itself through a small hole between the clouds and highlighted the area around the cabin for the briefest second. A figure clothed in flowing white moved along the edge of the light and vanished when the clouds closed.

He was wet when he got off his knees. The sight of his deep knee prints in the soft dirt triggered a thought that he might be going crazy. He shook his head. *I'm out here in the mid-*

*dle of a cotton field in the rain on my knees, praying and seeing angels.
I'm definitely slipping off the track.* The downpour reached him,
and he started sprinting for the cabin.

The water was standing in small puddles, and he was trying
to miss some of them when he rounded the corner of the cabin.
The cats had abandoned the front porch because they could stay
drier under the house—or because of what was on the porch.

He got a glimpse of something white against the dark gray
of the wall and tried to stop. His feet went out from under him,
and he skidded across the front yard as if he were sliding into
home plate from fifteen feet out, ultimately colliding with the
front steps.

He stayed on his back, oblivious to the rain and mud, chest
heaving, looking up at the porch to get his first glimpse of a
heavenly being.

The angel came to the edge of the porch, unmindful of the
driving rain, holding her sides and letting her laughter spill
down the steps.

He lifted a muddy hand in greeting; the angel grinned and
wiggled her fingers at him.

Missy Parker was home from Europe.

He rolled over and got to his feet. There was no need to
hurry in out of the rain—every part of him that wasn't wet was
muddy, and he'd lost a shoe in the slide. He put the bundle
with the Bible in it on the porch and went back to get his shoe.
When he bent to retrieve it, he went down face-first. She was
leaning against the wall of the house now, laughing and holding
her hair back in a fruitless effort to protect it from the wind.

He got up, held up a finger to signal that he would return
shortly, and strolled toward the lake. He went in the water up
to his waist and rinsed himself off; she waited, then welcomed
him back to the porch with a smile.

"Hi."

"Hi."

"I'm back."

"You were gone?"

She wrinkled her nose. "You're not mad at me for laughin',

are you? I mean, you aren't goin' to throw me in the mud or the lake or somethin', are you?"

"Why should I? I slid across there on purpose."

"Then I feel honored that you would put on a welcome-home show for me."

"You should. I'm normally a very serious person."

She grinned. "You look serious."

"What are you doing home? Polly said you'd gone to Switzerland."

"Three days was long enough for Switzerland. The huntin' club has a fish fry every Fourth of July, an' I've never missed it."

"You came from Europe to Mississippi for a fish fry?"

"It was a good excuse. I was ready to be home, an' I'm goin' to a semester of summer school. I'll be finished at Ole Miss in December."

"Well, come in an' we'll celebrate with a cup of American coffee." He handed her the bundled Bible. "Carry this."

"You're all wet."

"I'll pretend I just got out of my private pool."

She followed him inside.

He glanced at the clock. "Why aren't you in church?"

"I slept late."

"So you decided to punish yourself by coming out in this mess?"

She swept her hand down the front of a puffy-sleeved white blouse and a matching full skirt. "I brought an outfit like this to Roosevelt's daughter. I walked down to their house an' almost got caught in the rain on the way back. It's from Greece." She did a model's turn.

He remembered the shaft of sunlight. "You look exactly like an angel."

His compliment melted her smile at the speed of her thoughts. *I cannot encourage this man. He's smart, good-looking, friendly, an' funny, but he's not a Christian.*

He saw the change and didn't understand. "Are you okay?"

"I'm fine."

"Did I say something wrong?"

"No, no, I'm fine. Really." She took a step toward the door. "I have to go."

Rain was beating against the window. "Have you lost your mind? You'll get soaked to the skin."

She thought, *Slow down, Missy, an' make sure you don't burn any bridges. If you go flyin' out of here, he might get his feelin's hurt.* She said, "Right. I guess my brain's still in another time zone. Coffee sounds good."

He dried his arms and chest and put water in the teapot for instant coffee. When he unwrapped the Bible, she said, "You've been readin'?"

He dug a dry T-shirt out of a pile of disorder and put it on. "Every day."

She touched the edges of the blue note sheets. "Did the notes help?"

"I honestly don't know." He was squishing around the kitchen, getting out cups, sugar, and milk. "I think the Bible is well written, Missy, but that's all. I just don't see what you see."

"Have you talked to Mose?"

"And Leon and Evalina and everybody in your family."

"Mmm."

He turned his back on the coffee preparations. "It's the Christianity thing, isn't it? That's why you were going to leave just now."

"It is. I guess I'm a little too jumpy. Sorry."

"Do you think it's right for Christianity to stand between you and me?"

She looked down at the Bible. "Not for bein' friends."

"How about more than friends."

She looked up. "Uh-uh. It won't work."

"Why not?"

"Because I won't date a man who's not a believer."

"Polly's a Christian, isn't she?"

"She says she is."

He took a step toward her. "What does that mean? You don't think she's a Christian?"

"It means only God an' I know for sure if I'm a Christian.

No one else can really know. Polly says she's a Christian; that's all I know."

"She'll date me."

"I won't."

"I think you're being stubborn."

"I intend to be."

"Why?"

"Because if I date a man who isn't a Christian, we'll end up havin' this kind of conversation every time I take a stance on somethin' that's important to me."

The teapot's whistle signaled the end of round one; the points went to the girl.

Coffee was steaming in front of them before he looked at her and smiled. "I'm sorry. My mother would come back and kill me if she knew I'd invited you in here and treated you like that."

"It's okay." She put her cup on the table and rang the bell to begin round two. "Come back from where?"

The smile became a thin, hard part of an angry face. "That's not very funny."

"An' you know I didn't intend for it to be. My point is, your mom believed in God. She thought she was goin' to heaven."

The girl wasn't being mean. "You're right." He nodded. "Sorry."

They gave part of their time to silence. Then she said, "I went to Belgium an' Germany."

"How was it?" He didn't care.

"The most impressive thing I saw was the devastation."

"This is something you're telling me to make a point about God, right?"

"The Second World War was started by a man who didn't believe in God or heaven or hell."

"I'm not planning to start a war, Missy."

"If you're right, an' if there's no heaven or hell, then whether you seek peace or war doesn't make any difference."

"That's ridiculous."

"You're doin' too much readin' an' not enough thinkin', Pat. You're not considerin' the consequences of being an atheist."

"Thinking won't make me believe there's a God."

"Go the other way an' consider what disbelief can cost."

"The world doesn't need God to make it a good place."

"Really? What about the Holocaust? Was the murder of six million Jews wrong?"

"Of course."

"Well, if you think Hitler was wrong, then you need to come up with a good reason for your conclusions, 'cause right now they're based on a belief that good and evil exist—that means there has to be a moral law. If there's no moral-law-Giver—there's no moral law. If there's no moral law—then one of the greatest atrocities in history was no different from me killin' a turtle out there in that lake."

"You have no idea what you're saying."

"One of us doesn't, that's for sure. I'm sayin' mankind has dignity only because God created us. You're sayin' man is a biological accident that becomes whatever he makes of himself. I'm sayin' that either there's an eternity on the other side of our last heartbeat, or what's on this side of death is a wasteland."

"That kind of thinking borders on being stupid."

"Hardly." She took a sip from the cup and declared her victory in the second round. "Stupid is when the master of debate ignores the obvious, loses his temper, becomes inarticulate, an' says unkind things to his student."

"Your premise is all wrong, Missy."

"My premise is flawless, an' you know it." She wasn't playing a game, but she smiled to let him know they were still friends. "Say you're sorry an' that I won."

"You didn't win."

"I did too win, an' you know it; that's why you're mad. Say you're sorry."

He planted both hands and leaned almost to the middle of the table. "I'll tell you wh—"

She cut off her smile and put a restraining hand an inch from his nose. "You so much as whisper one single, solitary cuss word, hotshot, an' this conversation's over."

He sat back in his chair and breathed at the ceiling.

She said, "Now, say you're sorry, like a sensible person."

"I didn't do anything to be sorry for."

"Would your mother agree with that?"

"That's hitting below the belt."

She was winning the third round. The smile reappeared. "Tough. Say it."

His eyebrows met over his nose. "No."

Three to zero. "Take me home."

He threw up his hands. "Okay, okay. I'm sorry."

"Too late. Take me home."

"I said I was sorry." He knew he sounded like a seven-year-old boy, and that made him angrier.

"*After* I told you to take me home. Let's go."

"Good gosh." He glared at her. "I suppose *gosh* is a cuss word."

"Don't say 'cuss,' professor, say 'curse.'" The winner—and undisputed champion—of the Cat Lake Debating Society's first competition was prissing to the door.

The rain quit by the time they got to the car. She rode with the window down so she could smell the washed air; he sulked. The cotton already looked better, the lake refreshed. When they pulled into the driveway, she said, "If you promise not to throw any furniture, you can come over tonight an' we can play canasta."

"I'd like that, but I've already got a date with Polly."

"Well, have fun." She was unfazed. "Oh. Are you comin' to dinner today?"

He looked at his clothes, then his watch. "I guess not. Thanks."

"Okay. Maybe I'll see you tomorrow."

"Mmm."

She was out of the car when she remembered something. "Wait! I brought your last note with me instead of mailin' it."

She ran into the house and came back in a flurry of native Greek costume, holding a blue envelope at arm's length and wrinkling her nose. "Excuse the smell. It was in my makeup case an' my perfume must've spilled on it."

It was an generous answer to part of his cotton field prayer—sort of. The thing reeked.

He went back across the lake and banged his bumper into one of Mose's pecan trees when the car objected to being handled carelessly in the mud. He got out of the car and slammed the door. The answer to his prayer was back from Europe and getting ready to have fried chicken and hot homemade rolls at a meal to which he was invited; he was on his way to a peanut butter and jelly sandwich by himself. He took the other answer to his prayer inside to read it; within minutes he carried the blue notepaper back outside because the stench was giving him a headache.

"Where's Pat?" Old Mrs. Parker looked at Missy.

"He said he wasn't gonna eat today."

"Why not? I made an extra dozen rolls."

"His clothes were dirty, an' he was mad at me."

Granny stopped eating. "What did you do to that boy?"

Missy put her fork down so she could use her finger to point in the direction of the people she inventoried. "*That boy* is closer to thirty than he is to twenty; an' *you* are *my* grandmother, not *his*, an' *I* don't share."

Old Mrs. Parker rolled her eyes. "It can't hurt to be nice to him."

"It can if he thinks we're gonna be anything but acquaintances; he's not a Christian."

Bobby Lee said, "Amen."

Granny said, "Well, I made an extra pie, too. Why don't you take some of this food over there after we eat."

Missy put the pointer back to work. "No, ma'am. You can take it, or let Momma do it, or Evalina. I'm not takin' that *boy* to raise, an' I won't let him think I am."

"My lands, Missy, it's a bunch of rolls an' a pie, not a dowry."

"He's a big boy, Granny. He can run down rabbits an' eat 'em raw for all I care."

"Missy Parker, you ought to be ashamed of yourself."

The girl's father spoke. "She's right, Momma. Leave 'er alone."

Missy grinned and wrinkled her nose at her grandmother.

Pat held an open textbook in front of his face and thought about the events of the morning. Everything at Cat Lake had been fine right up until the minute Missy showed up.

Hunger finally got the better of him, and he went to the kitchen.

The good news was, if he had to choose one meal to live on for the rest of his life, it would be a peanut butter and jelly sandwich with ice-cold milk; there was an art to making a good PB&J, and he was a master. Maybe having Missy home wouldn't be a total disaster.

By the time he'd finished practicing his culinary skills, his attitude was almost in high gear. He was humming along with the radio when he opened the refrigerator door and was reminded that he forgot to buy milk the day before. There was also an art to punting a PB&J, but he *hadn't* mastered that. He ended up skipping his favorite meal, and while the Parkers ate pecan pie, he cleaned streaks of peanut butter and globules of jelly off part of the ceiling and most of the front window.

If God was real, He was laughing at Pat Patterson.

At three o'clock, he heard a rifle shot and went outside. The wet ground was steaming in the sun, and the cats and birds were back in their places. Up on the bridge, a man took aim and fired into the water. Pat put his hands in his pockets and walked up to the bridge, picking his way around the mud puddles.

The man watched him approach and spoke first. "Howdy."

"Hi. Having any luck?"

"A little."

The man looked older up close, but not aged. Pat put out his hand. "I'm Pat Patterson."

The man cradled the rifle in his left arm and shook hands. "I heard about you. I'm A. J. Mason."

This was the man Mose mentioned to Pat, the one in the middle of the war at Cat Lake. "You were out here when Missy was almost bitten by that snake."

Mason turned his full attention on Pat. The interest

seemed to subtract years from his age. "That was a long time ago. What'd you hear?"

"Nothing, really. Mose Washington said I should get you or Missy to tell me about it because you saw it up close."

Mason was giving Pat a candid once-over. "Well, I was sure there."

"Mose said there were demons in some snakes. Do you believe that?"

"I ought to. I saw what they did."

"It had to be a fluke. There's no such thing as demons."

Mason took the contradiction with grace. "Word is you're David Patterson's brother. Is that right?"

"Did you know David?"

"Some—he came to church up in town." Mason didn't take his eyes off Pat; it was as if he were trying to solve a problem and Pat held the answer. "I know he did a fine job of protectin' the girl from that Hull fellow. Did it twice."

"I haven't heard much about that, either."

He continued to search Pat's face. "You ever wonder why?"

The question didn't register with Pat. Mason reminded him of someone, but he didn't know who. The man was just one more copy of a hundred men he had seen around the little town—long-sleeved dress shirt buttoned at the neck, no tie, felt hat, clean shoes. But this man was different.

Mason interrupted his thoughts. "You're the college teacher, aren't you?"

"That's the plan, but I'm not quite there yet."

Mason's gaze went to the north end of the lake. "I'll tell you somethin' that happened that day that you might find interestin'. An angel spoke to me an' warned me about what was fixin' to happen."

"An angel?"

"Yep." Mason turned back to watch the boy's face. "Spoke to me more than once."

"What'd he say—or she?"

"Sounded like a he. He said, 'Be ready.'"

"I don't believe that."

Mason apparently found out what he wanted to know about Pat. He gave his attention back to the lake.

Pat said, "Are you going to tell me what else happened out here?"

Mason decided to give the man one more chance. "I'll tell you this—I cried on an' off for a month after it was over."

Pat waited, and when Mason didn't say more, he said, "That's it? You cried?"

"Most folks around here would say that's pretty much."

"And you won't tell me any more?"

"Nope."

"Why not?"

"Waste of breath."

"Why did you tell me about crying and about the angel?"

"'Cause of what your brother did. Figured I owed him somethin' for helpin' the girl. I wanted to see if maybe I was wrong about you." His shoulders rose and fell. "I wasn't."

"Wrong? Wrong about what?"

Mason leaned back on the rail—relaxed and calm. He propped the rifle against his shoulder. "Your brother was a good man—a smart one. But I'm almost seventy years old, boy, an' that's too old to be wastin' my time on fools—an' that's what you are."

Pat could almost feel sorry for an old man who refused to understand reality, but he wasn't obligated to let anyone call him a fool. "That's a little harsh, isn't it?"

"Maybe. An' I'm proud for how you took it." The old man had better things to do with his time; he pushed himself off the railing and started for his car. "Nice visitin' with you."

Pat's day wasn't going downhill; it had somersaulted off a cliff. He'd managed to get rain-soaked and mud-covered, then wasted thirty minutes while being taken down a notch by Missy. He'd gotten a headache, bent the bumper on his car, and been forced to miss out on dinner and Old Mrs. Parker's rolls. Now this old geezer had called him a fool, and he was tired of trying to act polite.

"You're kind of stubborn about this God business, aren't you? There are well-educated people all over the world who can explain why your beliefs are a waste of time—they're just superstitions."

Mason was standing by his car. "The educated people can talk, sonny, but they can't explain away facts. God's right here, an' He's more patient than me. He says He's not willin' that any should perish—even you. You might want to pull away from those educated people an' those college books and think about why He would allow a lynch mob to crucify His Son for a man who doesn't care about Him. Like I said, He's more patient than me—an' so is that girl. If it was me, I'd kick yo' hardheaded back end clear to next Christmas."

Pat decided to let the superstitious old goat know there was a difference between being intelligent and being a pushover. He was seven inches taller than Mason and outweighed him by eighty pounds. "I guess I'm learning to hold my temper as I get older. As for kicking me anywhere, if you were a few years younger I might teach you some manners."

Mason nodded slowly while he gave serious consideration to Pat's offer, then chuckled. "You tell Missy Parker I was carryin' a gun when you told me that." He put the rifle in the car. "She'll say I must be gettin' older myself." He touched the brim of his hat and drove off.

Pat chewed the corner of his mouth and watched the car until it was out of sight; there was something he'd missed. He put his hands in his pockets and walked over to the bridge railing, thinking. *It was a question*, he thought, *and I ignored it. Something he asked me.* It would come to him if he quit trying to remember. He put the thought aside and went back to his books.

From beneath the bridge, a voice said, *Do we use him now?*

Not yet. As long as he depends upon himself and refuses to believe in us, he is our ally. For now, he does our work for us.

Can he not harm her?

He will suit our purposes as he is. We can wiser use those who bend their will to ours—the ones who hate her—to harm those she loves.

CHAPTER TWENTY-THREE

The Central Delta Hunting Club was getting ready for its annual fish fry.

The land behind the brake belonged to the Parker family. The club's "lodge" was a shabby old shotgun house. Behind the house, a solid-looking old barn provided alternate—and quieter—sleeping quarters. During hunting season, the men who wanted to drink and gamble stayed in the house; the ones who wanted to sleep stayed in the barn. The ramshackle appearance of the clubhouse didn't bother the members who stayed there, because drinking, playing poker, and shooting dice took precedence over aesthetics.

Leon mowed the grass around the clubhouse, turning it into an acceptable place for the picnic lunch that would be served to about three hundred men, women, and children. At eight o'clock, cars and pickups started raising dust on the road by the Parkers' houses—men going back to town for things forgotten, others getting to the scene early to help with the cooking and drinking. The members assigned to do the cooking had been at the clubhouse since dawn, building fires under the black cook pots, heating the grease, and drinking moonshine. By noon, the grease was hot and the cooks were stewed.

Bobby Lee volunteered to supply part of the food. That meant Evalina was in charge of getting side dishes ready and overseeing their transport. Missy stayed out of the way while Evalina stood on the back porch, drying her hands on her apron and giving directions to her fifty-something-year-old son and his white assistant. "Boy, y'all go 'round to the front an' load them chests of ice first, then come back here an' take this slaw an' put it in the back end of the truck."

"Yessum."

"An' put Roosevelt an' Pat in the back with this stuff so it don't get tumped over on that old road through the brake, you hear?"

Leon said, "Yessum," for the fifty-ninth time.

Roosevelt Edwards had shouldered some of Mose's responsibilities at the gin while Mose was in prison. That meant he had become part of Evalina's fish-fry task force. Emmalee Edwards arrived with her daddy to help out, but also with an ulterior motive.

The girl and the men loaded the truck as ordered, and the pickup sagged when Roosevelt and Pat climbed in the back. Emmalee started to get in with her daddy, but Evalina stopped her. "You sit up front with Leon, baby. That truck won't take no more weight in the back."

Emmalee looked at Missy. "You goin' with us, Miss Parker?"

"I'll be along, Emmalee. You can go with them or wait an' go with me."

Emmalee, dressed in jeans and a white blouse because she knew that's what Miss Parker would be wearing, said, "Is it okay for me to wait, Daddy?"

His daughter was beautiful. A tall thirteen-year-old, she was already telling her friends she was going to go to college and be just like Missy Parker. Roosevelt nodded at the black copy of the Parker girl. "Stay close to Miss Parker, baby, an' do like you're told." Emmalee was a sweet child, maybe too sweet, and that's why Roosevelt liked for her to be around Miss Parker. Miss Parker was a fine young woman, but no one who knew her had ever said she was sweet.

The truck left with the food and the men, and the Edwards girl got closer to Missy and stayed there. In fact, she got so close that Missy said, "Are you scared, Emmalee?"

"No, ma'am." She watched the cars full of white folks passing by up on the road. "Only just a little, I guess."

"What are you scared of, hon?"

"I never been around so many white folks at one time. I'm scared they might all be lookin' at me."

"People are always goin' to look at folks that're special, Emmalee. An' you're old enough to be thinkin' about being special."

"Special how?"

"By knowin' God an' makin' Him known."

"Did Miss Pip tell you that?"

"Pip an' the Bible told me what God says, an' He says what I just told you an' a lot more."

"Will you teach me how?"

Missy took the child's hand. "No, I won't. But I'll do what my Pip did for me. If you're willin' to learn, I'll teach you how to teach yourself. If you don't want to feed yourself, I can't help you."

Emmalee was earnest. "Yes, ma'am. I want to learn."

"Then you learn this." Missy took a small stack of three-by-five notecards out of her purse, flipped through them till she found the one she was looking for, and handed it to Emmalee. "Here. You memorize this an' let me know when you can say it letter perfect."

Emmalee read the card. "Psalm sixty-one, verse two. 'From the end of the earth I call to Thee, when my heart is faint. Lead Thou me to the rock that is higher than I.' This is to keep me from bein' scared." She couldn't have been more excited if Missy had handed her a dollar. "It's beautiful. How long do I have to memorize it?"

"You need to start learnin' a verse a week."

"Do you do that?"

"I try, but I'll do better if I have you to help me stay at it."

The child was in danger of dividing down the middle from excitement. "You mean we can help each other?"

"The Bible says we're supposed to do just that, an' that'll be our plan. Can you do it?"

"Yes, ma'am, Miss Parker." Emmalee was ready for heaven, because life on earth was as good as it was going to get.

"If we're gonna be friends an' help each other, you have to call me Missy."

Emmalee thought she was going to faint.

The two men who followed the truckload of ice and slaw to the fish fry hadn't crossed the Cat Lake bridge in more than a decade. The driver said, "You think they'll remember us?"

The man in the passenger's seat cursed and said, "Who cares? Like your momma said, they're nothing but trash."

The father and son hated everyone and everything, even themselves. They were mean every hour of every day, and at eleven that morning they were well on their way to being drunk. The father said, "Stay close to me, and don't start any trouble."

The son sneered at his father and mouthed a string of curse words.

U.S. Congressman Halbert Bainbridge was lying about being in Mississippi on government business. He was there to show off his big car and make his kinfolks jealous. When he bragged that he "might just drop in" at the fish fry, his kinfolks laughed at him.

"Yeah, Hal, you go on an' try it," said Tub Pommer. "Them Parkers'll spot you for what you are right quick an' send you packin' in that fancy car."

The demon of Cat Lake listened to the father-son conversation and said, *I know these two, and they will do our bidding. We will use the young one on behalf of our cause.*

The fish fry was the same every year. Heaping mounds of steaming fish and huge bowls of potato salad, slaw, and hush puppies were arranged on long tables. Men in white shirts; ladies in summer dresses; girls dressed like their mommas; and rowdy, ketchup-splattered boys filled paper plates and sat in folding chairs or on the ground to eat until they were miserable.

The club's barn cats came out to declare a one-day moratorium on the scorn they felt for humans and made themselves available for bribes. Ever-present dogs let it be known that they had not declared a moratorium on chasing cats. Cakes and pies, baked by some of the best cooks in the nation, waited on the dessert tables for that moment when the picnickers would be ready to make their move from misery to agony.

Missy, with her African-Siamese twin, visited her way through the crowd to the serving tables. Emmalee worked on memorizing her first verse while Missy got away with weaving through the cooks' territory behind the serving line. Missy filled their plates, and the two friends escaped to a quiet area in the shade down by the barn.

Miss Parker was worthy of the girl's devotion. While they ate catfish, she encouraged Emmalee to expend whatever effort it took to know God well and to excel in school—basically the same things Emmalee's daddy often told her, but they made so much more sense coming from the mouth of her wise new friend. Every time Missy changed positions, Emmalee waited a few seconds then fixed her sitting position to duplicate the white girl's. The black child was two inches taller than her idol—long and graceful, with a shy smile.

When they had their fill of fish, Missy left the girl to make another foray for food. She exercised her royal rights and returned to the cooks' hallowed ground to take her pick of the desserts. Emmalee stretched out to watch the clouds play tag and work on memorizing her verse.

Emmalee was almost asleep when a cat, a huge tom, streaked past her on its way toward a hole in the side of the barn. When Emmalee stood up, the dog chasing the cat turned aside and the tomcat disappeared into his sanctuary. The dog jogged back to where he came from, thankful for the intervention that had rescued him from catching the cat.

Emmalee stepped close to the barn and heard faint mewing sounds coming from the other side of the wall. She picked up some scraps of catfish and walked to the front of the building.

When she stepped into the gloomy interior of the old structure, the warm smell of leather and dry hay came to her. Leftover harness rigs for mule-drawn wagons cluttered the front wall; fifty years of trampled straw and manure cushioned her feet. She took short steps toward the sound of the kittens, bent over at the waist and holding the offering in front of her. From deeper in the grayness, the mewing sounded more desperate. She tiptoed past scattered hay bales, creeping farther and farther from the light, barely whispering, "Kitty, kitty, kitty." Particles of dust drifted across the brightness from the doorway.

Polly Ragsdale, with three boys in her wake, stopped Missy and demanded that she go to Greenville with them. "We can go swimming first and go to the movies tonight."

"Who's that?" Missy was looking past Polly at a face she was supposed to know.

The three boys turned to look at a red-faced fat man. The stranger was overdressed in an expensive suit tailored to hide a soft belly; it failed miserably. A life of malice toward his fellow man marred his face.

Polly kept talking about the movie.

The fat man was waddling through the crowd, looking for someone.

The youngest of the boys answered Missy. "That's one of Tub Pommer's kinfolk that live in the Ozarks or Smokies or someplace. Tennessee or Arkansas, I think. He's some kind of a rich politician or somethin', but he's just as sorry as Tub."

Missy asked Polly, "Where's Pat?"

Polly pointed back toward the cabin and sniffed. "He left ten minutes ago. He's probably wrapped around a book by now."

"Here, kitty, kitty, kitty." It was too dark to see into the old stalls. Emmalee crept past the ladder to the loft, trying to peer into the darkness, moving in the direction of the kittens' cries.

Something she couldn't see moved in the shadows. The

rustle of clothing against straw was accompanied by a shrill growl from a frightened cat. Whatever moved was only a few feet in front of her. She heard the cat spit and growl again, and somewhere off to the side, a man cursed—a white man. The child froze when the man said the forbidden words. It was dangerous for a young black girl to be in a place like this with a man—white or black—and this one's voice sounded mean. Fear, heightened by her isolation in a dark place with a mean white man, reinforced her need to be out of the barn. The glare from the wide door blinded her when she turned, and she tripped over a loose bale of hay. She stumbled, put her hands out to protect herself, and spilled the fish scraps and herself into the thick dust.

More dust filled the still air when Emmalee scrambled to her feet, providing a drifting screen that outlined the shadow of the man standing between her and the door. She backed away from him. He followed.

Polly was pressing Missy. "Well, are you going or not?"

Missy wasn't listening.

One of the boys said, "What's on at the movies?"

Another said, "Who cares?"

A string of screaming children and barking dogs made a racing loop around them and kept running.

Missy talked to the youngest boy while she tried to figure out why she didn't like the clumsy-looking man. "What's his name?"

"Bridges or somethin' like that."

The fat man's gaze fell on Missy, and she heard a little girl's voice say, *Well, if a evil man comes up again, an' I can't whip 'im by myself, y'all can help.* She nodded to herself. "Halbert Bainbridge."

"That's it. You know him?"

"We met a long time ago, but he doesn't want to know me."

Bainbridge let his eyes linger on Missy, wet his thick lips, and went back to his search. He looked nervous.

Subdued light from the big door fell on a trembling kitten in the man's hand. Emmalee said, "I'm not but thirteen years old." The first tear washed a streak through the dust on her cheek.

The man nodded and said, "Nice." It was the most horrible word Emmalee had ever heard.

He came a step closer, and she saw the knife for the first time. She said, "I want to go to my daddy."

"Soon."

Her teeth were chattering. "I want to go now."

He shook his head. "After."

She backed into one of the stalls and trapped herself. Tears zigzagged down her cheeks when she shook her head. "I'm gonna scream."

"If you do, I'll kill you."

The kitten mewed, and the mean white man bent to put it on the floor. When he straightened, he said, "Are you going to scream?"

She was having a hard time getting her breath. "I want my daddy."

"Maybe later."

He jabbed the knife into the post by his shoulder.

"What time are y'all goin'?" Missy asked.

"Right now." Polly needed to get to the Greenville pool so she could show off her new two-piece bathing suit.

"I can't go right now. I brought Emmalee with me."

"Let her ride home with Roosevelt, Missy. We're in a hurry."

"I have to tell her first."

Polly rolled her eyes. "She'll figure it out for herself if you're not here. C'mon."

Halbert Bainbridge had looked for his stupid son everywhere but in the old barn. He stood in the brightness and peered at the vague shapes in the barn's interior. "French? Are you in there?"

"Get out of here and go on back up to the clubhouse. I'll be along in a minute."

Bainbridge waddled far enough into the barn to see his son's back. "Let's go."

"No." French Bainbridge didn't turn around.

A black girl's voice said, "Please help me."

Bainbridge took quick steps to where his son blocked the girl's escape. The girl's white blouse was barely visible in the dark reaches of the stall. Bainbridge hissed, "You idiot! Are you insane? You can't do that here." He instinctively looked over his shoulder to see if anyone was near.

French pulled the knife from the post and turned. "I told you to leave me alone."

From the front of the barn, metal jingled. Bainbridge and his son looked against the glare at a small figure holding a singletree. A husky voice, soft with pent-up anger, said, "Halbert, I thought we told you to stay away from here."

French said, "Well, well. It's our tasty little baseball player. Come on in, Blue Eyes. You can have your turn before your little friend."

Halbert Bainbridge cleared his throat and said, "Now, there's no need for anyone to get excited here."

From behind Bainbridge his son whispered, "We have to kill them both."

The older man's face was shiny with sweat. "Let me think."

The son turned and jerked Emmalee to him. He put the knife to her throat and told Missy, "Drop the club, cutie, or I cut her throat."

Missy took a step closer and recognized the boy. It was the one who had pushed her down on the bridge. "Bub, you so much as muss her hair an' I'll knock your fat daddy's brains all over this barn."

French Bainbridge tightened his grip on Emmalee and grinned. "Promise?"

Even the father thought it was funny. "I'm afraid my son

French doesn't care if you kill me or not." He turned and grinned at his son.

Missy didn't know they were both crazy until that moment. While the man was distracted she took another step, poised herself like a baseball player, and swung the three-foot piece of oak. Bainbridge turned in time to see the blow coming but not in time to completely avoid it. The old piece of wood, a veteran of thousands of miles behind a thousand mules and horses, adapted well to its new role and drove the fat politician to his knees by the ladder.

Missy stepped back and assumed a batter's stance. "Do we all still think this is funny?"

French was sniggering. His father was holding his shoulder and cursing. "I think you—you broke my arm."

"I was aimin' for your head, fool. Now tell him to turn that girl loose an' get out of here."

Bainbridge struggled to his feet. "You don't get it, do you? My loving son would pay money to have me killed if he knew he wouldn't get caught. That means I'm no good to you as a hostage. You're trapped, girlie."

A huge shape—slightly smaller than a thunderstorm but just as black—cut off the outside glare when it moved into the opening behind Missy. It said, "You reckon yo' trap'll fit over me?"

Missy sidestepped to let Roosevelt closer to the men.

Bainbridge leered at Missy. "He can't help you. We still have the girl."

Something rumbled inside Roosevelt, and he started forward. Missy rested a hand on his arm and said, "Hold it, Rose." She pointed at Halbert Bainbridge. "Make him stand there." Bainbridge wasn't planning on moving.

Missy went to the front wall and came back with a coil of rope. She threw it at Bainbridge's feet and said, "You thugs think you're holdin' the trump cards, but you've already lost. If you hurt that child, Rose an' I will beat you both unconscious with this singletree, an' I'll scream rape. Those men out there will come in here, an' if you aren't already dead they'll string your carcasses up to one of those beams with that rope. Now, you can walk off or you can die, right here, right now."

Bainbridge knew immediately that what she said was true. "Let her go, French. We can't win."

"But I've already won, old man," French hissed. "I get to kill this cute little thing *and* her little blue-eyed friend."

Missy had to act before the demented pair could formulate a plan. She said, "Rose?"

He kept his eyes on the man holding his daughter. "Ma'am?"

She nodded her head at the older Bainbridge. "If he tries to touch me, I want you to kill him. Will you do that?"

Mose had told Roosevelt more than once that Missy Parker was the finest white woman ever born, and Roosevelt had just watched his daughter and the young woman walk through a crowd of white people as if they were best friends. If a black man killed a white man in Mississippi, the black man would be lucky to live out the week, and Deacon Roosevelt Edwards of the Mount Pilgrim Church didn't want to die, but he almost worshiped Mose Washington, and he greatly admired Missy Parker. He prayed to God as he stepped closer to Bainbridge; his warm breath washed over the father of the man who was holding his daughter. "Yes, ma'am, I reckon I'll kill 'im grave-yard dead."

Bainbridge was a wretchedly poor judge of men. "You stupid black ape, you touch me and you'll be dead by sundown tomorrow."

Openhanded lightning came from the black storm and exploded against the white man's fat cheek; an angry rumble of thunder followed. "I done touched you, whitefolks. If you speaks again, *you'll* be dead *tonight*."

Missy was busy with French. She didn't crowd him, but she waited for an opening, watching him as a mongoose would watch a cobra. She said, "It's no use, French, give it up. You can't whip the whole world. The law's not gonna do anything to you for threatening a black girl, so back off."

French sneered; spittle ran from the corners of his mouth. "You take just one more step and I'll kill this girl, and I'll cut you and him and as many as come along. What do you say to that, Blue Eyes?"

"I say, I've got God on my side."

When she said the sacred name, French growled. Missy hadn't thought about demons until that second. Now she knew—demons possessed the man, and she was in a life-or-death battle. It also occurred to her that she had forgotten to pray.

"Emmalee?"

"Ma'am?"

"I want you to pray to God."

"Yes, ma'am."

"Fervently, now. You know what that means?"

"Yes, ma'am."

Foam bubbled on French's lips, and the growl became animal-like.

Because they expected the girl to pray silently, her soft voice surprised them all. "Dearest God, I'm scared. I'm standin' on the edge of the earth, an' I call to Thee because my heart feels faint. Please lead me an' Daddy an' Miss Parker to the Rock that is higher than—"

"Yahhh!" The demon-driven man yowled and stomped his foot like a spoiled child. From the stall behind him, an eerie shriek—the shrill snarl of an enraged animal—filled the barn. French Bainbridge's reaction to the scream was to abandon the black child, howl even louder than the animal, and leap into the air.

The tomcat, forgotten but still hungry, had tracked the pungent fish scraps Emmalee had spilled to their resting place in the stall behind the crazed man. He had gulped his first mouthful when the white man's foot landed on his tail. The tomcat screeched loud and long—just before he sank his pain-powered teeth bone-deep into the ankle of the offending foot.

French released Emmalee and Missy saw her chance. As he bent, she started her swing. The end of the long piece of wood connected solidly with the man's head. French Bainbridge went over backward, unconscious and bleeding, onto the leftover fish scraps. Emmalee ran to her daddy and jumped into his arms.

Halbert Bainbridge was backed against the ladder to the loft. "Is he dead?"

Missy ignored the question because she didn't care. "I don't think I'll let you ruin the fish fry, Halbert. Go get your car an' bring it down here. You can haul him back to wherever you live." Bainbridge was shuffling toward the door when she said, "If you try to run off an' leave him here, I'll turn you in to the law. Understand?"

Bainbridge left the barn holding his arm, whining and cursing to himself.

Missy said to Emmalee, "I need for your daddy to stay just a couple more minutes, then y'all can leave. Okay?"

"Yes, ma'am."

"You're a brave woman, Emmalee, an' a real prayer warrior, an' I feel honored to have you for a friend."

The child wiped her tears and stood straighter.

French was breathing and mumbling and bleeding profusely from a three-inch gash when Bainbridge returned with the car. Missy and her friends stood by while the man loaded his semiconscious son into the backseat.

Missy went to the driver's door as Bainbridge got in. "You were warned once to stay off this land, Halbert. If you ever come back, we'll assume it's because you want to hurt somebody, an' I'm promisin' you right now, somebody on this place will kill you." She pointed at the backseat. "That goes for you an' yours."

Bainbridge's fat lips were trembling, but he managed a snarl. "Well, I guess you think that makes me real scared."

"I know you aren't scared, Halbert." She pointed at Emmalee. "She was scared. You're just a coward."

Halbert Bainbridge would never come back to the Parker place. French would.

CHAPTER TWENTY-FOUR

I told him if he ever came back on our land—him or his—we'd kill 'em an' claim self-defense."

Bobby Lee said, "Next time you might want to consider gettin' the sheriff in on it."

"At the time I didn't want those two around Emmalee anymore—or me either, for that matter. If the sheriff got into it, it'd just be their word against Emmalee's. An' if they'd lied about Emmalee, Rose might've done somethin' that would get him sent to Parchman."

Bobby Lee nodded. "You might be right."

So far, the fish-fry incident filled the conversation at Sunday dinner; Missy did most of the talking.

Pat listened to the one-sided exchange in silence. When a lull came, he said, "What's a single tree?"

Bobby Lee said, "Singletree. It's part of the riggin' you use to hook mules to wagons. It's made out of oak—three foot long, big as your wrist, with steel hardware on each end to hook up the trace chains. They've been used more than once to settle a difference of opinion."

Pat frowned at Missy. "You were lucky you didn't badly injure Bainbridge."

Missy moved to the edge of her chair; she gripped her fork like a sword and pointed it at Pat. "Badly injure? He's—"

Bobby Lee rested his hand on her arm. "I think you better let me help you answer." He turned to Pat. "What would you've done?"

Pat started, "Well . . ." He looked at Bobby Lee, then at Missy. "I guess I don't know. I wasn't there."

Bobby Lee said, "Me neither, but I think it's a good idea to be real hard on men who do bad things to little girls. An' if a man's father stands aside an' lets it happen, then we need to get rough with the father."

"You can't mean you'd kill him?" Pat addressed himself to Bobby Lee.

"That would depend on him, or them; I'd kill 'em both to protect a child."

Quiet came to the table until Old Mrs. Parker said, "Pat, can you stay after dinner and play canasta?"

The change of subject was a relief. "No, ma'am, thank you. I've got a date with Polly tonight, so I better hit the books this afternoon."

"Some other time, then." She got up to take some dishes to the kitchen. "Who wants pie an' who wants cake?" She winked at Pat. "An' who wants both?"

Pat drove; Polly was responsible for running the radio and looking good. She sat on one foot, station-jumping and singing along with whoever came over the speaker, letting her hair blow in the wind. Whoever cut her hair apparently had a guide to determine the perfect hair length for girls riding in '58 Chevy convertibles. Peavine watched the car pull up in front of the Dairy Freeze and got three more pounds of hamburger out of the refrigerator; having Polly Ragsdale parked at his curb would double his sales.

After the carhop took their order, Pat said, "Nice car. I could live with having a convertible."

"Thanks. I like it myself."

"What do you not like?"

"Boredom."

"What's the cure?"

"I don't know, but I won't find it within a hundred miles of here."

"Thanks."

She giggled. "Except for you, idiot."

Two men wearing wedding rings stopped to ask about Polly's family. The first carload of boys pulled up by the convertible, and they all got out for a short visit. Four hamburgers, two malts, and three dozen amicable male visitors later, Pat said, "Let's ride around."

When they were on the street, Pat asked, "Do you ever get tired of the attention?"

"Does it bother you?"

"It could if I wanted to be alone with you."

She turned the radio down and took his hand. "We're alone now."

"And I like it. How about you? We had thirty guys come by the car while we were back there. Does it ever get on your nerves?"

"I'm used to it." She didn't smile. "My prom-queen days will be over in a year or two. I guess I'm just enjoying it while it's happening."

"Will you miss it?"

She shrugged. "Who knows?"

The young people in Indianola burned a lot of gas on Sunday afternoons; Pat and Polly did their part.

For the next few weeks, Pat's life centered on his study materials; working for Mose and Leon kept him fed. His social schedule included an occasional weeknight date with Polly, the same for canasta at the Parkers'. Weekends allowed two definite dates with Polly, plus Sunday dinner with the Parkers. Missy commuted to summer school at Delta State.

At midmorning on a Saturday, Missy stood on the porch and banged on the door. His car was out front, but Pat wasn't home.

She walked around the cabin. If he was out in the cotton field or on the other side of it, she'd never find him. She was trying to decide what her next move would be when he strolled out of the field twenty yards from where she stood.

"Hi."

"Hey. What're you doin'?"

He motioned behind him. "I go to the woods sometimes to read the Bible. There's a quiet place over there."

"Pat, you amaze me. It doesn't make sense to me that you're so faithful."

Her remark didn't set well with him. "I'm not faithful. It's something that needs doing."

"Well, the Christian world could use more people who think it needs doin'."

"Mmm." He couldn't bring himself to care what Christendom needed. "What're you doing?"

Pulling a tooth should be done quickly. So should this. "I'm the bearer of bad tidin's—Polly's on her way to Jackson."

"We've got a date."

"She didn't have time to come tell you, so she called me an' asked if I would."

He frowned. "What's in Jackson?"

"The High School All-Star game."

He stopped. "She's gone to a ball game? We made this water-skiing date a week ago."

He was waiting for her to say something. She raised a solemn right hand. "I'm innocent, judge. I'm just the errand boy."

The "errand boy" was wearing white shorts and a too-big T-shirt; her bare toenails were perfectly painted pink, with a light dust coating.

He mumbled something to himself.

She said, "I'd love to."

"What?"

"Join you on the veranda for coffee."

"Humphf."

She was sitting with her heels hooked on a chair rung when he brought the coffee out to the porch.

"Thanks." The cats had disappeared.

"We've had this date for two weeks." He didn't sit. "When's she getting home?"

"Late. There's a dance tonight." She sipped the coffee and made a contented sound. "A minute ago you said a week."

"What?"

"When you made the date." She kept the cup near her lips and looked innocent. "A minute ago you said a week ago; just now you said two weeks. If you get really mad, will you testify that y'all made it last spring?"

"Funny." He didn't laugh.

"Sorry."

"She's going to a dance?" He sat down.

"I should've warned you not to trust her."

His head came up. "I thought she was your friend."

"She is, but she's also the one who stole my fiancé."

"You were engaged?"

"Mmm. Tanny Britlyn. The only boy I've ever kissed." She tasted the coffee. "It was a long time ago."

"When?"

"Fourth grade."

"And you still remember it?"

"I take proposals seriously."

Talking to Pat about things remotely close to marriage was a mistake, and she had just made it.

"Maybe you take everything too seriously." He sounded like the calm before the storm.

She threw up a wall. "I don't see how you get any studyin' done. I'd spend all my time out here on this porch."

And he changed directions. "It's nice enough."

She closed her eyes. "It's the nicest place on earth."

When she opened her eyes, he was looking at her feet. She said, "I go barefooted sometimes."

Her feet were small and cute. The nail polish suited her. "Aren't you afraid of snakes or something?" He asked the question so he could prolong his study.

"Junior was the only one of us scared of snakes."

He wasn't interested in Junior. "And you haven't been kissed since the fourth grade?"

"If I have, it wasn't worth rememberin'."

"Maybe you're kissing the wrong men."

She could shut him up with ten words, but that wouldn't build bridges. "Relax, prof. I ain't kissin' nobody."

"You ought to try it. It's changed since you were in fourth grade."

Good gosh, Lord, bein' nice to this dope is like tryin' to pet a porcupine. "Gettin' back to the current subject—Polly said she'd come over tomorrow an' explain everything."

He wasn't interested in Polly either. "What're you doing tonight?"

"Dad's out of town, so I'm stayin' close to home. You wanna come over an' play cards with the womenfolk?"

It beat sitting in the cabin. "What time?"

"Shoot, come for supper. We'll eat around six."

He had three bacon-and-tomato sandwiches for supper and got his teeth kicked in at canasta.

Missy walked him to the back door.

"So. Do you think I should keep my date with her tomorrow?" he asked.

"Ask Ann Landers."

"From your perspective?"

"From my perspective—no."

"Why not?"

"Because you're not a Christian."

"That matters?"

"Does to me."

"You're kind of single-minded on this, aren't you?"

"I hope I always will be."

Seconds passed. "What if we put the religious issues aside, and you answer based on what you think as a woman?"

"I won't do that. I can't."

What a snot. "You don't bend much, do you?"

"Should I turn my back on what I believe to suit you?"

"Look, I'm a nice guy. I don't play the piano, but I do okay in other departments."

When she didn't speak, he said, "Well?"

"You're not nice. You're an arrogant snot."

The recollection of his recent assessment of her jarred him. He said, "Then why do you waste your time with me?"

"Because I'm committed to be your friend." The confidence of what she had become warmed her. She knew she was his friend, and she knew he knew it. She smiled. "But bein' my friend doesn't keep you from bein' a snot."

"The feeling's mutual."

"I know. G'night."

"Night."

On Sunday afternoon, he heard a car drive up and walked to the door in time to watch Polly step out. He couldn't put his finger on what it was, but something about her appearance made him assume that she usually brought out the big guns when she was going to apologize; *breathtaking* couldn't quite describe her.

He waited without speaking.

She said, "When a girl stands you up, you're supposed to act like you don't care. That way, she won't think she's got you wrapped around her little finger."

"Then I don't care." He had to smile. "I decided to be nice when I figured out I probably wouldn't get away with killing you."

She stayed by the car. "Does that mean we're still friends?"

"We can be close acquaintances while you're on probation. How's that?"

"Close enough to take me swimming at the country club?"

He drove. Polly looked beautiful and played the radio.

The Sunday afternoon crowd at the club's pool made room for them; they soaked up sun and visited.

"Missy said not to trust you."

She didn't even open her eyes. "She's still mad about Tanny."

"She said you stole him."

"He couldn't help himself. But he paid a high price."

"Tanny?"

"She beat him up at recess."

"Sounds to me like he made a good trade."

She grinned. "Spoken by a man who's never had to tell his buddies a girl gave him a black eye and a bloody nose."

"She bloodied his nose?"

"The principal ended up taking him to the hospital."

When the unmarried couple laughed, the young wives chasing their children around the pool smiled at them. Polly smiled back.

A three-year-old boy led his attractive mother in a race past their lounge chairs. Pat said, "Pretty."

"Mm-hmm."

"You're not jealous?"

"I don't have to be. I know what I look like."

"Good point." He watched her face. "Missy says I shouldn't date you because you're a Christian."

No reaction. "Okay."

"Are you a Christian?"

"Oh sure."

"Why isn't it important to you?"

"It is, but not to the point of studying the Bible and memorizing Scripture, or ditching you."

Two college-age boys came by. They were concerned about the well-being of every member of Polly's family, most of her friends, and the prospects of the Ole Miss football team. They finally left.

He picked up where their conversation left off. "Like Missy."

"Like Missy. In church she sits toward the front and takes notes. I sit in the back and daydream. She reads her Bible every day. I don't even know where mine is."

"But you believe in God."

"I know there's a God."

"How?"

"God made all the other birds and animals so that the male was the prettiest—the one that attracted the attention of the female. Then he made us." She opened her eyes and winked. "And my full-length mirror tells me He changed the recipe with boys and girls, and made us so we could enjoy it."

"You might make a good philosopher."

"I already am."

Mose was at the gin. It wouldn't be open on Sundays for another month, but he was just getting out of the house and letting the dog pretend he was hunting. Missy was sitting on the loading dock helping them watch the sun go down.

"He's leavin' in about a week."

"Mm-hmm."

"I knew he wasn't gonna believe. He's too hardheaded."

"Good thing ain't nobody else 'round here like that."

"You know what I mean."

"Maybe you doin' too much knowin' an' not enough prayin'."

She couldn't stay seated. "Dadgummit, Mose, you don't understand. He's a genius. He'll have a Ph.D. before Christmas; he's almost a professor. Every time I talk to him it's like arguin' with a textbook. I can't reason with him."

"Nobody said you was supposed to teach him or argue with him. You supposed to *tell* him. Tell him what you know. Let God do the rest."

"I've told him all I know."

"Tell him God's truth. He says His word won't return to Him empty, not without accomplishin' what He desires an' not without doin' what He sent it for. If He's sendin' out His words to that boy to draw him to Hi'self, then you can forget 'bout havin' to be smart. God gave us the words, Missy. He don't need smart folks to pass 'em on."

"What if he doesn't believe?"

"Everybody what knows about hell knows the answer to

that. They some fine men out there that just ain't gonna choose Him; he might be one of 'em.'"

"The thought of that just makes me sick."

"Good. We needs to be put out 'bout people goin' to hell, but the battle ain't fixin' to stop 'cause you don't like the way it's goin'.'"

"You're right. I'm goin' home to pray."

"Well, let's pray awhile here 'fore you go."

The dog trotted close enough to see the bowed heads and went back to his business.

Late Wednesday afternoon, she was walking across the bridge when she heard him call. She turned to watch him jog toward her. "Hey. Are you limpin'?"

"Hi. Football knee." He pulled on his shirt. "You going to my house?"

"Emmalee's." She held up a sack and pointed down the gravel road past the cotton fields. "Delivery service. You?"

"Headed home." The girl wore faded Bermuda shorts, a mismatched blouse, and used-up tennis shoes. A hole in the right shoe showed off two pink toenails; the little piggy that went to market and the one that stayed home were enjoying the sunshine. "You want company?"

"C'mon. When're you goin' back to Texas?"

"Saturday."

The word made her chest feel hollow.

They walked the road in silence for awhile. "Where were you takin' your Bible?"

He laughed. "I took it to work. Mose and Leon are still trying to get me saved." He smiled when he put quotation marks around *saved* with his fingers. "I think Leon's worried about me."

"Mmm." *That makes about twenty of us,* she thought.

"How come you're walking?"

She waved at the woods coming up on both sides of the road. "Bobby an' Junior an' I played all over this part of the place when we were kids. I just like being out here."

For the first time, he remembered what A. J. Mason asked him on the bridge. *You ever wonder why?* He asked Missy, "Why haven't you ever told me about what happened the day Junior was killed?"

The trees on either side of the road met over their heads; a soft breeze came out of the shadows and cooled her face. The sounds and smells reminded her of a hundred childhood adventures in the woods. "We camped out over here when I was five years old."

"By yourselves?"

"Not quite. We were almost in Roosevelt's yard." She laughed. "I ended up sleepin' on the floor under their kitchen table; Ellen said that was my tent."

He waited.

"I wish everybody in the world could've known him."

He stopped with her, and she looked back toward the bridge. She could see a bright June day and black water and hear the sound of the gun. And she could see him land in the water beside her, in the middle of the things he feared the most. She smiled.

"A. J. Mason was on the bridge with a rifle. Nobody knows how many snakes he'd shot—maybe ten or twenty. They wouldn't sink when he blew their heads off. They kept squirmin' in the water, bleedin' 'til the water turned red, tryin' to get close to me. I can still see Junior sprintin' across that old float. He jumped an' landed in the water right by me an' pulled me back to the float. He came out there in the middle of all that hell to get me." She stopped for a moment and wiped away a lone tear. "Pip held him while he died—Junior made her promise to tell me an' Bobby about Jesus." Another tear. "The last thing he ever said was, 'You tell my daddy I watched out for her.'"

She started walking again. "A. J. Mason cried on an' off for a week."

Pat said, "He told me."

"A. J. did?"

"About crying, not what happened on the bridge."

"Why wouldn't he tell you about what happened?"

"He gave me a test on angels. I flunked."

Pat told her about his conversation with Mason. He closed with the part where he told Mason he ought to teach him some manners, including the part about Mason holding a rifle while Pat threatened him.

She was open-mouthed with amazement. "Wow! He *is* gettin' old."

"He asked me if I ever wondered why nobody had told me about what happened at the bridge or when the Dillworth guy died."

"Mmm."

"Why haven't you told me before?"

"Maybe I knew how you'd react. There are some people who could've been there an' not understand that there were evil spirits at work."

He asked, "Can you give me a single reason why I should believe in something I can't see?"

"Probably not, but consider this. If *I* was a spirit being an' I wanted to win a war against the world, I would try to convince people that I didn't exist."

"That's too simple."

She didn't smile. "Yeah, an' way too easy."

"And you think there's going to be a war."

"Pat, the war started a long time ago, an' I know Who the winner's gonna be—I've read the end of the Book."

They walked the rest of the way to the Edwardses' house without speaking. When they reached the house, she said, "Be gentle with Emmalee, okay? She's still a little gun-shy around men."

"I don't need any thirteen-year-old friends. I'll just wait out here."

"Oh, for gosh sakes, c'mon. She won't bite."

"Humphf." *If I had wanted to mollycoddle teenagers, I'd have skipped getting my doctorate.*

The screen door burst open before Missy could knock. "Hi! I won—oh!" Emmalee stopped when she saw Pat and managed to slip behind Missy while clinging to the door.

Missy took her arm and eased her back into the open. "Em-malee, this is Pat Patterson."

Emmalee's training took over. She put out her hand, looked the man in the eye, and said the words just like her momma taught her. "I'm pleased to meet you."

Pat showed what he hoped was a warm smile. "Thank you. The pleasure is mine."

The smile apparently worked; traces of shyness lingered, but the initial shock was gone. Her daddy said this white man was Missy Parker's friend. "You work with my daddy at the gin."

"That's right."

She tried a tentative smile. "An' you teach at a real college."

Talking to a teenager was a chore he hadn't signed up for. He decided he could use her to practice talking to dull people at faculty coffees. "Soon, I hope. You're interested in college, aren't you?"

She forgot about being shy. "That'll be up to Daddy an' God."

Missy held out the sack and rescued him. "I brought you a present."

Emmalee peeked in the sack and her smile turned to laughter. "Missy! It's note cards! A whole hundred!" She grabbed Missy and hugged her fiercely. "Thank you, thank you, thank you! They'll last me a whole year." She remembered another lesson in manners and stepped back from the door. "Y'all come in."

Inside, Missy included Pat in another conversation that didn't interest him. "Emmalee's been learnin' a Scripture verse a week. She's gonna start doin' two a week."

Again, Pat practiced sounding interested. "Good girl. Can you recite one for me?"

The protégée reattached herself to Missy. Pat managed not to sigh.

Missy said, "Do last week's."

Emmalee relaxed her grip on Missy's arm and forced herself to make eye contact with the tall man. "First Corinthians one, eighteen. 'For the word of the cross is folly to those who are perishin', but to us who are bein' saved it is the power of God.'"

The two girls waited while Pat made a note in his Bible. He said, "What about this week's?"

Emmalee picked a card from the table and said, "I don't know it good yet."

Missy held out her hand and said, "Maybe I can prompt you."

Emmalee reached past her to hand the card to Pat.

He said, "What do I do with it?"

She ignored the frown. "You can help me."

He looked at Missy, and she gave him a you're-on-your-own smile.

Emmalee took a breath and said it perfectly. "Isaiah fifty-five, eleven, 'So shall My word be that goes forth from My mouth; it shall not return to Me empty, but it shall accomplish that which I purpose, an' prosper in the thing for which I sent it.'"

Pat read aloud the last words from the card. "'And prosper in the thing for which I sent it.'"

While Pat studied the card, Missy reached into the bag and brought out a piece of paper. "This is the thing about Joan of Arc I promised you."

Emmalee got more excited. "I'll copy it an' bring it back to you this week."

"How about comin' to the house for dinner day after tomorrow?"

Missy and Emmalee made a date for lunch on Friday to review their memory work and pray.

When they got to the road, Missy turned to smile and wave good-bye to Emmalee. Pat frowned and ignored the little girl on the porch.

They walked slowly, moving along the parallel cuts in the gravel. They were halfway back to the bridge before she spoke. "What can I say to you that hasn't already been said?"

"About God?"

She nodded. "Mmm."

He didn't want to hear any more. "I've been here almost three months, Missy. I've heard it all, some of it twice."

"It scares me for you to leave here without believin'." She was poking along with her hands stuffed in her pockets, kicking at rocks with her scruffy tennis shoes.

"Well, you gave it the old college try."

"Can we still write to each other?"

He didn't want to answer. He had come to Mississippi to spend time with her, and it hadn't worked. It was time to move on. "I'm not sure."

"Oh?"

"I've tried to see your truth. I can't. I need to get on with pursuing my own."

"Your own truth?"

"Mmm."

She walked more slowly, thinking. "Pat, truth is truth. What kind of reasonin' would support havin' each individual person arbitrarily select a belief system an' declare it to be *his* truth?"

"Why not? I'm sincere about what I believe. I have standards—high standards—but you don't think I'm good enough for you."

She didn't frown or raise her voice. "You're crammin' my criteria for a relationship into holes where it doesn't fit. This isn't about datin', it's about destinies. You want to believe there're as many destinies as there are people. I know for a fact that there are only two."

"That's too narrow, Missy. Christendom is melting away while the world watches because of inflexible attitudes like yours."

"Christendom is not what's goin' to melt, Pat. An' it's not *my* attitude, it's God's. An' you're tryin' to juggle destiny, datin', and world religions all in one argument." She tried a smile. "Pick one thing an' stick to it."

"Okay." He stated his first priority without smiling. "Dating."

"We've never dated."

"I want to change that."

The smile was gone. "If you know I'm your friend, that's enough."

"Not for me. You're different from any woman I've ever met. You're bright, fascinating, and beautiful." He was looking at her. She was looking at the road. "To tell you the truth, thoughts of you keep me awake at night."

"I'm genuinely honored, but I can't. I'm sorry." Her face color-matched itself to her toenail polish. "I can't date a man who's free to change what he believes as often as he changes his toothbrush."

"I wouldn't do that."

"You can't know that. You may feel that way now, but you don't have any place to anchor your conviction, Pat. An' the place you happen to be standin' at any given moment is your only navigation point. A sensible woman can't date a man who can't tell where he's standin' or where he's goin'."

"Then maybe it's time for you to be less sensible."

She didn't want to wave her arms, but her hands managed to get out of her pockets. "Are you listenin' to either one of us? You're askin' me to turn my back on the only security I'll ever know, to let a man who doesn't believe in compasses guide me through a jungle."

He set up his big question by asking, "Then how close am I to meeting your criteria for someone you would date?"

She slowed and stopped, took in a breath, and let it out. The hands went back in her pockets, and she kept her eyes on the gravel. "An eternity away."

He played what he thought was his trump card. "Okay. What if I become a Christian?"

Not sounding incredulous took some work. "So you an' I can date?"

He nodded.

Instead of answering, she prayed. *Lord, You said the preachin' of Your cross is foolishness to those who are perishin', an' this man is livin' proof. Father, datin' him might be nice, but I've never wanted anything as much as I want to see him in heaven.*

Pat was impatient. "Well?"

Her arms straightened so that her hands were jammed farther into her pockets. Her hands were clenched into fists, and her chin moved back and forth. "It doesn't work that way."

He wanted her to quit looking at the rocks and look at him. "You're making too big a thing of this, Missy. I don't see why you can't bend enough for us to start seeing each other."

Her voice lowered without her help. "How important is it to you?"

That was something he really hadn't thought about.

Her whole body relaxed. If she faced him and looked into his eyes, he would say whatever it took to sway her. She kept her eyes on his chest. "Would you have me be different?"

He could remember only two times when she had looked directly into his eyes—once when he'd made that stupid remark to her at the hospital and the second time on the front porch of the cabin when he made her angry. This time she wasn't angry; she was solemn, and she wasn't looking at him.

In that one suspended moment, while he watched her wait for his answer, he knew one thing: He didn't want to go back to Texas without a reason to see her again.

"I think you ought to do what it takes to give us a chance."

"I'm sorry to hear that."

"That means you won't."

"It means I'm not interested in comformin' myself to a man who might decide to change shape before supper."

When they got to the bridge, she forced herself to say, "You want to come to the house? Granny made a chocolate cake."

He thought, *That's good. If you keep feeding the guy dessert, you can treat him like a leper.* He said, "No, thanks."

She knew he was going to turn her down, but she had to ask. "Can I write to you when you get home?"

"I can't see how it would help." He was tired of the notes, the conversations, and the Bible. "Let's let it go."

He went to the cabin.

She walked across the bridge to her house feeling cold and empty, the same way she had felt when she'd known David was dying.

Saturday was three days away.

CHAPTER TWENTY-FIVE

Friday was frying-pan hot. A feeble breeze, laden with humidity, came from the south and went unnoticed by the men at the Parker Gin. August was teaching Pat that the temperature in Texas might go higher than in Mississippi, but the days would never get hotter. He asked Mose for a lunch break at twelve thirty to take a long dip in the lake; three other hands heard the request and decided they'd rather swim than eat. Mose gave his blessing.

Missy and Emmalee met at noon, both wearing white blouses and jeans, both barefoot. They sat in the Parkers' air-conditioned dining room and talked about boys and school, had prayer time, then said their verses to each other over sandwiches and sweet tea. After dessert, Emmalee gathered up her Bible and notes, and Missy asked if she wanted a ride home.

"No, ma'am. I'm gonna stop over at the gin an' see Daddy."

Missy said, "C'mon, I'll walk over with you an' say hi to Mose."

"Can we meet next week?"

"Probably. Let's wait an' decide on Wednesday."

Mose and Roosevelt met the girls outside the gin office.

When Roosevelt reached to hug his daughter she squealed and hid behind Missy. "You're too sweaty!"

Roosevelt laughed. Sweat ran in rivulets down his face and arms; Mose's khaki shirt was sweat-stained brown everywhere but the pocket flaps and the tips of his collar.

When Emmalee came out of hiding, Mose said, "Yo' daddy says you memorizin' two verses a week now."

"Me an' Missy both. We're gonna learn a hundred verses by the end of next summer."

Mose approved and Roosevelt beamed; both clapped. Emmalee ducked her head.

The racket brought the dog out from under the loading dock to see if he were needed. He passed close enough to the group to make sure none of the items in Emmalee's hands were edible and moved on to the shade on the east side of the office.

Missy looked around the loading dock. "Where's Pat?"

Mose pointed at the lake. "Him an' some of the boys took lunchtime to cool off."

Missy looked where he pointed. "In the lake?" Her brow darkened.

The dog pricked his ears when he heard her tone.

"They'll be fine," Mose said.

She walked to the east side of the dock; the dog and Emmalee followed. Over in front of the cabin, three black men were walking out of the water with their overalls on; a white man was out in the lake, floating on his back. The black men sat down on the bank to put on their shoes, laughing and enjoying the short recess from the heat. The white man floated a few feet from the bank, spitting water into the air like a small whale.

Two figures clothed in brilliance stood in the spirit world next to Missy and her friends. The taller one spoke. *Now, my leader?*

Very soon. Send me Pat's guardian.

What of Emmalee, leader?

When I have spoken to Pat's guardian, have hers come to me. Go.

The tall angel touched his sword to his chest. A different angel stood instantly in his place, his sword touching his chest. *Here am I, my leader.*

On the far side of the lake, the black men waved at the white one and moved off toward the county road. The white man rolled onto his stomach and moved at a leisurely pace for the bank.

Missy let out her breath when Pat reached the bank and started pulling on his shoes. Emmalee waited until the man got his shoes on and said, "I'm goin' home now, Daddy."

Missy and the men watched the young girl weave her way through the trailers parked in front of the gin. She turned when she got to the road to smile and wave, and the dog got up and trotted down the steps. Emmalee walked toward the bridge. The dog trailed behind.

The black men who had been swimming passed her on their way back to the gin, still dripping water and laughing. Roosevelt, Mose, and Missy watched everyone speak and smile. The black child kept moving.

She was on the bridge when she checked to see where the white man was; he was still on his way up to the road. She shortened her steps and the dog caught up. When she was almost to the middle of the bridge, she checked Pat's progress again. Still too far. She took three more steps and dropped her memory cards.

Roosevelt said, "That child can outrun a rabbit, but she drops everything she touches."

"She didn't drop those. She turned 'em loose." Missy was grinning. "You watch."

Pat Patterson was on the far end of the bridge now. The dog— who had been watching Emmalee's recovery of the note cards—turned his attention to the white man and moved closer to the railing.

Pat was still a few steps away when Emmalee picked up the last card. She straightened in time to unleash the day's biggest smile and said expectantly, "Afternoon, Mistah Pat. Sure is hot, ain't it?"

"Well, would you look at that." Roosevelt was shaking his head and smiling, "She's flirtin' with that boy. I ought to tan her britches."

"I'll have a little talk with her next Friday," Missy laughed. "Maybe she can give me some pointers."

Pat almost smiled as he passed Emmalee. "Hi."

Missy said, "Dadgum his hide, he didn't even smile at her."

The threesome could see Emmalee's shoulders fall when Pat kept moving; her chin sank to her chest, and she turned away from them. The dog came away from the railing and tripped her when she took her first step. She was facedown on the dusty bridge before the sound of her exclamation reached them. Pat was turning to see what had happened.

Missy turned for the steps by the office, and Mose said, "Just a minute."

"I'm gonna go help her."

"Uh-uh." Mose shook his head. "That dog ain't never come close to gettin' under my feet or nobody else's. Let's wait here a bit an' see what happens."

Missy looked at Roosevelt.

The giant smiled. "It'll be okay; she ain't tough as you, but she's learnin'."

Pat was walking back to the girl, and she scooted back to prop herself against the railing; the bridge around her was littered with white note cards. The dog came and sat at her elbow, and she put her arm around him. Her jeans and white blouse were covered with dust.

"Are you okay?"

"I 'bout . . . got the breath knocked outta me." She didn't want to blame the dog. "Sometimes I'm clumsy."

"You want me to go get Roosevelt?"

"No, sir. I'll be all right soon's I get my breath back."

She moved to stand up, and he turned to pick up the cards. "I'll get these."

"I can help. Missy says you goin' back to Texas."

"Yep. Tomorrow."

"When're you comin' back?"

"I'm not."

She didn't understand. "How will you get to see Missy?"

"I guess I won't."

"How can you be her boyfriend if you don't come see her?" She stooped to help him pick up her notes.

"I'm not her boyfriend."

The note cards were momentarily forgotten. "Why not?"

He thought she might be the most innocent looking snoop he'd ever seen. He smiled for the first time. "She won't date me because I'm not a Christian."

It wasn't smart to challenge a white man, even the friend of a friend, but she couldn't let it pass—her teenager's mind was imagining something almost as dangerous as angering God. She pretended to turn her attention back to the scattered cards. "Does yo' momma know you'd joke about somethin' like that?"

"I wasn't joking."

She abandoned the note cards. "You're not a Christian?"

"No."

"But everybody says you're smart—you're almost a college teacher."

"I don't have to believe like Missy to be smart. I just don't agree with her."

"Why don't you?"

"Because I don't believe in the exclusivity of Christianity."

"I don't know what that *exclusive* word means."

That's why we have dictionaries, he thought. His smile had disappeared sentences earlier. "It means that I believe Hindus and Buddhists and Muslims have a right to know God as well as anyone else. Everyone gets to choose what they believe, even if they don't believe in God."

"Those people—those Hindus an' things—the ones you say can know God, are they Christians?"

"Of course not." Trying to explain belief systems to a little girl was getting old fast. He picked up the last of the materials and straightened. "That's what I mean. People don't have to be Christians to know God—that would be exclusivity."

"God don't believe that, Mr. Pat."

He handed her the Bible and worked to fit the cards together without getting them wet. "You can call me Pat."

She reached for the cards. "Lemme read you what God says about that exclusive thing. John fourteen, six. 'Jesus said to him, I am the way, an' the truth, an' the life; no one comes to the Father, but by Me.'"

"Emmalee, all those other people can't be wrong. There's a whole world full of people out there—millions and millions of good people—that don't believe that they have to rely on Jesus."

She studied his face for a long second, then held up a finger and said, "Just a minute."

The spectators on the dock watched Emmalee turn and look at the lake, wait a few seconds, and turn back. From a distance, the little girl's body language was reminiscent of a young colt's—everything that wasn't long legs was enthusiasm.

"What'd she do?" asked Mose.

Missy and Roosevelt both smiled and answered. "She prayed."

Mose said, "Then that's what we ought to be doin'."

Emmalee turned back to Pat and pushed her Bible into his hands. "Hold this." She shuffled through her cards.

Pat cursed to himself—the whole country was full of Bible-crazy people. He'd spent three months being set upon by Bible-thumping zealots: the fifty-year-old yardboy, a gin foreman who probably hadn't gotten past fifth grade, and an exquisite beauty who could melt men with her eyes. Now he had been attacked by an eighth-grade girl who had probably never been more than twenty-five miles from home. He tried to hand the Bible back to her. "Emmalee, I need to get back to the gin."

"Just a minute. This is more important, an' Mistah Mose won't care. I promise." She found what she was looking for and pulled a card out of the stack. She cleared her throat; beads of sweat sparkled on her forehead and under her eyes; she held the cards against her dusty blouse with both hands while she introduced her subject. "Joan of Arc was just a young girl 'bout my age when she was captured by the British soldiers. They gave her a chance to save herself if she'd turn against her king, but she wouldn't do it. A man that's smarter than me said this is what she said just before they burned her at the stake. Listen: 'Every man gives his life for what he believes. Every woman gives her life for what she believes. Sometimes people believe little or nothin', an' yet they give their lives to that little or nothin'. One life is all we have—an' we live it, an' then it's gone. But to surrender what you are, an' live without belief, is more terrible than dyin', even more terrible than dyin' young. But there's a worse fate than livin' without belief—it is to live with a firm commitment to that, which at the end of life, at the portals of eternity, turns out to have betrayed you.'"

Not bad for a kid. "Well, that's beautiful, Emmalee. Thanks for reading it to me."

"No, that ain't beautiful—it's nice, an' it's truthful, but John three, sixteen is beautiful. Listen: 'For God so loved the world, that He gave His only begotten Son, that whoever believes in Him should not perish, but have eternal life.'" She held her cards to her chest and closed her eyes. "*That's* beautiful, an' His Son will never betray you."

They watched Emmalee talking earnestly, holding her note cards and leaning toward Pat, lecturing. And they watched Pat occasionally shake his head politely but firmly.

Missy saw it first. "Look."

Emmalee was watching Pat—holding her cards to her chest. Pat was staring into the distance. Neither spoke. A full minute passed, then two. No one spoke.

Pat walked past Emmalee to the railing; he rested one hand on an old ladder nailed to the side of the bridge and stared out at the lake.

Mose watched the two on the bridge and said, "Y'all be prayin', now."

The angel appeared with his sword in his fist, his fist over his heart. *Here am I, my leader.*

The leader moved closer to the two on the bridge. *The moment is upon them*, he said. *Summon the legion.*

The angel at the leader's elbow disappeared, and six thousand angels materialized around the two small humans on the bridge. The angels stood in ordered ranks, facing outward, each one carried a sword brighter than any earthly mirror. *Ready.*

The archangel nodded and smiled. *Good.*

The wind that had been from the south became quiet. The dog stood, pointed himself north, and tested the air. The cypress trees on the north end of the lake felt it first—the wind was changing.

Pat looked south down the length of the lake, hearing again the words she had just spoken; it all made sense. From behind him, the gentlest breeze cooled his back. "I've been doing it all wrong, haven't I?"

He couldn't see her, but she nodded. "Yes, sir."

"God sent Jesus here for me, didn't He?"

"Yes, sir."

"That's what everybody's been trying to tell me," he whispered.

She didn't say anything.

"What do I do now?"

She stepped close and rested her hand on his arm. "If you want to tell Him you believe, you need to pray."

He nodded because he didn't trust his voice. When he managed to speak, he was hoarse with emotion. "It doesn't make sense for Him to do this for me. I'm . . . my brother was a good man. I'm—" He remembered all the thoughts he'd had about the people who had tried to be his friends. "I'm not good."

"Nobody's ever gonna be good enough to come to Him. You come to Him an' accept what He did, an' He makes you clean."

Pat looked at the lake. *He makes me clean.*

They watched him saying something to her. She shielded her eyes so she could look up at him and rested her hand on his arm while she answered. He nodded and knelt in the dust by the old ladder.

"Have mercy," Roosevelt whispered.

Emmalee knelt by him and took his hand. "My daddy says for me not to hold hands with a boy yet, but he'd want me to hold yours so you won't be by yourself. Understand?"

He nodded. The breeze on his wet clothes felt cool, but that wasn't why he was trembling. He gripped her hand between both of his. "I don't know what I'm supposed to say."

"You have to tell Him you know you're a sinner an' you're sorry, an' you should say you believe in what Jesus did for you, an' you want Him to be your Savior. An' if I was you, I'd thank Him."

And that's what he did.

Mose and Missy and Roosevelt watched the tall man and the little girl bow their heads and pray.

When they were standing again, Emmalee took his hand and walked with him toward the gin.

"Mose—" Missy's voice broke and she wiped her eyes on her sleeves.

"I see 'em, honey," said Mose. "Just like me an' you."

The three on the loading dock walked down to meet Emmalee and the new Christian. Mose and Roosevelt shook his hand; Emmalee jumped up and grabbed her daddy around the neck, sweat and all. Missy stood to the side, waiting.

When Pat and Missy made eye contact, he blushed. He said, "I was wrong."

"Shoot." She laughed when she said it. "You're the only person in twenty miles that didn't know that."

He took a step closer. Sweat or lake water dripped from his hair. "I've changed my mind."

She kept their conversation in the group. "We saw that."

"I don't mean about God."

Every time she laughed, it sounded like she was having fun. "Oh?"

He laughed with her. "I think it will be okay if you write to me."

Missy's eyes sparkled when she winked at Emmalee. She told Pat, "I don't have a reason to write to you anymore."

"Then I'll see if I can come up with a good reason—and I'll write to you."

Emmalee squeezed her daddy's hand and giggled.

Pat Patterson, soon to be Ph.D., wrote to the girl soon and often after he got back to Texas, and she wrote back.

Just before Thanksgiving, he got one of the familiar note cards. It included an invitation to spend the Christmas holidays with her family; the pale-blue sheet carried just the faintest hint of perfume.

French Bainbridge had no interest in anyone's future plans but his own. She didn't know it, but French was planning a date with a cute little eighth-grader and her best friend.

CHAPTER TWENTY-SIX

The Christmas holidays came to Mississippi, and so did Pat Patterson. He and Missy spent most of their waking moments together; she took him to meet people he didn't know, they played canasta with the family, and they spent long hours alone in front of the fireplace.

Other than by folks at Cat Lake, the first anniversary of Pip's death was noted by few people. Christmas came and people gave presents. Mose rode down to Jackson, intending to stay with Pearl for a few days, but got restless and came home the next day. The first day of the New Year brought colder weather and found him poking around at the gin.

"Mose, what on earth are you doin' out here?" Bobby Lee had come over to see why Mose's truck was parked at the gin. "There won't be anything to do for another month, an' the cold's liable to freeze you hard as one of these machines."

"It is a bit chilly, ain't it?" The dog had gotten out of the truck because he thought he'd rather be with Mose than be warm; now he was having second thoughts. The wind whipped around corners and carried the cold into all the cubbyholes. "I reckon I'm just havin' a hard time findin' somethin' to keep me out of trouble."

"Well, come over to the house, an' me or one of the kids will whip you in a game of checkers."

Mose declined. "I been figurin' on movin' back out here. I believe I might go over an' do a little work on that old house." He could play checkers with Bobby Lee at the gin, but going into his white friend's house for a social visit wasn't something he was ready for. The two men hunched their shoulders against the wind and visited until the cold drove Bobby Lee back to his house.

Pool Pommer, Tub's oldest, came from a passel of good-for-nothing offspring that ran long on boys and short on brains. He was short, thin, and—seasoned by two trips to Parchman—rat-mean; money for staples—food and snuff—came to him from stealing and running a moonshine still. The moonshiner had never heard the word *genealogy*, and he didn't know how he and Halbert Bainbridge were kin, but he knew they were some kind of cousin, and that was enough. When the phone rang in his shack, the caller was French Bainbridge.

Pool's kinfolk said, "I need you to come to Greenwood and pick me up."

They talked for less than a minute. Pool hung up, pulled on a greasy hunting cap and a worn-out coat, and got into his truck.

Mose's little cabin didn't really need much work. One or two boards on the porch could be replaced, and a couple of spots on the roof might need attention in the spring; otherwise, the house was snug and neat. He got the fireplace going and spent the afternoon reading his Bible, pausing now and again to pray. Outside, the north wind sucked the smoke from the chimney and brought cold, clear air to chill the lake.

A short way down the road from the Cat Lake bridge, things in the Edwards house were not as peaceful.

For the ninth time, Roosevelt Edwards told his daughter, "You can go to the church meetin' with me an' Momma, or you can stay by yo'self, Emmalee. It's too cold for you to be out on the road."

For the tenth time, the teenager begged, "Please, Daddy, please. I can run down to their house in just fifteen minutes. I've timed it myself. Me an' Missy can do all our Bible verses, an' I can see Pat." She sat on his lap, a hand on each of his cheeks, pointing his face at hers. Desperation charged her need to make him understand that this was probably the most important moment in her life. "She hasn't gotten to see me but once since Christmas, an' I need to tell her all I've learned. Okay? Please."

Roosevelt and Ellen Edwards had two grown children. Their boy Milton was in the Marines; the older girl was teaching school. Emmalee had come along when her brother was seven and her sister was nine, and the two older children practically spoiled her rotten.

Roosevelt, whose 350 pounds of muscle fit neatly around the child's little finger, resorted to the only thing that had ever assured him victory over his teenager. He said, "El, come in here an' tell yo' daughter what to do."

The girl's momma walked out of her kitchen, took two seconds to point her expression and an emphatic finger at the girl, and went back to her work. The father-daughter negotiations ceased, and the girl withdrew to her room.

The guardian angel that stood at Mose's shoulder said, *He is a good man.*

The angel's leader said, *He is.*

Mose's angel said, *I am ready, my leader.*

As are the others. He nodded for the angel to act. *Glory to our God who sits on the throne, and to the Lamb.*

The late-afternoon smoke that came from the cabin's chimney drifted to the south. The wind across the lake was dying with the day's sun, and ice was reaching out from the shallows around the cypress trees. Morning would bring the Mississippi Delta a record-low temperature.

Mose was watching the sky color itself a darker blue and enjoying the fire. He felt Pip's warm hand on his shoulder, and she said, "You've got time to go over to that huntin' club an' maybe get us a rabbit, an' I'll be makin' up some biscuits while you're gone."

"I reckon I can go right this minute." He reached back to pat her hand.

When he moved, his Bible slid to the floor and the sound woke him. He left the Book where it was and sat back to warm his heart with the almost-real memory of her touch. The coals in the fireplace glowed, and her words came back to him. *Go over to that huntin' club.*

He finally stirred when the dog left the fire to nuzzle his hand.

He bent to pick up the Bible, then brushed off its cover while he repeated the words to himself: *Over to that huntin' club.* He looked out the window at the waning daylight and thought, *Me an' her both knows there ain't no rabbits at that huntin' club.*

He banked the fire and slipped on his wool stocking cap; the big coat came next. The two homecoming presents Pip bought him over a year earlier were ready to go—the Redbone hound was waiting at the door; the loaded shotgun was out in the truck.

The calm, frigid air carried the sound of someone crossing the Cat Lake bridge when Mose walked out to his pickup. He recognized the truck crossing the bridge but couldn't tell who was in it. *Most likely jes' Pool Pommer an' some other white trash.*

The passenger in the truck saw Mose but didn't notice him. French Bainbridge had his mind on other things.

Pool said, "What're we gonna do when we catch her?"

"You don't need to worry about that, Pool," he sneered. "You just need to take me to where she is."

Mean people aren't necessarily brave people. "Have you seen her pa? He's bigger'n a horse an' twice as tough."

"That's why I brought this." French pulled out a nickel-plated .38. "I call it my horse-killer."

The humor suited Pool and he giggled. His eyes stayed on the handgun while he estimated its value. French saved them from running into the roadside ditch by yelling at Pool to watch where he was going. Pool swerved and snickered. He calculated that he could sell the gun for enough money to buy two weeks' worth of food and snuff, maybe even some beer. He didn't know how much sheepskin coats cost, but the one French had on looked expensive.

"We got to leave here early," Ellen Edwards called from the kitchen. "Y'all come on to supper."

Roosevelt took his place at the head of the small table, and he and his wife waited for Emmalee. When the girl whose world was ruined sat down at the table, she kept her eyes on her plate.

Roosevelt looked at his wife and winked. He reached for his girl's hand and his wife's and said, "Emmalee, baby, would you bless the food?"

The girl jumped. Her daddy had never asked anyone else, not even the preacher, to say the blessing at their table. She looked up to see both her parents waiting with their eyes closed, and her hands started to shake. Her daddy squeezed her hand gently, and she said, "Lord, I thank You for—" She stopped to get her breath. "—for a whole new year, an' a whole past one. An', Lord, I thank You for blessin' me with Momma an' Daddy." Tears tickled the sides of her nose. "Forgive me for bein' hardheaded. All I want, Lord, is for You to grow me into a woman they would be proud of. Amen. Oh! An' thank You for the food."

Emmalee ate her food and listened to her momma and daddy plan their evening. She made a New Year's resolution to not be so much trouble.

The dog made a circuit under the trees while Mose got the shotgun and a flashlight from the truck. Mose made sure the gun was fully loaded and put three more shells in his pocket. The shotgun was a 12-gauge, a secondhand but exceptionally well-cared-for Winchester Model 97 that had belonged to A. J. Mason. Mr. A. J. had wanted to give Pip the gun, but she had insisted on paying for it; he did manage to get away with selling it to her at a small fraction of its worth. Mose showed the gun to the dog and turned toward the empty cotton field behind the cabin.

The hound saw the gun and decided he was happy to be out in the cold air as long as he could hunt. He padded back and forth across the field, stopping occasionally to sniff the air and make sure Mose was still coming. He had learned that there wouldn't be any game in the cotton field, but they were making for the woods of Eagle Nest Brake, and the brake was home to rabbits, quail, and deer.

Behind them, sparse gray smoke from the chimney rose straight into the sky, turned pink in the late afternoon sun, then leaned gently toward the south.

French decided they would walk right into the Edwards house and take the girl.

They were making their fifth trip down the road in front of the house. Smoke came from the chimney; Roosevelt's pickup sat in the front yard, and they could see people moving around in the house. The heater in Pool's old truck didn't work, and the temperature in the cab was a breezy sixteen degrees. Pool was sweating under his coat.

For the third time he asked, "How close do you think we ought to git?" He had yet to hear the answer he wanted.

Pool had seen Roosevelt up close and knew the man wasn't going to let them take his daughter while he was still alive, and if they killed him they'd have to kill his wife. The thought of killing didn't bother either of the men; the possibility of getting caught bothered Pool. The last jury he encountered had deliberated less than ten minutes before sending him back to Parchman. Any twelve men in the county would put him up there for life if he killed a kid, even a black one.

"I told you, we can pull up in the front yard, stupid. Why would we want to go stomping around in the woods in the cold?"

Meanness overcame fear, and Pool's cunning surfaced. "Don't be callin' me stupid, French. It ain't your car folks are gonna see parked at their house—that's why you left it in Greenwood."

"Well, then, stop wherever you like. Just get it done."

"You just hold your horses, French. It ain't dark enough, yet."

French Bainbridge held his horses and the .38. His anger was taking the upper hand, and he thought about shooting Pool right then, but he needed the idiot to drive him back to Greenwood.

Roosevelt started putting on his coat. "Baby, it's time to leave."

"Go out an' start that truck an' let it warm up some."

"I'm doin' that, but you needs to hurry up."

The gun rack by the door held the truck keys, two old hats, and a single-barrel shotgun. Roosevelt took the keys and went out.

There was plenty of daylight left when Mose and the dog got to the brake and scared up their first rabbit. Mose had a good shot at the animal but passed. The dog was disappointed not to hear the sound of the gun, but Mose wanted to stay quiet 'til he saw what was waiting for them at the hunting club.

The two cousins were almost even with the house when Roosevelt came out. Thick, white breath clouded behind him like steam from a locomotive.

"Look at that." French grinned. "He's leaving."

"That's good. We'll wait 'til he's gone an' go git the girl."

"Right. Go a mile or so down the road and turn around. We'll make a quick visit to this sweet child and go looking for her playmate."

When Mose and the dog came through the edge of the brake, they were directly in front of the hunting club's cabin. Mose told the dog to come to him, and they walked the short distance to the house together. The dog adopted Mose's cautious attitude and sniffed at the air and ground as they walked. They stopped a few feet from the building and Mose said, "Listen, now. If they's somebody here, we wants to see them 'fore they sees us. You understand me?"

The dog heard the caution in the man's voice and barely woofed. He followed the man's gaze and gave the house a thorough going-over. It was deserted. The smell of wood smoke was filtered to the them through the woods to the north.

Mose pointed at the woods. "Roosevelt lives right through yonder, maybe a mile. That smoke's comin' from his place."

The dog looked at where the man pointed and back at the man. The dog also smelled a covey of quail huddled somewhere in the same direction. He waited for the man to send him to flush the quail.

Instead, the man said, "C'mon. We bes' go look down to the barn."

Emmalee was curled in her daddy's chair under a warm blanket with her stack of memory-verse cards. Her momma said, "We'll be gone at least two hours, hon. If you needs anything, you call up to the church." The Edwardses had a brand-new telephone, and her momma believed in using it.

"Yes, ma'am."

Her daddy came through the door with an armload of firewood. "Baby, everybody likes that new blouse, but you won't need to burn up all this wood if you'll go put on a sweater. You hear?"

"Yes, sir. I'm goin' right now."

Ellen was going out the door. "Let's go, Rose. I don't want to be late."

Her daddy said, "You gonna be all right here by yo'self?"

"I'll be fine, Daddy. I'm almost fourteen years old, an' I can take care of myself."

"Mm-hmm." He kissed the top of her head and followed his wife out the door.

It was still light enough for them to see the exhaust from the truck when the house came in view again. They passed and French looked back to watch the front door open. "The man and woman are leaving."

"Good. It's just us an' the girl."

"Give them a couple of minutes to get gone, then turn around."

The inspection of the barn turned up a snoot full of dust for the dog and one or two startled cats. Mose walked back outside thinking maybe he'd come on a wild-goose chase. *Well, the trip won't be wasted if we finds us a rabbit on the way home.* He spoke to the dog, "We'll make another turn around this ol' place an' go back to the fire." He pointed toward the back of the barn, and the dog loped off.

The last bit of the daylight was trying to hide behind the trees in Eagle Nest Brake.

CHAPTER TWENTY-SEVEN

Emmalee hadn't put on her sweater yet. Her new white blouse was a Christmas present from Missy, and if Missy happened to stop by the house, Emmalee didn't want it hidden beneath a sweater. She had gone almost all the way through her stack of memory verses.

Pool stopped the old truck down the road from the house and they got out.

French said, "You got a knife?"

Pool didn't know anybody who didn't carry a knife. He produced it without seeming to move his hand.

"Keep it in your pocket. She can't hurt us, and we don't want blood all over us."

Pool's breath came in short, white puffs, and he started to shiver. "Are you gonna have that pistol out?"

French nodded. "In case there's someone in the house we don't know about. I don't plan on shooting her. You do like I said, and keep that knife in your pocket for now. Understand?"

Pool didn't like being told what to do, but he wanted to get in the house where it would be warm. He nodded so they could get going.

"You go in the front door. I'll be coming in the back. Don't hurt that girl. Understand?"

What Pool understood was that he was helping French, not working for him, and he'd pretty much had his fill of his rich cousin's willingness to order him around. "Can we just hurry up 'fore I freeze?"

Mose stopped at the corner of the clubhouse and looked around. He thought, *In the dream Pip said, "Go over to that huntin' club." But there ain't no rabbits or nothin' else over here.*

He took off the stocking cap and eased down to one knee by the side of the house. *Lord, I done a foolish thing here. I come runnin' off over to this cabin without so much as a howdy-do to You. I reckon I'm gettin' forgetful in my old age, but I don't want to leave You out when it comes to decidin' how to use my time. You know I loved that woman, but next time I'll call on You 'fore I go galavantin' off over the countryside.*

Emmalee was going over her last verse when she heard the sound. Something outside the house broke a twig or branch. She got out of the chair and pulled the blanket close around her. The only creature that would step on a stick hard enough to break it was a man. She looked out the front window and didn't see anything, but she got to the side window in time to see a dim outline scurry from the woods to the house; someone was trying to sneak up to the front door. She moved to the front wall by her daddy's gun.

Scuffing sounds came seconds later, telling her that someone had come up on their porch without calling out. That meant whoever was outside wasn't friendly. She tried to take the shotgun off the rack, but she was still holding her memory cards. She dropped the cards and backed across the room with the gun leveled at the front door.

The door handle turned slowly, and the door eased open. Dirty fingernails came around the edge of the door, followed by a dirtier hand. The next thing the girl saw was a white man's thin face peeking into the room. "Good evenin' to you. It's just Pool Pommer." His grin showed crooked brown teeth.

Pool could see that the shotgun wasn't cocked. He held up his hands and stepped into the room. He was easing sideways, showing his teeth, watching the gun and measuring the distance to the girl—weighing the odds of rushing her before she could cock it. While he deliberated, Emmalee took the gun's hammer with both thumbs and pulled it back.

The snuff-stained smile disappeared—Pool started waving his hands and shaking his head. "Wait! Don't shoot! Don't shoot! I run outta gas out here." He took another step into the room.

Emmalee relaxed only enough to take the pressure off the gun's trigger. She was going to ask him where his car was when someone bumped into the kitchen table. *One of them came through the back door!*

Pool heard French make the noise and watched the girl's eyes telegraph her understanding. Her cheek snapped back to the stock; she looked at him down the top of the barrel and centered the bore on his chest. Reason told Pool's brain that running and screaming wouldn't help, but it didn't tell his feet or his mouth.

Emmalee squinted her eyes against the coming shock, felt the trigger moving under her pressure, and watched the man screaming and scrambling for the door—trying to escape the inevitable.

From the back of the kitchen, French watched the girl bring the gun to bear and tightened his grip on the pistol.

Pool ducked, trying to throw off the girl's aim; adrenaline assaulted his system when the gunshot came. He had taken two steps, racing head down for the safety of the great outdoors, when the shot came; the walled-in eruption from the gun snapped him to a sprinter's posture. He closed his eyes instinctively to wait for the pain and accelerated for two more steps— head back, arms pumping, eyes closed—and ran full tilt into the unforgiving edge of the open door.

Emmalee's world stopped, then started again. Her gun

hadn't fired—it wasn't loaded. She realized that the person in the kitchen had done the shooting.

Pool was on his back by the door.

She had to run or they'd kill her.

Mose was kneeling with his head bowed when he heard the bark of the gun. He stood and walked a few steps toward the woods before stopping. The dog was nearer the woods, his floppy ears up, intent on the darkness to the north. Mose stepped closer to him and said, "That wasn't no shotgun, boy. That's a pistol."

The dog whuffed, and Mose said, "Well, we ain't gonna get no rabbit, so we'll just go up here a piece an' see is anything goin' on."

Whoever had come in the back door had a gun, and she was trapped if she couldn't get outside. She abandoned the shotgun and broke for the only opening that offered escape; no one could run into a door that hard and stay conscious. Pounding footsteps reverberated from the back of the house. She jerked her daddy's chair so it fell into the only path through the front room and increased her speed. Someone was close behind her, running through the room, and Pool was trying to sit up. As she ran past the man on the floor, he stuck out his arm, made a grab, and got a handful of fabric. She screamed and slowed. Pool twisted his hand to embed it in the material and jerked hard.

The blanket came off her shoulders and settled over him like a shroud.

And Emmalee was almost at the door.

Mose and the dog were in the edge of the woods when they heard the scream.

The dog stopped and Mose came alongside. Mose opened

the shotgun's action and felt with his fingers to make sure there was a shell in the chamber while he and the dog listened.

Only the cold quiet of the woods came back to them.

French was only steps behind her. He hurdled the chair, tripped, skidded across a layer of widely broadcast three-by-five cards like a man on ice, and fell into the tangle created by Pool and the blanket. The heavy fabric of the blanket and his flailing cousin captured the city boy, and he screamed profanity while he fought to free himself. By the time he made it to his knees, the girl was off the porch and halfway across the yard, her white blouse clearly visible against the black of the woods. French pointed the pistol at the middle of her back and pulled the trigger at the same time that his cousin, still at war with the blanket, kicked his arm.

The shot went wild and so did French.

The two hunters didn't confer when they heard the second shot. The night had brought the shots and scream from somewhere near Roosevelt Edwards's house. The dog put his nose in the air and picked up his pace, and Mose started to jog. They were less than a mile to the south.

Pool beat off the blanket and sat up. His top lip was split all the way through, his nose was smashed flat, and both of his top front teeth were snapped off. The girl was gone, and French was standing at the edge of the yard, waving his arms and cursing at the woods on the far side of the road.

Pool struggled to his feet and staggered down the steps. French quieted enough to come back and blame everything on him. "You gutless wonder, what'd you run for?"

Pool was recoiling from the touch of his own fingers, trying to explore the damage to his face. "Back up. If you hadn't got trigger happy, I wouldn't of run into the door an' broke my nose." The last three words came out as *brogue by node*.

"I shot the gun to scare her, you stupid fool. She was getting ready to blow you in half with that cannon." French was waving the pistol under Pool's broken nose.

"Well, it wasn't loaded, an' I didn't need yo' help." Pool tried to back away, wincing when he touched his teeth. "My front teeth is broke."

"You sorry redneck! I've got a gut full of your sniveling." French grabbed Pool's coat and drew the pistol back to strike him; a hard sliver of ice against his cheek transformed him into a statue. If Pool moved his hand, the razor-sharp blade would go in all the way to French's teeth.

Pool's inclination to whine became cornered-rat meanness; his whispered breath smelled of wet snuff. "I'd pull in my horns if'n I was you, Cuz. I didn't go to no fancy school; I done my learnin' in Parchman. When a man hits me, I hit back." He waited for French to lower the gun but kept the knife where it was so French could sweat a little. "Now. You want to go catch that sweet little girl, or you want me to make yo' face pretty?"

French spoke without moving his mouth. "Catch the girl."

The biting cold had stopped Pool's bleeding and was freezing the feeling out of his face. "C'mon, then. She'll go straight to that ol' huntin' club shack."

French Bainbridge needed his cousin to track the girl. Teaching him a lesson about hitting back would have to wait.

Emmalee thrashed through the woods and brush until she realized she was making too much noise. Seconds after she slowed to a walk, the reality of the cold began to set in; gulping the frigid air burned her lungs and chilled her body; uncontrollable shuddering, brought on by the terror of the white men's attack, was multiplied by the harsh temperature. She tried to quicken her pace without making any noise. The temperature was fourteen degrees and the night was dark.

She'd covered only a few yards when she heard them come into the woods behind her. They weren't worried about making noise, and they were traveling faster than she could, almost shouting at each other as they came. She stopped to listen and recognized the voice of the white man who trapped her in the barn during the fish fry; as soon as they got close, they'd see her blouse and catch her. And the white man would hurt her.

The thin material of the blouse Missy had given her, besides offering no protection against the cold, was a white flag against a black background. If she hadn't been worrying about covering up Missy's present, she'd be the color of the woods in her black sweater. She could take off the blouse and her dark skin would make her almost invisible, but the thought of the man from the barn finding her in her underwear brought cold tears. Her shivering became body-jerking tremors.

She angled away from her original path, moving as fast as she dared.

Mose and the dog were closing on the commotion that had moved into the woods. The man was getting ready to stop and listen when the dog angled off to the left. He spoke to the dog and they slowed, moving at a pace that allowed silence. The sound of men's voices was going to pass to their right.

"We should've caught her by now."

"Not if she's runnin'. She'll be at that ol' shack or in that barn."

French remembered the barn and smiled. "We'll see."

They moved faster.

The chattering of her teeth would have given her away had the men stopped to listen. They passed within twenty feet, cursing each other and her.

She tried to draw herself into a tighter ball. The leaves she had swept over herself to hide the blouse slowed the onslaught of the cold, but didn't stop it. The body heat that wasn't lost to the air was claimed by the frozen ground. She couldn't go back to the house, she couldn't get out on the road, and her Daddy couldn't find her if she stayed where she was. She was a helpless little girl trapped in the woods by evil men, and she was going to freeze to death a few hundred yards from her warm bed. A tear slipped off her cheek, fell to a dry leaf, and froze.

The dog stopped and tested the air with his nose. When Mose came close to him, he crept forward, picking his paws up one at a time and putting them down carefully. Mose followed.

She wasn't at the hunting club. The clubhouse was padlocked, and the barn was empty.

French turned back the way they had come. "C'mon. She's in the woods."

She had stopped trembling. Her arms and legs were numb. The sounds of the men had faded to the south, but they'd be back. The cold was her enemy, like the men. She didn't know how long she had been in the woods, but she was going to have to move or die.

Pool had been stomping around in the woods for almost an hour, and he was through. His front teeth were killing him, he didn't want the girl, and his coat offered no more protection than a wet flour sack. French and his big sheepskin coat could have the cold *and* the girl.

A thought came to the girl and she closed her eyes. *Lord, would You forgive me for forgettin' You? I've been so scared I forgot to pray. If I stay here I'll freeze, an' if I move those men will get me. My life is in Your hands, Lord, right where it's supposed to be. I know I'm not supposed to want to die, but I guess I'd rather freeze to death than move out there where those men are, 'cause they're gonna kill me anyway. I'm askin' that You take me to You or send somebody to help me, an' I'm waitin' right here 'til You do. Amen.* She was warmed by the knowledge that God would save her or let her come to Him.

Seconds later, she felt warm breath come to her face and smiled without bothering to open her eyes. God sent an angel for her, but the angel was going to have to carry her because she was too tired to walk. When the angel touched her face with something warm and wet, she opened her eyes, expecting to be surrounded by bright light. She wasn't. She looked into the eyes of a hound dog.

She could barely make out the man leaning over her, but she recognized Mr. Mose Washington's voice when he whispered, "Don't say nothin', baby. We got to be real quiet, now." He was taking off his coat.

She nodded.

He pulled her to a sitting position and propped her up while he got his coat around her. "Okay, now. We can't go nowhere 'til I takes care of them men. I know you're cold, but you got to wait here." He helped her lie down and fitted the stocking cap down over her ears. Holding the coat open, he whispered, "Git in here, Dawg." The dog came near, and Mose put him inside the coat with the girl. "Lay down, boy. There you go. Hold him close to you, baby. He'll keep you snug an' warm 'til I gets back." He bundled them in the coat, scattered handfuls of leaves over them, and picked up the gun.

She had to ask. "Are you comin' back?"

Mose leaned over her. "I'm just one old man, baby, but I promise to do what I can."

A small hand came out of the coat, took the front of his shirt, and pulled him close. She closed her eyes and whispered, "'Not by might, nor by power, but by my Spirit, says the Lord of hosts.' Zechariah four, six." She touched her fingers to her lips and touched his forehead.

Mose put the gun down. The woods and the world waited while he knelt for a quiet moment over the bundle in the coat. When he finished his prayer, he picked up the gun and became part of the cold night.

Pool was breathing through his mouth because his nose was swollen closed. Every time the freezing air passed across the exposed nerve-endings of his broken teeth, he moaned.

French trailed behind him, spewing curse words at the dark, the woods, the girl, and his cousin. There was no way he could find the girl by himself, and Pool was doing more whining and less tracking. The girl was gone, and he was going to have to come back down here and do this all over again. His perfect plan came apart because of one person, this sniveling lowlife that was stumbling along in front of him. He pulled the .38 out of his pocket and quickened his pace.

Mose stood in the dark, listening while the two cursed and moaned their way toward him. He brought the shotgun up and eased back the hammer. And waited.

A piece of the darkness on their left watched as the two troublemakers drew near. Mose saw the twinkle of bright metal when French extended the handgun toward his cousin, and he listened as the human predator made two crucial mistakes.

Pool stopped moaning. The sound of French's breathing had changed; his cousin was closer than he needed to be. When he heard the click of the gun hammer, Pool reacted. French pulled the trigger just as Pool turned and hit him a glancing blow on the jaw.

The muzzle flash of the gun turned the forest into a short-lived black-and-white photograph. When Mose's eyes readjusted to the darkness, Pool was on the ground, holding his chest. Pool looked at Bainbridge and whined, "What'd you shoot me for?"

"Because you need to be dead." French walked around him and started for the old truck.

Mose remained a part of the woods, watching the man who

did the shooting take a few steps, drop his pistol, and sag to his knees. Blood covered the front and side of the sheepskin coat.

Mose separated himself from the night and stepped closer to the killer.

French looked into the darkness to see the black man standing over him. "I'm cut."

"Yes, boss."

Bainbridge fell on his side and rolled onto his back. "Help me."

"It's too late, boss." Bainbridge only had seconds to live.

"Well, don't just stand there. Do something."

Mose knew the man for what he was, but he offered him respect because he couldn't risk offending him—the man's eternal life was at stake. "Can't nobody help you but God, boss. You dyin'."

French died with a stream of profane words on his lips.

Mose walked back to see about the other man. When he got close, Pool said, "Who's that?"

"Mose Washington, Mr. Pool."

"Come closer."

"That man back there got his throat cut, boss. Where's yo' knife at?"

"Here." The knife glittered and fell into the brush at Mose's feet.

Mose knelt on the freezing ground by the white man. "Is you hurt bad?"

Pool held his hands against the front of the thin coat. "Bad as it gets."

"You want me to get you to the doctor?"

The man's teeth were chattering; his head moved back and forth. "We wouldn't get to the road. I'm all tore up inside. My legs is already numb. I'm dead an' can't nobody do nothin'."

"God can, boss. He can save you."

"From dyin'?"

Mose considered his next words. "He can give you a life that don't never end, boss. He says so."

"How's He gonna do that, boy?"

"Can I tell you 'bout Jesus?"

Pool's bloodied and frozen lips tried to sneer. He rasped, "Why would I want to hear 'bout Jesus from some ig'nernt nigger?" He dismissed Mose by turning his face to the cold sky.

Mose was gentle with Pool for the same reason he had been gentle with Bainbridge; he was the only man standing between the white man and hell. " 'Cause the nigger is kneelin' by yo' side willin' to tell you, boss."

Pool shook his head. "Don't be runnin' on with this foolishness, boy. Jesus don't want me. I ain't never lived nothin' but a bad life. I know it, an' He knows it."

"He says He died for every wrong that's ever been done or gonna be done, includin' every one of yours."

Pool closed his eyes and frowned. "I reckon not. I ain't ever been in a church but once, an' that was to steal whatever I could get my hands on. An' that man layin' over there ain't the first one I've killed."

"God knowed we was gonna sin, boss, that's how come He sent His Son to die for us. He says if you'll believe in His Son an' ask for His forgiveness, He'll take you to His heaven. It's called the gospel, an' it's the truth."

"A man can't live his whole life bad an' then turn good at the end. Even a idiot knows that ain't right."

"He tells us different in the Book, boss. He says, 'Not by works of righteousness which we have done, but accordin' to His mercy He saved us.' That means nobody's good enough to take His gift . . . not now, not tomorrow. If you couldn't never be good enough, then it don't matter when you take the gift . . . when you was little, or right now."

Pool was looking at the stars again; he knew what was fair. "It'd be like I's doin' it 'cause I'm dyin'."

"He'll know an' so will you."

When Pool didn't respond, Mose said, "Time's short, boss."

"What do I do?"

"You got to pray to Him."

"Pray?"

"Yessuh."

"I ain't never done that."

"I can help if you like."

"Would you do somethin' for me?"

"What is it?"

"You reckon you could hold my hand?" Pool's hand was cold and bloody. Mose held it and bowed his head.

Pool said, "What now?"

"Tell Him you know He sent Jesus to die for yo' sins."

Pool started, "God, I know Jesus come here an' died for my sins."

"An' that you know you a sinner."

"An', God, I reckon I'm the biggest sinner that ever was."

"An' you accept Jesus as the One who saved you."

"God, this don't seem right—that You'd do somethin' like this for a man like me." Mose felt the man shudder. "It just don't seem right, but this good man says it's the truth, an' I believe it. I thank You for Jesus, an' I accept Him for savin' me." He held Mose's hand harder and said, "God, I been a bad man all my life. An' this here is the most special thing anybody ever done for me. I'm genuinely obliged to You."

Mose said, "Amen," and so did Pool.

Mose opened his eyes. Pool was looking at the stars, smiling. "I ain't got long."

"Can I do anything for you when you gone?"

Pool nodded. "Would you tell that little girl I'm sorry?"

"Yessuh. She'll be proud to know she'll be seein' you in heaven."

"Heaven?"

"Yessuh."

"I'm gonna go to heaven?"

"Yessuh. If you meant that prayer, you gonna wake up lookin' at Jesus Hisself."

"Lookin' at Jesus Hisself," Pool repeated. His eyes went to the black man. "Will you be comin' along?"

Mose was still holding his hand. "Yessuh, boss, I'll be there by an' by."

"I ain't got no right to ask, but you reckon you might do one other thing for me?"

"Yessuh."

"I'd be obliged if you could see fit to come an' see me every now an' again when you get there. There'll be good folks there, an' I don't reckon they'll want to be around such as me."

Mose smiled. "I'd be proud to be yo' friend, an' them other folks are gonna love you, too. You wait an' see."

Starlight sparkled in the man's eyes; wonder came to his voice. "Somebody's gonna love me?"

"Boss, ain't nobody in heaven what knows how to do nothin' else."

Pool Pommer couldn't hear Mose. He was listening to the voice of the One who had loved him from eternity past.

Mose stayed by the man's side long enough to say, "Thank You, Lord," then went to get Emmalee.

CHAPTER TWENTY-EIGHT

When he got Emmalee to her house, Mose called the church and told Roosevelt that he and Ellen needed to come home. The Edwardses got to their house and comforted Emmalee while Mose told them his plan. After the four of them rehearsed their story, Roosevelt and Ellen brought order back to their house while Mose walked down the road to the Parkers'. The dog—the first ever inside the Edwardses house—slept in the bed with Emmalee that night.

Bobby Lee called the sheriff's office, and Mose took a deputy to the bodies by way of the hunting club road and told him most of what he'd seen. Nobody mentioned Emmalee or the Edwardses house.

Missy drove down to the Edwardses house the next morning, passing law-enforcement vehicles and the coroner's station wagon on the way. She picked up Emmalee and Ellen and took them to Jackson to see Emmalee's sister; they would be gone most of the day. The men investigating the crime scene would be finished and back in their warm offices before the ladies returned.

When Missy left, Pat got in his old Chevrolet and drove to Greenwood. He went to the hospital and tracked Red Justin to a patient's room on the second floor. "Morning, Red."

"Well, good mornin' to you." Red excused himself from the patient.

When they were in the hall, Red said, "Did you ask her yet?"

Pat took only a few seconds to be amazed. "I'll ask her this afternoon."

Red rested a gnarled black hand on Pat's shoulder. "I'm right proud for you, an' I thank you for comin' to tell me."

"I also came to ask you to pray for us."

"Let's do that right now." Red put both hands on Pat's shoulders. The two men bowed their heads, and the old black man prayed aloud while people moved about their business in the busy corridor.

When he finished, Red said, "An' I'll be prayin' for you every day I live, for yo' effecti'ness in the battle."

Pat said, "Thank you—and I for yours."

The wheels of the county's bureaucracy turned slowly in mild weather; they became nearly stationary when the mercury moved below the freezing mark. The bodies of the two dead men had been in the county morgue twelve hours when the sheriff's phone rang. Congressman Bainbridge's office was calling from Washington.

Both men reflected the proper gravity until the sheriff happened to mention to the congressman that his son was killed in the Parkers' woods. Congressman Halbert Bainbridge immediately launched a cursing tirade against the sheriff, his county, and the Parkers and was starting on the state of Mississippi when the sheriff hung up on him.

Bainbridge sent aides from his office and punched the button for his private phone line. His only Christmas present from his family was a little late in arriving, but it was definitely worth waiting for.

The phone rang twice and his wife picked it up. "What is it?"

If he gave the information in small snippets, the exquisite pleasure he felt would last longer. He tried to sound somber. "French is dead."

The woman said only one word. "How?"

"Murdered."

There was a prolonged silence; she knew what he was doing. "Tell me all of it."

Of the four people he feared most, one was now dead. The woman he was talking to was the most dangerous of the three remaining. "He and Pool murdered each other last night in Mississippi. He was on the Parker place when it happened." He saved the best for last. "Pool cut French's throat and he bled to death."

The woman hung up.

Bainbridge tilted his chair back, closed his eyes, and savored the memory of the brief conversation.

Estelle Bainbridge turned to her middle son. "French was killed last night."

Ollie wanted to laugh out loud but matched his tone to his mother's. "What happened?"

She told him.

As long as he could keep her thinking he was loyal, he would be the favored one. He planned for a moment, then said, "I'll transfer to Mississippi State for the spring semester. It's time to let the Parkers know who the big boss is."

She ran her fingers through his hair. "I knew I could depend on you."

Late afternoon brought warmer temperatures, and Pat walked to the old cabin to visit Mose. He was on his way back to the Parkers' when the girl pulled into her driveway.

They met in the middle of the bridge.

"Hi."

"Hi."

"You've been gone a long time."

"I'm back."

"That's what you said when you came home from Europe last summer."

"You remember that?"

"I think I remember every word you've ever spoken."

"Mmm." She stepped closer and looked up at him. "How long are you stayin'?"

"For as long as it takes."

Her eyes were night-sky dark and warmer than the sun; she didn't blink; she didn't smile. "That won't be long."

"No."

She breathed deeply, taking in the clean, cool air. She turned to her lake. "Almost every good thing in my life happened on this old bridge, or close to it. God has made it a special place for me."

He smiled. "Me too. Will you miss it?"

"I don't know."

He touched her cheek, and she leaned her face against his hand. "Your hands are warm."

"Is that good?"

She touched his nose and said, "As long as your nose isn't cold."

"Mmm."

"Pat?"

He was tracing the outline of her cheek. "Hmm?"

"I'm hardheaded."

He took her hands in his. "I know."

"And stubborn."

"I look forward to seeing how God will use that."

"What are we going to do about this old bridge . . . an' the lake . . . an' the cabin?"

"We're going to thank God often for the way He used them in your life and mine." He looked into her eyes and saw her heart and made his vow. "We're going to remember what took place here, and we're going to thank God every day for what Mose Junior did. And we're going to ask God to let us spend the remaining minutes of our lives knowing Him and making Him known."

She smiled. "Then I guess we better go tell Momma an' Daddy."

He smiled back. "I told them this morning."

"Mose?"

He tilted his head at the cabin. "I just told him."

"Good." She let go with one hand and pointed toward the cabin. "I want to get married next week. Right out in front of Mose's old house. Is that okay?"

"I think that would be just about perfect."

She looked across the black waters of the lake at the pecan trees. "Where do you think'll be a good place to stand?"

He reached down and used his finger to sweep a stray tendril of hair into place behind her ear. His finger traced across her cheek and lingered there, touching her, memorizing the moment. "I've known where we were going to stand since the day I became a Christian."

She looked away from the lake and rested her cheek against his chest. "Fine. Then I'll just stand next to you."

The archangel's lieutenant watched the couple. *They have been strong.*

His leader agreed. *Indeed they have.*

The lieutenant said, *And Mose has been stronger.*

The archangel gave his attention to the cabin. White smoke came from the chimney; the setting defined peace. *The day is not far distant when he will be called upon to be stronger still.*

Spring was coming . . . promising peace.

THE END

Acknowledgments

What has transpired to bring this book to completion is nothing short of a miracle.

My manuscript would be gathering dust in a forgotten corner had it not been for the efforts expended by the people listed below. I am constrained by the inadequacy of words when I try to thank:

Mary Carpenter Greenway, my mother, for reading me a million books and stories. Anice Powell, my aunt, for another million stories from her imagination.

Diane Rhodes, Sarha Maldonado, and Carla Mercer, for never ceasing to pray. Carolyn Neighbors, for her encouragement, prayers, and English skills. Lloyd and Deanna Campbell, Doug and Cheryl Koeppen, Jim and Joan Roberts, and Richard and Durene White, for reading, encouraging, and praying. Durene White, for her selfless and exhaustive pursuit of perfection on behalf of the manuscript. Jamye Durant, for mentoring, praying, and guiding. Untold dozens of ladies who are in Bible Study Fellowship with Nan, people in our church, and our friends in the Monday night Bible study group, for their constant prayers and encouragement.

Bob Douglas, who showed me Mississippi's Parchman Prison Farm.

Randi Frazier, for always knowing which word to use.

Betty Aden, my sister-in-law, for her unflagging promotion of my writing.

Gary Terashita, for personifying what an editor and friend should be. Gary's wife, Kim, who was the book's champion before she was our friend. The entire team at Warner Faith, for making my words into a book.

Helen and Cody, Aubrea and Ron—our daughters and their husbands—and Kelli and James—our children by heart—for encouraging, praying, and believing.

My wife Nan. She sacrificed so I could write.

Our gracious God. No one can see more than I the presence of His guiding hand on this effort.

Readers' Group Guide Questions

1) How did you respond to the comment of Bobby Lee Parker, a non-churchgoer, in Chapter Six: "As far as he could tell, the men who went to church weren't any better off for going"?

2) What thoughts do you have about the demonic realm after reading *Abiding Darkness*?

3) How have you implemented the recurring theme of the book: Life's only worthwhile purpose is to know God and make Him known?

4) In Chapter Eight, were you able to identify with Pip's journey in her rocking chair? Have you been on a similar journey?

5) At the end of Chapter Eight, Missy thinks third grade is an affliction. Were any of your years in school an affliction? Which one(s) and why?

6) Reflect on the phrase from Chapter Fifteen, ". . . and didn't feel compelled to cram words into interludes of silence."

7) From Chapter Eighteen, is the phrase "Forgiveness doesn't have a facial expression" true? Why? Why not?

8) In Chapter Seventeen, Missy is sitting on the porch of Mose's cabin with Pat, wondering "if this is the most peaceful place on earth." Where do you feel peace and what is it about that place that affects you?

9) In Chapter Nineteen, Pat and Missy listen to the leaves whisper secrets. Describe what that means to you.

10) In Chapter Twenty-two, Missy tells Pat, "Well, if you think Hitler was wrong, then you need to come up with a good reason for your conclusions, 'cause right now they're based on a belief that good and evil exist—that means there has to be a moral law. If there's no moral-law-Giver—there's no moral law. If there's no moral law—then one of the greatest atrocities in history was no different from me killin' a turtle out there in that lake." Is her premise correct? Why or why not?

11) In Chapter Twenty-four, Missy tells Pat, "You're askin' me to turn my back on the only security I'll ever know, to let a man who doesn't believe in compasses guide me through a jungle." What do you think Missy had in mind when she used the word *jungle? Security? Compasses?*

12) Discuss the phrase from Chapter Twenty-seven: "Reason told Pool's brain that running and screaming wouldn't help, but it didn't tell his feet or his mouth."

13) Do you see the bridge as one of the characters in *Abiding Darkness*—a symbol of someone or something?

14) Do you see the lake as one of the characters in *Abiding Darkness*—a symbol of someone or something?

15) What, if anything, do you feel was the dog's role in the story?

16) Can you tie your feelings about current events in world history to the prospect of the presence of spiritual beings?

17) Which character appealed to you the most? Why?

18) Which man appealed to you the most? Why?

19) Which woman appealed to you the most? Why?

20) We saw forces of good and evil collide in the events centered on Cat Lake. Have you ever witnessed a struggle between the forces of good and evil? Tell your story.

21) How does the imprisonment of Mose compare with the imprisonment of Joseph in Egypt as recorded in the Book of Genesis in the Old Testament? Can you see how the upright behavior of faithful men, in circumstances where they are being treated unjustly, allowed good to triumph over evil?

22) Do you believe there is a constant battle being fought between God and his enemy, Satan? What about a battle between the forces of good and evil? Is there a difference?

23) Why do you think this story is set in Mississippi? What significance does the time frame of the story have?

24) In Chapter Two, the reader begins to see the nature and thoughts of the demon who seeks to destroy Missy Parker. Do you think that the depth and cunning that the author gives to the demon is accurate? Do you believe that the plans of the Evil One are this carefully laid out?

25) In Chapter Three, A. J. Mason is described as a Christian man, quiet and serious, not without a willingness to smile or laugh. He hears a voice that tells him to be ready. Do you believe that God speaks to today's Christians in this manner? If you are willing, share an instance in which this has happened to you or to someone close to you.

26) In Chapter Three, the reader learns about Junior's prophetic dream. Identify instances in the Bible in which God

communicates through dreams. Do you believe that God currently uses dreams to communicate with His people? If you are willing, share an instance in which this has happened to you.

27) Share your impressions of Missy Parker at the beginning of the book, after Mose Junior's death, and after she starts her Bible study with Pip.

28) In Chapter Six, A. J. Mason is described as a man who had "been shooting rifles and shotguns since he was old enough to understand what the trigger was for . . . training for this day . . . becoming a man who was ready." Do you believe that sometimes God uses our whole lives to prepare us for one moment? What impact would this belief have on your daily choices?

29) In Chapter Six, Horton prays this prayer: *If you're really there, and if you really got me out of that mess (in the war), I appreciate it. I reckon you're all we got.* Do you think God hears these kinds of confused and conditional prayers? How do you think He responds to them?

30) After her son's death, Pip asks why God would take a boy like Mose Junior. Do you think God did this? Do you think He allowed it? Why?

31) In Chapter Eight, the reader sees a thirteen-year-old Mose talking with Pap about heaven. Mose asks Pap about angels, and the old man tells him that the Bible says that each of us has a guardian angel. Where in the Bible is this found? Do you think this should be understood literally?

32) In Chapter Eight, the reader hears the advice that Pap has given to young Mose for as long as he can remember: "Boy, you need to do two things for your whole life. You got to know God better every day, and you got to make Him known." What do you think of this advice? Is it necessary to "make God known" in order to be a good Christian? Why or why not? What do you

believe happens to the Christian who does neither of these things, yet has made a sincere profession of faith?

33) In Chapter Eleven, the leader of the demons instructs his henchmen to possess Blue Biggers, to take over his will. Do you believe that this is possible, or do you think that certain people are predisposed by their natures to simply be available for evil's purpose?

NORTH

TO MOORES POINT
5 Mi.

COTTON FIELDS

GILMER'S
GROVE

PARKER GIN

OLD PARKERS

YOUNG PARKERS

COTTON FIELDS

CAT LAKE